INTO THE MOONBROCH

From the Azores to the Santa Clara Valley

INTO THE MOONBROCH

From the Azores to the Santa Clara Valley

DEBRA GOMES KORBEL

aventine press

Published by Aventine Press
55 East Emerson St.
Chula Vista CA 91911
www.aventinepress.com

Second paperback edition
Cover design by Sheri McGathy
Library of Congress Cataloging-in-Publication Data Names:
Gomes Korbel, Debra, author

Title:
Into the Moonbroch:
From the Azores to the Santa Clara Valley
Identifiers: LCCN 2023922583
ISBN 978-1-955162-30-2

O Sea,
How much of thy salt
Are Portugal's tears!

To win thy way across thy waves
What mothers mourned,
How many sons have prayed in vain,
How many brides have died unwed
That thou might've be ours,
O Sea!

Was it worth the toil?
All is worth the toil
If the spirit be not commonplace,
For he who would round Cape Bojador
Must be steeled to perils all unknown.

God gave to the sea the terrors of the Pit
— But behold! 'Tis the mirror of His Heaven, too.

-Fernando Pessoa (1890-1935)

Dedication

This book is dedicated to all first generation American immigrants and to my fun and feisty aunt, Donna Gomes Austin, my grandparents, Tom and Eva Gomes, and to a multitude of Portuguese cousins far and wide. You are the sweet bread of my life! Special thanks to my writer-uncle, Don Dugdale and my childhood friend Theresa Huether, for their valuable and precious feedback and support.

CONTENTS

Chapter 1 — 1902, Santa Clara, Winter in the Valley   1

Chapter 2 — 1878, São Miguel Island, The Azores   9

Chapter 3 — 1902, Santa Clara, Summer Adventures   17

Chapter 4 — 1878, Funchal, Madeira Departure   27

Chapter 5 — 1902, Santa Clara, First Impressions   37

Chapter 6 — 1878, The Atlantic, Azorean Sunset   45

Chapter 7 — 1902, Santa Clara, Watermelon Brandy   53

Chapter 8 — 1878, The Atlantic, First Moonbroch   61

Chapter 9 — 1903, Santa Clara, Spring in the Valley   69

Chapter 10 — 1878, The Atlantic, First Storm   77

Chapter 11 — 1903, San Jose, California, The McCallums   83

Chapter 12 — 1878, The Atlantic, Storm Recovery   91

Chapter 13 — 1904, Santa Clara, Rivalries   97

Chapter 14 — 1878, The Atlantic, Dead Calm   105

Chapter 15 — 1906, Santa Clara, Earthquake in the Valley   111

Chapter 16 — 1878, The Devil's Horns   119

Chapter 17 — 1907, Santa Clara, Aftermath   127

Chapter 18 — 1878, The Pacific, Darkness   133

Chapter 19 — 1907, Santa Clara, Summer in the Valley   139

Chapter 20 — 1878, The Pacific, Valparaiso   145

Chapter 21 — 1908, San Jose, Father and Son   151

Chapter 22 — 1878, The Pacific, Overcoming   157

Chapter 23 — 1908, Santa Clara, Autumn in the Valley   163

Chapter 24 — 1878, The Pacific, Outbreak   173

Chapter 25 — 1908, San Jose, Cannery Days   179

Chapter 26 — 1878, The Pacific, Grieving   189

Chapter 27 — 1908, Santa Clara, Biscoitos   199

Chapter 28 — 1878, The Pacific, Welcoming Party   207

Chapter 29 — 1909, San Jose, May Day in the Valley   215

Chapter 30 — 1878, Oahu, Landing   225

Chapter 31 — 1909, Santa Clara, The Grape Tower   233

Chapter 32 — 1878, Quarantine Island, Twins   245

Chapter 33 — 1909, Santa Clara, Flatfooted Luana   253

Chapter 34 — 1878, Kauai, Christmas   259

Chapter 35 — 1910, Santa Clara, Carnival of Roses   267

Chapter 36 — 1879, Kauai, The Jackel   277

Chapter 37 — 1910, Santa Clara, Auxiliary Ball   285

Chapter 38 — 1880, Kauai, The Evil Eye   293

Chapter 39 — 1910, Drawbridge   299

Chapter 40 — 1881, Kauai, The Sugar Mill   309

Chapter 41 — 1910, Santa Clara, Escape   317

Chapter 42 — 1882, Kauai, Diamonds   325

Chapter 43 — 1910, Santa Clara, Crossroads   333

Chapter 44 — 1882, The Pacific, California Bound   339

Chapter 45 — 1911, Santa Clara, Luana's Dairy   347

Chapter 46 — 1882, The San Francisco Bay   357

Chapter 47 — 1913, Santa Clara, Gloaming in the Valley   367

Chapter 48 — 1894, Kauai, Paniolos   379

Chapter 49 — 1914, Santa Clara, Julia's Gold   385

Chapter 50 — 1894, Kauai Girl   393

Historical Notes   401

Bibliography   403

Main Characters

The Mirante Family
• Miguel m. Maria * Fernandes
    Estela
    Ida
    Ana
    Paulo
    Domingos & Luana

• Anarosa * Fernandes m. Frank
    Alexio
    Stefan
    Julia
    Rose

The Terra Family
• Juvenal m. Marissa Gomes
    Jordao
    Sabina
    Renato
    Juvenal, Jr.
    Sophia & Sonia

The D'Angelo Cousins
• Gilberto D'Angelo
• Marcos D'Angelo

The Fernandes Family
• Gabriel m. Rose Amaral
    João *
    Maria *
    Cleta

• João * m. Colleen McDewey
    João, Jr.
    Jorge
    Tomás
    Mildred
    Anarosa *

The McCallum Family
• George m. Abigail MacIntyre
    Jackson *
Jackson * m. Olivia Moir
    Roger
    Samuel
    Susanna
    Celesta

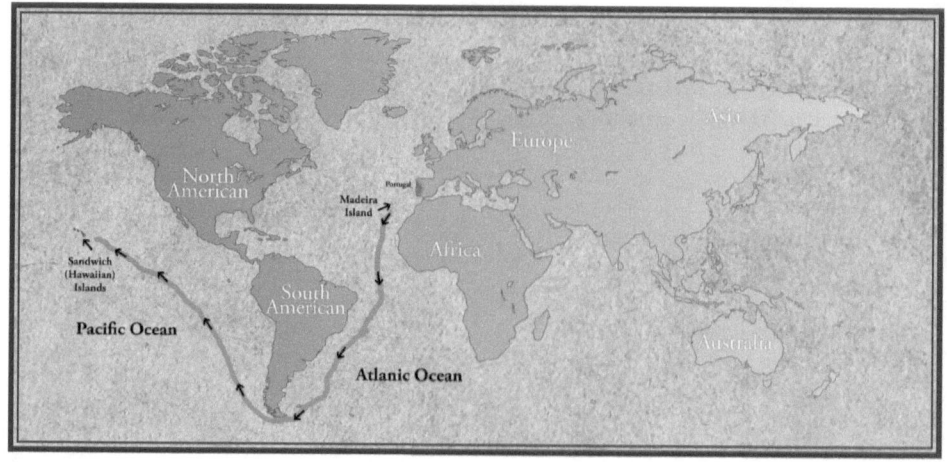

Azores to the Sandwich (Hawaiian) Islands

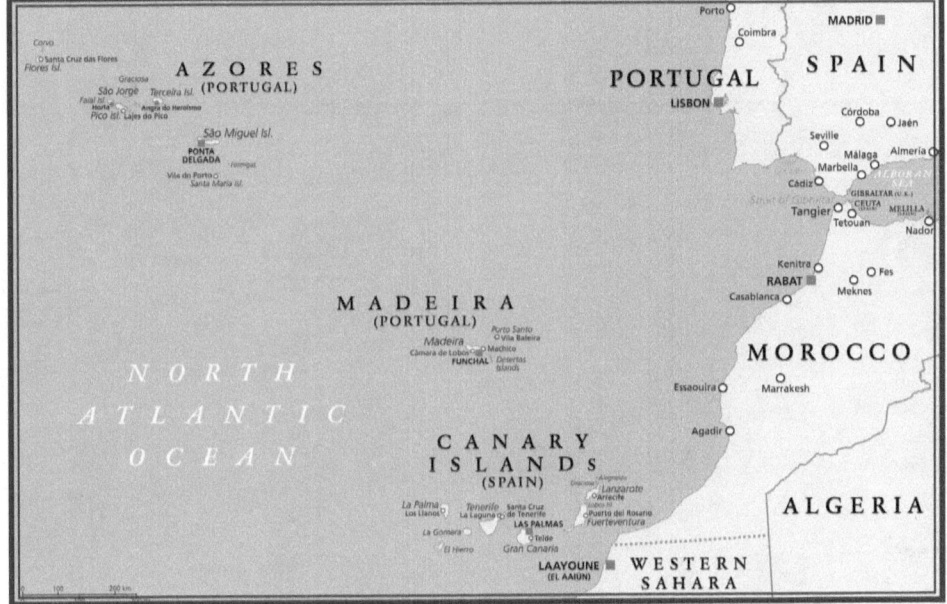

Azores and Madeira Island

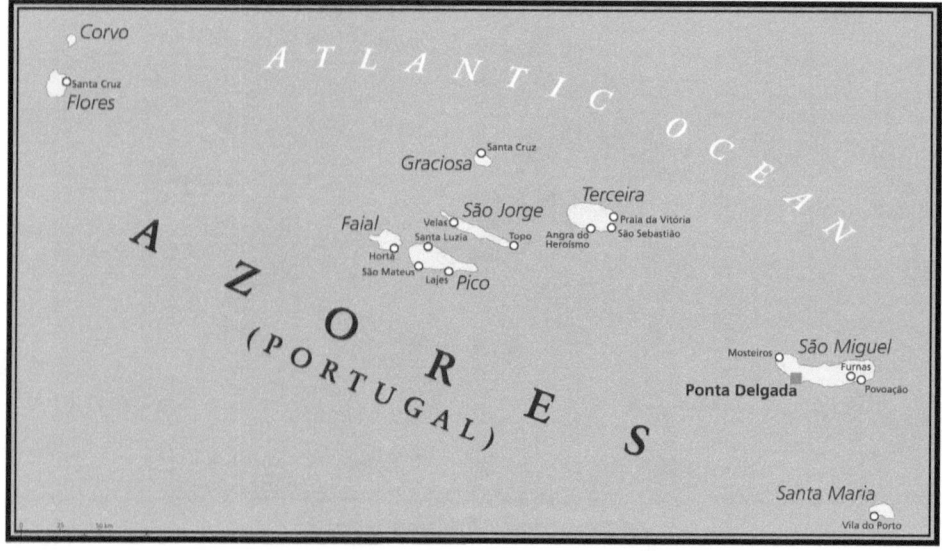

The Azores

CHAPTER 1

1902, Santa Clara, Winter in the Valley

Before the world came to them, and they realized that it had never really been theirs, there was a Valley. It was a Valley with as many opportunities as there were prunes and apricots. Where sorrel and mustard flowers blanketed the earth up to the sloping mountain ranges overlooking the San Francisco Bay on its southern shores and where cerulean skies are still the norm. Long before they first arrived, the Portuguese used to say that the streets were paved with gold, and so they came from many different directions to make good use of it.

Julia Estela Eva Mirante was born of immigrants who had sailed across turbulent seas in search of a better life. Anyone who looked at Julia, underneath a mass of auburn hair, could not miss the dark, penetrating gaze that seemed to dare anyone to defy her. Along with Julia came her brothers, Alexio and Stefan, a baby sister Rose, and an aunt Luana, whose pride in Julia could not be over-shadowed by an indifferent mother and a preoccupied father. Luana was not only Julia's auntie '*Tia*'; she was also her godmother '*Madrinha*,' and between them lay a sacred bond.

Now the twelve-year old Julia raced to keep up with her *Madrinha*, as they jumped off a horse-drawn trolley and snaked their way through the outdoor market around the Santa Clara college on a cloudy morning. Luana walked at a rapid clip, as the sky brooded over them with a handshaking fist full of rain.

"What are we after today, auntie?" Julia caught her breath, as she paced herself to keep up with Luana. She hooked her arm onto Luana's, knowing that the minute Luana hit the market, she was on a hunt no less heated than that of a stalking panther. On more than one market day, Luana had lost Julia in an absent-minded frenzy, and Julia learned that for every step her *Madrinha* took, she would have to skip three.

As Luana searched for prey, the violet fragrance from the flower stalls pulsed into the air, which left a taste of iced cotton candy. Vendors lined the streets with fruits and vegetables, household goods, medicinal remedies, and homemade clothing. Snake oil salesmen barked their wares, while puppet shows and candy displays enticed children away from the clasped hands of protective parents.

"Denims." Luana quipped, as she picked up the pace and glanced back at Julia. Julia responded by tightening her grip, sensing that Luana knew exactly where she was headed.

She kept a careful watch on Luana's every move and listened closely above the clamor. Julia knew from experience that her *Madrinha* never said or did anything at market that was not calculated to her advantage, especially when it benefited Luana's bakery business or enhanced her esteem in the eyes of her elder brother, Julia's father. The twenty-four year old Luana could barter better than anyone, even with vendors who refused to barter back; she was well known as a crackajack at sucking them into negotiation.

They approached a stall containing denim overalls, dungarees, and flannel shirts, every Valley farmer's uniform, except at funerals and Sunday services. Julia's father, Frank, had asked Luana to purchase work clothes for Julia's brothers and some of their farmhands. Fingering a pair of dungarees, Luana elevated her pitch, as she turned to Julia and made a show of her outrage.

"What is this, ninety cents? Why would anyone pay this, when everyone knows the exact same pair can be had from the Salvation Army for two bits?"

Julia ran her hand down the same pair and played along. "And, I could swear I saw that same pair at Smiths downtown for the same price." No sooner were the words out of Julia's mouth, when the owner, Mary Andrade, bounced out of a back stall. She was not going to let Luana have the last word around potential patrons.

"Why, Luana, you know these cannot be matched for quality with what you get at the Salvation Army." Mary chirped out her indignation. Luana was a long-time customer, and Mary rarely got the best of her, although she never ceased to try.

Luana ignored her and spoke to Julia. "What do you think Julia? Take a look at my dungarees. I could swear I got these at the Salvation Army two months ago. How do they compare?"

Julia eye-balled Luana's britches. "They look just as good as the ones on the rack. Why look! Even the same buttons and labels. Sewed on just right!"

Julia reached out and frisked the waistband. "Yep and they feel just as sturdy." Julia loved to play along and was growing more adept at it.

Mary was also somewhat familiar with Luana's game, but she needed to move her inventory along and wanted to hurry Luana away from listening customers. She crossed her arms and thought a moment. "Seventy-five cents is the best I can do."

Luana did not speak a word; instead, she began worming her way in the opposite direction. "Come on, Julia. I saw the same jeans at Farmer Dunham's stall, and it is still open." Behind them, they could hear Mary's harrumph followed by a sigh.

"Seventy cents, then. No less."

Luana finally turned to Mary with a twinkle in one eye. "Fifty cents or I'm outta here."

Another harrumph. "Luana Mirante, you are the squeakiest! Honestly!"

Mary huffed as she took a pair off the rack. Julia lifted her hands to her mouth to muffle a smirk, while Luana turned to Mary for the first time with a level gaze. "So, is that a 'yes'?"

"What size?"

"I'll take six pairs. Two size twelve, two size fourteen, and two size sixteen."

Mary's jaw dropped as she arrowed an evil eye at Luana. Julia, sensing an oncoming ruckus, quickly exited the stall. She could not keep from laughing. She knew Luana would be awhile, so she could pour a little local gossip into Mary's ears by way of consolation.

Julia skipped to the popcorn stand where, Fletcher Shumacher, a copper-haired, freckled classmate loitered. He sported a beetling smirk that he seemed to reserve especially for Julia, and he always smelled of tadpoles, even in winter. On another day, Julia would have walked in the opposite direction, but she wanted popcorn more than she wanted to avoid his smirk.

Fletcher spotted her. "Hey, little kanaka!" Fletcher flung the word at Julia, while he stuffed popcorn into his mouth. She would not look at him, but she made sure he heard the words she fired directly at him. "Shut your mouth, Spot."

Julia hit her mark.

Fletcher worked himself into a lather no less fiery than a bonfire. Julia turned on him just in time to watch the freckles pop out of his red face. She smiled at him sweetly and then snatched her popcorn and turned her back on him.

"Shut your mouth, kanaka!" He lunged to push Julia from behind, when a strong arm sprung out of nowhere, jack-knifed between them, and firmly took hold of his elbow. Stunned, Fletcher glanced up, as Luana peered down at him and pressed her thumb hard onto his funny bone. He winced. She was not a tall woman, but she was a strong woman.

He backed down.

"Don't ever let me catch you saying it again." His eyes still held a faint glimmer of his taunt, but he backed away and ran. "That's right, run as fast as you can, Spot!" Julia hurled the words at his back as a parting shot. She turned to Luana, and they laughed, much to the amusement of the gathering crowd.

"I hope he doesn't do that often." Luana remarked, as they headed towards the school.

"Every time he sees me."

"You don't put up with that, do you?"

Julia rounded on her. "You saw me, *Madrinha*. Did I look like I was going to put up with it?"

Luana observed the flare in Julia's eyes and backed off with a satisfied smile. Luana could not help but recall the first moment that Julia had won her heart. The four-year old Julia had been following her everywhere. Luana was standing at the wash basin scrubbing laundry, when she felt something coil around her legs like a garter snake. Startled, she glanced down at two ebony eyes, surrounded by a nimbus of ruddy-soft curls, peering up at her, as if she were the bright morning star.

"No, and I did not doubt you for a moment," Luana spoke decisively. That's all Julia needed, and they walked on, arm-in-arm. They made their way to the grocery stalls where Luana purchased flour, yeast, eggs, and sugar to make sweet bread for the family's weekend birthday celebration. When they were done, they waited for a trolley and headed back to the farm.

Just as they were entering the road surrounding the last acre of orchards, Julia's father, Frank, spotted them as he was pruning an apricot tree. He slid down the ladder and moved in their direction. "And just how did we make out at market today?" Frank spoke with a glimmer of a smile, knowing his sister's artful ways.

Frank, stood six feet tall, which was taller than most Portuguese men and with his blue-gray eyes, his was somewhat of a Viking stature. He was a man of few words, but when he spoke, those around him came to attention. His voice resounded like the bell of the angelus, suggesting something other than the poor boy whose parents had survived the life-threatening journey from Madeira island around Cape Horn to the sugar cane fields in Hawaii.

Frank put his arm around his baby sister, as they strolled to their farmhouse. Luana glanced up at Frank and spoke pridefully, "I kept it under five dollars and managed to get an extra pair for myself." When they reached the farmhouse, he waved goodbye. "I'll take a look at your loot later. Right now, I have to go down and check on the pigs. They broke out of their pen again!" Luana smiled and turned up the steps with Julia.

The farmhouse included three bedrooms, a parlor with a spinet piano, a large kitchen with a cast iron stove, and a wooden porch facing the east foothills and wrapping around both sides of the house. In front of the porch stood a pepper tree, knotting upward, dotted with tiny red berries, and shading the porch swing.

Towards the front of the house, looking out from a somewhat large parlor window, there stood a tiny but mighty sentinel named Pretty Boy. Wide-beaked with a salt and pepper beard and a blue-green overcoat, the parakeet kept watch from his brass cage. He liked to spout two often pertinent, and sometimes impertinent, phrases: "Oh boy, there he goes!" and "You're in trouble now, boy!"

Try as she might, Julia's mother, Anarosa, could not coax Pretty Boy into uttering any other words, and he never spoke when she wanted him to. Pretty Boy especially liked to gabble when someone was running in or almost out of the door, as if to scold them for leaving him. He repeated himself just once every time he spoke. When Anarosa puckered her lips for a kiss, Pretty Boy would reward her with one peck. If he refused, she would rub her lips with peppermint oil until he obliged her.

Luana and Julia listened for Pretty Boy's familiar refrain as they crossed the threshold from the porch. "Oh boy, there he goes! Oh boy, there he goes!"

Julia laughingly called back to him. "And here I go again. And here I go again," as she slipped through the front door and followed Luana to the back kitchen. She hoped that the feathered creature might some day pick up on her refrain, but he never did.

Though Luana was an unusually independent woman who owned her own bake shop with her twin brother, Domingos, she chose to live at her brother Frank's farmhouse. She struck a deal with Frank and Anarosa, when she first arrived in California from Kauai; she provided light house-keeping and babysitting for room and board. She spent the rest of her time working in a bake shop, until the owner agreed to sell it to her. Now, she and her twin brother Domingos managed the bakery together, and she divided her time between the shop and the farm.

She gazed down at Julia and realized the journey had been well worth it. My little Afilhada, Luana would say when Julia was her most charming, which was, in Luana's eyes, almost all of the time. But there was no crossing Luana when it came to what was best for her little god-daughter.

Julia could never stay in the kitchen for long. As soon as she was old enough to leave the farm on her own, she had discovered that there were many adventures beckoning from the outside world. Luana looked out the kitchen window and noted the dark clouds gliding in from over the westerly mountains, but Julia had already planned her escape, and Luana was quick to anticipate her next move.

"Julia, you must put on your raincoat. It will start thundering with flash floods."

Julia sniffed and drew up all of her five foot stature, "What is a little rain? Why should it matter?"

"Diabo Vermelho! (Little red devil) You do as I say and come back here!"

But Julia was too quick and knew Luana too well. With hands on her hips, Luana watched the two flint feet race down the garden path and shaded her eyes just in time to see Julia melt into the brume. She held Julia's red rain coat in her hands on the back porch, all the while she knew she would forgive her.

On this day, as Luana called after her, Julia fled down the tree-lined path and beyond the turnstile just in time to fade into the hedgerow that surrounded the first acre of fruit trees. Along that path she would find a row of poplars lining her road to freedom, for at the end of that road her closest friend, Therese, would be waiting for her.

Therese Janssen stood a clear eight inches taller than Julia, so Julia would always look up to her. Yet, they had learned to communicate with a single glance and were always guessing each other's thoughts. Every chance they could, they would make their way down the main artery of the little town, known as The Alameda, which ended at the college. Not far from the college, they would stop at Luana's bakery, called the Serradura, where they enjoyed sweet treats while they planned new adventures.

Today they managed to escape the pouncing rain by tunneling themselves between the pinions of crowded patrons under a mash of overcoats. Their faces pressed up against the plate glass encasement of Portuguese pastries, letting off steam from the mist clouding their view. Julia tracing an outline of her face and hair against the humid vitrine. Therese responding by adding horns and a tail. Giggling up more steam. Patrons shifting and grunting around them.

"How much were you able to get?" demanded Therese eagerly, which made Julia start to realize it was her turn to spring for the treats. Therese peered at Julia, whose eyebrows jolted upward in feigned surprise.

"Don't tell me — you forgot to bring the money! I knew it. You always forget! Why am I always the one who has to pay?"

Julia's eyes grew slightly downcast, and then she paused and looked up with a winning smile. "Don't worry. I'll find a way."

Therese did not doubt that she could, because she knew well that gleam in Julia's eye. Across the counter where customers were drinking coffee and devouring macaroons, Julia spied her Uncle Domingos who worked the bakery counter and delivery service.

"Watch this," Julia challenged, expertly wending her way around the waiting patrons to the other end of the counter. Therese rolled her eyes after her. She had no doubt that two hot Bolo de Bolachas were on their way with, perhaps, a hot chocolate or two.

"Hey, my little chickee!" exclaimed Domingos. "What are you doing out on such a day and in such mud!" Knowing that Domingos would give a full report to his sister Luana, Julia played innocent.

"Oh Uncle Domo, we were on our way to the confessional when we were caught in the rain..." she lied.

"To the confessional?" he smiled with amused accusation. "And what would my sweet have to confess? Have you been stalking the chickens again?"

"But you know it's not true and that I would never feed the chickens to the coyotes."

"Not even to save your cat?" He winked as he grinned down at her.

"Not even," she replied with a quick glance back at Therese, who gave her a look of 'hurry up.'

Uncle Domo towered over his niece with a knowing smile, glanced at the muddied pinafore and gave a backward glance at Therese. "And I suppose that such a drowned little rat could use a chocolate? Perhaps for two?"

"Oh yes," she exclaimed with bouncing eyes.

"And your favorite, Bolo de BoLachas, I presume?"

Uncle Domo required no answer; Julia's eager looks said it all. He quickly found a table in the back kitchen for the two girls and delivered the delicious treats with a sweeping flourish. He knew that Luana did not approve of his spoiling the girls or the attention that would be taken away from other customers, but he could not resist the dimpled smile of his favorite niece, as she licked the thick raspberry sauce from her cake with no thought of the scolding that waited for her back home.

CHAPTER 2

1878, São Miguel Island, The Azores

Like a monsoon rain, life can turn unexpectedly to test the mettle of a man's soul. Such a time had now come for Miguel Mirante. As he released the soil from his hand, along with the molded vine that would produce no grapes and no revenue for the coming year, he sighed with miserable resignation. He would not be able to pay his rents, and his family would lose their home on São Miguel island in the Azores.

So many crops had been blighted and many farmers lived in fear of starvation and ruin. And why should he be any exception? Why should the Almighty treat him any differently? Would the angel of death pass over him? These questions raced through his mind with ever-increasing insistence.

Some farmers had escaped the blight, but it was not likely in his case, given the proximity of his land to other failed crops. His hunched shoulders suggested the weight that he carried in his need to feed four children with another one on the way. How could he face his wife Maria? How could he tell her the truth? He reassured himself that heartache can flee and hope can be renewed. Surely, there must be a way.

Tomorrow they would celebrate a three-day festa dedicated to Senhor Santo Cristo Dos Milagres, and all the farmers and their families would travel to Ponte Delgado from every corner of their little island. There they would venerate a statue of Christ that was said to hold miraculous powers. It was known for its unique depiction of Christ as presented by Pontius Pilate to a roaring crowd, "Behold the Man." They believed there was power in the serenity of Christ's face, as it was juxtaposed to His bloody sufferings.

Miguel would pray for the strength to tell his wife after the festa, but he did not want to cast a shadow over their celebrations. When he returned to their farmhouse, he was greeted by his only son, thirteen-year old Paulo, who was not yet too big to run into his arms. As he scooped up his son and swung him up towards the sky, the boy's smile soothed his aching heart. His fatherly pride in his son always cheered him.

He pressed the boy to his cheek and quelled his thoughts, "Surely, the Senhor Cristo Des Milagres will hear our prayers once again," he reasoned with himself. "We will go to the festa tomorrow and our prayers will be answered."

He entered the front door of their cottage, and his eyes swept over its meager rooms. He did not see the threadbare furniture or the rug. He did not see the walls of plaster that were cracked in several places. He felt warmth and heard his family's joy in one another, and it was healing to his worried soul. Maria was preparing a meal of pork with sweet potatoes and collard greens. A bowl of orange persimmons rested on the table beside her as a backdrop to her bright smile.

Just as he bent over to kiss her, his eldest daughter, Estela, glided out from the bedroom in a ruffled full-length dress, which Maria had made especially for the festival. The sight of her took him aback. It was then that he realized that this sixteen year old would be a great beauty, which he could hardly comprehend.

"Who is this beautiful woman I now see before me?" He exclaimed as she made her entrance. Estela blushed, but he could not miss the pleasure in her eyes. Around her shoulders she wore a cape of brocade with silver sequins and flowers. The cape showed off her mother's exquisite handiwork, as it framed her heart-shaped face.

Estela's father encouraged her after dinner: "Go to bed and may you have sweet dreams that will brighten your heart tomorrow. You will be the loveliest of all the young women there!" Estela did not object, as she helped the other children to their beds. Given their excitement, they would all be hard-pressed to drift off to sleep.

In the morning, the household was up early preparing and bathing, cooking and adorning themselves. They all had a part to play. Maria baked her best sweet cakes of many kinds. Ida and Ana waited expectantly for Estela to finish entwining fresh rose petals into their braided hair, all of them dreaming about how they would spray baskets of petals along the path around the statue, as they marched through the square.

Paulo was eager to ride his burro alongside the other boys and gladly submitted to being dunked in the wash tub for a thorough scrub. Even Miguel would play his braguinha guitar to serenade the crowd as Maria sat proudly looking on with her sister and mother.

As the Mirante family wended their way onto the roadways in a cart drawn by two mules, they were joined by a slow, steady throng of friends and relatives approaching from every direction. The crowds resembled a stream of confetti sprinkling the island. Frivolity and music accompanied them on tropical breezes. Baskets overflowed with island flowers, hydrangeas and bougainvillea spilling out of straw hats. They carried their offerings of candles, flowers, and money to present to Senhor Santo Cristo Dos Milagres.

Festas were common on their cozy island, but none of them was as anticipated as much as this one. Half of the islanders would not return home until late into the third day or even the morning of the fourth day. It was not unusual to see people in the morning sleeping under apple trees or along the tressed vineyards. Mouths gaped open, heads thrown back, legs splayed, lying under trees. Empty bottles of jammy wine peppering the roadside.

All along the way, the young ladies dropped flower petals to create a path for the celebrants. Following close by were young men and boys on bicycles or burros. Some sat atop ox carts and wagons; they were swarming and calling out to the young girls, vying for their attention.

This was one of the few opportunities for young men to interact with island girls who were usually protected by close-knit families. Young girls rarely spent any time in the presence of the opposite sex, except their brothers, even during courtship. They were strictly supervised until marriage. But no one attracted as much attention as the eldest Mirante girl. Estela was determined to meet their taunts and propositions with dignified composure.

All eyes were on her and Estela knew it. Ever since she was old enough to remember, she had watched the parades closely, having been coached by her mother on how a young woman should behave. If a girl smiled or laughed at a particular boy, then the boys would try to capture her attention, and the taunting could become relentless or easily spin out of control. A father or brother might have to step in to subdue the riotous clamor. Estela did not want that to happen to her.

One young man almost fell off of his bicycle, as he clutched his chest and yelled out, "Beautiful one! Look at me! Look at me! My heart is yours." Estela fixed her gaze straight ahead. "I will die a thousand deaths unless you blow me a kiss." She refused to pay attention to the compliments and shouts. She kept her head high and her eyes averted. She focused on finding the plaza known as Campo de São Francisco, where the statue would be paraded around the courtyard. "Never give them the satisfaction of thinking you notice them," Maria had coached her.

The cascading crowd made their way towards the chapel at the Convento da Esperança. Several roads converged at the base of the plaza, and the crowd pressed forward with excitement, as they drew closer. Finally, Estela spotted the church entrance with relief. She had avoided a scene. Once mass was celebrated, the people poured into the streets, coiling their way in a slow, steady stream. The music was striking up, at first in a somber cadence and then rising to a crescendo of celebration, over and over, as the brotherhood carried the statue around the Campo de São Francisco. Those whose prayers had been answered from the previous year walked on their knees in thanksgiving all around the square.

Once the family left their wagon, they were immediately surrounded by those who knew them. The eight-year old Terra twins, Sonia and Sophia, grabbed each of Estela's hands and would not let her go. With squeals and giggles they led her into a large hall prepared for dancing that would take place in the evening after dinner. As they entered the hall, they stopped short to take in the enchanted world prepared for the night's festivities. Purple hydrangeas and jacarandas dripped from the ceilings, candle lights casting a purple glow, foxgloves and fuchsia bursting through the purple haze.

Estela laughingly twirled the twins around, as they glided over the dance floor and pretended to be little dancers. Their elder sister Sabina soon joined them along with their brothers Jordao, Renato, and Juvenal, Jr. They could have the entire floor to themselves before the adults would take over in the evening. For now, the eating and drinking would begin outside in and around the plaza, so the girls could have the hall all to themselves.

Jordao, who was two years older than Estela, had always looked down on her and spent his boyhood teasing her unmercifully. If she liked mangoes, he liked oranges; if she preferred pudding, he preferred cake; if she enjoyed playing a game, he let her know his absolute disdain for it. He loved nothing better than to get a rise out of her. She had grown up under his constant disapprobation.

But in a moment, that all changed, as he was drawn into the power of her nascent beauty and his own susceptibility to it. The disdainful remarks that would normally well up within him now caught in his throat, and the confident, cocky boy felt just a tinge of regret for his history of relentless teasing. He was now in her power, and he was ill-prepared for her to be as merciless to him as he had always been to her.

"So, Estela, do you plan to dance tonight?" A voice rang out from the far end of the hall. His name was Adao Oliveira and he was known to be the town flirt, the one who no young woman could resist. This was his first attempt at charming Estela, who had now caught his eye and might satisfy his unquenchable thirst for new conquest.

"That depends," Estela replied coyly, as she turned away from him.

Adao moved towards her, flashing white teeth splayed into an effulgent smile. No young woman in their community had ever been known to resist it, and everyone present was fully aware of it. Estela was about to set him down, but sensing Jordao tense up, she did not want to be altogether discouraging.

"Depends on what?"

"On who asks me and how I feel when the time comes."

Now Adao looked directly in her eyes, as he stood nearly eight inches above her with a bemused smile. Had it not been for Jordao glaring beside her, she would have returned the smile with a scornful one. Instead, she spoke lightly, "we shall see," as she pulled Sonia and Sophia after her. She figured that it was better to be protected in a cloak of mystery and leave both young men to glare at each other, than to show her true feelings. Not that she really cared.

While the young people were left to themselves, the adults were starting to take their places in the outdoor square, where lunch was about to begin. Miguel determined that he would forget the hopelessness of their situation and the dread of telling Maria, until he was accosted by his good friend and fellow farmer, Juvenal Terra.

Juvenal could not forget for a day that all was lost, and he plied Miguel with questions. "What will we do now that we know there will be no harvest? No way to pay the rents?" he insisted, as if he could pry an answer from one who was as hopeless as he. He had always looked up to Miguel and required his assurances and approval, but he could not keep his anxiety to himself, even on this day.

Miguel remained silent and thoughtful as he looked away. He could not see the way forward. He had no answer nor could he speak the truth aloud, as if giving voice to it would make it somehow more inevitable.

Juvenal pushed his cause one step further.

"I know a man from Funchal. He tells me there are boats ready to take anyone who is willing all the way to the Sandwich Islands and that these islands are a paradise. The skies are bluer; the sea is milder; the sand is softer; the air is sweeter. They want us there and the land owners will not treat us as if we are their beasts of burden, the way they do here. They are recruiting all who will come to work in their sugar cane fields. And you can bring the entire family. There is no end of work, and they will provide housing, gardens, and schools for the children."

Juvenal finally struck a chord in Miguel's heart. There were many ways in which life on their island was idyllic; it was a lush green paradise, where cows grazed lazily and where small-town life created a safe haven of comforts within tight-knit social circles. Yet opportunities were few; there were not enough schools for the children, and they were often needed for farm work anyway. Lack of space diminished any likelihood that he could ever own his own farm, let alone pass it to his children.

If the options for men were few, they were even fewer for women. Most of the men were confined to farming and fishing. Beyond marriage and children, there was no life for women, and many of them worked the farms while managing their household.

Miguel also thought about his son. In a few years, at age eighteen, Paulo would be conscripted into the Portuguese army. Who knows what war he would be carried off to or if he would ever been seen again? His love for his son gave him pause. "But leave my home? The land? My sisters and brothers? Everything I have ever known?" Miguel shook his head in wonder at the thought of it. To him, it would be like cutting himself off from the very air he breathed. Yet even his fears could not assuage his curiosity.

"Where are these islands? How far away? How will we pay and where will we live? Can we return if we don't like it there?" He had a thousand questions racing through his mind.

Juvenal answered him swiftly, as if the faster he spoke, the more likely his friend's decision would confirm his own. He desperately needed an ally to help him muster the courage he could not conjure up within himself.

"There is a man named Jacinto Pereira who lives in the Sandwich islands. He is one of us, and he will represent our interests once we arrive. He works with another man, Dr. Hildebrand, who has recommended us as good workers to the king of the islands. The good doctor is arranging boats to take us from Funchal, Madeira. We don't even have to pay money up front. We just have to bring our clothes and bedding. They provide the food, but we can also bring some of our own. We will stop at ports to replenish our food supplies, and we can even bring chickens onboard for our festas."

Miguel thought it sounded too good to be true, but he was intrigued and amazed at the generosity of such people. What could their motivations be? Why would they risk so much to bring them so far? He had never known the land owners of his village to be so generous; the idea was completely alien to him. He did not know about commerce and industry and trade and that there must be a return for their investment. He did not know what that return would be and the price to be paid for it.

But Juvenal planted one seed that would tilt the scale in Miguel's mind in favor of the journey: "Think of the possibilities: education for our children and savings that will allow us to return once the famine is over. We can send money back here to help our families survive in the meantime and then return whenever we want, because we will have the means. Perhaps we will even be able to purchase our own farms when we return instead of renting them."

Miguel looked at him thoughtfully. "Let me think about it some more, and we will talk again later this week. For now, let's just enjoy the day."

Later that night, Miguel lay awake staring at the ceiling, while Maria slept peacefully, his mind raced back and forth as he weighed all the imaginable pros and cons. He prayed. He tossed and turned. He realized that his options were few. Miguel knew he could not fail to clutch at any straw that might bring hope to himself and his family, as he stood staring at the edge of a precipice, the likes of which he had never known. And in that moment he also knew that he could not afford to stand staring too long, that he must look away to find the path ahead. "Senhor Santo Cristo," he prayed, "tell me if this is the way."

CHAPTER 3

1902, Santa Clara, Summer Adventures

Beyond the back garden wall of the Janssen farm lay endless adventures. It was a place where no grown-up would care to go, so they looked for ways to build barriers to it. Little did the Janssen parents know that their confines were not impenetrable.

Marie Therese Yvette Janssen hailed from a hearty stock of Dutch immigrant farmers who specialized in prune growing, the California prune originating from the work of a Frenchman, Louis Pellier, who successfully grafted a rootstock from the French prune onto a California plum near Mission San Jose. What followed was an enchanting purple-splashed Valley. Influenced by Pellier's efforts, Donald Janssen cultivated approximately three thousand prune trees out of the four and a half million across the Valley, a profitable business that enabled him to expand his farm along the San Tomas waterway.

Julia and Therese would disappear into the orchards through a portion of the wall that had crumbled and been replaced with a slotted wooden plank not far from several old water towers. They were careful to approach it from the row of poplars, along the back windows of the farmhouse. The rustling of poplar leaves from the Bay winds muffled the sound of their steps.

Julia and Therese rounded the red bottle brush that lined the back tank houses. As they slipped by the poplars to find the loose plank, Julia whispered, "Be careful — push from the top of the plank, so it doesn't fall out of place." Therese pressed the top gently so Julia could slip underneath. Then Julia held it open from the back of the plank and Therese followed.

Beyond the fence, the fragrance of high mustard grasses commingled with the fruit-pocked soil lining creek on its way to the San Francisco Bay. The creek was lined with row upon row of apricot and prune trees. Hot, pulpy apricots gushed from the trees like spider sacks, dripping down into the earth's crevices and nourishing the life below.

Julia ran for the first tree, "You take that one. I'll take this one. Let's see who can pick the most." They scrambled up as fast as they could, giggling as they threw the rotten fruit at each other and shoveled the plumpest into their burlap sacks. Afterwards, they fell exhausted on the soft grasses, where they would remain hidden from anyone who might pass by. The wind tickled their cheeks, as they looked up at what seemed to be a never-ending canopy of blue sky. They stuffed themselves with their best pickings, as they planned their future.

"I wonder if we will live in the same place when we grow up," Therese spoke wistfully.

"Don't be a pickle head! Of course we will," insisted Julia. "Don't you know that we will always be together?"

"How can you know that?"

"It's just something you know," Julia insisted.

Therese did not try to contradict her. Even as Julia spoke confidently, a coldness swept over her, and she looked up at the blue skies, as she mentally casted a line to the future.

Julia interrupted her thoughts, "Hey, do you know that big house near the school?"

"Of course! It's just about the spookiest house in town. I wonder who lives there and what it's like inside."

"Why don't we go find out?" Julia loved nothing better that to make a daring new adventure out of everything.

They took one look at each other, and reading each other's thoughts, they jumped up and ran for the swing that would catapult them to the other side of the creek. Therese grabbed the rope first and pushed off the strong boulder underneath the eucalyptus tree that held it. With one swing, she was safely lifted onto the other bank, and she tossed it back to Julia who followed.

They ran the entire way to the partially hidden Italianate Victorian and then hung panting and gawking at the house over a fence. It was a dark and lonely house. No doubt, it had once been a grand Victorian, but the bushes and shrubs were overgrown and the fine mahogany double doors, now white-washed, were half-hidden from sight. Three floors lay stacked like a wedding cake crowned with a cupola that seemed to act as a look-out tower, but no face ever appeared now from its dormer portal. The steps leading to the entryway were sagging and the railing was half missing.

Along with the dark pine trees that crowded their view, there was a scattering of tall palms that seemed to lean into the old house, as if they were being slowly sucked into it. Mourning doves and pigeons had blighted the fine carvings on the corbeling with their nesting. Even they seemed to have abandoned it. The only signs of life were black crows, trembling among the pines and cawing to one another. Their shrieks pierced the sky, acting as a portent to anyone who would dare to approach.

"Someone's gotta live here." Julia spoke her thoughts out loud. "I've seen the postman making deliveries. Once, I saw a man who looks to be a servant run to get the letters."

"But how could we ever get in there or find out who lives there?" Therese asked, almost to herself. The girls stood staring with quickening hearts, as they wondered how they could possibly pierce the gloomy hall.

"I have an idea," suggested Julia. "The only thing that gets in or out is the mail, right?"

"As far as I can tell."

"Then the answer is to follow the mail, right?" Julia looked amazed at her own genius.

"How are we supposed to do that?"

"We just wait for it. Every day we wait."

"And do what?"

"That's easy. We wait, collect the mail when it comes, read what we can, and then put it back before anyone comes for it. First, we find out when the servant comes out and then we allow enough time to get it back there. That way, we can find out who lives there. Brilliant, yes?"

"I swear you scare me to death sometimes," Therese sighed. "Honestly, who thinks of such things?"

"You're looking at her," Julia laughed. "Now, let's just wait and see what time the postman comes and what time the servant comes out for it."

"But this may take us all day," groaned Therese.

Therese was right. After two hours of waiting, they decided they would have to try another day. They closed the gates of the small school and started back to the Janssen farm, passing through the town cemetery along the way.

Beyond the grounds keeper's house, they noticed something they had never seen before. It was an open double door gaping out of what looked to be a basement. Peering down into it, they could see concrete steps descending to a level below the driveway near the stonemason's work yard. The basement doors were simply too enticing. The girls looked at each other and neither one said a word; they both knew what they would do.

Slowly, they held the railings as they descended to the wooden doors. Just beyond the doors was a single overhead light and beyond that, they could barely see three feet in front of themselves. Once their eyes became accustomed to the grayness, they opened wide eyes at each other. Before them lay winding corridors of underground concrete-slabbed tombs lining the walls on both sides. Some of them looked to be half-opened and cracked, as if an earthquake had shifted the corpses onto their sides and tilted each resting place in one giant, earth-moving roll.

Half expecting to find skeletal hands hanging out of their drawers, they held their breath. The air was heavy with a dank smokiness, like a grave that has been exhumed. As they rounded the first corner, they could not see from end to end, but they could tell the corridors continued onward. Curiosity overcame fear. Julia felt a strong temptation to reach out to draw a slab out of the wall, but Therese stayed her hand and then grabbed it.

Neither spoke a word and neither could resist the urge to see it through as far as they could reach. They could barely make out the names and dates on the stone drawers, noting that most of the graves dated back to a past century.

They heard a guttering sound, as the single light near the doorway popped and was snuffed out. A clutching darkness encircled them. They jumped and shrieked wildly, running towards the double doors, but they were now closed. Holding her breath, Therese pushed against them with one horrifying thought: had the gardener locked up and gone home for the day?

Anarosa was not one to give into fear, but twilight had been subsumed by black night, and there were no signs of her eldest daughter. She knew that Julia would sometimes run off for long periods of time, but she also knew that Julia was an independent girl who knew her way around. She never came home past dark.

Anarosa tightened her fists into two gnarled balls, pacing back and forth near the front parlor window. She was well aware that Frank would hold her responsible. He noticed her neglecting the girl and had mentioned it to her on several occasions. She would not admit it, but there was some truth to it. Anarosa felt no pang of remorse when Julia attached herself to Luana, and she consistently promoted her sons with little thought for her daughters. In Anarosa's mind, women served the success of their men, and even from an early age, she had taught her daughters to serve their brothers.

But Julia would have none of it.

Anarosa remembered the first time she tried to coax Julia into serving her brothers their breakfast. Even at eight years old, Julia flung her a disapproving look. "Why should I cook for them? Why shouldn't they cook for me?"

Stefan let out a guffaw in the background, but Julia's words startled Anarosa. It had never occurred to her that her daughter would resist what seemed natural to her. Anarosa had been a very compliant young girl, and she never thought to question her mother. She was always the "good girl" in her family and expected the same from her daughters. Julia's resistance frightened her.

"Don't you talk back at me! Where does that come from?" Anarosa fumed.

Julia said nothing; she just ran out and slammed the back door. What seemed obvious to Anarosa was unthinkable to her daughter. They seemed destined to always misunderstand one another.

Anarosa had lived a more pampered and traditional life than Frank. Her father, João Fernandes, came over directly from São Miguel to the east coast on a whaling ship. Once he married and started to raise a family, they all moved to the West Coast to start a dairy farm. Anarosa was the daughter of a Portuguese father who had won the heart of her American-born mother of Irish descent. Her mother's green eyes and strawberry hair were prized by the Portuguese men. To win such a woman was considered the sign of good fortune in America, and good fortune followed João Fernandes wherever he went. He was now a vastly successful dairy farmer who had moved from a San Jose farm to the Central Valley to expand his business.

Anarosa paced the room again, as she waited nervously for Frank to return from the ranch. When he arrived, she explained the situation. It was now eight o'clock in the evening, and there was no sign of her.

Frank turned to Alexio. "Go get Luana. She will know where to look for the girl." Alexio jumped up and found Luana on the back porch reading by lamp light.

"Luana, have you seen Julia?"

Luana looked up. "Not since this morning. Why?"

"Do you know where she's been today? When did you last see her?"

"I haven't seen her since breakfast. No doubt she's with Therese. Those two are inseparable." Luana put down her book and followed Alexio into the parlor. She read the worried look upon Anarosa's face, as Frank paced the room and then turned to Alexio.

"Alexio, take your brother and ride out to the Janssen place. Find out if they've seen Therese and if they know where they could be."

Alexio and Stefan ran out to the barn, and after saddling their horses, they headed west into the darkness towards the San Tomas Creek.

While plans were being laid for their rescue, Therese and Julia lay clinging to each other at the bottom of the stairs to the underground tombs, as close to the double-doors as they could manage. Shivering in the dirt, they were breathing heavily at the prospect of spending the night in the gathering gloom among the dead.

They had exhausted themselves screaming and pounding the splintered wood doors. Now, it had been at least three hours, and their dread was overwhelming. Clearly, the grounds keeper was not going to return.

"My parents are going to kill me," cried Therese.

"That would be the least of our worries."

"Oh, and like what could be worse?"

"I was thinking more about having to spend the whole night here. I'd rather face my mother now than sleep with the ghouls and spiders in this place."

"As creepy as it is, are you really afraid of the dead? I mean, do you believe in ghosts?"

"No more than I fear anything or anyone. If there are ghosts, we will be sure to find it out tonight. Now, that might be worth the bother of it all," Julia laughed looking on the bright side. "What stories we will be able to tell! And for all our lives."

"But it could be hours, maybe even days, before they open these doors again." Therese howled.

Julia peered at Therese and drew away from her to gauge the intensity of her fear. Concerned, she made up her mind to talk her out of it.

"Remember that time we put glue in Fletcher Schumacher's sandwich before lunch?"

"Are you kidding? I'll never forget the look on his face."

"Yeah, and do you remember why we did it?" Julia prompted her.

"Of course. He tormented you all year."

"Yeah, and I spent all year trying to think of a way to get back at him." Julia smiled with satisfaction as she rolled over the memory in her mind.

"What was it he used to call you?"

"What do you mean 'used to call me'? He still does."

"What was it?"

"Kanaka."

"But what does it mean?"

"It's a word used by some to describe the Portuguese who came from the Hawaiian Islands. It's also a name they use for native Hawaiians."

"But what does it mean?"

"Uncle Domo told me it's what they called the people who worked for lower wages than the white workers. Instead of paying the workers in U.S. dollars, they worked for a money that was worth a lot less. Kanakas." Julia shrugged. "And somehow that's a bad thing, but I really don't know why."

"And your family, they came from the Hawaiian Islands?"

"Not all my family. My father, Aunt Luana, and Uncle Domingos."

"Did they come by themselves? What about your grandparents?"

"My grandmother still lives on the islands with three of my aunts I've never met. My grandfather died working the cane."

"But how?"

"They don't talk about it, so it must be something really bad. I'd like to know someday. Even Aunt Luana won't tell me. It just makes her sad whenever her father's name is mentioned. And Luana is never sad, so it always surprises me when she talks about it."

"And your grandmother? She is still on the island? Which one?"

"She lives on Kauai. They tell me it is beautiful, a garden paradise. We should go there someday. Just you and me," hoping to take her mind off less pleasant things.

"How could we do that?"

"I don't know, but I'm sure we can find a way. Maybe we could find work there. We could stay with my relatives."

Therese thought about it for a moment and said, "But we'll be sure they don't pay us kanakas." And for the first time since they were locked up, Therese laughed.

"Yes, no kanakas for you and me." But Julia was not smiling when she said it. It was not in her nature to admit to any obstacle, not even a tightly shut basement door.

"Promise me something," said Therese.

"Of course."

"If we get out of this..."

"No — not 'if,' but 'when'!" Julia insisted.

"We will never be apart. We will always find a way to be together."

"Don't be ridiculous. Of course I promise, as long as you promise back."

"I promise back." And Therese promised before they both slid back into sleep.

As they slept, Stefan and Alexio rode back to the ranch with Donald Janssen, who was just as worried as the Mirante family. By the time they reached the farmhouse, it was nine thirty.

"We need to send out a search party tonight. This can't wait until morning." Donald insisted.

"If we're going to do that, then let's start at the Sheriff's house. He'll be home for the night, so we'll have to take all hands there," replied Frank. Frank gathered up all the farmhands and along with their sons, they rode off to the sheriff's house.

Sheriff Thomas Harlow answered his front door and listened to the story of the lost girls.

"When were they last seen and where?" he asked.

"It's been since early morning, maybe ten o'clock at our farmhouse. We know she went to the Janssen house to find Therese, but they have not been seen since that time." Frank responded.

Thomas looked at Mr. Janssen. "Do you remember seeing them after that?"

"No — I wasn't home, but my wife saw Julia come into the house."

"OK, give me a moment. I'll round up my partners, and we'll ride in separate directions to search the most likely areas." Looking at Frank, he asked what was the most likely area of town he thought they'd go.

"I think it likely that they would not go any farther than the farmhouse and around the Alameda, the Guadalupe, and the college."

"OK then. That's the area where we'll focus, but we should also search the creeks. Give me a moment to get dressed and gather my things."

They split off in separate directions. Stefan and Alexio searched the areas around the college. Looking at his brother, Alexio suggested "Why don't you take the area in and around the college, and I'll cover all roads within five miles of the school? Meet back here in an hour."

It was about midnight when Julia and Therese woke from the cold, shivering and dazed. Julia woke first, and she could hear a scratching sound, as if a tiny mouse was boring a hole in the wall. It gave her a chill, and every bone in her body ached from lying on the hard ground. Blinking to adjust her eyes to the dark, she whispered to Therese, "Therese? Are you awake?"

Therese started up abruptly with a pounding heart. She reached out for Julia and her voice betrayed a strain, "What time do you think it is? I just can't stay here a moment longer."

"I have no idea. You just have to hold on. Come morning, surely someone will come around and hear us." As they lay on the ground trying to get comfortable, Therese started up.

"Julia, I think I hear someone. A horse maybe." The whites of her eyes shown bright. They both fell silent, not knowing whether to cower or shout out.

"No, really! I'm not imagining things."

They jumped up and ran to the double doors. Their screams echoed across the quiet graveyard as they pounded on the double doors with all their might. Anyone within a mile could have heard them in the stillness and quiet of the tombs.

Riding through the cemetery, Alexio heard the muffled screams. Rearing his horse in the dark, he started calling out "Julia! Is that you? Julia, where are you?"

The girls kept up their screams. Soon, he found the double doors. Julia banged her fists until they were bruised all over again.

"How the devil did you get in there?" he cried out.

"Never mind! We'll explain later. Just get us out of here."

"Sit tight. I'll have to get help. If we can't find the grounds keeper, we'll have to pry the doors open. I'll be back as soon as I can."

Several hours later, Julia was safely back home. It was two o'clock when her mother finally put her to bed. Luana, feeling protective of her, got her some warm milk and took her off to bed, placing a hot water bottle under the mattress of the shivering child. Exhausted and relieved, her mother and father did not berate her, but Julia knew there would be a reckoning in the morning, and she was not looking forward to it.

CHAPTER 4

1878, Funchal, Madeira Departure

Looking like a row of stacking dolls waiting to be nested, Miguel and Maria held hands with their children along the dock at the port of Funchal Madeira. Beside them stood Estela, Ida, Ana, and Paulo, all dressed in their straw hats and white-starched Sunday best. They had arrived at Funchal from São Miguel two days prior to catch the first ship to the Sandwich Islands, so named by Captain Cook in honor of John Montague, the Earl of Sandwich.

As they craned their necks and shaded their eyes up at the large sailing vessel, known as a bark, their hearts swelled with the hope of another paradise. They had never seen any ship quite like it, and to them it was overwhelming, so expansive that they now believed nothing could touch them, as long as they were safe within its hold. Each of them held a canvas satchel with all the clothing and household goods they could carry. Maria clutched her growing stomach with an extra bag of sweet bread from yesterday's farewell gathering. It was not much, but it bolstered her with a sense of sustenance.

For Maria, there was no greater sorrow than saying goodbye to her seventy-five year old mother, Rose, in São Miguel. Years before, Maria's father had died, while working on the great railway connecting Lisbon to Carregado. That's when Maria and her mother became everything to each other. Given her few options, Rose moved her three children to São Miguel to live with extended family.

By the time Maria was twenty, she had fallen in love with Miguel Mirante, who was from Madeira but had traveled to São Miguel to find work as a farmer. Miguel knew that Rose would be uppermost in Maria's mind when he first approached her with his plan to move the family halfway across the world.

"Miguel, you cannot be serious. My mother could never survive the pain of it after all these years." Tears streamed down Maria's face as she considered all that it would mean to be separated from her mother.

"Hush, my love! Your mother has Cleta who has taken her in and cares for her. We will send money regularly to help them survive and then we will return and start our own farm."

Miguel convinced Maria that if they remained, they stood to lose everything, so they packed up their belongings and caught a boat to Funchal. Maria calculated that once they had saved enough money in the Sandwich islands, they would return to São Miguel, but she had no concept of the time or distance of the journey.

From the dock, Maria peered back up at Nossa Senhora do Monte, Our Lady of the Mount, the largest church in Funchal, situated in view of the harbor. She took in a view of the volcanic mountainsides that cupped the harbor, forming a protective escutcheon around it. She then swept her gaze back across the sea, eyeing the tiny fishing boats that bobbed up and down like sea horses ready to race, while the sun played staccato notes upon the blinking waters. She heaved a sigh and then followed Miguel up the gang plank of the ship.

As they showed their papers to the Steward, he instructed them through an interpreter and told them how much they could carry to their berth and how much must be stowed. They picked their most valued items and then handed one trunk to a nearby crew member, not realizing how long it would be before they would be able to access it again.

The Steward waved them onboard, and as they trundled up the gang plank, Paulo asked again about the land of pineapples and sugar cane. He never tired of hearing about it, asking his father endless questions, and Miguel never tired of embellishing his stories about it.

"What do their pineapples look like and how do they taste?"

"They say they are larger than ours and that they are the sweetest fruits of any other. Like golden pomegranates, only sweeter and juicier with no seeds to spit out. They say the nectar is so sweet, the bees cannot stay away from you after you eat it."

Paulo took this in silently while he punched his thumbs into his pockets and gaped at the beast of a ship that swallowed him up from the top of the gang plank. Standing two hundred twenty feet high, her three masts pierced the sky above him, and he could see no end to her sails. Her stays resembled an intricate web of cross-threads which held the masts and sails together. Facing the back of the ship, Paulo could see the crane that operated the anchors and the crew members who were loading the hold with supplies.

The First Mate, Joshua Roper, was busy overseeing efforts to prepare the ship, making a careful inventory of the cargo. It was clear that he commanded the respect and allegiance of the crew members, as he shouted out orders in a strange tongue which sounded like gibberish to Paulo.

The chief carpenter, Peter Oakes, was also busy making repairs. Hanging from the sides of the ship, crew members painted and caulked, securing the ship for the journey around the Cape Horn, known to the seamen as the "Devil's Cauldron." It was a place where the Atlantic and the Pacific, the two great titans of the seas, clashed into a perpetual maelstrom like fighting leviathans.

Nearby stood Captain William McAllister, an imposing figure of a man, six feet, two inches, in impeccable dress, from his black boots to his navy blue wainscot buttoned and neatly pressed. His thoughtful brown eyes under a rigid brow surveyed the entire ship with one glance. This was Captain McAllister's second trip around Cape Horn, and he was much more aware of the preparations required for a successful voyage. Satisfied that all was in order, he descended to his quarters but not before Paulo spotted him.

"Look *Pai*! Look! That must be our Captain."

"Yes, so it seems," Miguel rubbed his temples thoughtfully.

"Do you think we will see much of him?"

"Well, my son, a captain has many responsibilities. After all, our very lives are in his hands. He must ensure that all is working properly and that the ship is safe for us to travel. Every part of the ship must be checked and double-checked. He must also manage his crew. Their safety and well-being are also his responsibility. He stays below much of the time, as he plans our course and tries to anticipate danger."

Paulo listened carefully to all of this and considered how he might win favor with this Captain. It did not occur to him that the Captain would not understand his language. He would find a way. He was thinking of how he would like to be the Captain of such a great ship someday.

Once onboard, they were shown to their quarters on the steerage deck, which was situated below sea level. There were no portals, and the air was stagnant and stale. The immigrant quarters contained several long lines of bunk beds situated side-by-side. As a family of five, they were assigned two bunks. The girls shared one bunk between the three of them, and Miguel and Maria took the lower bed on the opposite bunk with Paulo above them.

The family hung all of their clothes and belongings on the bedposts and shared a few pegs on the wall behind their bed. They noticed that there was very little privacy, but they were able to string lines around their bunks on which they could hang clothing and some bedding. They would share a bucket as their latrine, and they were responsible for cleaning their own buckets and laundry.

Between the rows of bunks were tables lined with benches, where they would take their meals. Laid out for their afternoon meal were tureens of a milky soup containing a thin broth and bits of pork fat. Beside the soup, they were given hard tack, a hard bread with a cracker-like consistency. They would very soon find that this was the first of many similar meals to come. Yet, everyone took their first meal thankfully in anticipation of a new life. They gave thanks and shared Maria's sweet bread with the biscuits.

Across from them, Juvenal and Marissa Terra were settling into their bunks with their six children. It was comforting to know their most immediate neighbors, but there were many in the long room that they did not recognize. Following their example, many of them set up protective barriers made up of clothing and whatever linen they were able to carry.

"I don't mind the close quarters, but it would have been nice to know we would have so little privacy," Maria sniffed. "I would have brought more blankets and sheets."

Ever the optimist, her husband smiled and spoke hopefully, "But just think what good friends we will make here. Life long friends."

Maria looked over at him a bit incredulously. "Perhaps."

"Don't take friendship so lightly. We will need all the friends we can get for the journey and for building a new life. It will comfort us, as we consider the loved ones we have left behind."

"*Pai*, can I go now and explore the ship?" cried Paulo. He could not wait to break out. To him, the ship was a wonderland. Tousling his hair, Miguel replied, "But of course. I can't imagine you spending all of your time down here."

As Paulo bounded upward, it suddenly occurred to Maria that it would be difficult to keep him safe on this ship. While there may be less to worry about Paulo, what about the girls? They must lay down some rules.

She leaned into Miguel with a whisper, "I am not comfortable letting the girls do the same. They must be chaperoned at all times."

"I agree, my sweet, but we must be reasonable, " he raised his voice so that all could hear. "The girls cannot be confined down here for the entire journey.

The younger must always be accompanied by either one of us or their elder sisters. Surely, that is reasonable. Do you hear that girls?" He was not one to be cowed by his wife, but in this case, he agreed with her.

"Oh *Pai!*" Ida exclaimed. "Why must we be kept in a coop while our brother is allowed to run free? It's so annoying."

Maria was quick to reply, "You will soon learn that life is not the same for a girl as it is for a boy. You must learn to be on your guard."

"On my guard against what? Why should we not share the same freedoms?"

"Because there are those who would take advantage of you or hurt you, men and boys who are stronger than you. You are to keep watch over your sisters at all times. That is why there are separate quarters for single women without families. They are strictly chaperoned and kept at opposite ends of the ship from the young men, because they do not have family to protect them. Do not walk about the ship's lower compartments on your own, ever. You must respect the crew but always stay on your guard."

"But surely the Captain would never allow the ship's crew to harm us, would he?"

"No doubt it is not his intention, but we do not know these people, as we knew the families back in our village. Many of the crew are British, a people known for having their own way, and we do not speak their language. It's a whole new and strange world for us, and we are your family." She shook her finger at them for emphasis, "We are the ones who always have your best interests at heart. You must remember this."

Other than the occasional earthquake on their island, the girls were not really acquainted with fear. Their world had been nothing but one of happiness. Yet it seemed reasonable to them that they stick together until they could trust the people around them, so they did not argue.

"Then I would like to take the girls up on the top deck now, *Mãe*, so we can see the ship sail away," Estela responded. Maria gave them permission and told them they would join them in a half hour once they were settled.

By now, Paulo had already criss-crossed the top deck from one end to the other. Fascinated by crew members who crawled up the masts like spiders seizing their prey, he wondered if he might do the same. Then he heard a soft voice calling out to him.

"Hey kid! Pssst!"

Startled, he spun around to face a boy of about fourteen with thick, dark hair sticking out from his head in ropey strands. His coal-chalked face obscured his startling blue-grey eyes. The boy had popped his head out of an oak barrel, and the top of the barrel rested precariously on the nest of his hair.

"Can you get me some food?" The strange boy gulped.

Paulo was taken aback. "We had lunch down in our quarters an hour ago. Did you miss it? Where's your family?"

"Back in Funchal. My mother bribed a sailor to take me. I was so much trouble to her."

Paulo looked with intense curiosity at the young boy. It never occurred to him that a family would not care about their young boy. He would soon learn that not all families were alike and that not all children shared his happiness. From his pocket, he pulled out a piece of sweet bread reserved from his lunch. "Here, have some sweet bread." The boy grabbed it and swallowed it down in one gulp.

"Besides, I'm sure I'm not the only stowaway."

"Stowaway? What is that?"

"Someone who hides on a ship or a train or whatever without paying for it, and hopefully, without being seen."

"But aren't you worried what they'll do with you once they find out?"

"Well, they can't dump me in the sea. Once we're far enough inland, I'll be able to come out in the open more."

"What's your name?"

"Francisco," the boy replied. "Who are you?"

"My name is Paulo and I'm from São Miguel. I'll bring you food until you can come out in the open. Say, what do you think of those crew members climbing the masts? I'd sure like to do it."

"What's stopping you?"

Paulo shined a surprised but eager look in response.

Francisco gestured upwards. "I dare you. Go ahead. Who'll stop you? They won't even know you're not one of the crew members. And you'll have the best view of Funchal as we leave."

Paulo's heart thumped wildly as his eyes grew wet with the sea air. Without a word, he ran to the main mast, grabbed the lower stays, and started climbing. He was quick and nimble, but when he was halfway up the mast, one of the crew members spotted him and recognized that he was not one of theirs.

"Hey you! Boy! What do you think you're doing?"

Once the alarm was sounded, other crew members looked his way. He had drawn attention to himself, but he would not stop. He kept going without looking back. When he finally did look below, the crew and passengers appeared to be ants circling a drain beneath him, and he grew light-headed.

And then he saw the Captain, glaring up at him. This had not been the first impression he had hoped to make, but he was overwhelmed with the effort, the view, and the sheer thrill of it. While the way forward seemed effortless, it was another matter when he attempted to come down. He was like a cat caught up in a tree. He did not know how to position his feet and he froze.

After several attempts to persuade him to come down, the Captain turned to the Second Mate. "Go up and get him down. It doesn't look as if he can do it on his own. We'll have to delay our departure."

"And once I get him down?"

"Bring him to me immediately."

Estela and her sisters were just coming up to the deck when they heard the commotion. A crowd had gathered underneath the spot where Paulo had climbed up the mast, and they followed the trajectory of the collective gaze. Since there was nothing unusual about seeing a man or boy climb a mast, it did not register with the girls that it was their brother, although they realized the lad who was stuck was very young.

One of the Terra children spotted him first. "Look, it's Paulo!"

Estela leaned back, took a long second glance, and realized he was right. Feeling both frightened and infuriated, she called up, "Paulo! What are you doing up there?" Paulo could barely hear her, but it caused him to look in her direction. It also caused others to look in her direction and one pair of black eyes in particular. She called up again. "Come down here, at once!"

"I can't," he yelled. He was getting frightened and tired of holding on.

Before he could call for help, the Second Mate was behind him, speaking words of encouragement.

"Steady now, lad. Hold fast." Paulo could not understand him, but he knew his words were reassuring. The Second Mate safely tied a rope around him and secured it back to his own waist for safe measure.

"Now, wrap your left arm around my neck and when it's secure, let go with your right and hold onto me." The sailor pointed to his left hand and then to his own neck, and Paulo quickly got the idea. Soon, he was back on deck. Misty-eyed, all he could make out amidst the crowd was Francisco's smirk. His wounded pride would not allow him to glance in the direction of the stowaway again. He looked down and the next thing he saw were the Captain's boots.

"Just what do you think you were doing, young man?" He asked through the interpreter.

Straining upward, Paulo gulped and directed his words to the interpreter, "Learning to be a captain, like you." The Captain's expression softened ever so slightly.

By this time, Paulo's father had arrived to intervene. He turned to the interpreter. "Tell the Captain we are most apologetic, and it will never happen again," he said, while taking a strong hold of Paulo's hand.

After listening to the man's explanation, the Captain asked the interpreter to explain the rules of the ship, including areas of the ship that were off limits to the passengers. Slightly amused by Paulo's declaration of his young ambitions, the Captain added, that if Paulo really wanted to make up for his misadventure, he was welcome to help the crew by reporting to the Second Mate in the morning.

"However, let him know that climbing the masts will not be a part of his duties and that there is much about ship life that is not glamorous or exciting. He would be expected to work hard." The interpreter delivered this proposal with a slight smile, and Miguel thanked the Captain but declined to accept the offer on his son's behalf. Paulo, however, could not let the opportunity pass. "But *Pai*, I promise I will only do what I am told."

Miguel turned back to the interpreter in Portuguese. "Let me have some time to give it more thought. Can I assume the offer will remain open after tomorrow?" thinking that it may be a good way to keep the boy occupied.

The Captain nodded with consent, "As you wish," and retreated.

Miguel let out a long, slow breath and turned to Paulo, realizing that it was a good thing that his mother had not seen this stunt, even if he would have to tell her before others beat him to it. There was no doubt that Paulo had managed to create a sensation, and he had just made himself famous.

"I lost nine lives watching you hang from that mast. Never do anything like that again. You must promise me or I will have to keep you confined."

Paulo nodded, "Yes, *Pai*! But please let me help the crew. I want to be a sailor."

Miguel could only respond that he would think about it and now understood that there would be many challenges ahead as he ushered his children around the deck.

It was a beautiful evening, and the crew were just about to pull up anchor. The First Mate, Joshua Roper, barked out orders to the anxious crew. "Haul short the anchor! Yank on the windlass!" Immediately, two men scurried into action.

Once the anchor was up, the call came out to trim the sails. "Mr. Baker - make sail!" At his orders, the top men darted up the yard in unison. The bark began its sway.

"There's top-men aloft. Yank to the wind! Mr Lamb, take the wheel."

Paulo stood transfixed, head cranked upwards, as he watched the crew's feverish efforts. He did not understand their words, but he memorized their every move.

"Set your fore staysail and your fore and main top sail!"

Paulo looked up, until the sails billowed in the wind and the men disappeared into them. He clasped the trunk of the main mast, feeling as if he were riding a giant balloon flying towards the sun. Once they were in full sail, the wind died down, as the bark slipped into the horizon, and twilight fell upon them with a blanket of stars. All evening long, they swayed to the dulcet tones of strumming braguinhas and violas.

When Maria joined them, they linked arms and drew in a final glimpse of Funchal. For better or for worse, there was no going back now. As they gazed at the shoreline, a pair of malevolent eyes continued to survey them from on high, assessing their strengths and vulnerabilities. They were eyes that would not relent until the restless heart behind them could find a way around the father and the mother.

CHAPTER 5

1902, Santa Clara, First Impressions

Anarosa and Luana danced delicately around the question of how to handle Julia. Of course, Frank had his own opinions, which did not make matters any easier for Luana. Frank and Anarosa did agree on one point, that their eldest daughter required discipline and a firm hand. Luana was careful not to come between them; she was able to draw Anarosa out by refusing to take sides, and she listened closely to Anarosa's conversations with Frank as she worked in the kitchen.

"All I know is that she's wandering all over the Valley, and there's no keeping track of her. She's a wild child." Frank was expressing his frustration the day after they rescued Julia and Therese. "It's already well known that we had to call the sheriff to find her. The whole town is talking about it!"

Anarosa shook her head, "I know. It's not seemly for a young girl to be wandering around creeks and rivers, not to mention cemeteries, in the dark. Perhaps we ought to consider sending her away to my brother's dairy farm in Fresno."

"Send my child away?" Frank was appalled at the idea. "Maybe you just need to get a better handle on the girl!"

Anarosa now understood that in Frank's mind, it was her problem to solve and not his, and she quickly changed the subject. She sometimes suspected that Frank resented her carefree upbringing, one that was much easier than his.

It was not long after this conversation that Luana overheard Anarosa berating Julia.

"From now on, you will not leave this house until you have spent at least three hours in useful activity and that's after you have finished all of your chores."

"What? You mean three hours of piano and poetry? No thank you." Julia was defiant, even though she knew she stood on shaky ground. When faced with the reality of a new life under her mother's thumb, she was not going to give in without a fight.

"And no more running around creek beds. I had nightmares thinking of you being swept down to the Bay!" Her voice went low. "You are no longer a child. You will stay on the farm and learn to sew and play the piano, until you become a proper young lady."

"Why couldn't I do something fun like work at Luana's bakery or work on the farm? I'll even do some of the work that the boys don't want to do. Anything but stay inside!"

Alexio was nearby and had always had a soft spot for his younger sister. He understood Julia's need to be out of doors and was not against her helping out on the farm, so he could not help but insert himself in the conversation. "Why don't you let her help with the horses? Learn to ride? After all, it's time she learned."

"Riding is not exactly what I had in mind for a well bred young lady!" Anarosa persisted.

"Mama, many girls in the Valley learn to ride, and Julia is the perfect age for it. Every woman and girl should know how to saddle and hitch a horse. After all, what's she supposed to do in an emergency? And I know more than one young girl who rides in horse shows and even rodeos."

At this, Luana could not help but step outside the kitchen to add, "Haven't you seen the young girls who show their horses at the annual county horse show? They get to raise and groom them and then ride at the head of the summer parade!"

Alexio added another two cents, "And it would also be a great opportunity to show off our livestock and agriculture with other farmers. Think of what it will do for the family name."

Anarosa placed her hands on her hips and glowered at all of them, as it was clear that they were ganging up on her. She could not come up with a reasonable argument against their scheme. She also realized that taming Julia would never happen in a kitchen. Julia tried to feign an air of innocent indifference, even though she was thrilled at the thought of riding in the county horse show and the annual parade.

All Anarosa could say was, "I'll take it up with your father. But you will learn to play the piano, and you will not leave this house until your household chores are done. If you do not abide by these rules, you will not ride in the horse show and that's a promise."

"Yes, Mama." She tried her best to sound meek and compliant, but Luana could easily see the effort it cost her and gave Julia a knowing wink. Luana also knew that while Anarosa certainly meant to speak to Frank, her decision had been made, and Frank was not likely to put up an argument.

"How soon do we get started?" Julia turned to look at her brother, happy that she would get to spend more time with him.

"Whoa, wait a minute. I don't want you thinking this is only about riding in a fancy riding habit. You will be getting up with the chickens and working hard every day. It can be back-breaking work. You will start by working in the stables under Marcos's direction, and you will do whatever he asks you to do. Is that understood?" Alexio spoke with firmness.

"All I know is that I will do whatever I have to do to get out of the kitchen."

Alexio studied Julia with amused concentration. He had no doubt that she would do exactly what she put her mind to doing and that she would excel at it. Somehow, he could not picture her becoming the well-bred young woman of society envisioned by his mother. A debutante ball for his sister Julia? The very thought of it choked up a gurgling guffaw.

"Just keep in mind that it involves lots of cleaning up after them, keeping their stalls clean, hauling hay and oats, brushing and grooming."

"But when do I get to learn to ride?"

"First, you learn to care for them — and I mean really care for them — and then, when I'm convinced you have truly fallen in love with a horse, only then, will I teach you to ride her. If you do a good job, then we'll let you pick out your own foal come spring."

Julia's face brightened. "That means I may be ready to ride in the parade next summer, right?"

"It takes a lot more than just a few months to ride a horse!" But Alexio could see Julia's determination and did not under-estimate her.

"Let's go outside and talk to Marcos. You can start right away if he has work for you." Alexio jumped up and Julia followed, after glancing back a wide grin at Luana.

Marcos D'Angelo had been the farm's foreman for only six months, but in that time, he had gained the respect of all the farmhands and the Mirante family. Marcos's older cousin, Gilberto, was a long-time friend of Frank's, and together they had journeyed from what was then known as the Sandwich Islands to California.

Marcos began working with horses and cattle at the age of twelve and gradually gained a reputation as the keenest and most trustworthy horse master for miles around, despite his young age. By the time he was sixteen, he was working for the largest landowner in the Valley, Jackson McCallum, but had lost his position through the foul play of other ranch hands, which left a bitter taste in his mouth. His cousin Gilberto introduced him to Frank who hired him on the spot.

Marcos now looked over the thirteen-year-old Julia, taking in her flowered blue dress and pinafore, which were inappropriate for working in a barn. He was insulted at the idea of playing nursery maid to a young girl, a big come-down from managing almost fifty ranch hands. Nevertheless, he kept quiet, given what he owed to Frank and Gilberto. He determined to make the work as difficult as possible, in the hopes that she would easily give it up, and he would no longer have her under his feet.

"Every stable must be shoveled first thing each morning at six o'clock sharp. Do you think you can handle that?"

Julia pierced a glance up at him without flinching. She understood instantly that he was not going to make life easy for her. She also realized that his support was critical to her chance of success. Her response was direct and matter-of-fact, "Yes, I do." She met his steely blue gaze and held it there. Marcos turned towards Alexio, who readily perceived that it was not going to be Marcos's favorite assignment.

Alexio spoke somewhat apologetically, "I've told her that no task should be too small for her. Treat her just as you would any new hand. She needs to learn everything there is to know about caring for horses. Eventually, if she does well, we'll make a horse woman out of her."

Marcos handed Julia a pitchfork and pointed to a nearby shovel. "We've got ten stalls and they're all dirty. Start shoveling. When I return in an hour, I don't want to see one stool on the ground. You can use the pitchfork to bail in clean hay." He wasn't going to give her anymore explanations than he had to, knowing that it was unlikely she could clean them all in an hour. He turned on his heel before she could object or question him.

Alexio's expression creased into a grin. "I see you'll have your work cut out for you." She shrugged a response, and he returned to the house.

Julia surveyed the stalls and made a quick mental calculation. Ten stalls. That's not even ten minutes each. She had never picked up a shovel before, but with confidence born out of determination, she picked one up and began to shovel.

It was much heavier than she expected, and after scooping up one shovel of dung, she tottered forward as she looked for a place to pile it. She circled the barn, trying to find a dumping spot, lost her balance after tilting over, and fell sideways into manure. Marcos had not mentioned where to shovel the dung, and she had not thought to ask. Scrambling up, she looked over her scraped knees and filthy dress.

"What a mess!" A voice cried out from the hay loft. Julia turned around in the direction of the familiar voice. She fanned her hands over her eyes for a focused glance.

Julia shouted up at Therese, "Where are you?"

"I'm up here in the hay loft, watching every stupid move you make."

Julia looked again through the filtered sunlight seeping through the cracks. She could just make out Therese with her feet dangling off the sides of the loft. "How long have you been there and how'd you know where to find me?"

"Your brother told me you were in the barn, and I've been here long enough to see you try to shovel horse manure. Don't you know how to use a shovel?"

Julia ignored her taunts and cried, "Quick! Just get on down here and help me shovel out these stalls. It's gotta be done in less than an hour."

"But why?" Therese whined. She had just finished chores at home and was not relishing the idea of more work. She had her heart set on sweet treats.

"Just help me now and I'll explain more later. Look, there's another shovel in that corner over there."

"Where are we going to chuck it?"

"Let's just toss it out the front doors into a pile." Therese looked uncertain but immediately picked up the shovel and started hauling. They soon realized it was taking too long to run it over to the door.

"We've got to find a cart of some kind." Julia ran out and brought back a wheelbarrow. "This will help." The girls doubled their efforts and made fewer trips to the pile, running back and forth between stalls. Within a half hour, it was all out of the barn.

"We better sweep them out now and get some hay down here to replace what was there."

They were soon done, and Julia smiled to herself as she considered the impression she would make on Marcos. He thought he could outsmart her, but he would soon find that she was not such an easy mark. She imagined the look on his face when he saw what she had done.

"It was the only way I could get out of canning. And you know how I hate canning." Therese agreed and remarked, "I only hate it a little less than sewing. But why shovel manure?"

"Because I'm going to ride in the horse show, and I'm going to win so I can ride at the head of the parade."

"And just what does shoveling manure have to do with that?"

"It's what I have to do to get in the parade. Alexio even said I could pick out my own horse when the mares birth their foals in the spring." Julia tossed new hay with rigor.

Therese was starting to get the picture. "Does that mean we won't be going down to the *Serradura* bakery anymore?"

"Of course not." Just as she said it, Julia heard approaching steps. She did not want Marcos to know that she had help.

"Quick! Get up in the loft out of sight. We'll get to the *Serradura*, as soon as I get rid of my slave master." Therese scrambled up into the loft, just as Marcos made his entrance.

He glanced over the stalls with surprise, while Julia stood still and held her breath. He did not comment on her efforts, but he seemed impressed enough. "This is not where you dump the manure."

"But, you never said ..."

The twitch in his jaw stopped her in her tracks. "Next time, you need to ask. Now take the shovel, and I want it all out the back pitch door. Do you understand?"

"Aye aye, sir!" She could not help the sarcasm but regretted it, as soon as she saw his blazing eyes. She knew she had to somehow win him over or even her brother would not stand by her. While she had never learned how to catch flies with honey, she was beginning to realize it might come in handy in this case.

"That's right!" he growled. Do as I say and we'll get along just fine, but don't cross me, or I'll make your life a misery, and you'll never ride in a horse show. Now, do you know where you stand?"

Julia wanted to repeat her previous refrain but bit down hard to restrain herself. She did not notice the blood that trickled down one side of her lip, but Marcos did. He turned his back on her and went out the front doors. Julia reeled around and shouted up into the loft towards Therese. "Quick! Get down here or there will be no time for the *Serradura*."

Therese scrambled down and then took a hard jump. Together, they shoveled everything back into the cart, raced it over to the back pitch door, and dumped it outside in a pile. And then, with one mutual look of understanding, they made a run for it. Julia conveniently forgot that Marcos had other things for her to do.

They headed down the garden path, past the turnstile, along the poplars and up the Guadalupe River towards the Bay in the direction of the *Serradura*. After stuffing their bellies with chocolate and malasdas, they meandered down the street and back to the old house. Julia could not stay away, although there had been few opportunities since their misadventure in the cemetery.

The girls had managed to go back at least once or twice, but they had no success at stealing the mail. The butler was always too fast for them, as if he were sitting by the window waiting for the mailman. They surmised that he might be gazing out the window. To avoid detection, they looked for a new hiding place and found it at at a nearby tank house, just beyond the old house and well-sheltered by eucalyptus trees. They climbed up to the tank platform and dangled their feet off the sides while they waited for the mailman.

"If we're going to grab the mail, we will have to get closer. Why don't you wait for the mailman down at the far corner and signal me when you see him coming?"

"But how do I know which direction he'll come from?"

"Because he always comes from that direction." Julia pointed to the west.

"And how can you know that?"

"Because I've been watching and waiting on my own, when you weren't around."

Therese shrugged and climbed back down the tank house and ran a couple of blocks away from the old house. Then she returned. Huffing and puffing, she vaulted back up to the frame and announced that he was about six blocks away headed in their direction. The wind whipped up around them, creating a flutter from the sails and a grinding from the rotor, as they hunkered down and waited.

Within a half hour, Julia spotted the mailman. "I'm going down. I've got to get closer, if I'm going to beat the servant to the post box. I'll have to keep along the side and back fences, if I don't want to be spotted."

But Therese was having second thoughts, "I don't know. If the butler is waiting by that window, like we think he is, he is going to see you."

"Don't worry. I'll keep my eye on the window." Julia disappeared around the hedge and sidled up to the the house facing away from the convent, just under the front porch side window.

As the mailman approached the post box near the sidewalk, Julia thrust her head up into the window, but what she saw caused her to shrink back. A wizened gray face. Peridot-shot eyes peering out from a halo of snowy, long tendrils tied in clumps to one side. Piercingly grim and disapproving.

The old woman's words stabbed at Julia through a window screen. "What do you want, girl? I've seen you lurking about. Don't think you can hide from me."

Julia said nothing, but she did not run away. It was not as if she had never seen an old woman before, but her curiosity overcame her fear.

"What is it?" The old woman pointed to a statue of an angel on the front porch etched in stone. "Is that what you want? Take whatever you want. I have no need of any of it. Just leave me alone," her voice cracked from disuse.

Julia returned her gaze with a look of helpless curiosity. The old woman stared back and her eyes dilated, as she studied Julia's face. Then she disappeared, as suddenly as she had appeared. Julia walked away deep in thought.

When she returned to the tank house, Therese was waiting for her, not having seen the face in the window or Julia take the mail. Now she saw the look on Julia's face and knew that something had happened.

"You look like you've seen a ghost. What happened?"

Julia stood there thoughtfully. "I got caught."

"By the butler?"

"No, not the butler." She spoke slowly. "An old woman. She must be the one who lives there."

"Did you get the mail?"

"No, but I won't have to now. I saw what I came to see, and I will be back."

"You'll be back? But what for?"

Julia spoke thoughtfully and slowly, as she studied her feet. "I'm not sure how or when or even why, but I will be back."

CHAPTER 6

1878, The Atlantic, Azorean Sunset

Some say there is no sunset like an Azorean sunset. The same might say that, when the sun in its brilliance mounts the azure skies, it lingers enthralled for one moment longer, as it rises above these galvanic islands just off the north coast of Africa: Santa Maria, São Miguel, Terceira, Graciosa, Faisal, São Jorge, Pico, Flores, Corvo.

The Mirantes had never seen their islands from so many panoramas or even from a map or a globe. During their sail through the Azores, they caught one last glimpse of their homeland at sunset. Like starlings in a murmuration, they gathered from various parts of the vessel. Miguel pulled out his braguinha, and they softly sang words of their homeland:

O Gente Da Minha Terra

It is both yours and mine
This destiny that binds us together
No matter how much it is denied
By the strings of a guitar

When I hear the lament
Of a singing guitar
I am instantly lost
With a desire to weep
Come back
Oh people of my land

This sadness will I carry
And share with you my loved ones
As I bid you goodbye
And carry you in my heart

The immigrants established a nightly routine as the first week passed. When the crew were not performing drills and inspections on deck, they would dance under the starlit skies. To the Portuguese, dancing was as natural as breathing, the perfect past-time for any occasion. In sadness, in pain, and in pleasure, there was always the dance, whether slow and moving or brash and exuberant. The *chama-rita* circle was an unspoken invitation to everyone nearby, for those staving off nostalgia and homesickness and even fear, as well as for those who rejoiced in the new life ahead of them.

In those first few days, the weather was pleasant and mild, but some of the immigrants could not stop looking back with a deep sense of loss. Others were caught up in the excitement and could only consider what lay ahead. As they replaced the rigging and repaired the flax sails, the crew could hear a confluence of weeping and laughing or moaning and sighing.

One man had carried a marjoram plant onboard, holding it close, as he crossed the gang plank. It was a plant that grew wild all over his island, and its robust scent permeated everything around it. The herb was used generously in many native Portuguese dishes. It was as if he wanted to take with him the taste and the smell of his homeland, thinking that it could be bottled and transported.

"It's not likely you will be able to keep that alive on this long journey," remarked the First Mate when he saw him carrying it onboard. The man looked up at him with the wet and defiant eyes of a child clutching a beloved toy.

"Don't worry. I will keep it alive." He spoke it as if his own life depended upon it. He felt like a plant uprooted, and he knew he must be replanted, just as he would replant the marjoram. Mr. Roper wisely concluded that it was not worth the effort to prise it from him and simply motioned for him to come through.

Immigrant accommodations were nothing more than adequate, except for the food, which was barely edible. The immigrants continued to receive the same hard tack and gruel, even while it was whispered among them that the crew were given meat and some vegetables and that chickens were being raised on deck. There were even a few milk cows below steerage.

"We cannot survive on these paltry meals," grumbled Juvenal as he swung his spoon around the room. "Some of our wives are pregnant and need more for their strength."

Miguel nodded in agreement. "Surely this will get better." Even as he spoke, he wondered. If this continued, what choices did they really have?

Juvenal insisted, "But if we started our journey with so little, how are we to expect to receive anything better? We must address the problem now."

Listening in on the conversation, other families joined the bellyaching. By the second week, it was being whispered that the cook was withholding what should have been theirs and already buying favors with his gains. It was even rumored that some of the young women would cajole him into giving them food for favors.

The corpulent cook, Jack O'Malley, was called 'Slick' because of his greasy spoon and his greasy mouth. He looked as if he was always dipping into the cooking pot, and his apron, draped over an expansive belly, exposed the evidence for it. He also spoke out of two sides of his mouth, when questioned about the food rations. The cook spat out one story to the Captain and another to his detractors.

It was not long before alliances began to form, creating tenuous power structures like the tentacles of an octopus curling through their fragile floating world. Life at sea could suddenly be filled with over-heated tempers that might easily result in spontaneous outbursts. And, whatever one could barter with to make life at sea more bearable was often turned into a device replicated by others.

Of course, the crew had their own pecking order and protocols, but aside from the crew, the immigrants were the least powerful and the most vulnerable to malice and caprice. They all wondered who, if anyone, could be an advocate for them.

Paulo lost no time gaining the good graces of the crew, hoping he would be a sailor someday. He worked hard to understand their language, and when he could not understand, he watched them eagerly and imitated their moves. He became a steady and quick learner. During his first week, Paulo begged his *Pai* to take him to the First Mate to report for duty.

Mr. Roper took one look at the boy and glanced at his Second Mate, Wilbur Haye, known as little "Wills" among the officers and crew. Wills stood a mere five feet and five inches and was the shortest adult crew member on board. He sported a half toothless tobacco-stained grin and smelled of sardines. Over his bushy eyebrows he wore a woolen cap that appeared to have been knit during a past century. It was the only indication on his person that someone might have loved him once.

Wills was the guy who was given all the tasks that no one else wanted. Whether it was cleaning out the slop buckets, swabbing the decks, or minding the chickens, Wills was your man. He was also responsible for supplying the crew with equipment to do their work, and he performed some of a common sailor's drudgeries. He reefed and furled the topsails and repaired the ship along with the crew. When he was not sleeping, he spent all of his time on deck.

Mr. Roper turned to Wills, "Wills, take this boy under your wing and teach him everything you can. He cannot speak English, but he can watch and learn."

Wills squinted through his splayed, bony fingers, as he stared down at Paulo through the bright sun. "A' ye sure ittsa' worth the botherin', sir? I mean, uh, he's such a little 'un. What if he dunnot understand and falls overboard or even worse?"

"The Captain has agreed, so we must give it a try, Wills. Have the rest of the crew keep a half eye out for him. Make sure they don't abuse the lad and let him do whatever task you need. And make sure he doesn't get washed overboard."

"Aye, aye, Sir," replied Wills, all the while thinking, "If this lad becomes any trouble a'tall, I'll be done with 'em or give 'em nothing but a big dose o' the slop buckets. Mebbe I can even make a little bilge rat outta 'em."

Paulo could not understand all that had passed between the two seamen, but he stood as tall and erect as he could and saluted, just as he had watched them do, producing a half smile from Mr. Roper, as he turned his attention to other matters. And then, with one wave of the hand, Wills showed Paulo to the quarterdeck and pointed to the bucket and the scrubber and then the deck.

"OK, laddie, let's see 'ow long ye can last. This entire upper deck is yours to clean ever' day. Take the scrubber and be sure to keep the bucket refilled," he said as he motioned to each. Wills walked the four corners to show Paulo the extent of his responsibility. He then whistled at one of the crew to demonstrate the process.

Hal O'Grady ran over to Wills and readily took up the task. Wills then pointed at Paulo and then to Hal, "Now it's your turn. Show me, boy!" Paulo grin and then imitated what he had just seen with great relish.

"Ye seem to have all the monkey grease, little monkey. That'll do now. Keep it up," Wills said, as he walked away with a grin. And from that day, all the crew members referred to Paulo as that "little monkey," who had climbed the mast on the first day. They figured out the Portuguese word for monkey was "Macaco," and it soon stuck to Paulo like a sailor's tattoo.

It was some time before he could understand why they called him Macaco, but even when he had figured it out, he did not mind. Although he had never seen a monkey, he knew they were quick and strong and could climb the highest trees. He liked that idea, because it might mean that, eventually, he would be climbing the masts. He wanted most of all to be on the watch, so he could stand on top of the world to see it go by.

Paulo spent four hours scouring every inch of the deck, until he came back to the beginning and started again. In the meantime, the crew were told to keep an eye out, in case he tried to scale the mast again, but Paulo was too determined to make a good impression to repeat his mistake. If he had not been so busy, he might have noticed Francisco lurking nearby and eyeballing him.

"Why, boy. Have you got some more food for me?"

Paulo tilted his head sideways while on all fours. He went back to what he was doing but shot back at Francisco, "No one has food. You're going to have to bribe the cook or make yourself known. And stop calling me "boy"! I've had enough of your suggestions anyway."

"But boy!" Francisco grinned as he said it. "Have pity. I'm starvin'!"

Paulo rose to his feet to face Francisco. His first impulse was to slug him, but he thought the better of it. It was with a generous heart that he reached into his pocket and pulled out the last of the sweet bread his mother had given him. "Here's all I have left. Now, figure out another way to feed yourself in the future. Everyone is hungry almost all of the time." He tried to sound firm on the matter, but his resolve was as easily melted as his generosity was boundless.

Francisco took the bread and wolfed it down greedily. "I'll just have to find another way into the kitchen stores without being seen by Slick. You get me what you can. What do you say?"

"I don't know why I should, after all the trouble you caused me the other day. It got me off to a bad start with the Captain."

"Why should you care? So, you really want to be a sailor?" Francisco laughed. "That work you're doing now doesn't look like sailor's work to me! Why would you want to do that?"

Paulo paused and gave it a thought, "Sometimes, you have to do what you don't like to do, so you can do what you really like to do!" He turned back to his work bucket.

Francisco laughed at that. "Well, when I set out to do what I'm going to do, no one will keep me from it by making me do their dirty work. I will do it my own way in my own good time. Whatever I do will be mine and mine alone."

Noticing the glances of the other nearby crew members, Paulo got back on all fours and said, "Well, this is what I want to do, so why don't you just go away and leave me to it?" Francisco smirked but only said, "Whatever you like. But you have to have some fun once in awhile. Meet me at the lifeboats on the starboard side after dinner and bring me whatever you can spare to eat."

Paulo waved him off and then started to clean the entire deck a second time, but Hal O'Grady, noticing the extra effort, sought to encourage him. "Hey, Macaco. I think that is quite enough for today, little laddie. Ye've done a fine job. Now, go to yo' family and come back tomorrow right after breakfast. There's no end o' work on this floatin' bucket."

He pointed to his pocket watch to indicate time and tomorrow, which was the best he could manage by way of sign language. But Paulo readily understood, stood up tall, and gave his best salute in response. Hal responded with a salute and then a pat on his head for encouragement.

While Paulo was learning his first duties, the girls were trying to establish some sense of routine to their daily life onboard. Chores like bathing, personal grooming, and laundry had to be rationed carefully to coincide with limited resources and ship rules about where and when these activities could take place.

Each morning Kit, the cabin boy, would bring them a bucket of fresh water, and on Saturdays, they received a bucket each for laundry. That meant the daily bucket would have to be shared among them. Since there were six of them, they decided to dip one wash cloth one time and then they would all share it to wash their face and hands. Paulo would go last.

"Oh Lordy," Ida cried. "What is worse: to be dirty underneath your clothes, to have dirty clothes, or to have dirty hair?"

"I have to have clean hair," added Ana. "I couldn't stand to lie in greasy hair all night."

"Well, it'll take at least one or two cups to wash your hair and then one or two cups to rinse. If you can wash with one cup, you'll have some left over for other things," figured Estela, as she sighed. "One hair wash per week will have to do."

"Well, I don't see why *Pai* and Paulo need any hair washing," retorted Ida, as she ran her fingers through her hair, as if she were feeling for lice.

"But *Pai* will need to shave. Perhaps, the boys could share the remainder of their bucket on their day?" Estela probed thoughtfully.

Maria was not as sanguine about what would work with Paulo's bathing habits. "I'll ask your *Pai*. And as for Paulo, he would welcome not having to bathe at all, so I'll have to take charge of his bucket on his day and be sure he gets his ears and his hair washed at the very least."

"By the looks of him when he came in after scrubbing the deck, I would have to say he'll need washing every night!" cried Ida. "Why! Did you see him? I'm so glad that he's sleeping above us. I just hope that the smell rises upward! Maybe he could swim with the crew when we anchor."

And then after she had a moment to think more about it, she cried, "Oh no! And then he'll smell like a salty fish," cried Ida. And with that, they all had a good laugh.

Miguel walked in just in time to hear the ruckus. "What is that all about it?"

"Paulo either gets a bath or he will smell like a salty fish. Either way, you're the one who gets to sleep closest to him," chuckled Estela.

"Well, I will certainly look forward to that. The way things are going, we'll be lucky if we ever see Paulo. He is all over this ship. But I hear that he did very well today and enjoyed every minute of his first day."

"Huh!" snorted Ida. "I don't know how anyone could get excited about cleaning the quarterdeck. What is wrong with that boy?"

Miguel responded firmly. "Now, now. Don't ever discourage him. It keeps him happy and occupied, and he's learning what it means to be a sailor. This could only be good for him."

Just as Miguel finished his sentence, Paulo came in for dinner. As they sat around their hard tack and gruel, the grumbling resumed among their fellow passengers. There was barely enough to fill their stomachs, and it certainly wasn't getting better. Paulo had managed to sneak a little hard tack into his pocket.

Before his neighbors could provoke him into taking their part, Miguel jumped up and motioned for his family to accompany him on deck for their last sunset over the Azores. He was not going to worry tonight, and he was not going to get caught up in their mutterings. For Miguel, this was a solemn moment, and he was determined to enjoy it with his family. It was a final salute to their beautiful homeland.

CHAPTER 7

1902, Santa Clara, Watermelon Brandy

Anarosa stood speechless, as her eyes bounced around her kitchen. It had taken a good deal of bootlicking, but Luana had eventually talked her into using the kitchen for the week, and now it was run amok. Not that Luana had failed to consider the bakery kitchen, but Domingos was unbending. He insisted that he could not carry on the business of fine baked goods with sticky watermelon syrup and seeds underfoot.

Anarosa leaned back and sucked in her breath as she glanced around her kitchen, which now resembled a canteen. Watermelon rinds, bottles, seeds, copper vats, bags of sugar, and raisins. There was no room to sit. She spoke with an accusatory voice, as if she had never agreed to let Luana use her kitchen. "How many days will it stay this way? If I'd realized you were turning my kitchen into a distillery, I'm not sure I would have agreed." Of course, she was back-pedaling on their bargain, having been distracted with knitting a blue sweater for Frank's birthday, when Luana started prattling about watermelon brandy and how she would need to use the kitchen for an entire week. Why hadn't she thought about it a little more before she agreed?

Luana's eyebrows brittled and her hands clutched a watermelon rind, as she took up her cause. "Remember, I told you it would take at least five days. I didn't sugar-coat it. I told you the truth. But I also promised I would have breakfast, lunch, and dinner ready on time out in the dining room every day without fail. You won't go without a meal, and you won't have to lift a finger for it. Think of the break it will be for an entire week! That was our bargain, right?"

"And the sticky juice and seeds all over the floor boards?" Anarosa whined.

"You won't find a seed outside the watermelon patch." Luana spoke as she scraped up a patch of seeds from the table.

"Well, I hope it's worth it to you. I never heard of distilling brandy from watermelon, and I just won't believe it can be done, not for a second."

"Oh, trust me. It's been done and by several farmers right here in the Valley. The minute I read about it, I could not wait to try it out." Luana cooked up the scheme after daydreaming about how vials of the pearly fluid would make a stunning attraction in the corner of the *Serradura*. She had been growing quite an impressive patch of watermelons, and if she could perfect the art, there would be no end of new customers and a new stream of revenue. Perhaps she could exceed the amount of revenue taken in by the bakery, Luana reasoned.

Luana started the business of brandy-making by visiting Farmer Dunham, and she persuaded him to give her a lesson. As an incentive, she gave him baked bread for a month from the *Serradura* in exchange for sharing his methods, but he was so proud of his skill that he probably would have settled for much less.

"So how many ingredients will it take?" Luana quizzed the farmer.

"All we need is lots of ripe watermelon, water, sugar, and one secret ingredient," he declared as he laid out a large basin for catching the juice.

"And what might that be?" She fingered her locket greedily, as she waited for him to reveal his secret. With a blue-eyed twinkle, he easily gave way. "Raisins."

"And just how and where can I get them?" Luana stopped rubbing the locket and knit her brow. Farmer Dunham handed her a mail order catalog from Clovis, California. "There's a group of raisin producers right here in California. I order them by the pound." Luana could not wait to try it.

Julia was knee-deep in manure these days, so Luana recruited Rose as her assistant. Together they cut up twenty melons and removed the seeds before gathering the pulp into bags made of cheese cloth. The work was slow-going and gave them time for conversation.

"I noticed Julia is wearing her overalls everyday now," remarked Luana, as she sliced up watermelon.

"Yeah. Who would have thought. How'd you convince her?"

"I didn't need to convince her. After almost a year of stable work, her dresses were in tatters, and your mother told her she'd have to launder them herself and earn money to pay for new ones. That's all it took."

"Yeah, Julia has always found a way to disappear every Monday on wash day. She'll do anything to get out of washing and ironing. She's even traded with me for cooking and canning, which she hates only a little less than playing the piano."

"That's my girl," laughed Luana. "She's just not going to be the domestic type."

"No, but who would have thought she'd be a farmhand? Have you seen what Marcos has her doing? She sometimes works in piles of manure and smells like it too. I told her she can't sleep in our room without a bath every night!"

"I know. I have to help wash it out of her hair, and the only thing that seems to help is vinegar. And lots of it! But she does seem determined to ride."

"But Marcos won't even let her ride yet. She spends her time cleaning out the stalls."

"And she gets to watch them train the horses and break them in for riding. She loves that part. But I do agree that Marcos seems to be taking his time about letting her do more."

Once they finished cutting and seeding, Luana and Rose squeezed ten gallons of perfectly pink watermelon juices from the cheese cloth and poured them into cooking pots. Then they added the sugar and raisins.

"Now comes the hard part. The temperature has to be exact at each step to prepare for fermentation." Luana struggled to read her notes.

After a slow process of heating and then cooling, Luana aerated the juice, mixed up a starter, and then funneled the mixture gradually into pot stills. Then she added the starter and plugged up the pot stills to start fermentation. It was only then that she realized she could only produce small amounts because she was limited by the number of large-sized pot stills and the time it would take for fermentation to complete.

Rose looked at her curiously as she hesitated. "What's the matter?"

"We don't have enough pots to use up all twenty pounds of watermelon. Unless we can get more, we can only use five pounds of watermelon per week. That's not going to give me the numbers I need, but it's got to do until I can get more equipment and consistent use of a kitchen." Luana spoke with a sigh but seemed determined to work through the problem.

"What are we going to do with what's left? Mama's not going to like that at all."

"I figure we can just share the rest with the hogs until I can afford more equipment."

Anarosa walked in just as Luana finished her sentence. "It's lunch time, Luana, and I see that it is not yet on the table."

Luana jumped up. "I've got most of it ready to put together. Just give me fifteen more minutes, and it'll be ready. Rose, help me cut up the bread."

True to his word, Marcos did not make life easy for Julia. He grew so unendurable, Julia seriously considered going back to the kitchen to pit and can, but like a firefly melting into night, the thought soon faded. On this particular day, making watermelon brandy sounded like a whole lot of fun by comparison, and she experienced a pang of jealousy when she thought about Rose working with Luana. Then she reminded herself that she had to be persistent, if she was ever to be a horse woman.

Julia was in charge of grooming twelve horses who were kept in stalls overnight and used for family riding, but she had not been allowed to handle or ride any of them during the day. She wasn't even yet allowed to groom or feed them, but she had befriended them and loved to talk to them, finding that each one possessed a unique personality.

When no one was looking she would slip an apple in front of them, as she had seen her brothers do. She stood admiring her favorite, a beautiful buckskin mare with golden hair and a mane, tail, and lower legs all in black. Her name was Mattie. But she would never do for a horse show; she was too slow and lazy.

"But when can I ride?" she bellowed out in a fit of frustration that afternoon, when she could catch Marcos between his rounds.

"If I can't work with the horses, how am I ever going to ride?" She tried not to bother him too much, as he seemed to be constantly grumpy, but her patience was wearing thin.

He sliced her with a dismissive glance. "There's a lot you'll have to learn before you can sit your first horse."

"Fine, but I haven't learned anything new in three months. All I do is clean!"

This was the first emotional outburst Marcos had witnessed since the flash of rebellion at their first encounter. He sensed that she had more spirit than his best stallion, but he had watched her closely and noticed how tightly she controlled her emotions.

"Well, then. If you're going to handle horses, then you have to learn to tie ropes the right way, so you can harness and lead them out to the paddocks.

You'll also need to learn how to tie them properly to their hitching posts." He picked up several ropes and demonstrated how to tie a quick-release knot and a slip knot.

"We've got plenty of rope around here. I want you to practice these knots five times each day and leave them on this fence at the end of the day for my inspection. I'll pull apart every tie that is not right, and you'll do them over again in the morning. Then you'll untie them and redo them at the end of each day again."

Julia blinked as she quickly did the math and gulped.

"Now, let's see you do the first couple of ties."

Marcos watched her as she tried the quick release tie. Of course, she was all thumbs, and she could not remember the steps.

He leaned in to grab the rope back from her. "The trick is to hold the rope with your left hand until you pull the bight through all six inches on the right." He demonstrated it again.

This time Julia studied it closely. "Let me try one more time while you watch," she insisted.

Marcos stepped back and could see she was making progress. She managed to get the bight through, but she fumbled when it came to snugging the knot. Marcos flung a remark back at her, as he walked away, thinking it would keep her out of his hair. "Much better. Now, repeat it every day until you can do it in your sleep."

Julia was about to protest but bit her lip. Whatever would get her on a horse, she would do. She tackled the quick-release knot and then the slip-knot five times. Then she stood back and examined her work with a squint and with what she thought was a critical eye. "This is as good as it's going to get for now."

It was not long before she mastered the rope-tying, but instead of being rewarded with her first riding lesson, Marcos made her master the same techniques, only blind-folded. He seemed determined to delay her first riding lesson for as long as possible. The more infuriated she was by it, the more pleased he seemed to be.

Four days flew by and both Luana and Rose were exhausted. Fermentation was not the cause; it was all the cooking and cleaning. Not only did they prepare all the family meals, they were making lunches for the field hands. Luana soon realized that she was taking on more than she had anticipated, and she was neglecting her duties at the *Serradura*. Domingos was going to have to put up with it for a few more days.

Rose and Luana counted the hours and minutes until they could test the sweet liquid. After everyone had eaten dinner and left to do their evening chores, they tiptoed into the kitchen. Not because they had to, but because they couldn't stand the anticipation and were afraid of failure. As if their tip-toeing could change the result.

First, they checked everywhere to ensure that no one was around. After opening every closet, Luana took a syringe and extracted some of the pinky broth, dropped it into a clear glass, and took the first sip. Her face was a picture of amused contemplation. "Well," cried Rose. "What do you think?"

Luana popped her large gray-brown eyes wide open and then squinted slightly and puckered her lips. "It tastes like a sweet nectar! I just don't know about the alcohol content. It doesn't seem very strong. I'll have to test it further. I do know that customers will rip bottles of this stuff off our shelves! We won't be able to keep enough of it in stock, unless I can find a way to produce it in larger quantities."

Luana's eyes reflected delight, as well as greed. Rose stared inquisitively, believing that anything her aunt said was possible must be possible. "Let me try. Let me try!" Rose reached for her glass, but Luana pulled it away.

"Not yet. Let me finish off a few drafts, so I can test the alcohol content first." Luana had no way of testing it other than to experience it for herself, and she did not want to let Rose drink too much. However, she couldn't deny her a taste, given all the work she had done.

After two or three shots, Luana raised her glass and passed a verdict on it. "There's no way anyone could get drunk off of this stuff. But it has just enough of a taste of alcohol to make it appealing. Mothers will use it as a concoction to rub the gums of their crying babies. Grandmothers will nip at it between naps, and once they develop a sweet tooth for it, the men can use it as a physic. Maybe, just maybe, I could sell it to local saloons or even drugstores!"

Luana's greedy imagination was spinning out of control, while Rose was still reaching out for a taste. "Go ahead. It won't kill you." Those were Luana's famous last words.

Rose took a sip and then another. And another. Luana barely noticed her, as she grabbed more for herself. The sweet watermelon went down too easily; it was like drinking candy by the bottle. Both of them sat for nearly a half hour testing it. They pulled some leftover watermelon out of the ice box, and ate it while they drank. Before long they were dropping the rinds and spitting out the watermelon seeds. Watermelon seeds were hailing all over the floor, until Luana reached out and grabbed Rose's arm.

"No. We can't mess up your mother's kitchen. Let's just see if we can spit those seeds into that copper kettle over there."

With a blurry eye and a teeter totter on her rump, Luana gathered up a mouthful of seeds, and with one heave, she spit them five feet into the kettle. She performed this feat, as if she were chewing and spitting tobacco into a spittoon at Jake's Place. Located at the Mud Hen Slough right outside Alviso, Jake's Place was a backwater hole, but greatly loved by local farmers and their workers. A haven for grifters and wanderers, haranguers, political yappers, and star-gazers. One would think that Luana had spent some time there, but that's not something you would ever get her to admit.

Rose stared at her in awe. "Let me try that!" She filled her mouth full of watermelon seeds. Before Luana could stop her, the seeds were showering the floor. Both of them stared wide-eyed at each other and honked like geese. As Rose tottered upward to clean the mess, it took only two steps before she was sliding across the floor, landing face-first in sticky watermelon sludge. Slimed from head to toe, she reached up to find a head of hair full of watermelon seeds.

The hullabaloo brought Anarosa to the door in yet another state of incredulity. The floor boards were sluiced with brandy, seeds, and syrupy juice. Luana's cheeks shown with pink slime, as one lone seed tilted precariously on her left cheek, and her right eye shone brightly upon it. The house was as redolent as a brewery, and Luana was fuddled and filled with prospects for success.

Anarosa looked from one to the other when sudden realization came upon her. "Luana! Did you get my daughter drunk?"

Luana looked at her wide-eyed and stood her shaky ground. "There ish NO way to get drunk," she insisted, "on wata-melon branny." And then she screwed up her face into a picture of feigned civility. "She just slipped in juice. Nothin' that a hot bath won't cure."

Rose did not speak a word as her mother led her to the bath, but with one backward glance, Rose flashed a look of alarm on Luana's behalf. It would be morning before Luana was capable of sober reflection. As Luana tumbled into bed, she could vaguely make out the trills of Pretty Boy from the front of the house.

"You're in trouble now, boy! You're in trouble now, boy!"

Chirp, flap.

CHAPTER 8

1878, The Atlantic, First Moonbroch

Sometimes the Mirantes would remain on deck in the evening to watch the moon rise. Once they had sailed through the Azores and set out to cross the Atlantic, they spotted their first moonbroch, that somewhat rare event when a halo surrounds the moon. Sailors once believed that a moonbroch signified an impending storm. On this night, the moon appeared multi-layered, like a gauzy veil surrounding a nacreous orb. The Mirantes did not yet know the significance of these signs, but they would soon experience it.

"Look!" cried Paulo. "I see lights in the distance." After scanning the horizon, no one could see the lights, but Paulo insisted it was there, and he pointed towards the starboard bow of the ship.

"No, Paulo. There are no lights. We are far from land now. We passed into the open seas one week ago," insisted his *Pai*. "What are these lights? Can you describe them?"

Paulo spoke dreamily, "They look like a string of twinkling stars." He felt certain that there was a great celebration at the endpoint of this crystal strand, and in his heart believed that he belonged there, sensing it was his destiny. He unconsciously strained toward the bow, causing Miguel to reach out to steady him. His father's restraint brought on another sense of being shut out.

This was the first time on the ship that he felt constrained, and he was overwhelmed by what the Portuguese call "*saudade*," an unquenchable longing for something that is gone or missed or unattainable. He felt it now that he was getting farther away from all that he had known. He suddenly realized just how far he was from home. No one could see what Paulo could see, and they all laughed at him.

"Paulo, you must be dizzy from scrubbing so many decks and carrying slop buckets. Honestly, I think it is all going to your head. I am not certain that it is at all good for you," protested Maria, as she shook her head at Miguel for encouraging the boy.

No one could persuade Paulo that there was anything wrong with swabbing decks and pitching slop buckets or that he could not see the quivering stars. He loved being on deck with the other crew members, and they were including him in their conversations, as he learned their strange tongue.

"Mr. Haye told me that next week he'll teach me how to pick oakum."

"What on earth?" cried Ida.

"It's an important job. We pick bits of yarn apart and use it as caulking all over the ship. It holds the ship together. All the crew members do it, especially on rainy days when they aren't able to repair the rigging." This comment produced a gale of laughter.

"So, you're saying that this ship is held together by yarn?" Ida snorted. "Let's hope there's more than that holding us together when we cross through Cape Horn!" There was yet another spontaneous burst of laughter, which did not faze Paulo in the least.

"And I'm also going to learn how to make 'spun-yarn' from old junk. We pull all the junk apart and draw out all the yarn. Then we knot it together and roll it into balls. Mr. Haye is going to teach me how to use a machine that spins and rolls it."

Ida pinched in her eyebrows, as she looked at Paulo in disbelief but said no more. Nothing could dim the excitement Paulo felt about every sailor's task, and there was no task too menial for him.

It was not long before they all slowly made their way down to steerage and to their bunks. The immigrant quarters were below water level with no portals and very little lighting. The Steward supplied them with three or four oil lamps throughout the day, which were often shared by as many as twenty people. Without the lamps, they would have been trapped in deep darkness, even during daylight hours.

Some of the women would take up their knitting or sewing at this time of night, huddling together around one single lamp like a cluster of bees bearding a hive. At such a time, the gossip mill would churn in a low buzz.

One woman, Hilda Cabral, complained regularly about the mistress her husband Antonio had brought on board. "He promised me he would get rid of her once and for all," she spat every night in Portuguese. "With his honeyed, lying lips, he told me that, if I would just get on the ship with the children, we would make a new life together, and he would give her up. Now he visits that she-devil in the middle of the night right under my nose. He thinks I don't see, but I keep one eye open."

"And with his children sleeping just a few feet away!" exclaimed one woman. "What kind of woman would do such a thing?"

"Well, it makes me wonder what promises he made to her. Imagine, getting on a ship with no means of support to follow a man with a wife and four children," cried Marissa Terra, shaking her head in disbelief. "What a *baruta*!"

"I think you ought to get to that woman somehow, if for no other reason than to let her know that you know what is going on, and you're not going to sit back and just ignore it."

Hilda muttered under her breath that she would think about it, while the others offered their ideas on what she should do. Nothing could harness the combined indignation of so many women, as they bruited over such a situation. They exhausted the subject with head shakes, hand-wringing, and sighs.

"Perhaps we could all get together and start leaning on her," pondered a feisty, older woman named Regina. "Make life difficult for her."

Hilda looked up from her work with a quizzical expression. "How do you mean?"

"Little things. Mess up her bed or laundry. Make her comb disappear. Trip her or bump into her when she passes by. If we all find ways to cause her trouble, then maybe she might get the message that her behavior is not acceptable. What's her name and where is she?"

"Beatriz. She's in the single women's bunks at the far side, four rows from the back wall, the upper bunk. But I call her 'Jezebel!'" Hilda spit out the words, as she cracked the only smile they had ever seen on her sad, round face.

"Imagine that scumbag of a husband crawling up the side of her bunk like a baboon in heat! He ought to be dealt with as well," sniffed Regina.

"But how?" wailed Hilda, drowning in a combined sense of helplessness and self-pity.

"Don't worry, we'll figure something out." That ended the conversation for the moment, but they all knew they would find new and creative ways to make life a misery for both of them.

At the next table over, there were those who were learning English, telling stories, and reading out loud or to themselves. The ship's Steward had passed out a few English books, and other passengers had brought their own books in

Portuguese, which they shared and read to each other. Although the majority could not read at all, they loved to listen, and storytelling was a favorite pastime.

There was a man named João Amarel who spoke enough English to read the English books out loud and explain them to those who wanted to learn. João also served as an interpreter between the crew and the passengers. He was envied, because his position gave him influence with the officers. Whenever the officers wanted to communicate with passengers, they would call João. As a result, João knew much of what went on and was a wellspring of information.

But mostly, the immigrants loved to tell stories from their homeland, particularly stories that enchanted, enthralled, or terrified. The best story tellers would use hand motions and body language to act out their plots and characters with great drama. With little lighting, they could easily create shadows on the sides of the creaking vessel, as it pitched them back and forth. The wide-eyed children would gather around the storyteller and screech with pleasure.

Octavio was their most masterful storyteller, but he had to be in the mood. Every night the children would insist he tell them a story, but he would shuffle his feet and sometimes say no and sometimes tease them to work up their anticipation, as well as his own imagination. And then, with a huge sigh, he would shrug his shoulders and a faraway look would rise up through expressive eyes. He would begin his stories slowly and softly, as if in a trance.

"Once there was a man and his wife. They were so lonely and so sad because, after many years, they had no children. The wife cried day and night, swearing that she would be happy to have any child, even if it was no bigger than a bean. After some time had passed, she gave birth to a little boy who was, in fact, no bigger than a bean. They named him Manuol Littlebean. One day, she could not find him. The more she called, the more frightened she became, thinking that she had stepped on him or accidentally swallowed him."

As Octavio described the scene, he gave a big gulp and stomped his square foot on the floor, causing all the children to lurch back and cry out. "Little did the mother know that Littlebean had been eaten by the goat and was still alive in the goat's stomach. Littlebean did not know what to do, so he jumped around, causing the goat to kick and buck. The goat screamed and thrashed so wildly that the father decided to kill it and throw it in the street." Octavio thrust his hands on the floor and kicked his hind legs up and down, much to the delight of the listening children.

"At night, a wolf came and ate the goat, consuming Littlebean in the process. The wolf got such a stomach ache that he crawled into a robber's cave containing sacks of gold and threw up all over the sacks. Littlebean came tumbling out, looking dirty and chewed up but all in one piece. When the wolf saw him, he thought he had seen a ghost and ran away. Littlebean then ran home and told his father about the gold in the cave, and so they went to the caves and retrieved the sacks, making them the richest family in their village."

Paulo looked at Octavio very seriously and asked, "Did he get into trouble when he got home?"

"Not after he told them about the sacks of gold. They called him the cleverest boy who ever lived!" Octavio grinned wide with a wink, and Paulo's worried brow relaxed. Then the children begged for more. Instead, Octavio proposed a game called "Little Bean."

"I will be the wolf and you will all be little beans. But little beans can only crawl on their bellies. They cannot run, walk, or dance. I will count to ten and you will hide, and then I will come to find you. You can crawl away when you hear me coming, but if I catch you, I get to carry you off to bed!"

With that, Octavio moved their lantern to another part of the hold and closed his eyes as he started counting. All of the children scurried to hide; they hid under tables, under bunks and ladders, and even behind their parents. Octavio spent the next hour gleaning out all of the 'little beans' from their hiding places. As he came closer to a little bean, he would pant and growl as if he were a wolf, often startling them into shrieks.

Try as they might, they could not get away fast enough. As soon as he ran away with a little bean, there would be a scream followed by giggles. Other little beans made sounds as they scrambled. One by one, the children were carried off to their beds to dream of streets paved with gold, pineapples, and an endless supply of sugar and sweet treats. Within no time, their parents followed them into slumber.

While the passengers prepared for bed, the crew were on deck in the dog watches. Captain McAllister walked the weather side of the quarterdeck, while Joshua Roper inspected the lee side, and Will Hayes manned the weather gangway. The sea was calm, as the first watch positioned themselves. The remaining crew descended to the hold to wait their turns on the watch. Before retiring, the Captain instructed Wills to look out to the south and southeast for storm warnings, that part of the ocean which was known for its powerful gales.

"Mr. Haye, keep a sharp eye out, and if you spot the devil tossing darts at the horizon, take in sail and rouse me at once," he instructed Wills. Four hours later, when the passengers were deep into their dreams, lightening was spotted on the east horizon. Wills called down the watch and blew his whistle.

"Carry a message to the Captain. We're looking at powerful swells three points off the starboard beam to the east."

The Captain was called up and soon planted his feet on the galley way. By this time, a heavy rain had begun to fall, and all the men were called up on deck. After surveying the scene, the Captain spouted his orders, followed by a bell call from steerage.

"Sail trimmers to their stations! All starboard lines, ahoy!"

Immediately, a half dozen men scrambled to the top mizzenmasts and braced and reefed the top sails towards the back of the ship.

Simultaneously, another half dozen men scurried up to the topsails at the front and main masts. Standing shoulder to shoulder along the rain-drenched yardarms, the men struggled to bring the billowing sails under control, knowing that the worst was yet to come.

They were quickly sodden as they swayed back and forth over the waxing swells. Some of the seamen had no time to put on outer clothing, wearing their bed slops. Some shivered as violently as the ship. The sails ballooned hard in the wind. Arresting them required swift action and a deft hand, as they worked side-by-side to knot the reef points. Meanwhile, the strong winds whistled through their ears with a screech, as if the grim reaper was hard on their tails.

It was difficult to hear orders from below, let alone to hear one another. Yet, the most experienced sailors knew exactly what to do without hearing them. The least experienced took their cues from watching them. In some cases, the men held onto the mast with one hand while they furled the sails with the other.

As they turned bilious, the less initiated took turns retching over the masts until there was nothing left to hurl, leaving an aching hollow in the pit of their stomachs. Within thirty minutes, the ship was careening against tons of water hurling over the bow. Every hand at the ready. All the sails were in except the jibs and the main mast. Joshua Roper joined the helmsman at the wheel.

"Come up on the wind about three points off the bow on the larboard side" he shouted. "Keep the rudders down!"

Peter Oakes had a reputation for being one of the most adept sailors on the masts, but you would never catch him on a life boat during a Sunday recreation, for it was widely known that he could not swim. He could, however, climb the masts one-handed and in the worst of conditions. On this night, he wore his heavy trenches and carried a full belt of tools, none of which kept him from easily climbing the yard arms. As the men on the main mast struggled to bring it in, he made his way upward to assist them.

Wills stood struggling with his crew when he spotted Peter below, and he called out to him for help, "Peter, ahoy! Up this way! We canna bring 'em to heel!"

Peter scrambled in their direction, but just as he was about to reach them, the ship jolted sharply, tipping the vessel just shy of a forty-five degree angle. It happened as Peter reached out to grab the mast, propelling him forward and off balance. Startled by the lightening flashes around him, he plummeted into a whorl of swirling seas.

The row of men on the yard arms watched with horror, just in time to see the almost imperceptible bleep he made on the surface of the weltering waters. And then they looked wide-eyed at each other, knowing that there was no way that Peter, the landlubber, could save himself in his heavy equipment.

When all was quiet again, they could feel the loss of him, but there was no time to mourn, as they struggled and swayed in the leaden darkness. Best not to think of it now. Best to move on. And so they struggled in unison. Crawling along the yard arms, they coordinated and double-downed their efforts until finally, all was secure. Then they made their way quietly down the masts, back down to their quarters like grenadiers marching in formation.

As they fell into their sleep sacks, every man went quiet in the belly of the howling ship, reliving over and over the loss of their comrade. Thinking how slippery was their hold on life, until they could stand it no more and silence was broken.

"I suppose he went quickly, what with the lead he was carrying," was the first remark.

"He hardly knew what hit him, no doubt," was the second.

Joey Lamb sucked in his breath. "No, but we did. We surely did. It's all over for 'em, but it's not over for us. We live on in the memory of it."

There was one simultaneous sigh of assent before a long silence, a silence that did not last long. With the tipping of the bark, they were soon taking in too much water, so Mr. Roper called for all idle hands below to man the pumps.

Then came one loud clap of thunder announcing that the worst was yet to come. With that same clap, the ship lurched violently, and all passengers were thrown from their bunks with a collective thud on the stony hard floor boards. Everything that was not nailed down went with them.

CHAPTER 9

1903, Santa Clara, Spring in the Valley

Spring blew into the Valley that year with all the fascination of a cherry-jeweled Japanese geisha. Adorned with pink and white-blossomed tresses, she flung her deepest green and gold-flowered skirts across the Valley floor and struck a pose for summer. No one could take his eyes off of her with wildflowers and blossoms as far as the eye could see.

Rose's dark chocolate eyes and hair accented her pink muslin dress in concert with the visual feast before her. Hanging over the front porch, she inhaled the Pacific breezes banding with the perfumes from a nearby jasmine tree. As her eyes feasted on the groves, she imagined that the ground was covered in a blanket of thick snow, but the blossom flurries defied her imagination.

Behind her, she could hear the sounds of peck-pecking, as Pretty Boy dispatched his breakfast. She stepped back through the front door and listened to the familiar refrain, as she glided past his cage and into the kitchen, "Oh boy, there he goes! Oh boy, there he goes! Pretty Boy made no distinctions when it came to sex. As long as it was not that of his own kind. But when it came to Rose, he always added a whistle, a low kind-of wolf whistle. He skirled it for no one but Rose. Not even Anarosa. It always evoked the shadow of a Mona Lisa smile on Rose's face when she heard it.

In the kitchen she was met with another sound and a rich, earthy scent: the grinding of Arbuckle's coffee. It was Luana's new discovery, her latest culinary gambit to drum up business for the *Serradura* and to accelerate her aspirations for a dairy. It was fresh ground coffee any way you like it. With cocoa, without cocoa, sugar or no sugar, cream or milk or vanilla. The whole family had been recruited for taste testing.

Julia sat in her overalls with her hair tied back in thickly coiled braids, slowly sipping Luana's latest invention: coffee with a shot of maple syrup topped with thick foamy cream and another drizzle of syrup. Luana studied her face, yearning to hear that it might be the ultimate coffee sensation. Julia rewarded her with a smile and slowly nodded her head several times. Luana waited. "Well?" she cried impatiently.

"I think you may have something here. Too bad you can't bottle it and sell it all over the world."

Luana rippled her eyebrows like a caterpillar fighting dust and shut one eye while she dug into her thoughts. After a few moments, she remarked, "Well... maybe I will. After all, there may be a way."

Rose laughed. "Oh, will you never stop? Isn't it enough that you've sold dozens of bottles of watermelon brandy? And now blackberry and plum?"

"Not while I've got a bunny hair's worth of breath in my body. And not until I've got my dairy," she declared as she scooped up her bags of coffee and started out the door. "Now, Julia, help me get these bags over to the *Serradura*."

"Sorry, but I've got riding practice and the mares need tending. You'll have to get Rose or Stefan to help."

Julia had been riding for a year now and her whole world had turned to horses, no thanks to Marcos. In the end, she was forced to plead with Alexio to give her lessons. Marcos would have nothing to do with it, but he did continue to torment her with many, sometimes nonsensical chores.

Yet there was one compromise she would not make. Without Therese, riding could not be nearly as much fun, so Therese had learned to ride with her. After Julia's chores were done, they would ride the entire day, sometimes helping round up the cattle. Near the end of their day, they visited Luana's *Serradura* bakery, until they were completely exhausted. Riding had allowed them to crisscross the Valley even farther than before. Their favorite jaunt was over the Eastern foothills towards Mount Hamilton. Julia would test their limits, going faster and higher with each ride.

They loved to climb the heights overlooking the San Francisco Bay. From this prospect, they took in a stunning view, hosted by ferryboats sputtering up and down and across the Bay. Valley treasures were transported to San Francisco ports at a rapid pace. White puffs of smoke dotted the west side of the Bay from north to south, as iron horses chugged back and forth on the land side. This endless stream of production and industry would lay the groundwork for the wealth of generations.

For now, Julia only dreamed of how to find the perfect horse to enter the county equestrian show, securing her a position in the parade. It had to be the right horse, one that would turn heads and gain her status as a champion horsewoman. She was determined to enter the show in the next year, but the new foals from last year were too young and none of the mares suited her.

A black stallion became her obsession, one with a reddish hue and a fighting spirit. His name was Coal. He was kept away from the other horses and farmed out to stud. He belonged to Frank, but only Marcos could ride him. Only Marcos *would* ride him. Not even Alexio would mount the steed, even though he was as skilled a rider as Marcos.

But Julia was smitten with Coal. No other horse possessed his strength or his beauty, none that she had ever seen. And strength and beauty were what she required. Having very little awareness of her own crescive beauty, she was determined to steal it, so she slowly wooed him with patience and soft words.

She knew it was highly unlikely that anyone would let her ride the powerful stallion and that if she proposed it, she would face a wall of resistance, stern warnings, and threats, which made it all the more alluring. So she hung out over the fence around his paddock in the early morning hours, when no one would see her, when most of the work hands were at breakfast, and when Marcos and her brothers were usually at the farmer's exchange market.

She strategized on how to work up the courage to approach the stallion and win him over. She tried sugar, then apples and coaxing words. She spoke to herself as she advanced upon Coal: "Enter the paddock. Stand quietly. Slowly make myself known. Let him smell me. Let him hear my voice. Take the bridle in my hands. Hold it for him to see." She would even climb the tree above the paddock later in the afternoon, when Marcos was riding him, to memorize and imitate Marcos's every move.

Her strategy worked; in time, she tamed the beast. Much to her delight, Marcos never noticed her in the tree above the paddock as she whispered to herself.

She could never forget the first day that she mounted and road Coal. She slipped her leg around him and sensed his strength and the first touch of his glossy coat, his iron-like muscles adhering to her touch. He felt like a luxury. He reminded her of a very fine Belgium chocolate she once tasted when one of the patrons from the *Serradura* returned from that faraway place and prodded her to try some. She nibbled it inch by inch, until it started to melt on her tongue. Once she had tasted it, she demolished it in one gulp.

At first, it seemed impossible with Coal, but patience paid off. She moved cautiously as she tested him, balancing her weight against his, as well as his resistance and will. Until she realized he had little tolerance for hesitation, and he threw her down. Her mouth filled with an earthy plug of mud and sawdust, and she felt the foamy snorts of the stallion overhead. She made up her mind that this would be the last time that Coal would throw her.

She spat out the dirt, jerked her head around, and fixed her eyes on him. He snorted and stomped in challenge. She did not blink and he calmed, standing straight and still above her. She pushed herself upward, keeping her eyes locked onto him, as she moved his way and nuzzled herself against the right side of his face. Taking him by the reins, she spoke softly but firmly. "Let's try this again, but now, I tell you when I'm ready to get down. Do we understand one another?"

He did not move, and this time, she did not hesitate. She quickly slipped over and around him for the second time. With her thighs firmly clinching Coal, Julia pressed him forward into a lope. In an instant, she felt him surrender to her will. As she urged him into a trot, she could feel his powerful muscles undulating forward, and she gleamed triumphantly.

She now had to be careful that no one discovered her secret. She would find time when Marcos and Alexio were at the county market making trades and conversing with other ranch hands. Until she was caught and all hell broke loose. Frank, Marcos, and Alexio had come out to the paddocks early one morning to inspect the livestock before they went to market. When they spotted her, they could not believe their eyes.

"Come down, right now!" Frank barked, and in doing so, he startled the stallion who reared up. Without hesitating, Julia expertly tilted forward in the saddle while using her knees to apply gentle pressure, and then she gave Coal plenty of rein and time to recover. Her gentle but firm response tamped down his fear.

Marcos stayed Frank's hand as he started to make his way to the stallion in a panic. "No, it'll be all right. Let me handle him." Frank saw the wisdom of his advice and caught himself, while Julia realized that this might be her only opportunity to convince them that she could handle Coal. She kept riding in spite of their pleas. In fact, she put on a show. First, she skillfully guided him into a lope and then into a trot and then slowed him down, backed him up, and then turned him in a circle to the right and then to the left. Their reactions went from astonishment to anger. "What are you thinking?" Marcos cried out.

Frank sputtered. Alexio muttered. Marcos fumed. Nevertheless, they could not deny the horse's gentleness and tractability in her hands. They just did not want to admit it. They could not admit it. It defied all their preconceptions. Frank did not trust the horse, so he asked Marcos to get her down. Marcos approached the stallion and the girl cautiously.

"Julia, do as your father says." He spoke softly, as if he were trying to tame the beast and not the girl.

This was the first time Marcos had ever called her by her name. It was always "squirt" or "small fry" or when he was really mad, he stumbled into his Italian so she would not understand, "poco pest." But she understood his tone and hated him for it.

Her father called out her full name: "Julia Estela Eva Mirante! Right now!" And then, she knew she was in trouble. As Frank followed her into the house, she heard the certain pronouncement of her doom: "You're in trouble now, boy! You're in trouble now, boy!" Hop, hop; scratch.

She cried, she stomped, she insisted. Her determination was compelling but not enough.

"Go to your room!"

"But he's the one! He's the one!" She cried. Through her tears, she caught her father's fiery glance and knew she better not push it just now. There had to be another time.

Frank would not speak to her. As far as Marcos was concerned, she would never ride Coal again. She knew it and she resented him all the more. She plotted and consoled herself with plans of revenge against him, even though his were not the only objections. He had pushed her too far.

Several days later she found Frank alone, sitting in the living room. On her knees by his side, she begged him. "He's the only one who can ride with me in the County horse show. There is no horse as beautiful or as powerful. I swear he would never hurt me." One would think she was begging her father to accept an engagement to a man he loathed. In her heart, that's how it seemed; there was no other horse who would do. She probed for Frank's soft spot and found it.

In truth, he was secretly proud of her, although he would never admit it. He had finally realized that she was more like him than any of his other children.

Dauntless, gritty, and cunning. More so than his sons. And in that moment, he could not be more impressed, and so he gradually found a way to put aside his fears for her sake.

It was not as if Frank was unaware of the dangers Julia faced on a powerful but unpredictable horse, but he reasoned that with Marcos to coach her and the horse, he could fulfill her wishes. He also considered that if she had the skills and strength to tame the stallion without anyone's help, then she was ready.

Everyone knew that once Frank made up his mind, there was no argument. Anarosa tried to dissuade him, until she conjured up in her mind the extent of his brick wall and crumpled under its length and breadth.

Luana was triumphant on behalf of her favorite, but she would not dare let Anarosa know how she felt. Anarosa suspected it anyway. Ever since her disastrous "night of the watermelon brandy," Luana had been walking a very thin line with Anarosa. She now avoided walking outside that line. She had determined that whatever Anarosa suspected would never be proven.

When Frank broached the subject with Marcos, he was not expecting resistance. While the resistance was subtle, it was the first time he had felt anything like it from Marcos, and it surprised him. "Because I know your skill, I trust you to take care of my daughter. I want to see her in that show, and I want her to win."

"Surely you realize the dangers of a young girl on a stallion."

Frank deflected the obvious. "Are you confident you can control him? Has he ever thrown you?"

"He has thrown me, but not since his early years."

"So, I trust you to teach her everything you know about this horse. She loves him, Marcos, and I believe the horse will not harm her. She has convinced me."

"It's not her I'm worried about it. It's the unpredictable circumstances of a show and a parade. He's not used to being around other horses or crowds of people."

"Then we will have to find a way to get him used to other horses and ride him in a variety of places around the Valley, near trains and streetcars and more people. I trust you to prepare both of them."

Marcos would never say no to Frank, but he resented the trouble of it and blamed the girl, muttering to himself in Italian as he walked away.

"Perche quel po'di Pest. Che un po' sciocco!"

From this day forward he called her "Little Fool." Her smoldering resentment served her well, because it fueled her determination to prove him wrong. But worse than that, she would steal Coal's love away from him. Coal would be hers alone, and that would be her ultimate revenge.

CHAPTER 10

1878, The Atlantic, First Storm

The hold resounded with groaning within seconds after the ship fiercely seesawed to one side. Ida and Ana tumbled out of their bunk together and landed on the floor boards. Their cries were drowned out by others. Some who slept on top bunks were able to catch themselves before they went down. They were the lucky ones.

One lantern was kept alive during the night, until the cabin boy delivered newly trimmed lanterns each morning. That one dim light was snuffed out with the first lurch of the ship, leaving them all groping and calling for one another. Latrine buckets flew. Clothing and bedding wrestled with each other and entangled. Books and utensils bolted. Every dense object was instantly transformed into a potential deadly weapon. They felt trapped like fish in a barrel.

Parents called out for their children. Miguel and Maria heard from everyone except Paulo. The more they called, the more desperate and inconsolable they became. Their throats turned raw as their bodies flayed.

Just as they reached their bunks, the ship pitched sideways, casting them in the opposite direction. No matter how hard they tried, they could not hold onto one another. Some discovered that all they could do for stability was cling to their bedposts, and they gripped them, as if their lives depended upon it.

Those who had never been fishermen had little experience with seasickness. Many were heaving and could not find the slop buckets. Even if they had found them, the buckets would not stay in place. Soon there was vomit everywhere, creating a noxious fug that permeated every sucking breath. The crew were too busy with their work to be of any help.

Paulo sat upright with the first sign of storm warnings. He was keenly sensitive to the movements of the ship and its crew. He immediately felt the heated efforts of the men, as their feet drummed over the decks. He listened for the bell calling the crew to the watch. Without hesitation, he scurried down his bunk to the hold and up the main passageway. He was also thinking of

Francisco. Where would he be? He usually made his bed under or near the lifeboats or sometimes in the barrel where Paulo had first met him. Paulo checked both places, but there was no sign of him.

Given the febrile efforts of the crew, no one noticed Paulo, and he did his best to stay out of their way. He positioned himself near the helm where he could make out the orders of the First Mate calling, "lay yourself forward" and "lay yourself aft." He was transfixed, as he watched while they took in the sails. Craning his neck in darkness, he tried to make out their movements and was impressed by their agility and strength. Rolling thunder stunned him, followed by a ragged bolt of lightening etched across the horizon. He stood fixed in his position, like the stay on the main mast.

Wills spotted Paulo from the ratlines and hollered over the wind, "Macaco! Go back to yo' berth!" Paulo could not hear or see him, as he searched the gangway. Wills climbed down, took hold of him and yelled in his ear that he must go down below.

"But I want to help! How can I help?" Paulo cried.

"Ye would very likely be swept o'r board, laddie, if ye stay on the gangway. Go back down." Wills pointed downward, as he yelled over the upheaval. But Paulo would not budge.

Wills thought quickly. "I'll take ye down to the bilge to man the pumps. Wait there and hold fast!" Paulo returned an inquisitive look when he mentioned the bilge but did not question him. Wills knew that Paulo would not be of much use on deck, but he also knew the men would not pay attention to him below and that Paulo would remain safe in the hold. Grasping Paulo with his right arm, he led him far below, where all idle hands had been sent to man the pumps.

Once they were down in the belly of the ship, it was clear that they were rapidly taking in too much water. Eight men stood huffing over the pumps, while Mr. Swift, the man in charge, was busily barking commands as he stood with them in knee-deep, slimy water. Some would say that working in the bilge was like working in the belly of a whale. Not only was the stench staggering, the darkness and the heat created a swampy cauldron. Some of the men would routinely retch and then resume their work.

Wills called out, "Mr. Swift, can ye use another hand?"

Rory Swift blinked at the little monkey staring back at him with eager anticipation. He shouted, "I've got all the men I need for now at the pump.

Unless he can swim through sludge, I don't see how he can help. We suspect there's an open seam somewhere, but we cannot find it. The waterline is too high. If the lad is able to make a swim for it, he could be of use."

Wills explained Rory's instructions to Paulo as best he could, and Paulo jumped at the chance. "Just tell me what to look for and I'll find it for you," he insisted.

"Tell 'em to hold his nose and swim along the sides looking along the surface for anything that feels like a crack in the plank. And keep an eye out for water gathering in one place. Let me know if he finds anything." Rory turned away, thinking that Paulo would never find anything, but he was happy to get back to his work and keep the boy busy.

Paulo dove repeatedly down into the sludge and bobbed every few seconds up to the surface to take deep breaths, as he searched the length of the water line. He swam as though he were a seal swimming through an oil spill turning blacker with every stroke. But he worked rapidly and efficiently. Some of the men paused at their work to gaze in wonder. Anyone would think he was swimming in a clear spring fountain; nothing about it seemed to bother him.

"For land's sake, look at the little monkey go! The little laddie's gotta heart, he does!"

After much bobbing and weaving and long after the men had ceased to think of him, he rose to the surface and with one gulping breath, he cried, "I think I found something."

"Ye don't say! Let me take a look."

Rory followed him to the area where Paulo had just surfaced and examined all along the the belly near where Paulo had pointed. As Rory groped along just below the bilge water, he caught a large crack. "Yep, I think ye have found something indeed."

He turned to the men and spoke with command, "Gather me some oakum and a mallet with some leather casing and get it over here as fast as ye' can. We've got to plug er up, now! And the rest of ye, don't stop pumping."

Some of the men responded with hands at the pumps and some took to the buckets. In no time, others put together the caulking that would act as a sealant to plug the seam. Later, when the water had receded, they would fill in the plug with pitch, but for now, it would have to do. Within the half hour, it was apparent that their pumping was finally draining faster than the ship was taking in water. Once the water line receded, the crew cried, "Hip Hip, Hurrah! Hip Hip, Hurrah for little Macaco!"

Peering out of two blackened eyes under two oily brows, Paulo took it in with a slice-of-watermelon grin. Surely, he thought, they would let him climb the masts now. Just as that thought entered his mind, Wills appeared again at the entrance to the bilge. Hearing the news that Paulo had helped to plug the seam, he lifted him up and carried him on his back.

"Ye are wanted upstairs wee little monkey and not a moment to spare, as ya parents have been a'worry. Your father caught me on the weather gangway not just two minutes ago, and I promised I'd deliver ye' to 'em, so scramble down and be quick about it! But before ye do, take a moment to wash y'self, not that iddle matter once ye get down under."

With that, Wills took a bucket filled with storm rain and baptized Paulo. "Now there, that was ya first storm, and gawd knows it willna' be y'ur last. Scurry on down now."

While the crew were occupied, Francisco had been down in the storage area raiding the food supplies. He viewed it as a perfect opportunity to snoop around the stern. Before the hatches were tightly closed, he jumped under the poop deck near the Captain's quarters and waited until he was sure no one was around.

The Steward kept a stash for the captain's table just adjacent to the officer's quarters, which included some fine wines and whiskey. Not to mention poultry, salted beef, and cigars. Francisco was too greedy to resist it.

Paulo ran towards the hatch, but as he was about to reach it, he collided with Francisco. They could barely hear one another over the howling wind. Francisco showed him what he had found and offered to supply him with whatever he needed. Paulo's reaction was as indignant as it was fearful, and his fears were for Francisco. He knew that the punishment would be severe for theft and especially if the crew found out that the culprit was a stowaway.

"Don't you realize what you're doing? This will hurt the entire crew! The Captain will not quit until he finds exactly who did this. If you are not found out, then someone else will take the punishment for you!"

"Then all the worse for them because I will not be discovered!" Francisco was both arrogant and foolish.

"Put it back, I say!"

"What are you going to do about it? Are you going to tell?" Francisco spoke tauntingly.

"I will not sit back and watch the crew suffer for your wrong. You can be sure of that!"

Francisco lunged at him and before they knew it, they tussled across the deck, all while the vessel was pitching furiously. In the melee, much of the stolen goods were set free and began rolling. Wills spotted them from the weather gangway and scurried down to break them up. He caught Paulo under his right arm until he was swinging from his arm.

"Say, didna' tell ye to get below? Now, no more foolishness."

While he was struggling with Paulo, Francisco made a break for it and disappeared under the main masts. Wills paid no heed. "What is all this?" He looked around at all Francisco's booty.

"Someone was stealing from the captain's Steward, Mr. Haye. I was trying to stop him."

"Did ye get a good look at 'em? Who was it?"

Paulo was not one to lie, but something in him wanted to protect Francisco, knowing he could go under the lash or even worse. He hung his head as he replied, "No, sir. I just saw what he had and tried to get them back."

"Well, then, we better get these back to where they belong. Wouldn't ye say?"

"Yes."

"I'll take care of it. Just run down to ya mum. Promise now? No side trips."

"First, let me help you collect these stolen goods." Once, they had everything in hand, Wills disappeared with the bag of booty.

Within seconds, Francisco reappeared. "Why'd you have to do it?" He was furious.

"You just be glad they'll never find out now. You would have taken thirty lashes, maybe even more. You ought to be thanking me. Now, get away before you make any more trouble."

Paulo did not wait to see where Francisco was headed and made his way down to his berth. As Paulo descended into the hold, he could hear the moans and smell the stench. It was certainly not any worse than the bilge. Since he could barely see, he had to feel his way to his bunk, calling out as he tread lightly.

It occurred to him that if there was a hell, it must be like this, a place of deep darkness where you cannot reach the ones you love. Nothing lovely or beautiful resides there; it is all misery and alienation. He wrestled the thought away.

"Paulo! Paulo! Is that you?" His mother was beside herself.

"Yes, *Mãe*! I'm here."

"Where were you?"

"Don't you know I'd be helping the crew?"

"But they don't need your help, son. We need you here with us."

"Well, I saved the day. I found a seam in the bilge. It may have saved us from sinking."

Maria was sick with worry and the brackish taste in her mouth caused by nausea. So, she did not ask him what he meant or chide him further. She took him in her arms and rolled him onto the lower bunk between her and Miguel, as they continued to clutch the sides of the bunks and pitch back and forth. Not only were they living in a cesspool, it was filled with the lamentations of the seasick passengers who were freezing in their nightclothes.

Being island people, no one had adequately prepared for the gelid nights that accompanied the violent storms of the southern hemisphere. Much of the family's warmer clothing had been stowed far below. Along with their groans came the eerie sound of chattering teeth. Together, they tried to keep each other warm but had no idea that there would be two more days of misery.

CHAPTER 11

1903, San Jose, California, The McCallums

Jackson McCallum ruminated from his front parlor window which overlooked his vast lands abutting the eastern foothills of the Diablo Mountain Range. It was a stylish and well-situated room that set off to full advantage all that belonged to him. He drew a long pull of satisfaction from his cigar with the thought that he had achieved about as much as any man could be expected to achieve in this Valley. No one could match him for land, wealth, or prestige.

Several decades before, his father, George McCallum, had made his fortune during the California gold rush. Newly transplanted from his Highland village of Dunblane, George wasted no time once the calls for gold went out. He was always two steps ahead in any economic endeavor, someone who established himself early and knew just how to expand his assets.

Like many fortune-seekers of the time, he used his gold to buy large swathes of California land. Land that was dubiously forfeited by its original Spanish settlers in the melee between the United States and Mexico. It was too easy a matter to lay claim to what was once owned by those who no longer controlled the reins of power. As gold-rich investors gobbled up their lands, the Californios loped away with hats in hand.

For some time, the land lay fallow, as investors monopolized and hoarded land. Those who wanted to farm it were unable to do so, until the investors, urged on by commercial pressures, were forced to give way to those who would make use of it. The industry of canning and packing followed and was driven by the necessity to store and distribute greater yields. Once again, George McCallum re-invented himself to become a front-runner, and Jack profited by it. He ran the largest packing and canning centers in the Valley, and his sons, Roger and Samuel, would profit by it as well.

Yet, for all of his self-satisfaction, there was something more inside of Jackson McCallum, an indefatigable restlessness that dogged his late middle years. He was haunted by a sense that no matter how much he had achieved, it was somehow not enough and never would be enough. He simply did not know why.

He made a sudden start, as his wife Olivia joined him for tea in the late afternoon, trailed by their maid, Mathilda, who carted in the serving trays.

"Darling! You can't say you weren't expecting me." She examined him closely with cool gray eyes and spoke with a soothing tone. "You seem so lost in thought."

Tall, sleek, and elegant, Olivia McCallum was always impeccably dressed, manicured, and coifed. Ashen-gold braids looped around the crown of her head without a hair out of place. She made a quick study of her husband, always determined to detect anything in his demeanor that might represent a shift in the winds of his mood, hovering around him in the way that a colony of ants would safeguard its queen. There was nothing that escaped her notice or desire for control.

"But, of course," he dissembled.

Jack was not one to betray his feelings, especially to his wife. She had a long history of lecturing him on any point of dissatisfaction. He had learned to be high-spirited and grateful before her presence, which he doggedly avoided after breakfast and before tea. While *his* disapprobations were not to be tolerated, hers were to be elongated and dissected with all the long-suffering of a toothache followed by an extraction.

Jack groped for a benign and manageable new subject that would divert from his reverie. Anything properly provincial. "We're getting ready to wash the orchards, and I'm not sure we have enough pumps. I'll have to send Roger down to John Stocks before his inventory is out for the season."

"And while you're at it, we may need some new grafting tools along with those pumps," she quipped.

Olivia never ceased to amaze Jack with her detailed knowledge of farming. Not that she would ever be seen riding or roping or getting her hands dirty in the garden. She simply took a keen interest in knowing everything about everybody within her sphere, what they did, how they did it, and everything they said. To perfect her art, she became an inveterate eaves-dropper and gossip. It made him grateful that she could not be involved in the canneries; they were too distant and dispersed.

Olivia made her fortune when she met Jack. Her father, Abel Moir, was a doctor at the Quicksilver mines. The pampered daughter of a well-esteemed man, she was spoiled and grew to be endlessly ambitious. Jack and she grew up on opposite sides of the Valley, and it was unlikely they would ever meet, until she volunteered to help the women's auxiliary host a dinner at Santa Clara college where Jack was a student.

As soon as she spotted him, she set her sights on him, and he could not resist the come-hither look of the enigmatic, ashen blonde. Her success at snagging one of the most eligible bachelors in the Valley gave wings to her relentless vanity.

As Mathilda poured his tea, Olivia launched her nightly information-gathering campaign with a provocative salvo. "I think it's time that Tom Haley found a new position. I caught him asleep in the barn today."

Jack lowered himself into a cane back chair and drew on his cigar as he puffed thoughtfully. "That would be the fifth ranch manager this year. I can't afford not to give him some leeway. There are few good managers left in this Valley, and I gave up the best there is." Just as he spoke, their son Roger arrived, along with his brother Samuel and his sisters Susanna and Celesta. They had been out riding and had arrived late for tea.

"And who might that be, Father?" Roger inserted himself into the conversation.

"Marcos D'Angelo, of course."

"If the stories of the ranch hands are true, then I would think you would consider yourself well rid of him," said Olivia.

"That's just it. I never did believe they were true, and I'd fire every one of those ranch hands now to have him back. The entire operation is nothing but a pain in my backside. I can no longer trust anyone to manage it."

"I hear he found himself a new position." Olivia made it her business to know both the particulars of her own homestead and those of others as well.

"I'm surprised that anyone in the Valley would have him," said Roger. "I thought his reputation was ruined. Who was it who took him on?"

Jack now remembered how some of the other McCallum ranch hands had resented Marcos's position as his foreman given his youth. They contrived to undermine his efforts. When they could not sabotage his success, they sought dishonest methods. They planted stolen goods in Marcos's quarters, and through a series of intrigues, they managed to also plant suspicion in the mind of Jack McCallum.

Although Jack had his doubts about the matter, he investigated further and discovered the stolen items. Marcos pleaded his innocence, but Jack considered it easier to let him go than to take his side. He suspected foul play, but he was more concerned about looking weak in the eyes of the world than in exonerating his foreman. Marcos was told to pack his things and go immediately and without pay, leaving him with no means of support and a tarnished reputation. That's when he applied to Frank for a new position. Frank now took satisfaction in knowing that the McCallum's loss was his gain and that Jack somehow knew it.

"I don't know him well, but he's got small potatoes in this Valley. A "porta-gee" by the name of Mirante. Twenty-five acres around Santa Clara with a small stable and just a few head of cattle. It's quite a comedown for Marcos. I expect it's all he could find."

"I never particularly cared for him," Roger volunteered. "A loner, solitary and even somewhat unfriendly, but I suppose if you really wanted him, it would be no great matter to get him back. I bet we could strike an easy deal with Mirante."

Celesta surreptitiously eyed each of them and said, "Well, I think he's dreamy! The strong brooding type. And devastatingly handsome to go with it. Perhaps he even has a poetic soul?" As the youngest, she had to fight for her share of the conversation, and she was skilled at using provocation to get it. On this occasion, the only thing she was able to reel back was one long yawn from Susanna, as she was demolishing the last crumbs of her lemon cake. "Who cares about ranch hands, when I'm going to upstage them all in the horse show next week?"

The equestrian show for young women was all Susanna wanted to talk about. She had selected a dusty rose riding habit to offset her pale locks, her white hat and boots, and her horse, Misty. Misty sported a light orange mane, and Susanna thought Misty's coloring would set her own outfit off to striking perfection. This was her second year in the show, after winning the previous year, and she fully expected to win again.

"Well, if you want to win at horses, then Marcos is your man. No one knows more about them, and no one can teach you like he can," declared her younger brother, Samuel.

Susanna rolled her eyes drawled as she spoke. "Marcos, Marcos. He may be handsome, but he's not the only horseman in town. And besides, I think I've proven already that I know exactly what I'm doing."

"Either way, you are going to have to get that stain out of your riding habit." Celesta chimed in with the painful reminder that her riding habit was not fit to be seen.

Susanna groaned. "Mother, Mathilda was unable to get it out. What am I going to do? I was counting on wearing it. My only other one is two years old and faded."

"An egg yolk will do the trick."

"An egg yolk?" Susanna glanced at her mother incredulously. "Are you serious?"

"Yes. That's exactly what I said. I have a recipe from the apothecary who recommended mixing an egg yolk with alcohol or ox gall. He says there's nothing it won't remove from clothing, and then we just wash it off with soap using flannel cloth."

Before Susanna could object, the front door bell rang. "Mathilda, would you get that please?"

A messenger was shown into the entryway. He had been instructed to wait for a reply. Mathilda returned to the parlor with the missive for Mr. McCallum. Olivia made a study of her husband, as he groped for a letter opener and reviewed its contents. His expression displayed alarm, and he looked up at his wife whose voice was insistent.

"Well, what is it?"

"I must go to my mother."

"Your mother. That old bat! Whatever for? She doesn't deserve your attention. We haven't seen her in years." Olivia became wild at the thought of it. As Jack ran upstairs to get ready, he spit out a response through clenched teeth. "She's dying."

Olivia looked back at her children. All eyes were on her. Not one of them had seen their grandmother in at least ten years. They were not allowed to, for reasons they could only guess. She turned away from them, not wanting to betray her emotions.

"Finally," she thought to herself. "It will all be ours now." Somehow she had to make sure. Had to make sure that her husband would secure all that was left of the McCallum land and gold. No one really knew what was left. The old woman lived an isolated existence and never socialized with anyone. Olivia got up, paced, rung her hands and then quickly followed her husband upstairs. She found him collecting his things into an overnight bag.

"How do you know it's serious?"

"Doc Hanson wrote that he did not expect her to make it through the night. I must go to her."

"What is it?"

"Pneumonia."

Under normal circumstances Olivia would object to his going, but now everything must be secured in their favor. Jack had no living siblings, but after the distance between Jack and his mother, Olivia could not be certain it would all fall into his hands.

"You know what you must say?" She broached the subject straightforwardly.

"About what?"

"The gold, the land. Of course." It was not time to be subtle.

He searched her eyes as he looked up with an expression of disbelief. "At a time like this? Is that really all you can think of? Isn't it enough that you forced me into neglecting her all these years?" Olivia slowly lowered herself onto a divan and answered his last question. "Forced you? That's certainly not the way I remember it."

He looked straight at her without changing expression. "Either that or you would make my life a misery." Then he looked away, as he hastily opened his dresser drawer.

She ignored his gibe and repositioned herself. "But consider, dear, if it doesn't go to you, where will it go?" That gave him a start, as he thought through the answer to her question. He could not come up with an answer, and that was the problem. He swung around at her.

"What real reason do you have to believe that she would disinherit me?" He was almost afraid to understand her.

Now, she knew she had hooked him in and so she prodded further. "Do you really want to see it all go to charity or to some distant cousin in Scotland or God knows where? You must find a way to speak to her before she's gone. Whatever is left of her land holdings, she surely doesn't need them anymore. Much of the land hasn't even been worked for years."

Jack had to concede that what she said was true, but the thought of raising the question to a dying woman, the woman he had neglected for so long, was painfully distasteful to him. "I can't force her."

"Of course not, but you could convince her that the land and gold are better off in your hands for the sake of our children. After all, she may still have a soft spot for her grandchildren. How many acres do you think she owns?"

"At least ten thousand. Not just here, but all throughout the San Joaquin and Central Valleys."

"And find out where she has stashed the rest of the gold."

"It's not clear that there is any." Jack began to fidget as he finished the packing. The entire conversation was making him uncomfortable, but he could see that it was a necessary evil.

"Oh, come on, Jack. You know there is. Your father hinted at it several times before he died."

Jack finished his packing and glared at Olivia. "You never had any good reason to hate my mother and yet you do."

"No, Jack, you're wrong," she purred. "I don't hate her; I just find her company distasteful."

"Why, what did she ever do to you?" He flashed a rare burst of anger. He did not wait to hear her answer, as he made his way downstairs and out the door.

Jack returned late the next day, went immediately into his study, and shut the door. This was too much for Olivia. She was yearning to hear that the old woman was dead and gone. No more questions about the money or the gold. She had enough sense to avoid the appearance of cupidity by not rushing into the study, but she kept a restless eye upon the study door. Finally, the door opened.

She sat languidly upon the parlor sofa and did not move or look up, as Jack entered. Nor did she speak a word. For his part, he knew he must tell her everything, so he spoke plainly.

"The land is ours. All of it."

Her eyes sparked. "And the gold?"

"She would not speak of it."

"But it exists. How much?" At this point, Olivia could not disguise her greed, and because Jack shared in that greed, he pretended he did not notice.

"When I mentioned it, she went silent."

"You did not press her?"

"I could hardly pull the arm of an old woman on her death bed. I asked her twice. I knew that was enough. I could see the disappointment in her eyes."

"So, how did you get the land? Was there a change to the will?"

"It turns out that it was not in her will. She agreed to let me call her solicitor, and she simply signed it all over to me."

"Finally. We're done with her. But how vexing that she refused to hand over the gold. She has it; I know she does."

At this, Jack turned around on his wife. He could understand her greed, but he could not abide her cruelty and her baseless hatred towards the mother who had never shown anything but kindness to them. "You're wrong. She's not dead. She recovered." And with this comment, he made sure that she could see the look of satisfaction in his eyes.

CHAPTER 12

1878, The Atlantic, Storm Recovery

The ship and its passengers moaned on. By the third day, the storm had swaddled them in what seemed like a permanent state of wretchedness. How long could they hold on? They wondered and waited. Many of them did not dare go on deck, for fear of being washed away. For some, the yearning for fresh air and water overcame their misgivings. Those few intrepid held fast to the railings, as they made their way up for just one gulp of fresh air and a cup of rain water. Worse than that, there was no food or relief from the crew, who spent all their time struggling to keep them afloat.

The click-clacking of rosary beads and the murmurings of the Hail Mary co-mingled with their caterwauling. And then, Juvenal Terra cried out loud, "What about the statue of Senhor Santo Cristo dos Milagres? Who has the statue? We must find the statue!" His desperate cries caught the attention of everyone within hearing distance.

They knew that going back hundreds of years the statue was used to ward off the great earthquakes and volcanoes plaguing their islands. Experience had taught them to bring the statues to the town square to hinder or prevent the magnitude of the quakes. Or they would permanently plant them on their farmlands to warn them away. Almost every family had some version of that statue, and they all believed in its power. They now believed that it held power to quell the restless seas.

"The Savior will win over the beastly storm," Juvenal cried out in a calenture. "He will bring us calm waters." There were cries and shrieks in response. "Who will give up their statue? It must be thrown overboard! Who will help save us?"

One woman cried out, "Here it is!" She had been clutching it since the storm began. They persuaded her that it would do no good until it was thrown into the maelstrom. Fear caused her to clutch it tighter, but the laments of the others were brought to bear upon her fears, so she released it from her sweaty palms.

"Now, who will go on board? Who will thrust it into the sea?" Followed by silence. And then the cries became increasingly desperate.

Paulo spoke up. "I will take it. I know the ship. I can hold on."

"*Meu Deus!*" Maria cried, but Miguel gently persuaded her. "The boy has become expert at traversing this ship. After all, he came back safely to us, didn't he? And as long as he carries it, he will remain safe."

Maria slowly released Paulo. He grabbed the talisman and bounded upward. From the quarterdeck, he quickly surveyed the watch and made certain that he was unseen. After climbing halfway up the yard arms, he tossed it directly into the purling waters. And then he waited. Within the hour, the storm died down. He scrambled down and back to the hold. He could hear the cheers of his people, but it was not long before they all fell into an exhausted stupor.

When morning broke, Kit, the cabin boy, finally came with lamps and breakfast. As they took in the wreckage of what they now called home, they shook their heads in dismay. Personal belongings were scattered everywhere. Untangling them and identifying what belonged to whom was a chore. Much of their clothing and supplies needed cleaning and the floor scrubbing. After breakfast, they got to work.

The Steward came down to announce that bathing accommodations would be set up on deck after breakfast. The crew tied up sheets for privacy and provided barrels of rain water for washing. Everyone would have an opportunity to bathe and wash their clothes. They all agreed to take turns by family. When one family returned, the next one would go up. One by one they slowly went abaft to receive their baptisms.

When it was time for the Mirante family, Ida and Ada went first. They both slipped behind the curtain in their underclothes. Kit handed them bucket after bucket, and they washed each other's hair.

"Kit! You better keep your eyes shut or we will scratch them out!" Kit knew just enough Portuguese to feel the warning. To feign distaste for the task, he puckered up his face into an exaggerated moue, as he handed them each a pail over the draped clothesline. The air was icy, so they shivered their way through their bath, still grateful for the fresh air and the relief from nausea and noxious odors.

Kit assisted them throughout the morning and brought them lunch, and their hunger was acute. They were all famished. At the lunch table, the murmurings among the passengers about the inadequate food frog-jumped over each other. Those who possessed the means could purchase extra food when they reached Valparaiso, but there were others who were desperate to take action on behalf of their wives and children.

Juvenal Terra spoke first, "We need to let the captain know. I fear he is unaware, and I suspect that food is being withheld from us and hoarded, so that Slick can barter with it for personal gain."

"Yes, but how can we prove it and how can we approach the captain? He is always surrounded by his crew and we need an interpreter to help us." Everyone agreed that it must be done at the proper time and in a respectful manner. They all turned to João Amarel.

"João, we will need you to speak to the captain about our grievances."

"But how do we provide proof? I cannot go to the captain without some evidence."

Paulo had been listening in and spoke up, "If he's making deals in exchange for things he can sell, then we have to find his stash."

"What do you mean?" Juvenal looked doubtful.

"He must have money or bartered goods hidden away somewhere."

"Yes, but how do we prove he's providing food to ladies who give him favors? It's not like we can paint a picture." Octavio grumbled.

Paulo was determined. "That can't be all he's getting from this. We can set a spy on him and search his room, when he's not around. Maybe it's money. Maybe it's food - who knows?"

And then, Paulo thought of Francisco. He would make a perfect spy. After all, he reasoned, he knows the ship inside and out and has even been in the captain's quarters. "Once we find out where he's hiding his stuff, we will tell the captain who can search his belongings."

"That's not a bad idea, little Macaco. And just who do you propose will go looking for his booty?" Juvenal wanted to be satisfied on this one final point, before they put their plan in place.

"Just leave it to me. I know this ship and I know the crew's routine. I'll find a way." Paulo was not going to give Francisco away. Given Paulo's stature with the crew, they agreed that it was worth a try. After all, what did they have to lose?

The next day, Paulo looked for Francisco. They must first locate Slick's loot and figure out who else might be helping the cook. Not surprisingly, Francisco already knew Slick's habits, and he had observed how the cook pilfered the food. Not only was he provided with favors from certain unmentionable ladies, but sailors were giving him whiskey, tobacco, and sometimes coin for extra food.

Paulo was not at all surprised to find that Francisco had figured out how much he could siphon from the food stores without being noticed. What he did not know was where Slick might be hiding his ill-gotten gains.

"I'll help you," Francisco said, "but you must return the favor by providing me with food once Slick is found out. You've also gotta help me spy on him."

Paulo did not hesitate. "First, we lay in wait to see if we can figure out where he hides his booty. There are a few questions we must answer: What does he do the same time and the same way every single day? When he's not cooking and cleaning, where does he hang out?"

Francisco plowed his hand through his unruly hair and scrunched up his face while he gave it a thought. "Well, after the officers have eaten, he almost always plays dice at the back of the ship. Sometimes he stays up late, even after midnight. Especially on Sundays when the captain and the officers dine together."

"Let's try again next Sunday. I'll keep watch at the dice game, while you search his room. If he comes back early, I'll run ahead to warn you."

"You don't have to worry too much about that. He usually comes back deep into his cups. He wouldn't know I was even there."

"That's perfect. Try to find a hiding place — somewhere you can watch and wait in his quarters without being found out."

The following Sunday, Paulo and Francisco met on deck after supper and waited for Slick to pass by. It was some time before he left his room around ten, and then they followed him at a safe distance. For two hours they watched overhead, as Slick used one podgy hand to shake the dice furiously and the other to guzzle his grog.

When it appeared that the cook was completely soused, Francisco left and slipped into Slick's room. It took Francisco a few moments to adjust to the darkness, and then he made out a table, chairs, drawers, and a chest. He opened the chest and rummaged through it, trying to avoid dismantling its contents. It contained nothing that would suggest evidence of the cook's skulduggery. The same was true of the drawers. "After all, why would he hide it in such an obvious place? If he's got pelf, then it must be carefully hidden," Francisco reasoned.

He prodded the floor boards one by one, taking his time to try them every which way. He was just about to start on the wall planks, when he heard a rustling sound at the door; it was one very inebriated Slick. Where was Paulo and why hadn't he warned him? Francisco dove for a hiding place under the bunk. After knocking down just about every standing object in the room, Slick stumbled into his bunk followed by a mighty wind of flatulence.

Poor Francisco was pinned with arms at his side under the low-lying mattress, bulging with the dead weight of a drunken Slick. If that were not enough, he was perfumed by the mighty wind and could not move his arms to help him slide out from under the bed or avoid the noxious fumes. He would have to wait for Slick to roll over and wanted to cough but did not dare.

Pinched in for more than an hour, Francisco was barely able to breathe. Then he heard a roar. Growing inpatient and thinking it was an oncoming storm, he tried to shimmy out of position, but when he heard the roar again, he realized it was not what he thought. The roar became a sputtering gurgle preceded by a brief hiatus and then a crescendo into another roar. It now dawned on Francisco that Slick was not going to roll over, and his deafening snores would only increase at a faster pace. There would be no sleep for Francisco that night, as there would be no rolling over.

At the crack of dawn Kit arrived to drag Slick out of bed, a well-practiced daily routine between the boy and the cook. Breakfast was essential on this ship, especially for the captain and crew, but absolutely no one wanted to wake the cook. All knew that striking the bell was useless no matter the number of times they tried, so they gave this fearsome task to poor Kit.

First, Kit would meekly call out to Slick, "Uh, Mr. O'Malley. Issa' time! Wake up!"

Of course, this never produced a reaction, but Kit felt it his duty to start with a polite approach, repeating himself every five minutes for up to a quarter of an hour. When that did not work, he would draw near the snoring lump with trepidation and pull on his toes. This generated a roar and a sputter, a sure sign to everyone within listening distance that the wake-up process was underway, a great relief to growling stomachs.

After that, it was not uncommon for the hapless cabin boy to dodge around the room to avoid flying projectiles aimed in his direction. And then another toe-pull might be needed. On a very few occasions, those projectiles would find their mark, and the poor boy would wince in pain. Eventually, the lump would drag itself out of bed and Kit would run for it. Breakfast would now be served. The captain would smile as Kit ran past his cabin, and Wills would mutter, "Gawd be praised! Letta' nuther day begin!"

On this particular day, several toe-pulls were required, and each time Slick jolted, Francisco winced in pain. Finally, with one swift movement, Francisco was released from the underside of the mattress, and he made a run for it. He could not help the guffaw that rushed from his mouth, and Slick swung around at the sound."Fee Fie Foe Fum. I smell the blood of an Englishman!" Slick cried out. Little did he know that it was no Englishman but a Portuguese!

Francisco had the presence of mind to cover his face before he rolled out from under the bed, dodged around the sleepy giant, and took cover behind the galloping Kit. Slick bellowed, but he was in no shape to pursue the stowaway, his mind too foggy to know whether or not it was just a bad dream. It would take several slathers at the wash basin before he could think straight, let alone react.

While he was washing, Francisco searched the ship for any sign of Paulo. He knew that Paulo would be up early, working with the crew. It was just a matter of finding him, but it would have to wait until after breakfast. So Francisco slipped under the lifeboats, one of his many sleeping spots, thinking he'd just take a snooze until Paulo came out on deck. Instead of a snooze, he fell into a deep sleep that would last for four hours.

Once awake, he found Paulo swabbing the deck and turned on him. "What happened last night? Why didn't you warn me?"

"Sorry! I fell asleep. By the time I woke, he was gone."

"I was stuck under his bed all night, and he saw me in the morning, but I don't think he'd ever recognize me."

"But did you find anything?"

"Not yet. Whatever he's got is well hidden. We'll have to keep trying."

Francisco decided that on their next attempt, it would have to be Paulo who did the searching.

CHAPTER 13

1904, Santa Clara, Rivalries

The County horse show and parade were three months away, and Marcos was true to his word, now that he understood how much it meant to Frank. He rode Coal daily across the Valley. He had to ensure that the stallion could be controlled around crowds and traffic. Every day, he steered Coal down The Alameda into town and even along the rail tracks to expose him to city life. He knew he would eventually have to let Julia do the same, but it would not be without his assistance, and he knew that he somehow had to convince her it was for the best.

"My father says I can ride him now," she insisted every morning as he was about to take off with Coal.

"You've ridden him, but you haven't ridden him in a parade."

"I can ride him anywhere," she spoke as she looked up and started to grab the reins.

Marcos steered the stallion away from her reach and looked down at her with an icy stare. "Don't be such a little fool. You wait until I say he's ready and not a minute before. And then I will go wherever you go. You will not take him anywhere without me." He did not enjoy berating the girl, but her impetuous nature concerned him, especially when he could see that she seemed determined to defy him.

He wrapped his fists firmly around Coal's saddle horn, as he spoke and looked down at her from on high. Julia knew he was in complete control of the matter, which her father would support, and she resented her position of impotence. Marcos did not wait for her response.

"You know I can ride him on my own." She called out after him, as he left her in the dust. She was definitely not making headway on taking Coal away from him.

Behind the scenes, Marcos was making special arrangements for Coal during the show. Since he knew every ranch manager in the Valley, he easily discovered that Tom Haley was in charge of checking in and managing all the

horses during the show. Tom was also one of the judges, and Marcos knew
Tom was someone he could trust. Tom's reaction to the stallion being placed
in the show was just what Marcos had expected.

"How can you be serious? A fifteen-year-old girl riding on a stallion?"

"I couldn't agree with you more, but her father insisted, and her father is
my boss. So, I have to find a way to minimize the risk. Can you help me?"

"And this is his own daughter who will be riding him?"

"Yes. As strange as it sounds, he supports it."

"What do you have in mind?"

"First, the stallion enters the stadium from the south entrance, instead of
the north, where all the other horses will be lined up. And he doesn't enter until
the last minute and just before the girl is about to ride. I'll bring him in at your
signal. Can you arrange that?"

"That shouldn't be too difficult. What else?"

"We'll let her ride him in the stadium at least twice before the day of the
show. Would that be breaking any rules?"

"Not that I am aware. No one has ever asked before, so I see no law against
it."

"And when we start the parade, I'll come alongside just behind the stallion
on his left and another rider will flank him on his right."

Marcos was going to have to handpick two geldings the stallion could
tolerate and was finding this to be no easy matter. He had almost exhausted his
herd and was already having to borrow from other ranches.

"I'll need your help to find the right geldings."

Tom nodded his assent but could not help challenging him a bit. "You
know that will only be necessary if the girl wins."

Marcos paused a moment and gave off a confident air. "Oh, she'll win
alright. Don't you worry about that." And with that, Marcos walked away. Tom
scratched his head at the man's arrogance, knowing that the McCallum girl
would give all the competitors a run for their money.

As Julia fumed, Luana searched for ways to distract her. She realized that
the more Julia brooded, the less she was likely to be in the right frame-of-
mind, when it came time for the competition. As they sat on the front porch,
Luana frisked her thoughts for ways to distract Julia from her grudge against
Marcos, when an idea popped into her head.

"You're going to need a riding habit. One that will make you stand out. No more boots and overalls."

"But I can't ride in a dress."

"It doesn't have to be a dress, but you have to learn to look and ride like a young lady, and I'm going to make you a habit that will help you fit the part. And no more braids. We'll have to dress up that mop of curls."

Up to this point, Julia had not given it much thought, but Luana's suggestion channelled her energies in another direction. Julia considered what might be needed. "Therese can sew. Let her help you."

"I could use the help, but we must make some choices now. We need to choose the right fabric and just the right color."

It didn't take Julia long to make a decision. "It has to be white. That will be a nice contrast to Coal."

"I like that; it will also set off your bronze curls." Julia frowned. She hadn't considered how it would make her look, and it vaguely irritated her, but she did not argue the point.

"Tomorrow we will go to Smith's and pick out fabric. Let's invite Therese and make a day of it. We'll even stop at the *Serradura* for lunch." Luana made her way to the back door, and Julia followed her. Within minutes, Marcos trotted up on Coal, who snorted at the sight of Julia. Coal had broken a sweat, so Julia could see that he had been ridden hard. Marcos did not give Julia a second to open her mouth before he barked his orders.

"He's ready. Now we need to get you ready. You'll be up early everyday, starting tomorrow morning at six o'clock. Expect to ride all day and everyday for the rest of the week."

"But..." she started to speak. Before she could say anything more, he had left her in the dust again. It was getting to be his habit. Luana heard everything from the open window, as she sat reading under Pretty Boy.

"I guess our trip to Smith's will have to be put off to another day."

"Yes, and who knows when that will be."

It took a week before Julia was free to think about her riding habit again. Every night, she took a soak in the tub to ease the saddle sores, while Luana washed the stench out of her hair with vinegar.

On the morning of the show, Susanna McCallum took a final glance at herself in the looking glass and posed for the cameras in her mind's eye. Then she descended the winding staircase, as if her name had just been announced at a debutante's ball, and glided down to the breakfast parlor.

The bouquet of roses on the credenza sat in honor of her expected congratulations. The family was assembled for breakfast and each had a part to play in the show and celebrations. Not only was Susanna competing, but both of the young men had been entered into their own age-appropriate competitions. Olivia would be helping to host a luncheon after the parade, and they all fully expected to do credit to the family name by wrapping themselves in the accolades of all those in the Valley who really mattered.

"I see that the egg and ox gall worked well. Your riding habit never looked better." Celesta could not help remarking on Susanna's appearance, as she unfolded her napkin and cracked into a soft boiled egg.

"Thank you. I feel better than ever. I'm ready to take on every rider in the County, and I have an enormous appetite to prove it. Nerves of steel."

Jack glanced over his morning newspaper. "Of course, with Tom Haley as one of the judges, you will all have a great advantage."

Susanna smiled, as she pictured herself cantering on Misty in the front row of the parade. This year would be better than last year, she thought, as she recollected the homage paid her from the prior year. After the parade, there would be a barn dance. Last year she was never without a partner, the envy of every girl there. There could be no doubt that an even greater triumph awaited her this year.

Roger and Samuel sat watching, as Susanna entered the stadium on Misty in her dusty pink, both of them expecting their sister to steal the show. She handled the mare gracefully, as they loped during the first round and then increased her speed for the second round of trotting and galloping. With gentle control and dexterity, she slowed the mare and then stopped in front of the judges to back up and take her through several required maneuvers, turning the mare right and then left and then backing her up again. She finished with a bow.

Her performance was flawless, and the crowd broke into enthusiastic applause, as she loped the mare back to the north gate. She was followed by nine young women between the ages of thirteen and sixteen, all entering and exiting from the north gate.

As Susanna performed, Julia and Marcos stood with Coal at the south gate, waiting for the signal from Tom. Julia would be the last to ride, and she spent her time speaking softly into the stallion's ears. Finally, she heard her name called out from the bullhorn, "Julia Mirante riding Coal." Marcos helped her up onto the saddle and gave Coal a reassuring pat and a whisper. Then he looked Julia straight in the eye and spoke softly. "This day is your day. Go and get it." She was too surprised to react. The gate opened slowly, as she settled into the saddle.

The crowd let out a collective murmur, as the majestic stallion seemed to have floated in on a cloud. The girl in the long auburn curls under a low-fitting white cowboy hat did not escape the crowd's appreciation either. She sat straight in the saddle with her long locks slightly grazing her lower back, and there was much speculation as to who she was and where she came from. Together, she and the stallion made a stunning pair. Roger could not take his eyes off of her. No one could.

As Julia trotted and then galloped with the stallion, she spoke words of reassurance to him. "We can do this boy. Remember this? Just like we practiced." She did not worry about the crowd, although she could feel all eyes upon her. She was completely focused on her task, and like Susanna, she performed flawlessly.

There was only one slight but significant difference in their performances. After Julia and Coal completed the required maneuvers, she roweled Coal to maximum speed one last time around the circuit, his muscles undulating under his glossy coat. In that moment, Julia had never felt more powerful or exhilarated. Finally, she slowed him to a gambol and steered him to the south gate. The crowd loved it. As Julia and Coal exited, the audience erupted into another roar of appreciation.

Roger and Sam looked at each other with surprise and concern for Susanna. Frank and Anarosa looked at each other with pride and joy. Luana and Alexio beamed. Marcos stood unruffled and unsurprised.

There was a long wait as the judges deliberated. They took longer than any other competition, so everyone knew it was a very close call. Some realized that the crowd's reaction to Julia and Coal would be a decided advantage. Finally, the announcement was made, "And the winner is Julia Mirante riding Coal." The crowd went crazy, stood up, and started stomping, "Coal, Coal, Coal."

Marcos turned to Julia, who was still mounted, and then he opened the gate to signal her to re-enter the stadium. With his look and a wave of his hat, Julia read his thoughts. She exited the gate, cantered Coal slowly around the stadium, and waved with her hat to the crowd. The crowd roared. The entire scene threw Susanna and Olivia McCallum into a tizzy.

Olivia rounded on her husband as if the outcome was entirely his fault, "Just what are you going to do about this?"

Jack looked at her coolly. "And just what do you think I can do?"

"They had no business bringing a stallion into this stadium."

Jack shrugged and rubbed his chin. "I know of no rule that forbids it. You'll just have to accept the outcome. As a matter of fact, it was a downright clever idea, even if it was foolish." He refused to discuss it with her further, stood up, and walked away.

Roger ran down the stadium to find Tom Haley. He tapped him on the arm and turned on him full-face. "What happened Tom?"

"What do you mean what happened?" Tom shrugged. "You were there. You saw it. At least part of the competition is based upon the response of the crowd. Their performances being equal, the rest of the judges went for the crowd-pleaser. Nothing I could say would stop them."

Roger had to admit he was right, but his sister would never hear it from his lips. In the end, Tom had voted for Julia and Coal, but the McCallums never needed to know it. Tom eased his conscience by telling himself he had not told an outright lie. Just as they were finishing the conversation, Roger spotted Marcos attending to the stallion.

"So, that's who's behind all of this!" Tom followed Roger's gaze.

"Yep. Marcos D'Angelo. Who else could tame a stallion so a girl could ride him? He went to a great deal of trouble to prepare that steed, not to mention the girl. There's not a better horse whisperer in all of California."

Roger deflected the compliments on Marcos's behalf and moved in Marcos's direction. He could not resist the opportunity to have a few words with the former McCallum ranch manager. As Marcos was brushing down the stallion, Roger approached him.

"So, I see you've come down in the world, eh, D'Angelo?"

Marcos glanced up to see the person confronting him and refused to make eye contact, so he locked his gaze on the stallion. He answered unnervingly. "I wouldn't say so."

"Well, there are quite a few who *would* say so," Roger insisted.

Marcos again refused to grace the deprecating comment, as he averted his gaze and continued to sweep the stallion's soft coat into perfect glossiness. Marcos was a year older than Roger, and while they had never been particular friends, they were peers. They had ridden together on several occasions. Roger waited for Marcos to defend himself, but he remained silent, while Roger's curiosity got the better of him, and he filled the silence.

"Who's the girl?" he asked flatly.

"You heard her name, didn't you?"

Marcos focused on brushing down the stallion, but he was not insensitive to the other man's interest in Julia. It bristled him and that took him by surprise. He never liked surprises, especially from his own heart.

"What kind of fool puts a girl on a stallion?"

Marcos's eyes narrowed, but he again refused to take McCallum's bait. "The kind of man who knows his daughter and who knows his stallion, I expect." At this, Marcos turned his back on McCallum and would say no more, as he led Coal to the parade. Roger's eyes followed him out to the exit, and from that day, the young men held no love for one another.

Julia could feel two eyes boring into her back as she led Coal in the parade. Cheers followed them down the parade route. She and Coal sat in front of the rest of the young women who had competed against her. Julia knew she had made an enemy of Susanna McCallum, but it did not faze her. She had never heard of Susanna before that day and did not care about her good opinion. She was determined, in any case, to enjoy this moment as she proudly guided Coal down the parade route.

Marcos's eyes were also upon her, as he and Alexio flanked Coal with two piebald geldings. He carefully scanned the crowds for anyone who might approach her or the stallion. The cheering as she passed down the parade route was almost deafening, but he would never let anyone know just how proud he was of her, especially not her. When the parade was over, the family crowded around her, and Frank helped her down from her mount.

"I knew you would do it, honey. Now, is it time to get ready for the dance?"

"Papa, do you mind if we skip it?"

"Skip it? This is your day to shine!"

"Yes, but I've had enough shining, and I don't really like to dance." She shrugged a shoulder and looked at him through pleading eyes.

"But they're all dying to meet you. You'll be the bell of the ball!" Frank looked at her intently, realizing that this daughter was never likely to be anything but a tomboy. Alexio, however, was not surprised. He laughed again at the thought of his sister in a ballroom or even, in this case, at a barn dance.

Marcos stepped in. "I'll take her home with the horses if you all want to stay." Everyone agreed, and Luana joined Marcos and Julia.

At the dance, Roger McCallum looked for the mysterious girl on the stallion but never found her.

CHAPTER 14

1878, The Atlantic, Dead Calm

The watery atmosphere reposed into a windless calm for an entire week as the bark idled parallel to the South American coast. The crew sapped all of its energy preparing the bark to pass around Cape Horn. They spoke of it with such dread; it was as if they were sailing with Odysseus and preparing to meet Scylla and Charybdis at the Strait of Messina.

On the third night of dead calm, the moon hung low and blood red, peering down at them like a rawboned vulture on a draggled rock. Just as the Mirantes ended their nightly stroll, Paulo hung spellbound over the side of the ship.

"*Pai*, I've never seen a red moon. What does it mean?" He exclaimed in awe and wonder.

Maria shuddered and wound her arm around Miguel's, while Miguel cast about for the appropriate answer. She had never seen a blood moon and her superstitious nature presumed that it was a bad omen.

"We are far from home in another part of our world. We should expect to see new sights and wonders."

"But is it the same moon as the one we saw on our island?"

"Yes, indeed. The moon does not change, but its position in the sky and our position on the earth can change. The atmosphere around the moon also changes, in the same way that it changes around us."

"And will we be looking at that same moon when we reach our new islands?"

"Yes, always the same moon and the same sun and the same earth and the same God who made them. All people who have lived on this globe share all of this in common. It reminds us of our shared humanity." That seemed to quiet the boy who stood there for another half hour pondering the thought.

Now that they were nearing the Horn, it was the crew's job to ferret out the cracks and crevices and to check for structural weaknesses in the ship. It was Mr. Haye's job to ensure that the crew took full advantage of these days of calm. Leisure time was confined to late afternoons, when crew members would sometimes swim or refine the art of building ships in bottles.

When they woke in the morning during that halcyon week, the passengers heard nonstop drumming as the ship's crew hammered oakum into every soft spot they could find and then poured hot tar into the oakum to cement it. All hands were on deck the entire week. Pounding mallets, swishing paint brushes, cranking cargo. Calls from above and below and before and aft harmonized to echo the sounds of a bustling port city.

Working from top to bottom, crew members were hoisted aloft to tar the main and fore masts, strengthening them to survive the hellish passageway. They would also tar the shrouds, back-stays, and lifts. They could not afford to pass to the Pacific without their masts and sails.

"Mr. Hayes, that's where I want to be. Can't I tar the main mast?" Paulo was intently watching the process, dreaming of climbing up and down the halyards.

"No laddie. It's one o' the toughest jobs on the ship, and only the toughest can risk it. Not one drop o' tha' tar can touch t' deck, and ye have to work the oakum into the tar while youra runnin' up and down those trunks. It takes all but three hands. Then ye have to ride down hangin from the halyards while youra tarrin' with oakum in the other hand."

Paulo still struggled to understand the Yorkshireman's English, but he knew the word 'no,' and he got the general gist of what was said from Mr. Haye's tone of voice. Paulo squinted upward, as he watched the men dangling above him in the hot sun, tar buckets in one hand and oakum in the other. Any spot missed would have to be redone.

"Now, I told ye we'd be a' pickin oakum. Let me show ye. Before ye can ever tar the mast, ye musta' work with oakum."

Mr. Hayes laid out a pile of old rope and junk and showed Paulo how to pick it apart and put it together using tar. Paulo spent three days doing nothing but picking and tarring the oakum. It was grueling work, but Paulo determined to do it better than anyone. They would use it to make yarn and then thread the yarn through spun-yarn winches.

The spun-yarn winches could be felt and heard throughout the ship like hiving wasps. The crew used them to draw and knot the yarn from the oakum into multiple threads and then form balls of yarn that could easily be reused for repair work. At times Paulo would be called upon to stretch out the yarns along the deck as it was spinning, while two others managed the wheel and spindle.

This was also a busy time for the carpenters. After losing Peter Oakes, they were pressed to find a replacement. Orders requesting an able sea carpenter, who could meet them in Valparaiso, had been sent with a passing ship. The remaining carpenters were rebuilding the steerage. They were also working on the immigrant quarters, building wood storage under bunks and securing tables, where they could store their belongings.

"I told you the ship was held together with yarn. You didn't believe me and now you know it's true. That's what you're hearing all over the ship, the pounding of oakum," insisted Paulo at dinner.

Ida rolled her eyes. "Too bad we can't eat oakum. I've been starving ever since the storm. The food is horrible. When are you going to figure out whether Slick is hoarding our food?"

Miguel flashed a look of concern. "Make sure you are extremely careful. One false move could get us kicked off this ship. Or worse. No one should suspect you of thievery."

"Don't worry, *Pai*. I will be careful. I know Slick's schedule, and I will not make a move until he is too busy to notice me. He's working in the bilge all day today."

Miguel shook his head concerned that Paulo would meet with trouble. It was during peak work hours that Paulo decided the time was right to inspect Slick's cabin for his contraband. He looked for Francisco after lunch to ask for his help and found him hanging over a taffrail.

"Slick is down below today. I heard Wills say he would be pounding oakum into the lower seams until the sun sets."

"Who else is around?" questioned Francisco.

"I've checked all around the captain and the cook's quarters. Everyone is out on deck or under the hold today. I just need you to stand guard while I go in."

"If I see someone coming, I'll knock twice on his cabin door. Remember, I never found anything in the floor boards or in the furniture, so don't waste your time there. First, try the wall planks, especially above his bunk."

They tested the cabin door and Paulo moved directly towards the walls around Slick's bed, while Francisco stood guard. After prodding the wall seams, Paulo found two loose planks above the bed. He popped his head inside and discovered a shelf containing a large box. Inside the box, he could see a stash of coins, extra food supplies, jewelry, and even carpentry tools and ship equipment.

"Francisco, come in here for a moment. What do you think?"

"That's got to be it. Now, it's just a matter of setting a trap that will give him away to the right person." They hurriedly replaced the box and the planking, closed the door of the cabin, and made their way on deck.

"Before we go to João, I think I can talk to Wills. I can trust him and he trusts me. Let me see what he thinks." Francisco agreed and disappeared, while Paulo bounded up to the quarterdeck where Wills was tarring with the rest of the crew.

"What is it laddie?" Wills detected concern on the boy's face.

"I need to talk in private." Paulo looked up at him.

Wills blinked. "I canna' stop me work now, Macaco," looking down at his tarred hands. "Meet me after the dinner bell. I webe' here on the quarterdeck."

Wills was ready when Paulo returned later in the evening. He took him aside and looked at him with all seriousness. "Coome lad. Some thins a' botherin ye? A' can see."

Paulo took a gulp. "We're starvin Mr. Haye."

"Starvin? Who?"

"All the passengers. We get nothing but gruel and hard tack for every meal."

Wills scratched his head. "Nothin else? Yo'a sure?"

Paulo shook his head up and down. "Nothin but."

"Well, that be worse than th' crew," Wills replied. "Why wooda' tha' be?"

"We think Slick is hoarding the food to trade for money and other things, and we have the proof."

"Proof? How?"

"I found it in his cabin. In the planks above his bed. He has a stash of money, jewelry, and supplies. We think he trades food for whatever he can get and then we get nothing. You'll also find ship equipment that has gone missing. We figure he's going to sell it when he gets ashore."

"We? Who is we?"

"My father, some of the other passengers."

"What d'ye think I can do for ye?"

"Talk to the First Mate or maybe even the Captain?" Paulo spoke hopefully.

Wills knew there was a risk, but if what Paulo said was true, then the Captain would surely want to know.

He tousled Paulo's hair. "Now, ye' don't be a'worry about this. Ole' Wills 'ill take care o' it."

Paulo grinned largely, his slice-of-watermelon grin.

"Get on with ye, now." And he patted him on the back side, as he darted back to his oakum.

Two days later, an inspection was announced. The First Mate, Joshua Roper, would be inspecting all quarters. The pretense for the inspection was that there was an outbreak of lice on the ship, and they wanted to ensure that none of the crew or their bedding were infected. Slick made the mistake of thinking he would be exempt. When they headed toward his cabin, he could not have been more surprised, and he scurried after them. After turning over the bed clothes, Joshua tapped over the boards above the bed and felt two of them give way.

Slick stood growling under his breath. Before Joshua could find the booty, Slick shouted, "Just wait a minute there. What do you think you're doing? There's no lice to be found in the walls."

Joshua Roper glanced over his left shoulder with a look of sarcasm.

"No lice? Are you sure Jack? Cuz we've been finding it everywhere." With one more pound, the secret compartment was exposed. "Well, what do we have here?"

Slick's face turned a noxious yellow-green. Joshua had come with two other crew members who stood by the door, so there was no escape. As Joshua pulled out an expensive piece of equipment, he looked over at Slick.

"And just how were you going to use these to cook, Jack? They're worth some money, aren't they?"

Slick spluttered excuses, and his gaze shifted nervously under quivering brows.

Joshua muttered under his breath just loud enough for Slick to hear, "The Devil take you then." Then he motioned to his men. "Tie him up and take him below. And then go find someone else onboard who can cook."

That evening the immigrants enjoyed chicken and vegetables in their soup, and nothing ever tasted so good. They also consumed loaves of bread instead of hard tack.

"How'd you manage it, Paulo?" They plied him for details.

Paulo did not know the details. He only knew that his friend, Mr. Wilbur Haye, had taken care of him. Next day, he looked for him on deck.

"Mr. Haye, thank you so much."

"You won't have to a' worry about food anymore laddie. The Captain found a new cook."

"No more Slick?"

"No more Slick - at least not in the galley."

"But he's still on the ship?"

"Yes, but not for long." Plans had been made to take Slick back to the mainland once they reached Valparaiso.

"All you have to know is that your meals are going to get better now, and Slick will not be the one cookin' em."

Just as Paulo was about to start picking more oakum, a red-footed bird with a long beak and a triangular wingspan made a startling appearance. As it hovered over the ocean, Paulo cried out. "What is it, sir? What is it?"

"Why, Macaco, issa' booby bird. Have ye not heard o' em?"

"But he has red feet, and he's so funny looking! Why is he hanging in the sky like that?"

Wills wound his arm around Paulo's shoulder and pointed upward, as they watched him float on the wind. "Now, wait for 'em to make his move. Ye must be very patient."

Paulo waited and all the while he did not take his eyes off the bird. In a flash, the booby bolted, striking the water face-forward, but unlike other seabirds, he disappeared. The bird could swim like a fish once below its surface.

Wills stayed close and whispered into Paulo's ear, "Keep a watch, laddie. Hold fast. Donna' take your eyes offa' the water."

After several minutes the booby again pierced the water's surface, clutching a large fish in his gullet. As his red web feet flopped behind him, Paulo stood gaping, until the booby flew into the quavering sunset.

CHAPTER 15

1906, Santa Clara, Earthquake in the Valley

There is nothing like the stillness that precedes the roar of a large-scale disruption of the earth. On this particular occasion, very few appreciated that stillness when the Valley floor moved suddenly and expansively, as if a giant living underneath its surface had carelessly turned on his side with a yawn. It took place at five-twelve on the morning of April 18, when most were sound asleep, unaware, and ill-prepared.

With that roar, entire blocks came down, followed by cries for help that might never come and the desperate scratching and clawing of those who would never make it out from under a rubble of brick and mortar. It was later reported that this giant moved the ground up to twenty feet and from eight to fourteen feet horizontally in some areas. The redwood trees in the Santa Cruz mountains shifted so violently that they spit out umpteen splinters and spread across canyons, as they cast about for new ground.

Like her brothers and sisters who preceded her on a tumultuous voyage, Luana fell out of her bed with a hard thud, followed by the mementos of her Hawaiian home. China rattled in its glass encasement. Books shot down and around. Bricks crumpled. Plates flew through the kitchen. Pretty Boy screeched and hopped on one foot, as his cage spiraled into a swirling waltz. "You're in trouble now boy! You're in trouble now boy! You're in trouble now boy!" It was the first and only time he would repeat himself more than once.

Luana screamed, as she struggled to untie herself from her bed clothes and groped, in a daze, towards Julia and Rose's bedroom. She could not control the juddering of her lantern as she slid along the walls. She grabbed the girls, wrapped them in her blanket, and rushed them out to the front porch. All the while, the house clacked around them like an overblown teapot on the boil.

Frank and Anarosa stumbled after them, as they grappled with their robes and yelled for the boys. Sleepy-eyed and bewildered, the boys came careening outside. From the porch, they could barely make out the undulating orchards melting across the landscape in the gray pre-dawn troposphere. The trees looked as if they could sprout wings and swarm upward in a colony like bats. Instead, many of them uprooted, as a low rumbling mooed below the earth's surface.

In the distance, they heard a clanging gong. It echoed repeatedly and then stopped abruptly. Much later they learned that, as the steeple of St. Patrick's crumpled, the church bell jettisoned from its spire and bounced onto the road below, landing on its base across a concrete pile of detritus, followed by the plangent calls of the fire station carillons. Gas and water lines bursting, hose carts unraveling, buckets splashing. The sirens wailed across the land like a mother who has lost her firstborn. Water towers collided, while people ran everywhere. A sense of fear filled the air, while every tongue tasted an acrid combination of smoke and metal.

Anarosa instinctively gathered her children, as Frank and Marcos ran to inspect the barns and the livestock. They skittered over the ground swirling around them and found the horses restless, stamping, and snorting. Chickens flapped. Turkeys hopped four feet in the air. The dog barking seemed endless.

Marcos caught Frank by the arm and pointed upwards, where the water tower was swaying, as though it were a palm tree in a tropical gale. They froze, horrified, as they realized there was no point in running for the tower. If it came down, they knew they could not save it and might well end up under it. As these thoughts flashed through Frank's mind, both men held their breath, waiting for either the earth to stop shaking or the tower to collapse. Thankfully, by the time the quake subsided, the tower was still standing. Knowing there could very well be aftershocks, they ran to inspect the structure.

"What do you think? Will it hold?" Frank questioned, as they examined it carefully. Marcos rounded the frame looking for any sections that might have been compromised.

"It looks stable enough for now, but I will work with the men to reinforce it." Frank knew that he could count on Marcos. Once the livestock were inspected and secured, they all noticed billowing smoke streaking the skies across the Valley horizon. Clanging fire wagons resounded, as fires continued to erupt out of the traumatized Valley.

Anarosa's mind raced, considering all of the potential disasters in the distance, and her initial thoughts were for her family. She knew they would need staples, such as flour and sugar, and she ran to Frank in a panic. "Please, take the horses and wagon and find out what groceries and supplies you can gather from the local markets. Who knows when we will be able to stock up again." Frank agreed and they all ran to the house to get dressed into their work clothes, knowing that there would be a long day ahead of them.

Miguel and the boys made their way towards San Jose, as Luana's thoughts turned to the state of her bakery and to Domingos. "I've got to find out if the Serradura is still standing and check on Domingos." One glance towards Julia was all it took. Luana saddled and mounted her mare and then reached out to Julia lifting her up on the saddleback, and they bolted towards the Alameda. Luana was worried about her twin brother who lived at the back of the store in a one-room apartment.

While Rose and Anarosa, went in to clean the house, Marcos worked on the windmill pump and the water tower with the help of a few farmhands and a pile of lumber. While they were finishing their work, Marcos spotted several men approaching on horseback. He scrambled down to greet them. It was Sheriff Harlow and two other men Marcos did not recognize.

"Marcos, how is the family?" the Sheriff politely inquired. Marcos explained how Miguel and the boys had gone to town, but there were still a few of the farmhands left.

"We need all the help we can get. The Agnews Insane Asylum has almost completely collapsed. There are many trapped in the debris fighting for their lives and others who are disoriented or have run off. There are also quite a few gas lines that have ruptured and fire is spreading rapidly. I'm looking for volunteers who can join a rescue crew. We must account for over one thousand patients and one hundred attendants."

Marcos made a quick calculation. "I can bring about ten to help. And I'll leave word for Miguel so that he can help when they return."

"I'll go get more help. Can you bring supplies and tools? And water? We need water and medicine for the wounded. Whatever you've got."

"We'll be there, Sheriff! Count on it."

Marcos immediately rounded up all available farmworkers, and Anarosa and Rose helped load a wagon with water bags, shovels, pick axes, barrels of pickled vegetables and canned fruits. They headed north towards Agnews. Marcos and his crew soon found that the Alviso Road was crowded with men and women rushing to the aid of the asylum and that their progress was painstakingly slow.

When they finally arrived, they took in a scene of chaos and hysteria. The sounds of moaning men and women trapped under beams and debris filled the dense air. Bodies were covered and strewn over the large front lawn, while nurses tried to comfort the survivors with blankets and whatever food and medicine they could find.

Several of the doctors who lived on the premises had already been identified among the dead. One doctor and his wife barely made it out by climbing down a fire escape. Students from the Santa Clara college began the dreadful work of unearthing bodies, covering them, and rescuing the living, but it was clear that they needed much more help.

Marcos led his own men. "Wherever you hear cries for help, start digging. Watch out for falling debris or structural instability. We don't want to lose any of you. Work in twos but spread out, so we can rescue as many as possible. Even if you don't hear cries, make your presence known as loudly as possible. Some may be too weak to cry out."

There were not enough stretchers to carry the wounded, so they used blankets to cradle them and gathered them together on the lawn where attendants, volunteers, and nurses washed their faces and hands and give them water. The wounded were crying out in pain, but there were not enough doctors and attendants to render aid or comfort. Marcos recognized that, while much of the medical supplies were lost in the rubble, they should mobilize helpers to salvage anything that might be usable.

More students arrived from the Santa Clara college, and Marcos put them to work searching for medicine and supplies, which they gathered in a heap on the front lawn, close to the survivors, attendants, and doctors. Nurses sorted out medicines for the doctors and assembled makeshift splints and cloth from leftover bedding. Sheriff Harlow arrived with a team of newly deputized volunteers and ordered them to guard the surviving patients who were mobile.

After five weary hours of digging, Marcos and his crew finally took a break, surveying the wreckage across the front lawns. There were no more cries for help; all was eerily quiet from underneath the toppled structure, once the largest building on the southern part of the Valley floor. Marcos paused to wipe his brow wondering where they would all stay while they were recovering and how they could be kept from running away. The landscape resembled devastation that was akin to the aftermath of a war.

"I think we should start building makeshift tents for the survivors," Marcos suggested to Sheriff Harlow.

"That's a good idea, but supplies are limited. We'll also need more deputized men to guard the encampment and find temporary shelter for them."

"Let's send out some of the students to the Santa Clara homesteads to collect blankets, lumber, kerosene lamps, and whatever food can be spared. We should also salvage food supplies from the wreckage." Marcos spoke with a command that the Sheriff appreciated.

"Perhaps some of the residents can provide temporary housing for them."

Sheriff Harlow jumped on his horse to round up the student volunteers, while Marcos gathered a handful of nearby volunteers to forage for food supplies. It took three more hours to gather what was left of the kitchen supplies and several more days to collect enough food for the survivors, with the help of the college and the Santa Clara mission.

Meanwhile, Frank and the boys headed in the opposite direction. As the Mirantes trundled into downtown San Jose, they discovered that most stores were filled with hoarding patrons, but they managed to buy enough to fill their wagon. There was so much hoarding that Frank asked Stefan to take the wagon back to the ranch, while he and Alexio walked to the Vendome Hotel, where many were trapped under a portion of the hotel that had collapsed while they were sleeping.

"Bring the wagon back once you've helped your mother stock the food," he cried out, as Stefan turned the wagon back in a northerly direction.

Like Marcos and his crew, they were forced to use their bare hands to uncover those who were trapped under the rubble, and the work was as backbreaking as it is slow-going. It was careful work, because any wrong move could bring down an entire ceiling or wall, collapsing the structure over the pinned and powerless survivors.

The smoky air from the scattered fires commingled with silica dust, so that the sound of ceaseless coughing filled every room. As Alexio and Frank were carrying out two survivors, several volunteers approached them with another problem.

"The ground has cracked all around the Santa Clara Water Works, and the large water towers have fallen. We need the water for the fire wagons and a rescue team to release the people trapped in the flooded areas. Bring every man you can spare." Alexio followed them onto the fire wagon, while Frank remained to carry out the survivors from under the hotel. Within a half hour, Stefan had returned to help. In all, they rescued eighteen people from the hotel by end of morning and found one dead.

In addition to pulling people out from under fallen structures, they worked with the firefighters to douse the flames, pail by pail. There simply were not enough people to help, given that the wreckage stretched from San Jose all the way to Stanford college, where numerous students had been crushed under a dormitory roof.

It was not until the sun was sinking in the western skies that the Mirantes took a break. Alexio had returned, and as they sat by the roadside, they watched as seven bodies wrapped in canvas were carried out of a nearby lodging house. All seven inside had been scorched in a fire ignited soon after the quake hit.

"How many did you rescue at the water works?" Frank asks Alexio.

"Maybe twenty. A few drowned." Alexio stared blankly as he picked at a cut on his left index finger.

They sat staring into space, coming down from a combined shot of adrenalin, shock, and exhaustion. The scenes they had witnessed this day would be forever etched in their memories. Stefan cried out, as the ground shook once more. They had been experiencing sporadic aftershocks, and with every shake, they felt a deeper sense of their own mortality.

"Sheriff says that many will be left homeless. We need to get back to the farm, so we can figure out how we can help accommodate as many people as possible." Frank spoke slowly but with resolution.

Luana's mare broke into a sweat, as they rounded a corner on their way to the Serradura. At least it was still standing. After tying up the mare, she reached for Julia, and they ran into the shop, but once they entered it, the store looked as if it had been burglarized and was strangely silent.

"Domingos! Domingos!" Luana cried, as she ran to the back kitchen and then to his room. She felt a wave of panic when she could not find him. At the same time, she was relieved that the bakery was still intact. It would take them hours to clean everything, so they went to work right away.

The bakery relied on brick chimneys for heating, and many chimneys collapsed in the quake. Thankfully, the bakery chimney, while damaged, was still operational, and the ovens were cast iron ovens. Yet, everything was covered in dust and debris. Luana remained uneasy, as the minutes ticked on with no sign of Domingos.

After five hours of lifting, hauling, sweeping, and repairing, Domingos finally came back, drunk and disheveled. Silently, he sat down in a corner and stared glassy-eyed into a dustbin of space, as his left arm hung over a box of inventory. Luana started to lash out at him, but in an instant, she intuited that something was terribly wrong and held her tongue.

Domingos was not given to hard liquor or even beer, and she had never seen him drunk. She turned away and vigorously applied her broom to the floor, sweeping as if her life depended upon it. An icy coldness came over her like hard winter frost.

Julia could not look away. She was dumbfounded by the appearance of the uncle who was always joking and making her laugh. "Uncle Domo, what's wrong?" Julia broke the silence, but Domingos just sat blinking and staring like a bootless owl in the night who cannot screech in the face of danger. Luana's broom wobbled in her hands at this next long pause.

Now Julia stood still, as frozen and watchful as a foretopman on a great ship, unmoving and insistent, facing the storm head on. She could not look away.

"What has happened?" Julia insisted he speak, and after one long tug on his arm, she clung to him. Finally, Luana stopped the nervous twitching of her broom and turned to face her twin. She spoke gently. "Go on Domingos. Tell us. What have you seen?"

Domingos drew in a long breath and gathered his thoughts, struggling to find the right words and the courage to speak.

"Bodies. Mangled bodies." He muttered.

His reply produced panic and hyperventilation. Luana sank into a chair, dreading the worst, while Julia cried out and tugged harder. "But we left everyone well at the farm. The water tower and the house were all right when we left!" Julia cried.

And then it occurred to Luana. "What about the aftershocks? Did something come down in the aftershocks? Surely it did not touch our family?"

Domingos gathered himself up from his slouch, as if the effort could provide fortitude. "Not the Mirante farm." He spoke slowly, "The Ja — anssen farm."

"What do you mean, the Janssen farm?" Julia wailed.

"The water towers were right over the house. All down. Everyone... everyone gone." He murmured softly, as he gripped the bottom of his chair and wagged his head from side-to-side.

"Nooooo! It's not true. It can't be true." Julia started to run out the door, but Luana grabbed her and wrapped her strong arms around her in a powerful embrace. Julia plunged into a lament that could awaken the shaken tombs she once visited with Therese.

"Noooo! Come back. Pleeease come back! Don't leave me. You promised." Julia started again to run out the front door, but Luana tightened her grip. Finally, Julia ceased struggling, and the tears came, hot and horrible. Luana felt it, too, as if her own heart were breaking all over again, reliving the day her father had died. Crushed. Pierced through.

CHAPTER 16

1878, The Devil's Horns

With preparations in full swing, the bark continues its slow idle down to the seafaring underworld. As it closes in on the Rio de la Plata, the crew keeps up a feverish pace, while the Captain agitates between his maps and his calculations. He wears a path from his cabin to the stairs to his lookout on the quarterdeck, back and forth with nonstop perturbation.

It is simply not an exact science. There are no reliable methods or instruments that can predict the temperature or the gales of the Tierra del Fuego archipelago in Chile, what some consider to be the starting point of the cauldron around the Devil's Horns. Unpredictable weather exacerbates their emotional churning.

The Captain debates regularly with his First Mate, Joshua Roper, on matters of timing and navigation. Mr. Roper shakes his head and throws up his hands, as he studies the charts in the Captain's cabin. "What we really need is a seer. You know there's no telling. Conditions can change in the blink of an eye."

Not only are weather conditions unpredictable, but there is no telling how long it will take to reach the starting point. Ships are known to sit idle for months before making any real headway around the Cape, given icy weather conditions and unexpected currents. Mr. Roper points to the Magellan Strait on the map and looks imploringly at the Captain. "We could follow Magellan's lead by taking his strait. A calmer alternative."

"Calm perhaps, but not necessarily safer," the Captain counters as he shoots a faraway gaze out of the porthole. "There's no guarantee we can avoid the williwaw winds in the straits, and the straits are too narrow to allow us to correct our course on a moment's notice. It's a gamble either way."

Mr. Roper presses his point one step further. "But the ice storms can capsize us at the Cape, or worse yet, suck us into a polar vortex."

"Even if the straits are less prone to ice storms, the Cape is the wider route. It gives us the leeway we'll need to avoid crashing upon the rocks or ending up in a frazil. Besides, I'm more familiar with the Cape. Experience is always an advantage."

Mr. Roper is inclined to take the route considered by some to be less tempestuous, but the Captain's pride in his own seamanship won't allow him that luxury. The Captain cannot admit to his men or his peers that he is choosing to take what is considered by some to be the easier path. The challenge is too much for his ego to resist; it is the grand prize among seafaring men to conquer not only the Horn but the fear of it within themselves.

Joshua finally relents. "It's your call Captain. Just tell me when and how to best prepare the men. They've not all been round this Horn, you know. Some are sore afraid, for all they've heard. We must show 'em that we, at least, are fearless in the face of it."

The Captain paces the room as he considers his First Mate's counsel. "Yes. Yes. I agree. If they sense any uncertainty from the officers, then fear will consume this ship like a spark on a tinderbox."

Joshua nods his head slowly in accord, as he continues to study passageways around Tierra del Fuego on the map. He rakes his long fingers through his thin, bony scalp, a nervous habit when difficult decisions are being made.

"We just don't know how long we'll be experiencing this calm. I expect that as we reach the Rio de la Plata, we'll have to start buttoning up. The collision of rivers in the basin can act like a rip tide. How long before you think we'll be there?"

"We've got two days at the most. Keep the watches ready to trim the yards," replies the Captain.

"Aye, aye, sir."

It takes them three more days to arrive at the Rio de la Plata basin, and the persistently calm weather catches them by surprise. This is the convergence point of Uruguay, Paraguay, Argentina, and Brazil. The confluence of their multiple rivers flowing into the basin acts like a natural aquifer, often resulting in precipitous weather. On this day, the calmer waters allow them to enjoy the rare sight of aquamarine rivulets in the basin.

As they continue their preparations, Wills considers what could be done with Paulo. "Do I put him down in the bilge again?" Paulo had been a great help during the tarring down of the ship, and Wills knows he cannot confine him to immigrant quarters. So, he lays a plan to keep him on the watch, knowing that he must discuss it first with the boy's father. He spots Miguel the next day on the starboard side of the leeway and grabs João to interpret for him.

"Eh, Mr. Mirante!"

Miguel turns with a quizzical look at Wills.

"I jus' wanna tell ye'. Yor little laddie has been a great help to the crew."

Miguel smiles naturally at any mention of his son. He turns to João, the interpreter. "Tell Mr. Haye that I'm glad to hear it. We're very thankful for all he's learned from the crew. And for your kindness to him."

"I was a' thinkin about how he might hep' us during our turn about the Horn."

"Yes, I know he'll want to be by your side, but I do have my concerns about his safety."

"Ay' a figured as much." Wills gropes for the right words. "But ye' probably know that ye' canna' hould the lad down. Many of our crew isn'a odda than he be, and heeza' longin' to be on the watch."

Miguel nods his appreciation of that fact, but he finds it difficult to concede, given the unpredictable gales they will face.

Wills gently persists. "I donna' plan to have 'em on the yardarms trimmin' the sails, but I woulda like 'em to keep a lookout by climbin' the main mast. We need someun' small but strong to relieve the crew, and I believe he's a'ready for it, ye' see. He would' na be up there all the time. Only some of the time. We would have to work with the lad ahead of the gales to get his footin' right. Would you be a 'willin?"

Miguel shakes his head. He knows how much Paulo wants to be on the watch, but it is hard to let him go. "I cannot do it. I cannot give my consent. I'm sorry, but it's just too dangerous. Just about anything but that."

"As ye' say. Your'a his fatha, and isn'a for me to gainsay ye'." Wills does not push further, but he is disappointed for the boy.

Miguel continues to feel disappointment too. That night at dinner, he gulps it down with his hard tack. The little boy inside is crying out to him. "I'm not too young to start learning to be a man." He remembers the man straining to break free of his little boy inside so long ago. He can hear Paulo's arguments on the other side of his conscience. "I'll be careful, *Pai*. I can do it. I know I can. Pleeease."

Finally, he gives into that inner little boy calling to him and turns to Paulo. "What would you say if I told you that Mr. Haye wants you to be on the watch — he wants to prepare you to climb the main mast?"

Maria gasps, but Frank gently takes her hand under the table, as Paulo's eyes grow bigger. "He spoke to you about it?"

"Yes, he approached me this afternoon. You'll have to start practicing right away, if you're going to be ready for the Cape."

Paulo makes an involuntary salute, gulps down his dinner, and bounds up to the lee side of the quarterdeck, where he knows he will find Wills. "Mr. Haye! Mr. Haye! My *Pai* says 'yes'! He says 'yes'!"

Wills looks at him, as he is running down the gangway with his arms up. There is a twinkle in Wills's eye. "Are ye' sure, little laddie?"

Paulo gasps and speaks as best he can in his broken English. "Yes! He just told me."

Wills puts his hand on Paulo's shoulder and looks him straight in the eye. "Then, thou'd bess na' los a' minute. Yo' meet me here at the mornin' watch. Listen for six bells and comma' runnin'!"

"Aye, aye, sir."

At dawn, Paulo takes in his first glimpse of the horizon from the mizzen mast-head, clear and bright, as they traverse tranquil seas. Hal O'Grady works with him, giving Paulo heavy outer garments as a true test of what he will be facing in strong gales. After one or two trips up and down the mast with Hal, Paulo is ready to find his feet on his own. And so he does, all day and all night long. No one can get him to come down for lunch or dinner.

Paulo feels as if he has been catapulted into a new world, where anything is possible and everything is accessible. Where a little island boy can become the captain of a great ship.

The men on the dog watches call out to him.

"Macacoooooo! When are you comin' down?"

"Ahoy there, Macaco. Save your nine lives!"

Paulo simply grins and waves at them. Nothing they say matters to him. He is riveted by the stunning expanse before him.

Like an ice skater's blade over a stone-cold lake, they glide over smooth waters, as the full moon swings low. The man in that moon seems to be lying on his side prostrate, waiting to enfold them. Paulo leans forward to meet his embrace. He can make out what looks to be a nimbus dotted with starry lights around the old man, similar to what he had seen in the distance once before. As the dogged winds lick his cheeks, he readies himself, believing that this time his heart's longing will not be denied.

What has become routine and ordinary to the crew, who climb the masts as a duty, is nothing but delight to the heart of this young boy. Those who look on from on high find themselves caught up again in their own little boy in the light of his glee. It is midnight before Paulo makes his way down to his berth and tumbles into a peaceful slumber.

For three more days they sail upon tranquil seas under crystal skies. After they pass the Southern Tropic, several of the crew pinpoint the Magellan Clouds. Captain McAllister keeps a nightly vigil on the galley way with Joshua Roper at his side, watching and waiting for the first glimpse of this extraordinary phenomenon. The Magellan Clouds light up the night skies with three very distinct and astonishing star bursts of liquid crystal, akin to the Milky Way, but looking as if they are routinely triggered by a slow-motion firework.

"Have ye never seen 'em before Captain?" Wills catches up with the Captain and Joshua Roper during the deepest night watch. It was a rare sight to spot the Captain on deck at such a time. He is joined by an eclectic group of stargazers, who are all clutching various sundry telescopes, spectacles, and light boxes, as they gather from the four corners of the ship. The Captain slowly collapses and draws down his telescope and sets it aside, while he shakes his head in wonder. "This is the first time. The last time I was here, the cloud cover and the storms were already upon us."

"Look there," Joshua Roper interjects. "It's the Southern Cross directly ahead over the starboard bow!"

The Southern Cross make up four brilliant stars, as though they are liquid diamonds, all of which transcend the brightest orb across the Southern Hemisphere. Once they all identify the four salient stars, their imaginations having etched it on their minds, everyone on deck falls silent. They all know that it is just one glimpse in time and likely one that they may never see again. The icy night cannot chase them away, as the fog leaves puffs of frozen air in the wake of their breath.

The calm seas do not last long after they spot the Magellan Clouds. The next day, the weather takes a sharp turn. They first realize it when two dark clouds tremble away from each other and then abruptly collide and thunder down on them with a massive roar.

The watch sends out its battle cry, "All hands ahoy! Tumble up here and reef the top sails!"

The skittish crew scale the yards, as if a ball of thunder is rolling up their tail ends. The longest part of their journey has finally begun. As the ship begins its sway, Wills completes a final inspection to ensure that everything on deck is latched, stowed, or nailed down. He wedges and nails down the hatches.

The passengers have also been busy securing their quarters against the coming onslaught. Having been through one violent storm, they now have a better idea of how to prepare. They stash and nail down whatever can be nailed down. Using sheets, bedding, and old clothing, they fashion slings and ties and secure them to their bedposts.

Small children are swaddled tightly to their parents this time. Extra food and water are stored and tied to their bedsides. Whatever they might be able to keep down and whatever would help them avoid dehydration. Lots of hard tack, water, and broth.

With the help of the carpenters, they secure lids for their water and slosh buckets and wedge them between their bunks. They are determined to do whatever they can to alleviate the noxious elements that plagued them in their first storm.The Steward helps them find their warm clothing and bedding that had been stowed in the lower hold. Then they brace themselves, praying, and telling stories. Anything that can take their minds off of the coming tempest.

The new cook also outdoes himself, knowing that the men will need sustenance. So, he fills the sailor's mess tubs, from which each man takes his salted beef on the run between watches. Some do not hold it down for long, as the bark gasps its way through bumptious waters.

It takes them five days of fighting against the boiling cauldron to round the Devil's horns. The ship is blown before the wind without sails and is driven off course for much of those five days. For captain and crew there is very little rest. With each attempt to round the Horn, they are slapped back as if an unseen hand is sweeping the seas against them. Sometimes they face what looks to be tidal waves, washing over the bow and engulfing them heave upon heave. Crew members fumble for footing. Gales whistle through them in rapid succession.

For forty-eight hours, the bark hurls up against unrestrained snow, hail, and sleet. No amount of clothing can keep the crew warm. Their stiff oil-cloth suits and southwestern caps only make it more difficult to reef the sails and climb the yards. Fingers frost-biting, toes tingling. The cook sends up flagons of grog, but even when they hold onto it, it is poor fare to seamen facing frosted winds. A rime encrusts itself over their beards and over the entire vessel, giving it the appearance of an undersea ruin frozen in time. Skies thicken like pea soup and then curdle into a cumulus.

After four exhausting days and nights, they finally reach the Isla Hornos, the tip of the Devil's Horn, two immense craggled rocks piercing a thickening smuir against a backdrop of snow-capped mountains. Daring them. Sucking waters beckoning them. Like Charybdis. Like Scylla. Terrifying the eyes on the watch. The bark careens on its side, taking in volumes of water, as they round her. Waves crashing over the bow. Exploding ice winds. Every shipman leaning hard. The Captain is glued and straining next to the wheelman, ready to spring into action.

The passengers dare not venture up on deck. They dare not move a muscle or whisper a syllable. Even the statue of Senhor Santo Cristo dos Milagres is now of no use to them, having been tossed in the previous storm. Strapped in their slings, they pray night and day. Curdling into fetal positions. Rooting their berths for life like an embryo sucking from its placenta. Endless sloshing and seeping water. Waiting for the deluge that will drown them in misery. They begin to welcome it. They begin to pray for it. Anything that might end the torment.

And then, Maria, with a tremulous voice, solemnly whispers in Miguel's ear what seems to be a final benediction. "Now I know the truth," she quavers. "We will never go back. I will never see my mother again." And Miguel makes no argument, as she silently bedews him with her tears.

It is deep into the night watch on the morning after the fifth day, when the gales finally die down. Wills is on the weather gangway as the bark hovers just beyond the Horn. An eery exhaustion creeps into the ship and its crew, as they slog into thick fog. After days of ferocious weather, a cold quietness settles into the bones of the bark and its passengers. Every so often a swell abruptly heaves up and tosses them up into a curl.

Upon the weather galley Wills listens and watches for storm warnings, but there is no sign of further disruption. Instead, he hears a low swooshing and moaning near the water's surface. He does not realize it, but they are surrounded by heavy breathing.

Taking a lantern, he peers over the bulwarks and is stunned to see not one, but a multitude, of orcas lumbering and heaving in the sluggish waters surrounding the ship. The combined breath of these wondrous animals rises up around them, creating a steam bath. The orcas seem to share the bone-weary enervations of the crew, as they heave their collective sighs into the midnight air.

Wills is mesmerized. He gazes up at the watch to see if anyone else notices. A myriad of wide-eyes peer down and around him with glassy stares, all hypnotized by the dark, sighing waters. They quietly glide with their escorts through the thickening brume and away from the dreaded Horn.

CHAPTER 17

1907, Santa Clara, Aftermath

A weary, dumbfounded silence fell over the Valley. The living were left to mourn and find a way to go on. They learned to envy the dead in their rest. Instead of keening, the funeral bells whimpered silently, unable to perform their service, tongue-tied from within their crumpled confines. Funeral upon funeral trudged through the streets without them.

The Sheriff's first priority was to repair the rail lines and roads which were desperately needed to bring in supplies for disaster relief and rebuilding. Marcos and the Mirante ranch hands volunteered to assist them. The U.S. Army also geared up relief efforts, and food distribution stations were set up across the San Francisco Bay. Working with the Red Cross and with local authorities, the U.S. Army brought provisions for many who were homeless.

Once repairs were completed, trains filled with supplies chugged in from all directions. Those whose homesteads were still standing provided land and hospitality. The Valley resembled an army encampment with tents stretching across its basin. Cook fires dotted the landscape and were, in some places, selectively prohibited due to broken gas mains. Those who still possessed working brick ovens and stove tops kept their fires burning to feed the needy. Fire fighters continued to struggle against spontaneous outbreaks.

The Mirante family worked feverishly to assist twenty-five families and individuals who inhabited their land in tents and makeshift shelters. Frank and the boys repaired the chimney and brick oven. Rose and Anarosa were then able to churn out soups, stews, and bread in mass quantities. Everyone contributed what they could. They were all relieved that the rainy season was mostly behind them and that sunshine splattered the Valley, as they sought to gain some sense of normality.

Luana, Julia, and Domingos lived and worked at the *Serradura* during this time, supplying the surrounding community with baked goods. Luana set up cots in the back room so that they could sleep in shifts and so that she could keep a close eye on Julia. They were given supplies and money from local philanthropists, as well as from the federal government. The local grocer, Tom Gomes, kept the bakery stocked by collecting rations of milk, butter, and flour from the Salvation Army. Much of the food stuffs were distributed through the store.

It was good that there was so much to do. It gave Julia an outlet for her grief, which had left her speechless. One week after the quake, they attended the Janssen funeral. All five caskets, wrapped in black crepe, were carried on three carts from the San Tomas Creek property to the Mission church for a funeral mass. Afterwards, they marched to the Santa Clara cemetery, where they laid their dearest friends to rest.

Julia stood as solemn and straight as the British King's Guard, swathed in black from her buttoned-down black boots and tights to her peach bowl hat joined in a rigid black bow around a tremulous chin. From behind a cascading lace veil, she maintained a solemnly hidden expression. They gathered outside the Mission church, watching intently as the five caskets were carried up a long flight of stairs, one by one, and then swallowed into the mouth of the dark, candle-lit sanctuary.

Once the procession had passed, Julia scrambled to the front of the church. Her eyes ranged back and forth in a desperate attempt to pinpoint Therese, as if she could hold onto her by force of will. But the caskets were indistinguishable from one another, the result of the hurried work of carpenters tasked with constructing hundreds of pine boxes all at once.

When the caskets were in place around the altar at the back of the sanctuary, Julia slipped into a spot nearby and Luana followed closely behind. Prayers for the dead were whispered, and mass was celebrated, but Julia did not hear a word. She was reliving over and over feelings of dreadful loss affecting her like a suffocation.

Outside, Julia walked beside the funeral carts with Luana close by. Down the street named for the city of Santa Clara, they marched to a dirge towards the cemetery, while Julia kept her eyes fixed on the caskets. Luana gently took her hand while they listened to the trumpets and percussion that accompanied their solemn procession.

As they rounded the corner of the old Victorian, two eyes peered down at them from up above behind faded curtains. Julia's eyes darted up involuntarily and locked into that gaze. She briefly raised her veil and paused until the curtains drew back. Luana paused with her and followed her gaze but did not ask questions, and then they shuffled forward.

Julia lowered the veil again and just as abruptly walked on with lowered eyes behind which she could not pretend that something essential about her world had not come to an end. Nor could she accept that her childhood was about to be buried forever.

Once beside the open gravesites, the caskets were identified, and Julia rounded on the grave where Therese was positioned. She knelt beside her, letting her tears fall on the hallowed ground. It would be the first of many times that she would kneel outside those underground tombs with flowers in hand. She lifted the veil and pulled it back over her hat.

Another pair of eyes fixed themselves, not on caskets but on the living. On Julia. Marcos stood at a distance with Frank and Anarosa, remembering a time when he had lost his parents at sea near Sicily. In one day, he had to learn to be a man, the oldest of eight children left bereft. He knew that look on Julia's face. He knew it only too well, and his heart struggled to rend itself from the memories and from her. The little boy in him would not be subdued.

As he started to choke back tears, he imperceptibly backed away from the funeral crowd, and then he walked towards the train station, and then he ran back to the homestead. He ran slowly at first, and then, as hard as he could. Back to Coal. Marcos rode him far and wide that day, not returning until the moon broke into the twilight.

Julia turned seventeen in the winter of the following year. When the next spring arrived and the funeral dirges had subsided and the makeshift shanties and tents were replaced with new homes and new opportunities, things seemed to return to normal. The Valley began to hum again with new buildings and new life. The Janssen farmland was sold. Such property exchanges made the Valley ripe for opportunists. And then there were old timers who cut their losses, sold out, and left to avoid further devastation, but it all started to feel brand new again.

Yet, for the Mirantes, they somehow understood that nothing could ever really be as it was. The ground had shifted, but in a very real way, they had shifted with it. Especially Julia. Everyone around her was acutely aware of it, Luana, and even more so, Marcos. It merely worried Luana, but in Marcos, it ignited sharp pain. For a long time, he avoided the sight of Julia and would not go near the house.

Julia stayed close to home. She rarely visited the *Serradura*. She grew quiet and pensive and even nervous. She was suddenly canning and pitting and doing all the things her mother had wanted her to do, just to keep busy. She practiced the piano every day, but she would not go near Coal or the paddocks. It was as if she had never known him.

It pleased Anarosa, but it did not please Frank, and it did not please Luana. They missed what they loved most about her: her fire; it was as if it had been snuffed out, and Coal was part of that fire. What she used to do with Therese, she could no longer do. Because she used to ride with Therese it was something she no longer wanted to do; the thought of going down to the paddocks only reminded her of Therese.

After chores were done, she would sit and read or sew for long hours on the front porch. She spent more time with Rose. Sometimes she seemed to cling to her, even pleaded with her to come sit beside her. She did not want to be alone.

Anarosa was cleaning out the kitchen one day, when she approached Luana coming from the back garden on her way to the *Serradura*. "Luana, what do you make of Julia? Why can't she snap out of it? Surely she's had enough time."

"Honestly?" Luana shook her head. "Give her whatever time she needs. I think she just has to work through her grief in her own way."

"It just seems too long."

"We can't force this. She'll get there. I don't worry about her, because I know she's strong. Each heart bears its own sorrow. We cannot bear it for her. Just so long as we understand that the little girl we have known is no longer there."

"I was talking to Gertie Cantell. She knows a very wealthy older woman who is looking for a companion, someone to read to her. Keep her company. Do errands for her. I'm thinking a little job would do Julia good. A way to keep her mind off of things."

"Yes. Having a place to go every day is a good idea. Any place that doesn't dredge up memories. A change of scene."

One day, Marcos came shambling up to the house on one of the geldings with Coal following close behind. He had not spoken to Julia since the earthquake. He stopped with horse and bridle just in front of the porch where Julia sat every day. Behind him, he had a leader on Coal who was saddled for riding. Coal snorted and whinnied when he spotted Julia.

"It's time to ride." He spoke kindly but with command. And then Marcos tried to make eye contact, but Julia averted her gaze and would not speak.

Marcos groped for words that might reach her. "He misses you. Ride him."

She shook her head and looked away. She could not resist her impulse to defy him. "No. I'm not ready."

"Then when?"

Julia looked down at her book and would not give a response.

"Well, then. We'll come every day until you're ready." And so they did. Until the day when she was ready, wearing her riding clothes, sitting on the porch waiting.

No one spoke a word. Coal nuzzled her. Marcos helped her into the saddle, and they road off. He led her up into the heights, and he took her to places she had never known. They rode every day and sometimes into the evenings, never speaking, just riding. Until she had seen every vista, dale, and glen and every moonscape across her Valley. Until its beauty seeped into her soul and became such a part of her that she knew she could never leave it. Until fear subsided and she could breathe again and find the way forward. Day by day. Ride by ride.

CHAPTER 18

1878, The Pacific, Darkness

Some people become destroyers, while others become those they destroy. Destroyers cannot live with truth or beauty; it must be crushed, and Estela Mirante was nothing if not a true beauty, both inside and out. But then, there are those who will not be destroyed, who live to triumph over their tormentors. The world cannot recognize such bravery; it does not.

She was now in his sights, and he would do the crushing. He watched her closely. He learned her routine, her habits, her friends, the sound of her laughter. He would lay in wait, for it would be a long journey, and there would be many opportunities. He also studied the father and the mother, observing their habits, and he began to gauge their level of carelessness. He surmised that he could definitely match them for wits and that would be their undoing. After all, who cared about these immigrants anyway? No one with any power on this ship would believe or defend them. He knew how the world worked. He would find his own way to feel powerful, even if for only a fleeting moment, a moment that would leave him with nothing but the illusion of power absent any enduring satisfaction.

Until one brilliant moonlit night, after they had rounded the Cape, when all was warm and dreamlike, he came to her with the intention of never leaving the recesses of her mind.

The Mirante and Terra girls spent these warm, summer evenings dancing on deck. They would make up new dances to songs and rhymes. There was one particular game they loved to play in their white night gowns. They weaved strings of cloth through their hair and then drew a large circle of rectangles on the deck with chalk including one single question mark and one single star. Then they would slowly dance along the circle chanting a rhyme.

Dance around the circle of my life
And make my dreams come true
String a chain of daisies
To the door of my heart

Unlock my secrets if you dare

Unlock my secrets when I fall down

On the last word, they would all drop to the ground. The girl sitting on the question mark would pose a question, and the one sitting on the star would answer it. The first person to land on the star was Estela and Sabina asked the question.

"Who do you love?"

Of course, Sabina was thinking of her brother Jordao. By this time, it was evident to everyone how he felt about Estela. Evident to everyone except Estela. Sabina wanted to find out if she could pry a secret from Estela's heart.

"But I love you all!"

At that, they booed her. Sabina grew more insistent. "But I know you love someone in particular," she probed. Estela did not budge, and she insisted that she loved many people and no one in particular. "There is no secret to reveal," she sighed.

"Ah, come on! We don't believe you. We know you love Jordao."

Estela only sighed. She knew everyone assumed there was affection between them, but in truth, she gave it little thought. She appreciated Jordao's feelings, but she had done nothing to lead him on.

"I wish I could satisfy your curiosity, but it would not be true. Come now, let's not waste time. Let's dance again, and this time, let's not be so predictable with our questions."

Again, they rose and danced and again Estela landed on the star. It was her sister Ana's turn to ask the question, and she thought awhile before she asked, "What do you most desire in all the world?"

Estela thought awhile, as she listened to the sucking of the water against the sides of the ship, "That we would find paradise for my family in our new home, and we would be safe and happy together always. There would be no fear and no separation."

Ida groaned. "Your answers are as bad as the questions! Can't you imagine something better than that?"

"No, actually, there is nothing better to imagine. You do not know what you are saying, because you do not know the value of what you have. We should not take security and love for granted, as if they are too commonplace to be the most valuable things we possess. They are anything but commonplace and anything but useless. Living on this ship ought to have taught you that."

"Let's try again," Ida deflected her impatiently. "And this time, let's be sure it's anyone but Estela who lands on the star. If it looks like she will, then we'll push her off!"

Everyone laughed and began the dance again. On the third try, Sabina fell on the star and Ida ask her the question. "If you could change anything about this life, what would you change?"

Sabina sat thoughtfully and spoke wistfully, "I would make sure that all children never cry from hunger or sickness, and no one could ever harm them or slap them around. All children would be protected in my world." As the moonlight caressed their tiny circle, no one could refute her words. They all silently agreed, as they became lost in their thoughts. It would truly be a different world, if the children never cried or had to endure abuse or love denied.

"It would be as if they all lived in a bubble." Ana remarked. They sat thoughtfully thinking about a bubble. "But when would it burst? How old must one be before they are launched into the world and no longer a child?" Ida wondered.

Sabina broke the thought-filled silence, as she jumped up and initiated a game of hide and seek so that the little ones would follow her down below. Estela looked out over the wide expanse made visible only by the full moon above her.

"When will you come down?" questioned Ida, as they all followed after Sabina.

"I'll only be a little while longer. I just want to enjoy the moonlight on the wide open sea."

Estela stared at the vee traced by the moon in the wake of the ship. It was not in her nature to regret or resent anyone, nor was it in her nature to blame anyone but herself when things went wrong. Her thoughts naturally turned inward when others accused her or when those closest to her were hurt.

Tonight was one she would never forget for its beauty, as well as for its dreadfulness. She sang softly to herself a song of home, little knowing that her song was overheard by another.

Soon, she made her way below, but as she passed the life boats, an unforeseen hand reached out and clasped her mouth from behind. He quickly drew back her hands and clasped them together behind her, as he dragged her underneath the canvas of the lifeboats away from the night watches and into a shroud of darkness. It all happened so fast, she thought she must be having a nightmare. Perhaps it was an incubus, something she had heard from the the the whispers among the women on the ship.

Her mind converged into a combination of horror and disbelief, as realization and pain stabbed her body and soul. Every muscle cried out to be free of her tormentor. But her tormentor was relentless and unyielding to all her struggles. He was prepared for them, choreographing every move and how it was to be accomplished. He relied on her ignorance, her naivety, and her innocence to protect himself and to rob her of her dignity. Deluded into thinking he could somehow seize it from her and take it into himself. It was the only way he could feel powerful against all those who had made him feel powerless.

Not understanding any of this, Estela struggled until she could struggle no more and collapsed in a heap, as he was done with her. Her mind went blank as she fainted, and then her tormentor melted back into the darkness, leaving her to the aftermath of humiliation and abject misery with which her tormentor had never been able to cope. Deceived into a fruitless quest for satisfaction, he would always have to strike again.

The ship drifted into the moon, as Estela fell into a nightmare. In her dream, she was shrouded in the knowledge that she was still not alone. Was that mocking laughter she heard buzzing around her? The sound crescendoed into a sneer that smote her heart with the deepest shame. Every day thereafter the visitation returned like bats attaching themselves to newly pitted recesses in the cavernous parts of her mind. As darkness slipped into dawn, a voice called to her. A light, faint and distant, rose up in her, slinging all her thoughts forward. "I must get up. I must go on. The day is coming. No one can ever know."

She had struggled within her whole being, and yet somehow she knew that the greater struggle was yet to be. She willed herself to move, her body aching in every fiber, the slightest movement seeming impossible. Her leaden hands involuntarily moved to her face to suppress the shame that flowed from her mind to her heart.

"I must not stay here. I must keep moving." An inner voice found its way to her. "But no one must know. I must get back to my berth before someone discovers I am gone. No one can know."

And then she put one step in front of the other, collecting her torn clothing as best she could, slowly, surely, and with resolution. And when she arrived at her bed, she fell hard on it and into a deep sleep. It would be the last one for a very long while.

At noon, Ida tried to shake Estela awake. It took several attempts to bring her to consciousness.

"Get up, you lazy thing! You missed breakfast, and now you'll miss your lunch! What were you up to all night? Howling at the moon?"

Instinctively, Estela reached up to touch her face, her neck, and her hands, concerned that somehow what had happened to her was evident to all like a rash that had broken out all over her body.

"How do I look?" she inquired quietly.

"What do you mean "how do you look"? You look like a bed rat who's been sleeping for fourteen hours! Your hair is a mess and your face needs washing. What do you expect?"

"But, do I look like me?" There were very few physical traces, nothing that could prove her attack was real.

Ida glanced at her curiously and spoke with some exasperation accompanied by an expression of disbelief. "Uh, no, you look like Paulo! What kind of question is that?"

Estela sighed and rolled over. Ida's sarcasm calmed her fear. She could hide and no one had to know. "I'm not well. I don't feel like eating. You can have my lunch."

Ida was surprised but was glad to oblige her, since she was always hungry. It took her about two seconds to bolt to the lunch table.

"Where's Estela?" Maria asked.

"She says she's not feeling well and that I can have her lunch." Ida quipped as she dished up a double portion. Maria thought it very odd since Estela was the healthiest of all her children, never complaining of aches and pains like the others. She determined to find out what was wrong, as soon as lunch was cleared.

Estela's was not the only broken heart on this floating, wooden world. There was another, one that no one would ever see or recognize. Her name was Beatriz. She did not understand why they called her "Bell," instead of her name. She did not understand why she found dirty water in her bed or soot on her newly washed clothes or why her personal items often went missing. Why the other women would not include her in their conversations or their walks on deck. She was never invited anywhere, and she heard whispers wherever she went.

Beatriz came on the ship thinking she would find someone who would love her and make her secure. He had promised to marry her when they reached the islands. It was not long after they boarded that she realized he was coming to bed late and getting up too early. Until she finally confronted him with a whisper in the dead of night.

"Antonio, where have you been? It's the middle of the night! I was so scared when I found you gone."

"Hush, my darling. The men stay up late. We talk, we smoke, we drink, and play dice. There's nothing to worry about." He lied through his teeth.

Beatriz would have to be content with his explanation, since she had no other choice. Back on the islands she had never had many choices either. She was a beast of burden to her drunken father who made her work while he drank. He beat her constantly, until she could stand it no more, and she ran away.

She found that running away solved nothing. It brought her more trouble and abuse. A young woman alone on the islands was an easy target. Whether she was home or away, she faced nothing but misery, and the women could be worse than the men. They assumed she had chosen her lot in life. They spat on her and called her "prostituta." No one ever stopped to ask her; they just assumed the worst.

Until she met Antonio, the first and only man who had spoken to her with kindness, who seemed to take a genuine interest in her. It was not long until she believed herself to be in love.

He had not thought through either his own feelings or what he intended to do when they reached the islands. He was fool enough to think she could work and help him maintain two households, but it had not occurred to him that she might become pregnant and unable. Now he was stuck in an impossible situation, and he did not know what he was going to do.

CHAPTER 19

1907, Santa Clara, Summer in the Valley

It was the peak of summer, when every day in the Valley was overwrought with frenzy, and every night sky was star-struck in deepest blue. To the young and strong, Valley summers seemed never-ending, and to those tested by time, they came and went too quickly. It was a season when the fruit bolted furiously to the ground or weighted down their hosts as if they were pack mules. Fruit pickers wrapped around thousands of trees, like clinging orangutans with arms akimbo, dotting the landscape for miles around. Deftly picking, repositioning, and picking again. These were the longest, never-to-be forgotten days.

Very soon, the cannery workers would do their peeling, pitting, and canning, and the steamboats would chug their booty all the way to San Francisco and out to the world. The smell of rotten fruit and sulphur settled in the air for weeks, and only the diligent reserved its plenty.

Rose stood taller over the butcher block this year. She was wiping down her forehead with the back of one arm while massaging a buttery wodge of dough with the other. Purple stains spluttered down her apron. Copious curls were tied in a cluster at the top of her head. She was learning to make pies for the *Serradura* bakery. Blackberries, cherries, apricots, apples. Luana was, once again, taking over Anarosa's kitchen, realizing that the time to find her own place was looming large on her horizon. Just not yet.

"Put more sugar in that dough, girl. It must be sweet." Every few minutes Luana would bark out her orders, and Rose would tolerate her drumming for the sake of a culinary education. Rose dropped a new ball of dough on the butcher block. Forgetting to flour her rolling pin, she rolled over it with one sticky stroke. The dough stuck to the pin, pulling off the block, and converging into itself.

"Try more flour. On the block and on the pin."

Rose poured flour all across the butcher block, powdering herself from her waist to the top of her head. Then she wielded the pin down and across the dough.

"Now it's too flakey. It's just breaking apart." Rose howled.

"Too much flour now, girl. Let me show you." Luana wiped her apron, took the dough, and threw it out.

"What? All my work!"

"We can't fix it now. Let's start over from the beginning." Luana insisted on perfection.

She deftly took the next batch of newly butter-spliced dough. She shaped it into a disc, smoothing out its sides to avoid over-handling it. Then she wrapped it up in paper and put it in the ice box.

"But, why the ice box?" Rose wondered.

"It has to harden just enough so it will not fall apart. Then we won't have to worry so much about the quantity of flour. Just remember to give it a little bit of flour. Just dust it, like so." Luana demonstrated by lightly sprinkling a palm of flour across the block. Rose sighed, realizing her hands were too sticky to wipe the curls from her forehead. She blew out the top of her mouth, angling upward. With one exasperated breath, the lock of hair over her eyes jettisoned into place. Then she leaned hard against the block. "I'm beat."

"Take a break. We'll leave the dough for a half hour, while I get some more ready." Luana was not usually so understanding, but she realized the girl was overwrought.

At just about that time, Alexio and Stefan poked their heads into the back kitchen door, wafting in the heady scent of stewed prunes and apricots. The boys were in a waggish way and had contrived a plan to bolt to the ice box without being seen, but Luana was too quick for them. She took one look at their boots and a hot flush seeped across her face. Their boots were caked into an amalgam of smashed ants buried in prunes, mud, and sawdust.

"Off with those boots, now!" Any trail they left would be hers to clean up. They dropped them sheepishly on the back porch stairs.

"Now, get out the scraper and start cleaning them before they become prune-petrified!"

Stefan rolled his eyes. Alexio groaned.

"Right now! And no lunch until you've washed up."

Stefan started pleading. "We're exhausted and we need food now." The look in Luana's eyes stopped them short.

"Not until those boots are scraped — and outside. Now!" The boys knew there was no denying Luana at such a time, so they scurried to comply.

Julia took a scrap of paper from her pocket, as she slowly rounded the college, wondering if the information in her hand was correct. When she reached Santa Clara Street, she could not find the house number from the piece of paper that Gertie Cantell had given her mother. She reread the numbers slowly, four-one-eight. She fingered the crumpled piece of paper and retraced her steps but still could not find the house. She double-backed towards the college, climbed the steps to a random house, hesitated and then knocked.

She listened and heard the sounds of muttering, scrambling, and childish giggling. The door opened a crack to reveal the harassed looks of a frazzled housewife by the name of Cathy Jacques. Cathy looked Julia up and down before speaking and then cracked the door slightly wider, curiosity getting the best of her.

"Yes, how might I be of help, miss?" Two pairs of toddler eyes peered up between her legs.

"Hello. My name is Julia Mirante. I'm looking for this address." Julie handed her the scrap of paper. "I can't seem to find the house number, but I know it must be nearby."

"Well, let's see. I'm not sure about the exact house number, but do you have a name?"

"Abigail. That's all I know."

Cathy ran a hand across her forehead and glanced down the block. "Well, that's gotta be the McCallum house, the old Victorian and barn near the school."

Julia gave a start. It had not occurred to her that it might possibly be the old house. She could not have been more surprised, as she reimagined the old woman in the window.

"Yes. The house numbers may be faded, but that's gotta be the one. No one has seen the old gal in years. She never comes out. What's your business there?" The woman now shot Julia an up and down glance that exposed her curiosity.

Julia side-stepped her question. "Do you know her well?"

Cathy settled in as she shifted her weight and shoved a toddler behind her legs. "No one does. Not now anyway. I've heard there was a time when she was well known around these parts, but no longer. I've also heard that she's better known as Abbie, Abbie McCallum, at least to those who once knew her well."

Julia thanked her and headed in the direction of the school, biting her lip thoughtfully. "Abbie," she spoke it out loud, as if the name could tell her the whole story. As if a person, perhaps this particular person, could be known by her name. She whispered it again, playing it over in her mind.

With each step, her heart fluttered around her chest just a bit faster. "I wonder how long she's been alone. What must life be like day after same day and how would it change a person to face such solitude and monotony? And for so many years? Like one who lies helplessly prostrate, just waiting to die." These were questions she was determined to answer.

She approached the house from the front and stepped inside the uneven picket fence gate, as it squealed on its hinges. She turned back to re-position the gate. Slowly, she climbed the uneven wooden stairs leading to the imposing front doors. She pulled on the doorbell, knocked, and waited. And knocked again. She heard sounds of soft scuffling.

Finally, the door opened. A lone servant poked his head out of the door, shifted his eyes left and then right, before fixing his eyes upon Julia. Astonished to see a living soul before him and seemingly suspicious, he croaked. "Yes?"

"My name is Julia Mirante. Gertie Cantell sent me."

He looked doubtful. "And what could your business be?"

"I'm here for an interview with Mrs. McCallum. Uh, Abigail McCallum. She's requested a companion. She does live here?" Julia was not certain how to describe the position. She really did not know what it would require. He opened the door and beckoned her inside without further introduction. She entered a spacious front parlor with high, vaulted ceilings. The room smelled of redwood and rose oil. The servant turned to her slowly. "Wait here." He did not motion for her to sit down, so she remained standing.

As soon as he was out of sight, she twirled the room with one sweeping glance, while angling her head upward towards the vaulted ceiling. The parlor was like an art museum, covered with life-sized oil paintings, mostly landscapes. Windows on another world filled Julia's imagination. It was as if one painter had been commissioned to depict every vista, valley, and glen of the Scottish Highlands. The effect was astonishing. The family portraits were hanging on the opposite wall. She gazed up at generations of handsome Scottish warriors and gentlemen in navy-green kilts hilted with bucklers and swords. Buxom Scottish lassis at the peek of their beauty smiled mysteriously down at her.

Above the mantel hung a portrait of the mistress of the house. It was a portrait of an young lady doused in a Scottish moonbroch. Despite her youth in the painting, Julia recognized the woman she had seen in the window. Those piercing peridot eyes spoke to her with a perceptive gaze. The artist had perfectly adorned her with eyes that were windows to the soul of a woman who knows what it is to love. Julia did not know how long she stood before it. It seemed that moments melted into hours as she waited in wonder.

And then Julia's glance swept downward to the smallest painting on the wall. It was the only painting that was not a portrait, a painting of a young Dutch girl about fifteen years old. She was dressed simply in a short, silken togo hugging her loosely and secured with a rope around her waist. The girl was lying on her stomach on a grassy knoll overlooking a mountain landscape. On her face was a dreamlike expression. Her arms lifted her up to see more, as if she were gazing at the highlands of heaven far away.

There was something other-worldly about the girl. Her face glowed with contentment; she was in a state of perfect peace. Julia wanted to be with her, longed to be content like the girl in the painting, to live in that same serenity. But she was stuck somehow in the thought that she was really on the outside looking into something in which she could not take part. Through tears, Julia somehow realized that she was looking through a portal into Therese's new life, and it pierced her soul. Her heart was torn between her happiness for Therese and the ache she felt without her. Julia staggered backward.

A cracked voice broke into her revery. "Well girl? What is it you see there?"

Reality snapped Julia back from the vision, as she swung in the direction of the voice. But the face she saw standing there was not disapproving. Instead it betrayed a faintly tender understanding. Julia could not speak, and Abbie McCallum could not miss her tears. Julia wiped them quickly with the back of her hands. This was the first time she had cried since the funeral. To deflect from her tears, Julia blurted out. "I thought I recognized a friend. In the painting."

"Was she the one who used to come with you to spy on me?" Abbie had recognized Julia, even though she was now six years older.

Julia nodded, unable to to hide anything.

"Was she the one you followed in the funeral procession after the great quake?"

Julia nodded again. More tears. Finally, she choked out what was heaviest on her heart. "I never got to say goodbye."

"It's all right. I understand. She understands. Now you need to understand. You must have faith. You must believe that you will see her again. That you will join her when the time is right, even though she will not come back to you here. Can you do that girl?"

Julia gulped and nodded, uncertain but very much wanting to trust this woman she had just met. Abbie held out a beautiful Scottish Madras-laced handkerchief. Julia hesitated. Abbie pressed it into her hands. "Consider it yours." Julia nodded her thanks.

"Now, young lady. Follow me upstairs. There is much that I would like to show you."

CHAPTER 20

1878, The Pacific, Valparaiso

It was a day to celebrate when the bark slipped into the port city of Valparaiso along the Chile coast. The Devil's Horns were soon forgotten by those who looked forward to a new life, although they would become fodder for stories passed down from one generation to the next. As the bark glided into the Bay in full sail, it was a sight to behold. Had they been ashore, the immigrants might have come to appreciate the beauty of their bark, fluttering into port with full wing-span like a butterfly lit up on a warm summer's day.

The passengers draped themselves over the taffrails, waving and cheering. The bark was soon hedged in by engorged canoes, filled with natives in light sea craft bursting with treasures. The canoes were colored with sun umbrellas and baskets filled with the catch of the day, the soft bronze skin of young girls and women adorned with feathered locks and escorted by tropical breezes. Barkers called out the price of goods and services, coveting the sailor's pay and his hunger for food, grog, and women. Not every crew member would go ashore, but those who could were in need of a break after their hard labors.

Kit sounded the bell as soon as the port came into view. Paulo claimed the best spot, positioned on the mizzen main-mast from six o'clock until their ten o'clock arrival. The Mirantes were up early so they could secure a spot on the right side of the ship facing the port. All joined in except Estela, who remained below.

With all the fanfare, there was still an underlying air of disappointment among the passengers. They would not be allowed to disembark. Strict orders were given to guard the gangway, and the Steward would check the papers of everyone coming in and out. Some of the passengers grumbled that it felt as if they were in jail, but there were some very good reasons.

After all, they had been contracted for service. Their passage had already been paid by their future employers. The shipping company would be held responsible for any missing persons, a circumstance the Captain was under strict orders to avoid. The Captain was also held to an uncompromising schedule; they could not afford to wait for anyone who might wander.

Since they would not be allowed to go ashore, the passengers placed their orders for food and clothing with the Steward. Maria ordered extra foodstuffs and blankets to supplement their still somewhat meager meals. They also purchased chickens to be raised by the cook.

"Look, Miguel, it looks like Funchal!"

It was good to feel close to solid ground, after so much instability. It gave Maria some sense of comfort about the islands they would soon call home. Miguel wrapped his arm around her, as they slowed into the port.

Far down below, Estela sat sewing by lamplight. Alone. They had all tried to talk her into joining in their fanfare, but she begged off, insisting that she wanted to finish her sewing project. Most of them found it hard to believe that she would miss the sights and sounds of land after such an arduous journey at sea. They wondered but did not press her.

The day before they arrived in Valparaiso, she menstruated, much to her relief. Now she could feel safe, because no one would ever have to know. She would never have to speak of it, and she could spare her family her anguish and humiliation. Nevertheless, it lived on inside of her like a parasite gnawing away at her insides, her deepest fear being that it would never go away. It felt as if it would never get better.

Until they reached the islands she would have to contrive new and better ways to deflect them all. She knew that they had all recognized a change in her behavior, and she was only able to feign sickness for so long. So then she tried keeping a stiff upper lip, putting on a smile, acting gay and nonchalant. She did whatever she could to dismiss their concerns, so that she could stay out of the light and out of range from his evil eyes.

She imagined that he was triumphing over her at a distance, and she was not entirely wrong. He did not wonder why she hid below. He counted on her devastation and relished the thought of it. She did not see it that way. She could not stand not knowing who he was, while he knew who she was. She would look at every crew member and wonder and accuse each one in her mind. What was the point of telling anyone when she couldn't identify the man? Would the captain even listen to her story? It seemed impossible to her.

A deep, smoldering rage filled her up and acted on her heart like burning acid. She contrived to invent some tiny bit of mental relief by way of imagination, but there seemed to be absolutely no way out; true justice could not be conjured. Behind every mental portal there was only the same unsettling proclamation of retribution and justice denied.

She understood that there would be no recourse in law, so how could she possibly share her anguish with her loved ones? If she did, then she would only be subjecting them to a bitter cup. She could not desire it. No, she thought, she must find a way to bear it alone. She must spare them the degradation of her fate. In the stillness of the night watches, she thought she would go mad with it, as she dreamed of revenge that was impossibly out of her reach. This was the hardest part.

While everyone was looking forward to their stop in Chile, perhaps no one had anticipated it as much as Antonio Cabral. He considered it to be the only way he could free himself from the impossible situation he now faced: a querulous wife and four children and a needy mistress with child. He pictured nothing but endless days of slave labor ahead of him, and he refused to wear those chains, so he sought to rid himself of them.

The question in his mind was how he could get past the steward on the gangway. This would be his only chance before reaching the Sandwich Islands. He considered looking for an opportune moment, when the steward's back might be turned, but that was risky. For one thing, it might never happen, and for another, he would have to plant himself somewhere unseen that was very close by. The gangway was fully open to the men on the watch from up above, as well as to the many passengers who kept their eyes on all the interesting activities from ship to shore.

Then he figured out a way. While most of the crew members would be onshore during those forty-eight hours, there would also be other crew members who would be on duty, repairing the ship and stocking the cargo. Small boats were trudging back and forth all day long to pick up food and supplies. What if he offered to join them? Especially those who rowed the cargo back and forth? It was not difficult to find someone who allowed him to help with the hard labor of lifting and rowing.

He disguised himself as a crew member and spent an entire day lifting and carrying the cargo for them. The common sailor did not ask questions of him. He speculated that he could convince at least one of them to go into town with him on the final journey, just after dark, so he could slip into a crowd once on shore.

"What do ya' say fellas? Who wants a trip into town tonight?"

"Too risky. The Captain will have our hides."

"Not if we're back at the first light of dawn with a fresh stock of cargo. They'll never know we were out all night. Is anyone counting?"

Sam Malone looked at him and considered.

"He's probably right. It'll be dark when the last load comes in. We'll just bribe the dockhand to look the other way and come back early in the morning with the first shipment. No one will be the wiser."

There were four men on the boat. Only a crew member named Sam would risk it, but the others agreed to keep mum. When the last journey to shore was finished, Sam and Antonio mizzled their way into the darkness on shore. Sam came back in the morning, but no one ever saw Antonio again, and no one from the immigrant quarters even missed him.

No one but Hilda and Beatriz.

Hilda was the least affected by the absence of the man who had given her nothing but grief. She considered herself somewhat lucky to be rid of him. She eventually came to the conclusion that there was nothing to be done. He was either dead or deserted, and either way, he was no longer of use to her. Her children were old enough to work the cane fields, and they had the support of an extended family, so she knew she could make her way.

Beatriz was another story. She was more vulnerable and heart-broken and had no family to help her. She was filled with fear as she considered the plight of a single, pregnant young woman on an unfriendly ship. After all, he had planned to marry her in the islands, which had given her some sense of protection. Now, how could she work once they reached the islands? She now realized that even if the Captain would delay the ship to find him, Antonio did not really want to be with her and would find another way to desert her when they reached the islands.

So neither woman bothered to report him missing and neither spoke a word to the other. By the time the crew discovered the missing passenger, it would be too late to recover him, and the men who rowed him ashore would never reveal how it happened.

Two days later, they had just left the Bay of Valparaiso, when the watch bell struck at three AM. The night was dark and serene. A fog-covering made the deck an easy hideaway. First, she must find something heavy to secure herself. There must be no opportunity for a rescue, and she must make a clean break into the water to avoid being heard by the night watches. She searched for something that would keep her from floating in the icy water. It must be quick and it must be sudden. A heavy chain draped around her waste. An iron anvil tightly nestled in her hands.

She took one step. Then two. She heard a rustling in the darkness. Someone might spot her. Then she stopped and hid under the gangplank. Waiting. Heart beating. Breath bating. Afraid. Afraid of life and afraid of death and darkness. Which was the greater fear? Which one would win her over? For two hours, she battled between both. And then she climbed up again and took one step and then another. Until it was a walk and a swoon into outer darkness, slipping, disappearing into a bleep on the waters. Surging down. Freezing. Bubbling, gasping, struggling, gurgling. Finally, stillness.

A whistle sounded. And then a bell. An attempted rescue ensued that was eventually aborted. It was too late. The crew member could not identify the person who had fallen from the gang plank. He was not even certain if it was a man or a woman.

Questions were asked that could not be answered, so the Captain ordered that everyone on board must be counted. It took a full day to complete the check-in, and when it was over, two missing persons were identified.

Even still, there were many questions that remained: Which one had jumped overboard? Did two people go overboard, and how would they ever know? Antonio was suddenly safer, since the Captain was not likely to send a search party back to Valparaiso as long as he had some reason to believe he was at the bottom of the sea. But that was something Antonio would never know.

CHAPTER 21

1908, San Jose, Father and Son

Julia followed Abbie up an art nouveau staircase banded by vine tresses laced with pomegranates and treble notes. They came to a landing overlooking a library with rows of bookshelves covering every wall from floor-to-ceiling. Two narrow windows gaped out from the south-facing wall over the back garden. Cane-backed chairs, window box seats, and a plush sofa lounge provided comfortable roosting places.

A baby grand piano, stippled with dust and marked by disuse, was stuffed into a corner by the fireplace, and velvet curtains darkened the room. The only sources of light were the fireplace and one solitary Tiffany lamp. Julia stood gawking. She had never seen so many books in her life; a banquet of delightful possibilities opened up to her. Abbie observed Julia closely and picked up a volume from the nearby sofa table. "So, here is where we'll spend most of our time together. Do you read, girl?"

Julia nodded in the affirmative. "But I don't see how we can get any reading done in such darkness. Do you mind if I pull back the curtains?"

"Do what you like, but when you leave, put it back the way it was. I do not care for the light."

It occurred to Julia that she did not even know what to call this lady.

"How would you like me to address you, ma'm? Mrs. McCallum?"

"No, absolutely not. You must call me Abbie."

It also occurred to Julia that she did not want to be called "girl," so she put herself forward. "And I am Julia."

"Yes, so I've heard. I also hear that you are quite the horsewoman, young lady. Gertie tells me she's never seen a young woman ride like you. I understand that you gave my granddaughter quite a comeuppance. Is that true?" So, the old woman did have contacts in the outside world. Probably a select few. Julia felt slightly apologetic.

"I never saw it that way, but I did win the young women's competition almost two years ago. I never met your granddaughter, but she was definitely my strongest competitor."

Abbie smirked and clawed back a stray clump of hair from her forehead. "I've no doubt she was. You needn't feel guilty about it. As a matter of fact, you should be proud of your accomplishments. So, how else do you spend your time? What are your interests? Your pursuits?"

"My family has a farm and a bakery. I spend most of my time outdoors with the horses, but I enjoy helping out at the bakery when my mother lets me."

"And do you play?" Abbie leaned on the piano.

"Yes, I play some, but I am really not what you might call proficient."

"The first thing you should understand about me is never to presume that you know what I would think or what I might call anything. I will decide for myself what is proficient. You just need to play for me. I have some of the best music in my library, and you are welcome to practice and learn from it as much as you like."

"Thank you, m'am. And what else can I do for you?"

"Please, call me Abbie." Julia nodded and Abbie grew suddenly fatigued and turned her back to Julia. She parted the curtains and surveyed the garden, bringing the conversation to an abrupt end, as she devolved into a tone of cold formality.

"That'll be all for now. Come on Tuesdays and Thursdays, promptly, from one to three o'clock. I'm sure we'll find plenty for you to do."

She pulled the cord to call for her servant.

"Now, if you'll excuse me, Howard will show you out."

Jackson McCallum lay prostrate, hearing voices but unable to speak or respond. Not able to lift a finger. He could not feel his feet, and his hands tingled. He faded in and out. When he was aware, he did not want to know or hear what they were saying, but he had no choice. He could not exercise his will; that was the hardest part.

A wife he could not trust became even less trustworthy. She was now the wife he felt certain was triumphing over him, perhaps eagerly anticipating his demise. How had it come to this? The children he thought loved him did not sound so loving. Where were his business partners, all those who had toasted with him every New Year's Eve? He could feel his life ebbing away. Did they know?

Sounds came out of an echo chamber. There were scrambling servants, plumping pillows, rustling sheets. Glasses of water to his lips. Handling him. Cleaning him. He heard the careful low-toned advice of doctors. He listened in on a symphony of whispers and sighs. Of course, they could not be sure of what he could actually hear, so they often spoke of what they ought not to have spoken.

"He may last a week. He could live for months."

"I've seen men his age back on their feet within a week."

"Hey Jack. We're missing you. Can't wait to see you back on your feet."

"Father. Can you hear me? Where are you? Come back to us."

"What was it got him?"

"Stroke."

"When did it happen?"

"He was in the barn saddling his horse. Nothing strenuous. It came on suddenly."

"The doctors say he has a good chance of survival."

"What do we do about the harvest?"

"Who will complete the land transaction? How do we move forward? When do we call in the lawyers?"

Life kept spinning around him. He tried to enter into it, but it was as if he was reaching through a tornado to catch the wind. His mind's eye faded from gray to white and then grew black. He could not speak. There was so much he might have said. He understood that he had suffered a stroke, but he felt nothing. Not depression. Not anger. Just helplessness.

When he was lucid, his life was passing before him. There were certain parts he did not want to see. His boyhood loomed the largest, his childlike heart beating hard against his breast. There was a time when little Jackson McCallum watched and waited and learned. And there was no one he looked up to as much as his father, considered a great man of his time.

George taught him well. He was a busy man, an important man. There was always one more mountain to climb, one more legal war to wage in his insatiable quest for more. Once his fortune in gold had been made, it was not enough in and of itself. He would use it to seize all he could, one land grant at a time. After California fell into the hands of the United States, there were years of what seemed like endless land disputes. The Californios lacked the surveillance methods, as well as the documented history, that might prove their ownership of the rancheros.

Men like George McCallum used the legal system of the day to lay claim to it, while the rancheros were hard pressed for the money to pay the taxes and hire the attorneys who could defend them in American courts. George had the means and influence stacked in his favor. He was rarely around, but when he was, Jack never took his eyes off of him. He longed to impress his father, because he did not know that his father was a man who could not be impressed. By anyone.

He possessed one seminal memory of his father that he could never forget. The memory of it lodged in his brain like a stray bullet that had barely missed a main artery and remained inoperable. Jack was eight years old when it happened. There was a man named Jose Aiello who had once owned over 600 acres, which came under dispute with claims made by George McCallum. The lawsuit over the land languished in the courts for ten years, and during that time Jose had continued to live on the land raising cattle.

A less tenacious man might have sold out, cut a deal with George, as so many others had done. But Jose cleaved to his land, as if it were his own body and soul, having invested all he had to work it.

Jack remembered his father ranting and raving about the man; he seemed obsessed with him. There were many nightly tirades about it at the dinner table as he stewed over how he might jawbone the man out of his property. It galled George that any man would defy him and that Jose had found a way to scrape up the money to tie him up in court.

When the Court finally ruled in George's favor, he could not wait to rid himself of Jose and his family. The Court ruling laid out the terms of land transfer, and Jose had one week to remove all of his belongings, or they would be forfeit to George McCallum. Jose was able to remove his cattle, but there were ten horses remaining that he could not stable, so George moved them to his own homestead. When Jose was unable to find them, while he was still looking for space to stable them, he came to their homestead and knocked on the front door. With his hat in hand, he had come to beg for leniency.

"Mr. McCallum, please grant me another week. I know I can find another settlement."

Spitefully, George refused. "You've got twenty-four hours and then the horses are mine to do with whatever I please."

Jose walked away sadly, but he was able to find one of his family members who offered to help him. He came back the next day to retrieve them. But he was two hours too late.

"But Mr. McCallum, I have a place for them now. I can take them."

George took his rifle and shot all ten horses right in front of Jose and right in front of Jack, who never took his eyes off of his father from the large front parlor window.

"There! There's your horses. Now, take them, and get off of my land and never come back."

Tears streamed down Jose's face. George did not flinch. Jack stood still and watched his father return to the house, take the rifle, and secure it back in his gun rack. George turned, saw Jack watching, and looked him in the eye.

"Remember, Jack, never compromise. Never back down. The law is the law."

Jack blinked and never forgot, while the horses moldered in the blazing sun, creating a stench that putrefied the atmosphere for days, until his father hired men to dispose of them.

While Jack lay waiting to fade away, he thought a great deal about his father, who died when he was just twelve years old. He would never forget the day of his father's funeral. It seemed that the entire Valley herded into and around the little Episcopal Church in San Jose. The church was heavily perfumed with enormous clusters of pink and white carnations. The smell of them sickened Jack. He would not allow them anywhere in his house or near him after that day. He did not want them anywhere near him now.

His father and mother had recently moved into the Italianate Victorian. His father's body was laid out in the downstairs parlor, robed in his best flannel suit. He lay under the painting of his great grandfather, Roger McCallum, who stood swarthy and strong in his tartan of deepest blue-green.

As Jack lay there helpless, he thought about the little boy gazing at his great-grandfather and then down at his own father. The little boy wanted to touch his father. He reached out and then shrunk back. He couldn't do it. He felt numb. Nothingness.

Looking back, he realized that he had no real connection with the man. He had tried. He had watched and waited, but his father was incapable of seeing his little boy. Incapable of finding value in him. And so, when he passed, Jack felt absolutely nothing. To this day, he felt nothing. When he could think, he lay there and wondered why.

He knew his wife was lost to him, but what about his children? Do his children feel nothing? He couldn't be sure.

Of one thing he was certain: out of all those things that had seemed so important for so many years, hardly any of it seemed important from where he lay now. The land, the gold, the power struggles, the men he'd hired and the men he'd fired. Marcos D'Angelo. He knew he'd been unfair. How many others were there like him? He couldn't count.

The truth now loomed large. About everything. Why couldn't he see it all before? What once made him feel triumphant now only made him feel small and petty. The raging waters of regret tumbled over him in his helplessness. Mocking him? Regret had always been a stranger to him, until now.

And then there was his mother. She was the only source of real love in his life, and he had cut himself off from it and for really no good reason other than to appease a spiteful wife. Olivia had never liked his mother. Also for no good reason. He remembered the day he brought Olivia home to meet his mother. The women mentally circled one another like lionesses sparring over a kill. It was obvious that his mother took an instant dislike to Olivia.

He blamed his mother then, but he did not blame her now. He saw now what she saw then. Would she forgive him? How could he get word to her? He could not even ask a servant to fetch her. He knew Olivia would never send for her, even for a last goodbye. A single tear squeezed itself out of him and trickled down into his ear. It was the last thing he would feel, the only tear of his adult life.

Twelve days later, Jackson McCallum was laid to rest. The San Jose Episcopal Church filled to the brim, just like his father's funeral. The sickening-sweet smell of carnations was staggering. The funeral procession marched from downtown San Jose, traversed The Alameda, and ended at the Santa Clara cemetery, just beyond Abbie McCallum's house. As the procession passed the old Victorian, the curtains in the upstairs parlor parted.

His mother had not even been invited. She was not told that her son had died; she learned about it from the newspapers. Of course, the land had already passed to her son and would pass to her grandchildren upon her death. They seemed to have no need of her, not even to comfort her grandchildren. There was only the lingering question about the gold.

CHAPTER 22

1878, The Pacific, Overcoming

It had been weeks since Estela had come out on deck, and while she may have been able to fool others, she was not able to fool Maria. Maria was worried and concerned, but she would not speak a word of it to Miguel or to anyone. Her instincts told her that something was terribly wrong with her daughter. She did not want to suspect the worst, but a woman's intuition for such things can be uncanny. She knew in a way that only a woman could know, so she protected Estela by her silence and by deflecting the suspicious comments of others.

It was wash day and all the women were taking turns showering on deck. These days did not come often, and no one missed the opportunity. To refuse to come out was conspicuous. As they waited for their turn at the shower, Marissa Terra prodded Maria for answers. "It makes no sense. Who can stand to stay so cooped up in that hole without ever coming out for fresh air?"

Marissa posed it as a question, wondering if Maria would find it as strange as she did.

Maria refused to give her any satisfaction. "The girl is just going through a stage. She'll get over it."

"Well, I've never seen a young girl go through such a stage. They are all eager to be out on deck as much as they can be. Even Jordao has commented on how odd it is."

"Of course, he would notice. Does he never stop noticing everything Estela does?"

Marissa smiled. "Yes, I suppose you are right. Do you think she'll ever come round to him?"

Maria shrugged. "It's hard to say. I just think she's not ready."

Then there were the other girls. Ida was especially relentless in calling out Estela's unaccountable behavior.

"*Mãe*, whatever is the matter with her? Who would want to to stay down there and do nothing but sew?"

"The girl is growing up. Perhaps she is tired of your games and dances on deck. She is outgrowing you."

Ida could not comprehend it.

Pretenses were getting to be too much, even for Maria. So, while the others were out on deck this sunny day, Maria decided to slip below. She found Estela by herself and approached her cautiously. She sat at the end of Estela's bunk and spoke to her slowly and quietly.

"Stella, you are my daughter. No one knows you like your mother. What concerns you concerns me. You realize you can tell me anything?"

"Of course, *Mãe*." Estela kept sewing but put up her internal guard. She knew that Maria was the most difficult to fool, even if she had said less than the others; Estela had felt her mother's knowing eyes upon her.

Maria gently slid over and taking Estela's chin in hand, raised up her head to peer deeply into her eyes. She spoke simply but in a way that could not be ignored or denied. "I see something here that I have never seen before." Estela darted her eyes away, struggling to hide the pain that was lodged deeply.

Maria grew more insistent. "You can tell me. Whatever it is, I will understand. You need to know that I can help you, whatever the matter is."

Estela's expression ranged restlessly as she squeezed back the threatening tears. Maria did not need a specific answer. She wanted to make it easier for her by answering for her. "Has someone on the ship hurt you?"

It took a moment, but Estela decided not to fight her and nodded her assent.

"Hurt you in ways we cannot see?"

Estela closed her eyes and sighed deeply. And nodded again.

"I think I know how. Now, tell me. Is it anyone we know?"

Estela felt some relief in purging her secret. She looked up earnestly and shook her head in the negative.

"*Mãe*, I never saw him. Never saw him coming. I cannot identify him. It all happened in darkness. I wanted to spare you the pain I have endured. I beg you, please. No one else can ever know. Please." Estela pleaded, and Maria pressed two fingers to her lips.

"The first thing you need to know is that there is absolutely nothing about this that is your fault. Nothing. Can you believe that?"

Estela's face was filled with doubt. "I can try," she spoke weakly.

"Yes, you must try. And keep trying, even when it seems impossible. And it will continue to seem so."

Maria searched for this truth to register in Estela's eyes, and only when she sensed that Estela could receive it did she go on.

"Please don't distress yourself. I honor your desire for privacy. I also understand and appreciate your concern for us, but in return, you must understand that your family is here for you. Those without families have no life line when tragedy strikes. Not one of us is meant to travel the hard roads of this life alone. We need one another. Do you see that?"

Estela nodded slowly as she registered a wisdom she would learn to cherish. "Yes, *Mãe*. Yes."

"There is a woman on this ship who fell to her death when all was lost. We women do not speak of her now, but we were unkind to her, because we did not understand her. We now know that she had no family. No support in the storm. We are complicit in her death, and it is a terrible thing to realize. We might have helped her had we known. We might have been the family she lacked."

Maria now choked back her own tears. Then turned to her again.

"My brave and beautiful girl, you cannot face this without knowing that you are deeply loved. Had such a woman possessed what you possess, then she would have had a reason to live. You are not like her. You have every reason to live. Do you see that?"

"Yes. I can see, *Mãe*. I can see that." Estela smiled thinly but was listening closely. Breathing heavily as she began to think differently.

Maria smiled with relief. "God loves you. Your family loves you. You are surrounded by that love and wrapped up in it, so you can face life bravely, whatever comes."

"But what can I do with this anger? It eats away at me. Why is there no justice in this life?"

Maria nodded and took her hand. "We must understand that sometimes we find justice in this life and sometimes we do not. Either way, whatever this life has to offer in the way of justice will always feel imperfect; it can never satisfy. No matter how hard we try. It does not mean we don't try; it just means we may have to live with the imperfect but whatever it is, it is only justice delayed."

"Why must that be?"

"I don't know that answer. I only know that we must trust God for justice. His kind of justice, knowing deep within that it will come; it must come. You see, there is a channel inside all of us. It can be a channel for love or a channel for hate. If we allow bitterness to take root, then the bitterness will choke out the channel where love was meant to flow. And so we choose to forgive and leave true justice in God's hands."

"Forgive? How can that be possible?" Estela revolted against the very idea.

"You are right. It is impossible. For us mere humans, it is truly impossible. But with God, all things are possible. Trust Him to do for you and in you what you cannot do for yourself. Can you understand that kind of faith, that kind of love?"

Estela shook her head in wonder. "Not completely, but I will try."

"Pray for this man, whoever he is. His soul is terribly tainted. He dwells in deepest darkness. You can be sure that he will bear the pain of it, even though you cannot see it with your own eyes. Imagine that he has not had the family you have had. Perhaps someone has abused him. He has undoubtedly suffered in ways neither you nor I would ever see. He thinks he is strong, but he is weak and pitiful. In this, you will be set free from the terrible memories and the pain he chose to impose on you."

Maria continued. "I knew pain once. It wasn't the same as yours, but it was very real. I watched a wicked woman abuse my mother. We had no choice. We had no other way to make a living at the time. She tormented my mother relentlessly. I grew to hate her. I thought there was no escape, but I trusted in God, and He showed me the way to forgive her and that set me free from her, to the point where I rarely think of her anymore, and if I do think of her, I pray for her. Can you understand that in forgiveness is your release and a channel for God's power to make a way where there seems to be no way?"

Estela was amazed. "I think perhaps I can." And then Estela felt her mother's strength surge within her and knew that she could trust her and her words. Not that she had ever doubted her, but it came alive to her in a new way that she could not have appreciated before. "Thank you, *Mãe*. I love you."

Maria took her in her arms, and Estela let her tears fall for the first time. It was the first step in the journey to overcome so as to live with a heart set free to love. Estela rested in the assurance that although it would not happen in a day, it would happen day by day, and she would find her way forward.

Through all of this, Jordao never stopped visiting Estela. Smiling. Telling jokes. Bringing her card games to play and whatever presents he could find on deck to amuse her. He taught her how to play dice for match sticks. At first, she resented him and discouraged his attentions, but slowly, she came to appreciate his friendship, even looked forward to seeing him.

One day, not long after she had cried in her mother's arms, he came to her with a smile.

"There are porpoises surrounding the ship! They are jumping all around us in the sunshine. The sun bounces off their backs as they rise up in the sky. They are so graceful. It is such a sight to see. You must come and see them!"

She shrank back. "No — you go. You go without me."

Jordao saw her fear. While he knew something was wrong, he would not press her. He only wanted to help her, so he met her gaze.

"Whatever it is. Whatever makes you afraid, I will be with you. Hold my hand. Come up with me into the sunlight. Do not ever let anyone or anything steal your joy. The good things in this life are yours to embrace, but you must reach out to embrace them." He stood and held out his hand to her.

He was compelling, a breath of fresh air. She wanted to believe that what he said was true, so she took his hand. As they arrived on deck, she let him put his arm around her.

The dolphins gamboled in the sun, as if beckoning them to join in their play. To Estela, it felt good to laugh and to feel the sun on her face. It also attracted the attention of others. For an instant, she felt the chill of baleful eyes, but they soon shriveled back into the corridors of her mind, as Jordao joined her.

In that moment, Estela glimpsed a pathway through the darkness, the path she would take to the breaking of a new dawn. In her mind's eye, she saw the end of time; a time to be made new; a time when destruction and oppression would cease. She felt herself propelled forward, as if on angels' wings.

CHAPTER 23

1908, Santa Clara, Autumn in the Valley

The leaves were turning rosiny gold and Jack had now been gone for over six months. At first, it felt unnatural, but as time passed, Olivia realized that she now had no one to contend with and no one to play the part of her conscience. While she had learned she could wear her husband down on some matters, she knew that he possessed at least a tinge of restraint when it came to tormenting his own mother.

His death changed all of that. The way was clear and wide open to her now. She experienced a newfound sense of freedom. Olivia was determined, once and for all, to get her hands on what remained of the McCallum fortune.

This time she would use the one weapon she knew would strike hardest at the old woman's heart. Love letters. She went to the secretary and unlocked a drawer whose contents had long been forgotten. It was her final salvo, her last resort to lay claim to all of the gold. She gave no thought to the sorrow and grief they would cause or to the fact that she and her family already had more than enough to secure their comfort and prestige for generations to come.

She unfolded the first letter and scanned its contents: "no love like our love"; "no other woman for me"; "you make me feel alive again." She smirked at the prosaic phrases of a middle-aged man who had been besotted by a harlot.

She remembered wondering why he kept his own love letters, not knowing that he had already paid the woman off in exchange for their retrieval. How long had it lasted? Not long, no doubt, but it was long enough to devastate a much younger Abbie McCallum. Olivia felt certain that she would never get over it.

She also remembered the day that Abbie discovered the letters, when she had witnessed her mother-in-law's misery. Their relationship was still a cordial one at that time, and Olivia was shrewd enough to have secured Abbie's trust, at a time when she had something to gain by it. She entered the upstairs parlor and found Abbie weeping, something she had never witnessed in the staid and dignified older woman. She ran to Abbie's side with a pretense of deep concern.

"Mother, what is it? What could the matter be?"

Desperately needing the support that her daughter-in-law now offered, Abbie handed her one of the letters. As Olivia read it, she felt triumphant, vaguely realizing that this knowledge gave her power. Revealing nothing of her jubilance, Olivia turned to Abbie with a facade of sympathy. "He can't really love her. This woman is known for her moral turpitude. After all, why would he maintain possession of letters he wrote to her? Something is not right."

But Abbie did not hear her words; she was too blinded by misery. "I don't know what to do. Shall I confront him? Keep it to myself? Play the role of the injured wife? Use it against him? He'll only hate me for it." She shook her head at every possible stratagem.

"Say nothing. It will blow over. And do whatever you can to overwhelm him with your love. Exact revenge by yielding in him a tormented conscience."

Olivia prodded her with soothing words. She then resorted to a disingenuous means to create false hope, not caring if her words were true but very much wanting Abbie to hand her the letters. As Olivia placed a consoling hand upon her mother-in-law's knee, she whispered furtively as she made a study of her face. "He will soon realize that you are the only worthy woman in his life and throw her over. I promise you. Now dry your eyes and let's go shopping for some new dresses to cheer you. We will woo him back with your revitalized beauty. And let me take care of these letters so you are never tempted to wallow in them again."

Abbie looked gratefully at her daughter-in-law, sensing that there was some wisdom to her words, as she slowly handed over the letters. Much to Olivia's surprise, her words proved themselves to be true. George had already thrown the woman over.

After that day in the parlor with Olivia, Abbie witnessed a sudden transformation in her husband. He grew more attentive than at any time in their marriage. He even took her on a European tour to celebrate their anniversary. It went exactly as Olivia had said, and Abbie was grateful for her daughter-in-law's foresight, never suspecting the manipulative hooks that were intentionally being implanted.

Olivia pondered over these memories with a smirk. She could not help but wonder if George had ever realized that the letters were missing. She smiled as she considered why this would not have concerned Abbie. Olivia had assumed that a guilt-ridden man was not likely to have mentioned missing love letters to his injured wife. Nor would he be inclined to dwell on what had only become a source of shame that he had bought off in order to forget.

Now Olivia sat down to write a letter to her mother-in-law, in which she suggested that she would provide the letters in exchange for the gold. And why not request the family jewels while she was at it, knowing that Abbie possessed an impressive array of gems and diamonds? She would threaten to make the letters public, using them to bait the local gossip columnist. It was as simple as that. Olivia reasoned that it could not really hurt a woman who had no real need, at this stage in her life, for family gold and jewels but who would surely want to protect her dignity and honor. As she was finishing her venal missive, Olivia heard the front door slam. Roger was home, and she would invite him to play a much-needed part in her scheme.

Roger took one look at her preoccupied expression and suspected that she would be sending him on a mission of some kind or other. He fidgeted with his gold pocket watch, newly acquired since the reading of his father's will. It had been passed down from George to Jack and now to Roger, who was unaccustomed to its weight and its bulk.

"Good day, mother, and just what is on your mind today?"

"I have an errand for you of some importance." Her look was as guileful as the task she was about to give him. Olivia knew that Abbie would never receive her without suspicion, and she also knew that Abbie would most likely jump at any chance to see her grandson.

Roger examined her closely as he released himself from her embrace. "You mean I am to follow instructions without ever knowing anything about why you want me to do what you are asking, correct?"

"Exactly," Olivia gave off an appreciative smile in exchange for her son's anticipating her desires. She continued in a confident drawl, as she stepped away from him and retrieved the sealed letter and held it out to him. "I've been thinking that, now with your father gone, we should make some attempt to repair our relations with his dear mother."

With his back turned away from her, Roger helped himself to a glass of sherry from a crystal decanter. Despite the insincerity in her voice, he agreed with her stated intent, whatever her underlying motive. He had always cherished the memory of his grandmother. As a little boy, he simply assumed that his parents must have had good reason to cut her off, never questioning their veracity or motives. Now, as a young man, he was happy to renew a closer acquaintance with her, so he did not prod his mother further. He took the letter. "So, what do you propose? An invitation to dine with us, perhaps?"

His mother did not catch the subtle sarcasm in his suggestion; she was too intent on carrying out her purposes. "No, I think that would be too much, too soon. Rather, I think we should take small steps."

"And just what did you have in mind?"

"A simple letter of condolence and friendship delivered by your hand." She said it with a self-satisfied smile. Roger could provide no reason to refuse, but he did sense treachery, even if he had no proof of it. Something about it made him hesitate and so he held onto the letter for several days.

Roger put off his visit to his grandmother, dreading the possible confrontation, the angry words, and the bitterness that might follow. He had made many excuses to his mother until it became impossible to deflect her wishes. He sent a note ahead to inform his grandmother that he would come by early Thursday afternoon at two o'clock, believing that she rarely received visitors and wanting her to be prepared. He also knew she would be anticipating some specific purpose for his visit, given that he had not seen her in ten years.

Arriving promptly, he handed his hat to her servant, Howard, and asked him where he might be able to find her. Surprisingly, he would not be paying a visit to the sitting room on the ground floor, where he remembered she used to receive visitors. He was told to enter the upper parlor.

As he slowly climbed the stairs to greet her, he became aware of a change in the stale air of the old house. The air overhead was fresh, reminding him of the Pacific winds that tickle the mountain pines as they escort the sea birds on their visits to the Valley. And, for an instant, he thought he was dreaming.

The house was dimly lit under the overcast autumn sky, yet breaking through the dust and gloom, sunlight filtered through the upper parlor and down to the landing of the stairwell where he stood. As he ascended, through the open balusters, he caught a glimpse of lace cuff encircling a slender wrist poised on the arm of a sofa chair. He moved upward tentatively. It took a moment for his eyes to adjust and to realize that it was not his grandmother who was sitting in the chair. Curiosity propelled him upward, as he turned his head sharply at the top of the landing to examine a new presence.

Through the caning that encircled the chair, he could barely make out the soft muslin folds of her dress and the russet curls that framed her delicate profile. Her curls were adorned with a bonnet, criss-crossed with yellow satin ribbon and tied in a bow under a slightly dimpled chin. She tilted her head away from him as she recited from one of his grandmother's volumes of best loved poems, as if in a song:

I hear, I hear, with joy I hear!
—But ... there is a Tree, of many, of one,
A single field which I have looked upon,
Both of them speak of something that is gone;
The Pansy at my feet
Doth the same tale repeat:
Whither is fled the visionary gleam?
Where is it now, the glory and the dream?

Our birth is but a sleep and a forgetting:
The Soul that rises with us, our life's Star,
Hath had elsewhere its setting,
And cometh from afar:
Not in entire forgetfulness,
And not in utter nakedness,
But trailing clouds of glory do we come
From God, who is our home[1]

The words pierced him through, making him pause and back away. Hating the exigency of what he suspected to be a mean-spirited errand.

He vaguely remembered this room in its season of grandeur, and his mind quickly filled with rapid clips of those luminous days. They were days of tinkling dinner bells and gaiety, which were set against a backdrop of serenades from the dusty piano beside his now sleeping grandmother. Servants carrying plates of steaming hot dishes. Smiling guests in their best white dress. He felt

1 William Wordsworth, *Ode: Intimations of Immortality from Early Childhood*

a sudden ache for what was and for what should have been, as he considered what life had become for this grand lady.

Stepping back, he turned and moved slowly down the stairs. He could not stay and had to check his impulse to run. As he descended downward to the inquisitive looks of the servant, he reclaimed his hat, glanced up, and paused at the large portrait hanging above the downstairs mantle, a portrait of a very young Abigail McCallum. For the first time in his life, he truly saw her and felt her sweet and intelligent eyes upon him. The young Abbie stood with long, flowing hair upon a portico. In the background was the Stirling Castle with the River Forth in the foreground near her Highland home. What had become of those days?

In that moment, he knew he was a part of her and that she was beautiful both inside and out. Her piercing green eyes were a perfect reflection of his own. It struck him now in that moment that he had believed a lie, and he determined to know her better.

Inwardly shaken, he walked slowly as he reached the outer gate and then turned back to gaze upward to the light that filtered out of the upstairs parlor window. He carefully considered his next steps. To the west of the old Victorian was a barn, and he positioned himself near it, where he remained unseen. The autumn winds whipped the sails from the tank house overhead, and he buttoned his jacket to ward off a chill. One windswept tear seeped inexplicably from his left eye, as his hand caressed the smooth, polished gold of the newly acquired pocket watch.

Eventually, she came and descended the steps, closing the gate behind her and carrying the borrowed book of poetry. There were no indications that she was aware of his sudden exit or his presence near the barn, and he could not fathom why that realization compounded an empty ache inside. She was in no particular hurry, and he was struck by the lightness of her step and person. It seemed to him that there was no faltering in those steps. He left his horse tethered near the barn and followed her down and across the street towards the old mission. He longed to know more of her.

He knew little of the depths that this would lead to, never having pursued anyone or anything with equal certainty. And that years later, he would look back and never fail to understand those first steps. He understood less now that this would be the only time he would take this journey and so he did not hesitate. There could be no thought of hanging back but only vague feelings of longing mingled with hope.

He watched her as she rounded a meandering path lined with fir trees, and then he followed her. After crossing through the center grounds of the college, she took to The Alameda where, just beyond it, she crossed the street towards the *Serradura*. At this time of day the bake shop was filled with people, and the windows were steaming from the hot ovens and the mingled breath of its patrons. She opened the door and slipped inside, and its warmth filtered past him, along with an autumn breeze that twirled the leaves off a nearby maple. He waited and watched her through the windows.

From outside, he could see dimly that everyone knew her and greeted her. Clearly, she was well known here, and this was her neighborhood. Who were these people? He stepped forward cautiously, opened the door and entered, as one who arrives in a new land. He chose a corner table with his back to the windows but in a position to avert his eyes when necessary. He could not find her in the crowd, but all around him he heard the boisterous colloquy that was common among the Portuguese, a Latin language possessing both the passion of Spanish and the lyricism of French.

He ordered a coffee and a pasteís de nata, a delicate egg custard tart. He had to admit to himself that he had never tasted anything quite like it. It tasted of buttery rum and orange peels, as it melted in his mouth. He became vaguely aware of his own natural disinclination for just about anything outside his own provincial world, and he paused to question it for the first time. He did not linger on the thought for very long. It was not his purpose to draw attention to himself, except from that one person who had led him there. He realized that there was no hiding in a place where everyone knew one another, but the distinguished gringo in the corner could not be overlooked by such an inquisitive and familial crowd.

Gilberto leaned over the counter and whispered to Domingos. "So, who do you suppose that is and what do you think brings him here?" Not one to resent anyone who contributes to business, Domingos glanced towards the corner and shrugged. "As long as his money is green and his blood is red, it is of no importance to me." His eyes swept the corners of the room, as he wiped the last of a dozen newly washed glasses. This attracted Luana who, glancing to the corner and then back to the two at the bar, knew exactly who the man was. She could not have been more surprised.

"*Meu Deus!* He's only the heir to the biggest farm and fortune in this Valley. I've heard it said that he is just like the mother, famous for her relentless ambition for the family name and greedy to retain them for her eldest son. It is even whispered that she swindled her husband's mother out of her land and tens of thousands of dollars."

"How is that possible?" replied Domingos.

"No one knows, only that the old woman used to own all of the land holdings that are now in the hands of her son's heirs, while she lives as a recluse in the old Victorian house near the parish."

"Yes, I know who you are talking about now. It is also said that the old woman has stockpiles of gold and that no one knows where she hides it. I wonder what could have brought him here?" Renato spoke in a whisper, even though he mouthed it in Portuguese.

Luana shrugged, but she kept her eyes on the stranger, as if she could unlock the secrets of his heart. She thought highly of her ability to peg a man on sight. Was he an adventurer, an opportunist, a wanderer, or filled with nothing but selfish ambition or lust? Every female instinct in her suggested that there was a specific reason for his being here, and she was determined to find it out. The mere fact that he came to a place on the opposite side of the Valley from where he belonged suggested to her that his actions were nothing if not intentional.

Roger kept his gaze steadied towards the window, but he could not help glancing fitfully into the crowd every few moments. Until he beheld her. She was strolling out from the back kitchen with Rose at her side. They were laughing, as if they had just shared a delicious secret. Rose held a package of newly baked cookies just retrieved from the oven.

Now, he saw her straight on in the full light of day, and the recognition of his sister's rival jolted through him suddenly, like the beginnings of another, much stronger Valley earthquake. It had been three years since he had first seen her astride the majestic Coal, and though she had since matured, there was still something daring and playful in her manner. The scene now came back to him, his sister's indignation and her rival's serene indifference to it, making it all the more infuriating to Susanna. He remembered the girl's stallion, its dark beauty, which accented her own. The gaiety in her voice brought him to himself and he strained to hear more.

"Whatever you do, don't stop anywhere." Luana was trailing behind the girls, all while she was coaching a distracted Rose. "Your mother is expecting company and must have them for tea by four o'clock." With a backward glance, Rose assured her that nothing would keep her from meeting her mother's expectations.

Once Rose was out the door, Julia leaned against the bakery counter, and Luana quietly frisked her for information about the stranger in the corner. Glancing slightly backward towards that corner, she whispered, "Don't look now, but there is a man in the corner named Roger McCallum. Have you never heard of him?"

Julia resisted the temptation to glance back. "No, but he could be related to Abbie McCallum. You know, the woman I visit and read to every week? The one I told you about?"

"So that is who you visit? In that spooky old house? What's it like and what is she like?" Luana leaned in with greedy interest.

Julia stroked her coffee cup thoughtfully. "Well, not so bad actually. The house is full of old things that interest me, and she has a wonderful collection of books. She lets me borrow as many as I like. At first, she seemed unapproachable, but after awhile, I was strangely drawn to her. She has lived a very different kind of life, and I am learning a great deal from her."

"Well, try to find out why she gave all her land away to her son before she was even dead in the grave. And don't be obvious, but take a look at the grandson before you leave."

Julia's curiosity was piqued, and she asked Luana for another coffee, so she could linger awhile. His steady gaze waited for acknowledgement as she spoke to Luana. When it felt safe, she turned and glanced to the corner. Her eyes could not help but meet his in their earnest penetration. He did not turn away and neither did she.

What she intended as a glance turned into one long, curious, and inquiring moment.

On her part, it was stubbornness that held her there and an instinct that rises naturally to meet intimidation. On his part, he was determined to leave with the assurance that he was now firmly implanted in her thoughts. Little did he know how much more his heart would retain that gaze than hers. In years to come, he would wonder who it was who had turned away first.

Luana missed nothing in that one long glance and clearly understood what had brought the handsome stranger to her humble bakery. She was in no way surprised. Of course, her little *Avilhada* should have nothing but the best, but Luana considered whether all the fortunes of such a young man could really be what was truly "the best" for her Julia. Luana was struck by the realization that Julia was no longer a child.

One part of her wanted to warn Julia not to succumb to a man who would undoubtedly possess competing interests, when it came to choosing a woman in his life. The other part of her could not interfere with anything that might come in the way of good fortune to her favorite. She believed that Julia would know best how to hold onto her own heart, in spite of his many attractions. She was also determined that while she would not interfere, she would keep a careful and close watch on them both. She searched inquiringly after Julia, speaking in a whispered Portuguese. "So what do you think of him?"

Julia responded as she stared into her cup. "I think he seems far too sure of himself, and I imagine he is used to getting what he wants." She was somewhat taken aback by his boldness, but it would never occur to her that his gaze was inspired by admiration. She vaguely resented the presumption in his stare, as if he sought to command her. She had had enough of men who tried to control her, and her insides grappled with resentment.

"But, of course he is. He's very rich and very well known." Luana continued to hold her voice in a whisper.

"So, why did he look at me like that? I thought his eyes would bore holes into my soul." Julia recoiled again at the thought.

Luana did not want to plant the seeds of attraction in her niece by telling her what she suspected. Roger McCallum would have to do his own wooing, as far as she was concerned; she was not going to further his cause, at least not until she felt certain that his intentions were honorable. It occurred to her that not many men truly understand their own intentions when first struck by Cupid's arrow. She shrugged with a laugh. Let him be smitten, Luana thought. He'll soon learn that he's caught the tail of a tiger, and it will do him some good.

As she reached for the broom, Luana chuckled to herself. In the time it took for her to turn back to glance his way again, the tall, handsome stranger was gone. She wondered how long it would be before he returned, as she vigorously swept around the table where he had left his crumbs, and while Julia pushed him just as vigorously out of her thoughts.

CHAPTER 24

1878, The Pacific, Outbreak

They were now in the home stretch, and the excitement in the air was palpable. Once the bark broke off from the coast of South America, the Pacific seas cracked wide open to them like a meaty black walnut ripe for the picking. Nothing but blue horizon and endless oceans surrounded them. The way seemed clear; they now all felt a sense of invincibility. They had passed through the greatest storms and lived to tell the tale. Soon they would reach their new home.

As they journeyed north, temperatures turned tepid and sometimes hot. There was more dancing, more music, and bathing on deck. More chamaritas and gamboling dolphins.

Paulo spent most of his time with the crew. He even berthed with them once in awhile, when he was on the watch. He was learning to reef and furl the top sails now, and he was living up to his moniker, proving himself to be the nimblest runner up the yard arms. The more he learned about sailing the seas, the less he wanted to pick pineapples and cut cane. He was almost fourteen years old, and it was not unusual for boys his age to become merchant seamen. Miguel understood this and was concerned that he might lose his boy.

"Maria, I think we ought to prepare ourselves. Men on the seas grow up sooner than we are accustomed."

"What are you saying? Paulo will come with us. There is no question in the matter."

"I may not be able to stop him."

"But surely he is part of our contract. He must work in the islands for at least three years. Isn't that our bargain with the sugar cane growers?"

"The contract is for our labor, not the children's. Although the children can work, they will also be able to go to school. And besides, I've heard that the Captain can negotiate to purchase contracts if he chooses."

"Miguel, you can't be serious. He is still just a boy."

"When I think of how much he loves what he's doing and how many opportunities it will open up to him, I cannot refuse him. I never could have dreamed of such a thing at his age. The only thing I had to look forward to was the certainty of going off to war at eighteen."

Maria was dumbfounded. "How can you suggest it to him? We may never see him again!"

"Believe me, I am not going to suggest it. I have said nothing to the boy. I am just trying to anticipate the possibility."

"Wouldn't he need your consent?"

Miguel rubbed his hands together, but he spoke the truth that was in his heart. "I am not certain I could say no, even if I were asked."

Maria dared not say anything, but the look in her eyes spoke loudly. "I've lost my mother, my sister, my home, and now I'm losing my son? What have you done to us?"

Miguel did not know that she was also thinking of her little girl who was no longer a little girl, but a woman with a wounded heart.

The time had come for Francisco to make himself known. Since he did not want to work for the crew, he had held back and pilfered what he could for survival. Now that they were nearing shore, he would have to barter for a clean exit, so he could make a living once he was off the ship. He realized he was in a jeopardized position. He could be jailed once they reached port.

Paulo was becoming anxious for him, as the time drew near. "When do you plan to talk to someone on board?"

"It's getting late. I could just sneak off the ship."

"I don't think that will be easy. You saw how they guarded the gangway in Valparaiso."

"I did, but don't you know that someone *was* able to sneak off the ship?"

Paulo's face filled with surprise. "What do you mean?"

"There were two people missing when they counted passengers. Only one went overboard."

"But how do you know that for sure?"

"Because I know who he was. He told me what he was going to do and how he was going to do it."

"Who?"

"Antonio."

"Antonio who?"

"Cabral. He wanted to leave his wife and start a new life. He went to shore with the crew hauling cargo and never came back."

"But why can't you take his place?"

"I thought of that, but it's too risky. I don't have his papers, and his wife can identify me."

"Maybe I can speak to Mr. Haye. Ask him what they do to stowaways. And I'll find out if you can make a deal with the Captain."

"I don't want to work with the crew. I want to get off at the islands and find work. But talk to him anyway. He may know something we haven't thought of. Just don't give me away."

The music and dancing on deck came to an abrupt halt, and Paulo never had the opportunity to speak to Wills. Within a week, one crew member and two immigrant children were struck with measles.

There was no easy way to quarantine the sick, but as soon as the ship's doctor discovered the outbreak, he ordered they reserve a corner on the other side of the hold. The Steward brought sheets to partition off the area and marked the sheets with a red X, but they could not bring in fresh air or humidity. Pallets were set up behind the area, as more children fell ill to the virus. The stolid air and unsanitary conditions of their quarters fed the contagion. Paulo was the third child to succumb.

He was oozing with red eyes, hacking, sneezing, and burning with angry redness. The doctor on board could only do so much. He examined Paulo's face, chest, and the insides of his mouth and found white blotches in his cheeks.

"There's no doubt, he has contracted the virus. Keep him quiet. Wrapped up but not too warm. Lots of water and rest."

He turned to Paulo and spoke softly, "Rest your eyes as much as you can. Keep them closed."

Paulo nodded and closed his eyes obediently.

Maria would not leave his bedside in quarantine.

Paulo's hacking cough became worse, and every night, those around him labored with him in their thoughts. No one could sleep for the worry of him. On the fifth night, he started vomiting severely, and his fever rose so high, he became delirious.

"Miguel, we must get him more water. He's losing all of his fluids," cried Maria.

Miguel returned with another bucket of water. "If we need more, just let me know. The Steward showed me where to find it."

Miguel found a neckerchief and filled it with water and pressed it to the boy's lips and face. It ripped at his heart to see Paulo so placid and helpless, his beautiful, kind boy, who had been so full of life. He felt his face and neck and sensed life ebbing away without admitting it. He peered into Maria's weary, sad face and shared her pain.

"Go, my darling. Try to get some rest. I will sit with the boy until daybreak. You must try to rest or you will lose your resistance to the virus, as well."

Maria retreated to their bunk and slipped into a fretful sleep. Miguel had felt his boy floating away from him, but he had never imagined it would happen this way. He tried to pray, but no words would come to his mind or to his lips. "Please. God... please." He pleaded.

When the bell struck two on the watch, Paulo's breathing grew slow and regular. At half past the hour, his eyes opened and locked with Miguel's.

He spoke slowly and haltingly. "I.. I saw the lights again, *Pai*. I saw them... in my dreams. It is time for me. Time for me.. to go home." He spoke in broken, rasping breaths.

"Do not try to speak. You must remain absolutely quiet. As quiet as you can. So you can grow stronger and better."

"No, *Pai*. I know I will not get stronger; with each breath, I know I am leaving, but I don't want to leave you and *Mãe*." He faltered on this last word.

Miguel was dumbstruck by his son's certainty. It was the truth he had not wanted to admit. Now, he must live with it, and even worse, he must live with the fact that he had brought them here and was responsible for whatever may come. And now this, a loss he could not even grasp, let alone accept. How much more would he have to sacrifice for this new life?

"No, Paulo. You must not give up hope. You are strong. Please do not lose hope."

"*Pai*, there is ... one, last thing. A favor. Will you promise me you will do what I ask?"

"Of course, Paulo. Anything that is within my power to do for you."

It was now a great effort for the boy to speak, but he was in earnest. He pulled himself up with and rested on his elbows. "There is a boy, on board. He is close to my age, and he is all alone. His family did not want him. He sleeps under the lifeboats."

It took Paulo a long time to say these few sentences, and Miguel put his hand on his shoulder to calm him. "You must not exhaust yourself. Lie down."

"No, *Pai*. This is important. Please... listen." He gulped and paused.

"Go on, my son."

"Find him. His name is Francisco. He can take my place. Please, don't tell the crew I am gone."

"But they know you so well. How can I hide the fact?"

"Tell them ... I must rest down here. Wait until the crew leaves the ship. Once they are gone, then you go last with Francisco as your son. Please, promise me."

Miguel hardly knew what he was saying, only that he had to honor his son's dying wish. He could see that it took all of his strength to speak.

"Yes, Paulo."

"Wrap my body in the night. Slip it ... overboard."

Miguel choked at the thought. "I... I can't."

Paulo strained with what little strength he had left in himself. "Please. You must. They would bury me at sea anyway." He choked. "So, why shouldn't you be the one?"

Miguel could not utter a word. Tears scorching. Pain shooting through him. Blinding, mind-numbing pain, a portent of what was to come.

He took Paulo's hand, as he contemplated the aching, empty years ahead without him. Trying with all his might. Bobbing his head up and down to reassure him. Paulo squeezed his hand, smiling his slice-of-watermelon grin faintly, and then catapulted with a free-fall into the next life.

The bell struck four. Miguel reverently wrapped his son's body. He was not thinking about what he would tell Maria. How he would explain to her why she would not be able to say goodbye to her son.

His mind fractured into panes of grief like a sharp-edged stained glass window. Each shard pressing on one another in a pain-filled amalgam of pieces that will not quite fit together.

He wrapped Paulo's body securely and then held him in his arms with head pressed to his chest and eyes downcast. Slowly climbing upwards.

Jaggedly breathing. Soft footsteps under cover of darkness. Whispered prayers. Blessings and benedictions. Tenderly hoisting him, pressing him to his liquid cheeks one last time. Holding him for another hour while he grappled within himself for the courage to release him.

Gulping, he spoke his final words to his son, "Paulo, go with God."

And then to himself, "Holy Spirit, show me the way forward."

He gently let him slip down slowly, down into liquid darkness.

When all was done, Miguel made his way to the lifeboats, as if in a trance determined to fulfill his son's dying wish. He screwed up his courage and called out in a whisper, "Francisco! Francisco!"

Miguel waited and then he heard scrambling. A head popped out with hair streaming wildly in all directions.

"Who is it?"

"Are you Francisco?"

"Yes. Who told you where to find me?"

"Paulo. He is gone. You are now my son. Come with me."

Miguel reached out his hand and felt the uncertain clasp of a smaller one. They marched downward as if in solemn procession. Miguel pointed to an empty bunk. "He wanted you to take his place." And then, Miguel collapsed into determined forgetfulness.

CHAPTER 25

1908, San Jose, Cannery Days

It was June, a month when Valley people stay close to home or close to a cannery. Heads are down to ferret out blemishes or to avoid smashing pulpy fruit. Faces are sun-scorched and oily with exertion. A month when dogs and cows lay low to the ground scatting flies or shambling away from them. When mosquitos and raccoons are equally industrious and when housewives pour multi-colored produce into scalding hot bottles.

Anarosa was pleased that Julia was working with Abbie to pay some of her own expenses, but it was not enough, as far as she was concerned. Since Julia's eighteenth birthday, Anarosa's goal was to marry her off. Most girls her age were married or on the verge of marriage, but Julia showed no interest in marriage or men, something that her mother found difficult to understand.

Anarosa thought it did not help that the only time Julia wore a dress and fixed up her hair was at church or when she went to see Abbie McCallum. The rest of the time, Julia braided up her hair and slouched around in an old pair of overalls. She spent more time riding and roping with the boys or galloping off into the foothills on Coal with Marcos.

"How is that girl ever going to get a husband?" Anarosa clenched her hands, as she glanced up from the front porch, where she and Luana had been knitting after supper. Pretty Boy sat on Anarosa's shoulder, while Julia raced around the paddock roping a calf with her brothers. Their air of amusement ricocheted off the porch swing where the two women were sitting. Julia loved a dare, especially one that allowed her to prove her brothers wrong about anything she could or could not do.

Luana stood still, startled to realize that marriage was such a concern to Anarosa. The last thing Luana wanted was to see Julia married, at least not yet. It was too soon for Luana to contemplate, and she knew Julia well enough to know that she was not ready to marry and would never be forced into it. Anarosa just did not understand her own daughter.

Since the incident with Roger McCallum, Luana was all too aware that Julia was capable of attracting the opposite sex. Anyone with eyes could see that Julia possessed a rare kind of transcendent beauty. Julia also maintained an air of indifference towards anyone who might take an interest in her. Luana understood that these traits were an alluring combination, and she kept a watchful eye out for her.

"Why rush it?" This was all Luana could think of in reply to Anarosa's concerns. To Luana's way of thinking, the longer a woman remained single, the better. "Let her be carefree for awhile." Early marriage just meant more children, a harder life, and fewer choices.

"She's of no use to me at all." Anarosa muttered as she returned to her knitting. "And she won't do anything I ask her to do." She sighed as she settled back onto the swing and resumed her purling. Luana wanted to say "She's your daughter. She's not your work horse. Just let her be." But the words stuck in her throat. Luana still had to tread carefully around Anarosa to avoid threatening her sense of authority.

"Why don't you let her help me out at the bakery? I'll pay her a small amount. That should supplement what she's earning from Abbie McCallum."

"I was thinking the canneries."

"The canneries?"

"Yes. Why not? It's hard work but it's good money. It's also a good life lesson. It may even make her realize how hard she'll have to work without a man."

Luana searched Anarosa's expression, trying to gauge her level of determination. There was a look of self-satisfaction. When the canneries began recruiting for new workers, Anarosa decided to ship both Julia and Rose off. She made sure to discuss it with Frank first to ensure that he would be her ally. One night at dinner she asked Frank to raise the subject.

"Girls, your mother and I have arranged for you to work at the McCallum canneries this season."

Both of them bounced their heads up from their plates and darted a quizzical look at each another from across the dinner table. The objections caught in their throats. The boys were just as surprised. There seemed to be plenty of work on the farm. Why go looking for it, they wondered.

"What about our work here?" Rose was the first to respond. Julia still cared for the horses and Rose did the canning and sewing with Anarosa. Rose had also been learning to ride with Julia and was just starting to enjoy it.

"Also, what about my visits to Mrs. McCallum?" Julia put in her two cents. Julia was now at a point where she looked forward to her visits with Abbie. She felt that Abbie returned the sentiment and did not want to disappoint her. Anarosa had anticipated every possible objection. "There's no reason you can't do it all. You'll take the early morning shift at the cannery and have the afternoons free."

"I'm supposed to be at Mrs. McCallum's house at ten o'clock in the morning."

"I'm sure we can arrange a time for you to visit her in the afternoon. I'll just ring up Gertie Cantell and make sure the arrangements are to her satisfaction." There seemed to be no way around it; they would be sorting and slicing this year. The girls were not quite sure how to feel about that, but they had no further objections to raise, so they knew the subject was closed for now.

Stefan planned to drive the girls to and from the cannery. On the first morning, he hitched a wagon and waited outside, while Anarosa fussed over their dress. She had made them a set of cotton shirts and gathered skirts with aprons and bandanas to wrap their hair. Surveying herself in a mirror, Rose was ready to pitch a fit. "I look like a laundry maid."

"It doesn't matter what you look like. The cannery has their rules about how you should dress. Your hair has to be tied back so it doesn't get in the food. And you should be wearing comfortable shoes, since you will be on your feet all day."

"I hope no one recognizes me." Rose whined. "I'll never live it down." She was feeling more than a little uncomfortable in her new get-up, while Julia took it in stride, looking at it as an adventure. Besides, she liked the idea of earning more money. Like Luana, she would save every penny. Maybe someday she could help Luana with her dairy.

In truth, Julia did not think too much about the future, but she had become aware of her mother's push towards marriage, and all she could think about was finding alternatives that would keep her mother at bay. She tied up her long locks and wrapped the bandana tightly around her head with barely a thought of how she looked, and then she bounced outside and vaulted up into the wagon beside Stefan.

One glance at Stefan's face told her all she needed to know about what he thought of her dress. She projected a warning look at him. "Don't you say a word. Not a word." Stefan only smiled and grabbed the reins with a laugh, as Rose jumped up behind them. Rose sank down into the back seat, as they jounced off the farm and onto the Alameda.

When they arrived, there were crowds and long lines of new workers waiting to sign up for work. People were lined up outside five or six large sheds where the cutting and paring and canning work were done. Each shed was assigned a supervisor who was ready to train the new workers.

"What time shall I pick you up?" Stefan tossed out, as they climbed down to look for the right line.

"One o'clock sharp. Don't be late, alright?" Rose was anxious to get the first day over with and get home. She felt entirely uncomfortable with the whole venture. Stefan grimaced and tipped his hat. He knew it was torture for her, and he did not want to make it any worse, but he could not help but smile at their strange outfits.

Julia linked arms with Rose. "Let's be sure to stick together. I don't want to get separated today." Rose agreed, knowing that she was going to need all the moral support she could get. The lines were snaking around the building, so it was hard to know which one to join. Finally, Julia spotted a familiar face. It was Cathy Jacques, the woman who lived down the street from Abbie McCallum.

"Mrs. Jacques, do you remember me?" Cathy looked up and recognized her. "Oh yes, you were the young woman looking for Abbie McCallum, right?"

"Yes, I'm the one."

"Did you ever find her?" Cathy was more than a little curious about the incident, since the old woman was so reclusive.

"Yes, actually. I did. I work for her now."

"You work for her? What does she have you doing?" Cathy was intrigued.

Julia avoided getting into details. "Oh, I just help her out with errands and odd jobs here and there." Then Julia quickly changed the subject. "Can you tell me if this is the right line for beginners? This is my sister Rose. We've just arrived and we've never done any cannery work before. How do we know where to sign up?"

"Well, if you want to cut peaches and cots, this is the line, which is a likely job for a beginner. I'll save a spot for you if you'd like to get some coffee first." Cathy nodded in the direction of a coffee table where coffee and water were provided. Julia and Rose made their way to the coffee line and waited their turn. There was no cream or sugar, and the girls had never tasted coffee without it. Having skipped breakfast, they grabbed the coffee anyway and made their way back to Cathy who was holding a spot for them.

Rose took a sip of the scalding hot coffee. It smelled comforting on a cool morning. One taste and the look on her face spoke volumes. "Bleck! I don't know if I can get used to this."

Cathy laughed. "Have you never tasted coffee before?"

"Well, yes. But I'm used to Arbuckles with cream and maple syrup."

"Cream and maple syrup? Who drinks coffee that way? You've just got to get used to the taste of coffee for its own sake." She reached into her pockets and took out a small bag of beans. "Here, I carry these around. Chew on a coffee bean."

Rose and Julia shrank back with a disdainful look. "What? Chew on a coffee bean?" Their faces filled with doubt.

"No, really. Try it. You'd be surprised. It's just something you acquire a taste for — like anything else. Once you've gotten used to real coffee, you won't want it with all that sweet stuff any more. Put out your hand." She shoved her hand towards them and waited. "Just try it." Julia and Rose hesitated but then they each took one bean. Cathy waited. They raised their eyebrows at one other and then gingerly placed the beans in their mouths.

"Now bite down on it. You've got to get the flavor out." They both obeyed and flinched, their faces a study while they slowly masticated it. "It'll take awhile, but you'll get used to it." Cathy insisted.

Rose grimaced. "I don't think I want to get used to it."

"I challenge you. One bean every morning for a week, and you'll be drinking coffee black. Like everyone else. That's what grown-ups do." She looked around and sure enough, everyone had a cup of black coffee.

"Now that you mention it, that's how our Dad and brothers drink it." Julia sighed. "I guess we need some lessons."

"Yes, but Luana is not going to like it. She's sold on flavored coffees." Rose replied and Julia just shrugged. Then Julia remembered that Cathy was married with children. "Who's taking care of the little ones while you're working?"

"Oh, my mother-in-law. It's just until the end of August. You'll find that there are a lot of women here who work outside their homes during the canning season. The grandmothers take on the kids or the husbands who do shift work." Cathy introduced them both to her sister-in-law, Mary Aiello, and her sister, Terry Zuniga, who were both standing in line in front of them.

"Welcome! Is it your first time?" Terry asked. Both girls nodded.

"You'll want to pack a lunch or snack. You'll find you develop a ferocious appetite after standing over fruit for several hours." Terry thought she'd offer them the best advice she could, noticing that they both had come empty-handed. "Have you had breakfast?"

Julia and Rose shrugged. They hadn't even thought about it.

"Here, take my lunch and split it."

"No, we couldn't do that. You'll need it." Julia gently pushed it back to her.

"You won't last long without some food today. And the first day is critical. If they see you slouching or resting for even a second, out you go. And they spy on you constantly from an overhead platform."

"Yes," Cathy added. "We call it the "crow's nest" because the supervisors look down on us like a murder of old crows."

Terry handed her lunch back to Julia with a wink. "Don't worry about it. I can share my sister's lunch." Before they knew it, they were at the front of the line. After answering a few questions, they filled out some paperwork and followed a supervisor into a large staging area lined with tables covered with work stations.

Each station contained a chair, a box, and pruning knives. A rather large-boned woman by the name of Betty Newfarmer gathered ten new employees at a time to provide them with their instructions. All the women in Julia and Rose's group stood around while she boomed out instructions.

"My name is Mrs. Newfarmer. I will be your supervisor every day except on Friday. After I'm done demonstrating, every one will find a station. This group is in charge of pitting and splitting cots. Once you've filled a cart with cots, there are runners who will bring you new boxes. Do not stop at any time, even when the runner is removing your box. If the runner does not come back in due time, you can carry the box of cots to the next station and retrieve another empty box yourself, but whatever you do, do not remain idle.

Cathy leaned over and whispered to Rose and Julia, "Don't let them see you idle for one minute. One false move and you're out." Her eyes darted upward, and Julia and Rose followed her gaze to a second story walkway that cross-crossed the building above the work stations. There was no hiding anything under the overhead lights. "The faster you work, the better."

"First, you must always wear a head covering and gloves. Do not forget to bring them. If you forget, there are extras in the bin over to your right. Return them at the end of your shift. You will be allowed a thirty minute lunch break at ten o'clock and two ten minute breaks at eight o'clock and noon. Now are there any questions?" Everyone stood, as if at attention before a drill Sargent. No one spoke a word.

"Let me demonstrate to you how to slice and pit. Gather round." The crowd closed in and with one stroke, she split and pitted a cot. Rose blinked. She did it so quickly, Rose never saw the pit.

"Any questions?" No one moved or spoke. "Find a station and get started. When a buzzer sounds, that's your break time. Leave your gloves at the station and proceed to the picnic tables outside."

Julia picked up her utensil and did the best she could to imitate what she had just seen. Not surprisingly, it took her several strokes to dispatch the first pit. She grabbed another cot and sliced it. And then another. She glanced at the other women. She could see that some were more experienced than the others. Cathy was standing next to her and clearly understood what she was doing. Julia's box was only half filled when a runner snatched her box and then replaced it with another box. Julia tried picking up her pace and Rose did the same.

There was no time to glance up. How easy it would be to slice a finger if I tried, thought Rose. After an hour of slicing, Rose was tired and racked by the redundancy of motion. Every muscle was aching with the strain of holding her body in one position, especially her arms and her back. She took a moment to lean against the table, so she could reposition herself. After she had done this more than once, one of the supervisors stood next to her and spoke in a low voice between her and Julia, so that they could both hear. "If someone sees you do that from above, you won't be allowed back tomorrow." And then she just slipped away.

Rose and Julia worked faster. Finally, a bell rang, and they sighed and relaxed. While their group was strolling over to the picnic tables, Cathy asked them about the incident with the supervisor. "So what did the old battle axe whisper in your ears? I'm sure it wasn't anything pleasant."

Rose laughed, "I shifted my body once or twice and leaned too hard on the table, and she let me know I wouldn't last."

"Yeah, they do that to the newbies." Terry chimed in. "That's their way of putting the fear of God into you so you'll work harder."

"Yeah, those supervisors have to look as if they're actually doing something." Everyone laughed.

"Just keep both hands moving at all times. They don't want to see you doing anything halfway."

"I can't get used to it. You're so much faster than I am."

"Oh, you'll get faster. Believe me. Working eight hours at it gives you lots of practice."

Ten minutes flew by and a bell sounded again. They had to be back at their stations within five minutes. Lunch time was just long enough to gulp down their food. After that, Rose thought that the end of the day would never come. When it did, the last bell rang out, and she let out a groan. She could feel every muscle relax and then work their way into spasms. While Rose was rubbing the tension out of the back of her neck, she happened to glance up and saw something that immediately caught her attention. Cathy saw it as well, and they both glanced at each other and then back again.

Above them stood a very handsome and well-dressed gentleman in a light-weight brown sack suit, collared with a wide silk tie and a fedora hat. He was standing overhead and staring down at them. It took them aback. First, because no one else in the warehouse was dressed like him, and second, because most of their supervisors were women. Not only that, but the work was done, so why was he staring and at what? Cathy and Rose soon realized that he was not looking directly at either of them, but his focus was razor-sharp.

It was Julia. She had just pulled off her scarf and rolled her hair over her front shoulder. She removed her gloves and noticed that Rose and Cathy were staring at her. "What? Did I do something wrong?" She glanced down at her dress to see if she had stained or torn her clothing. "Whatever it is, I hope it's not a firing offense." Her good humor bounced around the now emptying cannery shed.

"Turn around slowly and look up." Rose spoke softly. Cathy and Rose were both dying to see what the man would do, if Julia noticed him.

Julia turned and looked up. There they were again, those startling green eyes just staring. It took her a moment to realize that she had seen them before. They seemed to beckon to her, and once again, she did not look away. What could this man want? There was something insistent in that stare, and then his expression changed. It softened and he smiled, as if he were privy to all of her deepest secrets.

He now noticed that others were looking back at him, and he seemed to come to himself. Then he turned away abruptly and walked back across the platform. As soon as Julia could gather herself together, she hastened away, and the other women chased her down.

"Do you know that man, Julia?" Rose was the first to ask, but everyone else was just as curious and kept up the pace.

"Not exactly." She marched outside, peering into the crowd, looking for Stefan on the wagon.

"Well, how exactly?"

"I've seen him once before. I think his name is Roger McCallum."

"Roger McCallum?" Terry gulped. "If that's who he is, then he owns this place and he pays our salaries. Have you actually met him?"

"No - not at all." Their female instincts were on high alert.

"You must know him. Why else would he stare at you like that?"

Julia skidded faster. It was bad enough that she had to encounter him again, but now she had to somehow explain something she did not understand to other people she hardly knew. She stopped short and clinched her fists at her side.

"I have absolutely no idea. Now, can we just forget about it?" She lanced them with a look of finality.

The others backed off, but Rose was not so easily put off. All of them were hanging onto Julia's every word. It seemed to them that Julia knew more than she would admit. "I think you just may have an admirer, Julia." Rose challenged her.

Julia snorted. "What? I don't even know that man." The thought of it made her indignant.

"Yeah, but I bet he knows you." Rose grabbed Julia by the arm and stared her down. "Don't you realize that if that is Roger McCallum, then he may just remember the time you whipped his sister in that riding contest. Did you ever think about that?"

Julia jerked her hand away. "Yeah, well, maybe he's got it in for me because I insulted his sister. But if that's the case, then he sure knows how to hold a grudge, because that was almost four years ago. It's a wonder he would recognize me."

Being a little older and wiser, Cathy could not help making another observation. "Yes, but you forget that he smiled at you. That's not the behavior of someone who's holding a grudge."

"Way to get into the good graces of the boss on the first day." Terry quipped.

Now, all Julia could do was laugh. "To think that I spent all day trying to stand up straight, just so I could keep my job, and now I'm going to lose it anyway, just because I insulted the boss's sister four years ago!" That ended the conversation, much to Julia's relief. It was time to head in opposite directions, so they said their goodbyes and dispersed into the crowd.

"Don't forget your lunch tomorrow!" Terry flung back at them, as she and Cathy faded into the crowd.

Julia and Rose jostled through the crowd looking for the Mirante carriage. They were surprised to see Marcos instead of Stefan sitting up straight in the driver's seat, but he did not seem to be at all aware of them. He was looking past them, even though they knew he must be there for them. He was staring intently at someone else. Rose and Julia turned to see who it was. "It's that man again," Rose remarked. "Why is he looking at Marcos?"

Julia grabbed Rose's hand and yanked her towards the carriage. "I don't know. Let's just get in and get away." She was in no mood to look back again at Roger McCallum. She had had enough of his stares.

"Marcos! We're here. Ready to go." Rose broke into Marcos's stare. He started, realizing they were both in the wagon beside him. "Let's go then!" He pulled the reins and circled in the opposite direction, away from Roger McCallum. Rose yanked around with a backward glance. She was amazed to see that Roger had not moved or turned away. He was standing there with hat in hand and his hair waving in the breeze over a slightly crooked smile.

Neither Julia nor Marcos spoke a word all the way home.

CHAPTER 26

1878, The Pacific, Grieving

They were just two days away, clipping across the Pacific's emerald seas, drawing close to journey's end. The immigrants would soon catch sight of their new home for the first time. After losing two young children, the Captain decided to gather everyone together to announce the estimated time of their arrival and a surprise celebration. Kit struck the bell to signal an assembly on deck after breakfast. Everyone converged under the Captain's shadow.

"Ladies and gentlemen, I have gathered you to announce that we are within forty-eight hours of landing. Upon arrival, we will be escorted into the Honolulu Harbor on the island of Oahu, which is the main entry port to the Sandwich Islands. However, there will be a two-week quarantine period, due to the recent outbreak of measles."

João Amarel repeated the words for the sake of those who had not yet learned English, and a low murmur burbled through the crowd. The Captain raised his hand to quiet them.

"Now, I know you are anxious to disembark and get to your new homes; however, the quarantine is for the protection of the natives. We must ensure that we are not spreading disease or sickness." He paused to consider what their concerns might be and how he might allay them.

"We are much aggrieved at the loss of two children; yet there is still reason to celebrate. We are grateful to our Almighty God that most of you are arriving safely. You have faced a difficult journey and overcome many obstacles with great courage. You have reason to be optimistic and much to look forward to, as you begin a new life." The Captain managed to stitch together a faint smile across the corners of his mouth, as he ranged a glance across the crowd. It was the first smile they had seen on his face since they had rounded the Horn.

"Tonight, we will hold a special celebration of thanksgiving. Our cook will serve up roasted pork with apples and potatoes, and there will be two glasses of grog for every adult. Those of you who wish to make your own contributions to our feast on board are welcome to do so. And we invite you to bring your musical instruments for dancing as late into the evening as you so desire." The crowd responded with cheerful, if not somewhat weak, applause.

One woman in the crowd turned to the translator. "Can we make sweet bread and roasted chicken? Some of us have been raising chickens on board since our time in Valparaiso." João repeated the question to the Captain in English.

The Captain answered affirmatively. "Yes, there will be one oven available to you throughout the afternoon, and we welcome your contributions. See the cook, who will help you gather whatever you need." The women murmured among themselves and began making plans to share supplies and swap recipes.

Anticipation was now high, even among the most weary. But for the Mirantes, there was nothing but silence and grief. A dark cloud had descended upon them and quickly overshadowed every bright thought that might otherwise light their way. They could not see their way through the darkness.

Even Ida was quiet, watchful, and pensive. Her mother and father were not speaking to one another. This was an experience so incongruous to what she had always known that it threatened her sense of security. It was something the girls had always taken for granted, given the light of their father's enduring optimism.

"It will not seem like a celebration without mother," Estela sighed, as they stood over the taffrail on the starboard side of the ship and watched the white caps break. She was getting used to coming onboard and enjoying it more often. The loss of Paulo, coupled with the rift between her parents, had become a distraction that helped drown out her own pressing sorrows. Caring for others would become her strength.

"But why can't she make an exception, just this once?" Ana wondered out loud.

"You heard what the doctor said. If she delivers now, the baby may not survive. She needs to lie absolutely still for at least three more weeks, until it is safe for her to deliver."

"How will she ever do it all? Her grief is such a heavy burden!"

"Yes, she's going to need our help once the baby is here. She is not strong." Estela realized how much her mother was suffering, now that she herself had experienced deep anguish.

"I just hope she speaks to *Pai* again," sniffed Ana. As the youngest girl, she had taken the rift between her parents particularly hard. She could not understand how it was possible, and she was shaken by it. Estela put her arm around her.

"Some things just take time. They love each other too much to stop loving now."

Ana spoke up out of a deep sense of her frustration. A thought that had been haunting her finally broke the surface of her heart. "But can you imagine *Pai* throwing Paulo's body overboard? How could he do such a thing?"

"Remember, he explained it all to us. It was Paulo's wish. Think about it. Could any of us deny him his dying wish?"

Ida chimed in with indignation. "But for what? So that laggard of a boy could take his place? I will never accept him as my brother. Never!"

"Paulo must have seen something in him. After all, we know they became friends, and we know that he helped Paulo find the stolen goods that Slick stashed away. Paulo must have had good reason to help him. We must try to accept him."

Ana peered deeper into the sea where her brother's body lay. "Now we are forced to play a false part. We become part of a lie to protect someone we hardly know and we're expected to treat him as a brother? And for how long, I would like to know?"

Estela put her hands on Ana's shoulders and turned her around to face her. "Ana, how can you be so heartless? The boy has been abandoned by his family. Paulo cared for him. Doesn't that make you want to try for Paulo's sake?"

Ana cast her gaze across the sea, as if seeking for that one spot where she could retrieve her brother. Then she let out a long sigh, as she realized she could never bring him back, no matter how hard she dreamed it or wished for it. "For Paulo's sake, I will try, but he will never be a true brother to me."

"That's all you can do, Ana. Just try. Everyday, just try."

"But why?"

"Why what?"

"Why someone like Paulo? Someone so full of life and love. Why did he have to die so young?"

Estela wrapped an arm around her. "These are questions that cannot be answered. No matter how many times we ask, the answer will not come back to us. Some say that only the good die young. It makes me think of him in another place, a much better place and that we will see him again."

Ana's face filled with sadness. "But it seems such a long, long time to wait."

"Never give up; never lose hope. It's what keeps us alive. Focus on the living but never forget those who have left us."

Ida chimed in with another thought. "And how are we to dance and celebrate tonight, as if Paulo never existed?"

"Because that's what he would want us to do, and that's what he would do. Just because we go on with life does not mean that we do not carry him with us."

"All I know is that I don't feel like dancing, at all."

"Then dance! Dance as if he were right there dancing with you. Pretend if you have to. Besides, *Pai* says that all we have to do is make a showing. It doesn't have to be all night. We just go to the dinner and dance one *chama-rita* and then we can leave." Estela began coaching the girls, a part she would play many times as they learned to adjust to life without Paulo.

"I know!" Ida cried out. "Let's all do one dance together to remember Paulo. He will be the invisible secret of our *chama-rita* circle tonight. We don't have to tell anyone why we're dancing together, but we will all be in on the secret." Ana's eyes brimmed with tears, as they all embraced. They saw their plan as a sacred tribute.

Ida had another concern. "You realize we may have to remain in quarantine longer than others because of *Mãe's* pregnancy, don't you? Some of our friends will go ahead of us to different islands, and we may never see them again."

"That would be the case, even if we were not delayed." Estela was quick to take their mother's part. She wanted whatever would ease her mother's burden. "Think what fun it will be to have babies around again! It has been such a long time." She had not lost her father's optimism completely.

As she was speaking, Sabina Terra joined them, along with the twins, Sonia and Sophia. "Hey you guys, my mother is gathering food to get ready for the banquet. We need more yeast and sugar. Why don't you see what you can dig up?"

Estela was glad for the interruption. "Perhaps we can do something to make it more festive, maybe decorations?" Everyone agreed it would be a challenge, but it was at least something else to divert their thoughts from Paulo. The Terras were the only ones who knew the truth about Francisco and were sworn to secrecy.

Sensing something wrong, Sabina smiled and said, "It will do us all a lot of good to dance again. But first, let's get to work."

When evening came, the sun's rays poured over and around the bark like liquid gold, as it slipped through a light fog and traced a yellow-shimmered reflection in its wake. When day turned to night, the sky dressed itself in a coat of starlight. The waters below lapped rhythmically against them as they were escorted by the light winds.

Every lantern on the ship was lit for their feast, many hanging brightly above and around the quarterdeck, the forecastle, and the promenade. The Captain arranged for several tables to be brought up from the lower decks. Joshua Roper arranged room for dancing all around the upper deck and quarter galley.

Glossy loaves of sweet bread in various shapes and sizes lined the tables. Rings, braids, loaves, crosses, and balls. Platters of arroz com feijao, linguica, jars of Portuguese pickles, sweet peppers and pearl onions. One woman made a bulo de mel, a seasoned honey cake. Normally, it would be topped with sliced almonds, but an extra layer of honey dressing would make do.

The ship's cook also did his best to contribute to their feast. He added his specialties of Jam Roly-Poly, Treacle-Dowdy, and Sea Pie. Numerous passengers brought Madeira wine to supplement the grog, which to most Portuguese, was considered barely tolerable. On this special occasion, Kit was sent below to retrieve the wine from the deepest storage holds.

"How can they stand this stuff? It tastes like goat piss!" Jordao spat out the grog the first time he had tried it and now stood on deck next to Octavio sipping it gratefully. The two men knew better than to turn it down. They had been drinking it for months, and by now they were somewhat accustomed to it.

Octavio leaned against the brig and whispered into Jordao's ear, "This is my last glass for now. This time we will drink the good stuff first and save the 'piss' for last. Once our fine Madeira wine is gone, we won't know the difference, anyway, eh brother?" He slapped Jordao hard on the back.

Jordao smiled back at Octavio, knowing he would always make the best of any bad situation. Then he glanced around the gangway, wondering when or if the Mirante sisters would make an appearance. These days he rarely spotted Estela on deck. She was so moody; he never knew what to expect from her. He began to wonder if she would make a good wife after all.

Octavio interrupted his thoughts, "Oh, to be in the grape fields, once again, eh Jordao? I remember those long September days. We would carry our grapes in large baskets and follow the sun to the vats."

"Yes, how I remember. "Then our fun would begin. We'd wash our feet and dance upon the grapes, until they were crushed and we were exhausted. We laughed at our knee-high grape stockings."

Octavio could not help but remember. He sighed as he placed a hand on one hip and mulled over his faraway thoughts. "It was the best part of the year. Now there will be no crushed grapes to bring to the wine press. Only endless sugar cane fields."

"Well, at least we know about chopping cane."

"Yes, we sure do. But the wine has always been the best incentive for chopping the cane. Now it will be for someone else and not for us."

"Do you really think that will make a difference?"

"All I know is that I will do what I have to and save every penny to buy my own farm. I know I can't work as someone else's hired hand forever."

Jordao agreed. "Yes, we will have our own, no matter the cost."

Octavio raised his glass. "No matter the cost."

The meal they shared that night was unlike any they had consumed since leaving Funchal. They broke sweet bread under tremulous stars. They enjoyed roast pork and chicken. There was not a hard tack or bowl of gruel in sight. They even lapped up a savory Portuguese fish stew, soaking it in crusty bread. The Captain and his crew toasted and celebrated right along with them.

A train of men, women, and youngsters appeared suddenly in traditional Portuguese garb streaming the galley ways and promenades. Colored in sashes, striped shirts, gathered skirts, and colorful vests, they set their celebrations ablaze under a canopy of shining moonbroch. Every musician had been called into service.

It was as if a fresh new wind had blown into the sails of their hearts. Lanterns were lit all around, casting shadows off the fascinating movements of their branguinhas, rajaos, and violas. A few of the men knuckled down on their accordions. They strummed and sang, as flickering light bounced off of their faces deep into the night.

When the first dance began, the Mirante girls were ready. They too had donned their traditional garb of striped gathered skirts under aprons and deep red waistcoats over white blouses as they came together in a tight *chama-rita* circle. When others tried to join them, they waved them away. "Let us do this first dance together," they pleaded politely.

On the first note, they clasped hands and formed a circle. Imagining Paulo dancing in the center of their circle, they felt his smile. Step-by-step, their hearts were soothed by the thought of his presence.

The old Chama-rita dance
Does have little to learn more
Than, lift a foot in the air,
Stamp the other on the floor!
I want to sing and dance
Stamp my foot on the ground
Dance with the prettiest gal
In a Chama-rita Round

Miguel watched them from above. Estela had told him how they were going to dance the first dance for Paulo. She begged him to join their dance, but he could not find it within himself, so he promised that he would look on. As he waited for that first dance, he thought about Maria lying down below, alone and haunted. She did not want him in her presence. Never had he felt so alone. He remembered the night he had let his boy slip through his arms. He felt tears choking up inside. "Bringing them on this journey was a mistake. It was all my fault." His thoughts preyed on him.

When the dance began, and he saw the radiance in his daughters' eyes, their beauty calmed him, which shown out of their love for Paulo. A surge of hope charged up against his sense of devastation and loss. He came to himself, when he realized that he still had much to live for. "Surely, Maria will forgive me," he thought as the tears threatened to break.

Maria lay below. She had insisted that everyone leave her alone, desperate for solitude. She could hear the strains of the braguinhas on the wind, causing her to lie as still as a slabbed headstone. It calmed her, while everything else in her felt numb. The baby did not move. There was no longer any room to move, and it felt as if there was no longer room in her heart to move. She tried to stop thinking, but over and over in her mind, she kept replaying the scene where Miguel let his son slip into the frigid waters.

Maria thought about how she had woke up startled on the morning Paulo left them. She was breathing heavily and perspiring profusely. She had been dreaming. Dreaming of Funchal. In the dream, she was standing on the warm sands along the harbor, and she could hear the crashing waves and the beaver-like fishermen preparing for their day. Her heart was relieved; she was home again. She turned towards the shore, and she could see her mother Rose in the distance smiling, waving, and reaching out to her. Maria held out her arms, but as she began to move in her mother's direction, a flock of seagulls swarmed around her, clouding her view. She tried to run, but her feet felt as though they were caught in quicksand. The birds swirled and screeched, threshing wildly. She fell down sobbing upon the sand.

In the midst of the dream Maria felt waves slapping against each side of the hull, along with the familiar jouncing of the bark. Reality had raked through the foggy dream to awaken her, but the thought of home kept pulling her back into her dreams. Back and forth. Until Paulo flashed across her mind, and worrying thoughts flooded in like robbers who had broken down the door. The thought startled her awake, and then she recoiled from that reality by swaddling herself in her blankets.

She remembered now, as she lay listening to the strumming braguinhas from the celebration above, how on the morning Paulo left them, she had turned slowly in the gray dawn light and felt the steady breathing of her husband. She could not fathom why Miguel was not with Paulo. He had promised to take her place and to take care of the boy. She turned and shook Miguel hard, but she could not awaken him. He was breathing heavily and laboriously, and she knew he needed rest, so she did not persist.

Thinking of Paulo, Maria had groped for a cloth to wipe her face and then dressed herself. She gathered some leftover food, bundling it into a satchel, and then retrieved a pail of water and a lantern. Making her way to the quarantine area, she was careful to avoid bumping anyone or stepping on belongings. She approached the cordoned area and slowly drew back the curtain that had surrounded Paulo. Maria panted as she realized he was not there, and her heart startled and sank. It was as if she knew the truth, but she did not want to know.

She panicked and scrammed back to Miguel for an explanation, paying no mind to the other passengers now. Bumping and jostling her way back, she rustled everyone she passed. When she reached Miguel, she shook him hard and felt, but did not hear, a wail well up from deep inside of her. Everyone around them awoke, including Francisco, who was lying in the bunk above them.

"Where is my boy? What have you done with him?"

Miguel tried to shake off the heavy sleep, but something inside of him resisted. He was thick with grogginess.

Maria's thoughts shifted. Why did Miguel leave Paulo? He had promised to take care of him. It was out of character for her to jump to conclusions, but she was in a panic, so the accusations came thick and furious. "Have you been drinking? Did you neglect our son? What did you do to him?" She pounded her fists on him until he was fully conscious. Miguel grabbed his bed clothes and bounced upward, wrapping his blankets around her, as if to protect her. He had to find a way to calm her, so he held her closely and firmly.

"Hush!" Miguel did everything he could to quiet her, but her cries rang around the barrel of the ship like a clapper in a bell tower. Everyone within hearing distance would know their business, and Miguel was ever mindful of his promise to Paulo. In the moment, keeping that promise outweighed every other concern he felt. It was the least he could do for his boy.

"Darling, listen to me. Come with me to the upper deck, and I will explain. We must speak privately." His voice turned solemn, and she followed him numbly. The deck was clear, except for a few men on the watch, who were high above them. He steered her to the back of the ship under the mizzen mast. He placed both hands on her shoulders and told her what she dreaded to hear, tears pulsing down his cheeks.

"Paulo is gone, my love. Our son died in the night. I was with him."

First, she let out a wail, and then she thrashed and paced. "Let me see him. My boy." She wrapped her arms across her now very extended stomach. She was just four weeks away from delivery, and Miguel worried for her health. She gasped out her next words. "I must see him one last time." Her eyes blinkered wildly and then landed on Miguel. "Where is he?"

He stopped her and caught her restless gaze. "You cannot see him again. It was his wish."

"What? His wish not to see his mother?" Her hands covered her face in deep distress. She howled, "Where is he? I must go to him." And then she started to run, but Miguel held her back, trying to brace her.

He quickly realized his mistake and shook his head furiously. The right words were eluding him.

"No — no, that's... not, what I meant." He gasped out.

"My son? I cannot see him? Hold him and lay him to rest?"

The reality of what he had done to Maria sank deeply into Miguel. His thoughts had only been for Paulo and for what the boy had wanted as he lay dying. What had he done? All of his well-prepared explanations now came back upon him like sad tunes of long ago, unfit to meet the desperate needs of the moment.

She bolted, and in his helplessness, he let her go. He could not find the words to tell her that their son was at the bottom of the sea in a place they could never go, fathoms away.

CHAPTER 27

1908, Santa Clara, Biscoitos

When Julia and Rose stepped down from the wagon after their first day at the cannery, they spotted Luana on the porch waiting to hear how it went. Aching and exhausted, Julia was not in the mood to talk. "Sorry Luana, I'll let Rose tell you all about it. I have to get ready for my next job." Julia was beginning to think she had taken on way too much work as she swept passed them to change her clothes.

Rose, on the other hand, could not make it past the front door without slumping onto the porch swing next to Luana. "Well?" Luana examined her, as she pulled off her bandana, "How'd it go?"

Rose groaned in response, massaged the back of her neck, and threw off her shoes to soothe her aching feet. "I wish I could tell you something exciting, but truthfully, it was the most monotonous day of my life. I'd much rather be baking at the *Serradura*. I mean, you stand for hours and just do the same thing over and over again. It's so tiresome. And I'm lucky I didn't slice my little pinky into the cot box! I almost fell into a stupor from boredom. When I finally got a break, I could hardly move. It's as if my muscles were seizing up the minute I tried shifting from one position to the next."

Luana put down her sewing with a sympathetic expression. "That sounds dreadful."

"You bet it is." Rose glanced down at Luana's embroidery and picked it up. "Well, this is looking sparky." Luana plucked her work back and prodded Rose for gossip. "Did you see anybody we know?"

"Not really. Julia knew someone who helped us figure out where to go. Her name was Cathy, and she told us to stop putting maple syrup in our coffee and to start eating coffee beans so we can learn to drink our coffee black."

"Well, that sounds even more dreadful." Luana rolled her eyes in disgust as she stabbed at her embroidery. "It doesn't sound like anything interesting happened at all."

Rose sighed. "Not really." And then she thought about it for a moment. "Well, there was this man staring at Julia."

Luana stopped and leaned in. "A man? Julia? Do tell."

Sensing Luana's interest, Rose sat up straight and groped her mind for embellishments. "Well, at the end of our shift, Cathy and I looked up. And there he was above us on the crow's nest. That's where the supervisors stand spying on everyone. The platforms are all over the building."

"What did he look like? Was he handsome?" Luana's curiosity was at such a peak, she almost stabbed herself through the embroidery hoop.

"Now that you mention it, he was. Very. And impeccably dressed, just like a real gentleman. Tall with light brown wavy hair. Cathy and I were surprised to see him there. We thought we had done something wrong because he was staring. Then we realized he wasn't staring at us at all — he was staring at Julia. But it turns out, he owns the place! Can you imagine that?"

Luana grew agitated. "Did he talk to Julia?"

"No, that's the odd thing about it. Julia says she's never even met him. He didn't even try to talk to her, but when he realized we were looking at him, he turned and practically ran in the other direction."

"How do you know he owns the place? Do you know his name?"

"Yeah — I mean after all, it's the same as the name on the building, McCallum. His name is Roger McCallum. It was Cathy who told us and she ought to know. She's worked there every summer for the past five years."

"Are you sure Julia's never met him before?"

"Well, she says she knows who he is because of that woman she works for. You know the one, Abbie McCallum."

Luana did not say anything more to Rose, but she was alarmed. Now Julia would be around Roger McCallum on a regular basis, and she, Julia's *Madrinha,* had no way of knowing what was going on.

Rose broke into Luana's thoughts. "And another funny thing happened, now that I think of it. When we came outside, Marcos and that man were staring at each other from across the front of the warehouse in front of a crowd. It was as if they knew each other and clearly did not like each other."

"How could you tell they did not like each other?"

"I don't know. Marcos just had the strangest look on his face. He seemed mad." Rose thought a moment. "Or maybe just concerned."

"Concerned about what?"

Rose shrugged. "I can only guess."

This was news to Luana, but she simply responded by saying, "Well, Marcos did work for Jackson McCallum, and I don't think things ended well for him there."

Rose sat up straight when she heard this. "Now, that's a mystery worth looking into. How do you suppose we can find out what that's all about? Maybe ask Marcos?"

"No, I don't think we should bring it up to him. Not if the two men have it in for one another." Luana and Rose looked at each other with the same thought at the same exact moment. Luana made the first move. "Well, just maybe I'll see what I can find out from Gilberto. You know, Marcos's cousin."

"And I'll find out what I can from Cathy. She seems to know everything about everybody." Rose smiled and added, "Between the two of us, we'll figure it out."

Now that Julia was working at the cannery, she had to rush to get ready to make it on time. On this day, she wanted to stop at the *Serradura* to pick up a surprise for Abbie. She saddled Luana's mare and down to the *Serradura* with her dress and bonnet flapping behind her. Luana and Rose watched her from the porch as she took off.

"There she goes again. Off to see that old woman in that spooky old house." Rose remarked. "Honestly, I don't know why she seems to enjoy it so much."

"Well, whatever it is, her spirits are very much improved since she first lost Therese. I really thought that she would never be the same."

"Now that you mention it, it's almost as if she's found a new best friend and that can only be a good thing for her." They both agreed and watched Julia ride off into the mid-afternoon heat.

Julia was bringing new ideas and conversation back into Abbie's life, while Abbie was introducing Julia to culture, art, and music. At first, their time together was guarded and formal, but it wasn't long before it was filled with surprising laughter. It all unfolded slowly and unexpectedly for both of them, creating a bond between them that neither of them gave voice to.

In the beginning, Abbie was simply looking for a companion, someone to read to her or shop for her, but mostly, it was a way to break up her long, endless days. After awhile, she looked forward to their visits. Their conversations flowed effortlessly. There seemed to be no end of things to talk about between them. Julia had become the daughter she never had.

Julia especially loved to bring Abbie small gifts from the farm and bakery. At first, Abbie was slightly taken aback by Julia's presents, but with time, she relaxed and learned to enjoy them. Julia's curiosity about Abbie, her life, and her house was limitless, which was naturally endearing to Abbie.

There were also gradual changes Abbie made to the house to accommodate her time with Julia. The baby grand piano was moved out from under its dust covers. Abbie no longer played, but she introduced Julia to new music and coached her to take her playing to a higher level. Julia would take the pieces that Abbie gave her and practice them at home. When she felt she had learned them well enough, she would take them back to Abbie.

Afternoon tea was ready when Julia arrived with Biscoitos cookies and laid them out on a platter. Julia removed her bonnet and smiled. "You are going to love these. Perfect for afternoon tea. Notice they are shaped in a circle like a wreath. They represent good fortune."

"How so?"

"The wreath is a never-ending circle representing the seasons of our lives. Just like winter, bad times come, but the circle of life always brings us back to spring and summer. The bad things do not last; they cannot remain."

"Is that something you've learned since you lost your friend?"

Julia spoke thoughtfully. "Yes, I think so. The sadness is still there, but it softens. It's no longer sharp; it's like a deep cut that heals and leaves a scar." Abbie seemed less certain, so Julia prodded a bit, "Haven't you found it to be true yourself?" A shadow passed over Abbie's face. "We're all different in the way we deal with pain. Some things can leave us crippled, not just scarred."

"But don't you think we can choose?" Julia insisted, but Abbie remained silent and looked away. Julia studied her face. Abbie seemed as if she had fallen into a trance, far away, lost in thoughts of long ago. Julia wanted to know about those things, but she had discovered there were certain topics that were not safe for Abbie.

On a couple of occasions, she had asked Julia to leave early. Julia learned that it would happen when their conversations bumped up against the hard edges of Abbie's memories. Julia sensed that Abbie was a woman who had been deeply disappointed by the people who were meant to love her, and she had learned to tread lightly around her emotional barriers.

After a long pause and a couple sips of tea, Abbie changed the subject. "What about that new piece you've been working on?"

"Chopin's Nocturne?"

"Yes, Opus 9, that's the one. Play it for me."

Julia put down her tea cup and reached for the music in her satchel. She drew it out slowly. The nocturne had left a deep impression upon Julia's heart, and she wanted to play it perfectly for Abbie. Julia hoped it might ease Abbie's mind now, perhaps bring her some peace from her sorrows. Abbie listened intently, as she sat rigid and straight upon the settee.

Julia began playing slowly with the lightest touch. She played it as thoughtfully as she could, and she thought she played it faithfully. She wanted to be absolutely true to the music, but it was not long before Abbie began to bark at her restlessly, as she stood upright and paced the room.

"Adagio! Adagio!"

Julia slowed down, but Abbie kept barking in an agitated manner, "Adagio! Adagio!" It was as if she had been caught up in some bad dream. Julia felt as if she was playing in slow motion. As she played on, nothing seemed to please Abbie, and she only seemed to grow more discomposed.

"Stronger now. This is a forte stanza." Abbie positioned her fingers as if she were playing the music and stretched out her fingers in a downward slicing motion. Nothing Julia did seemed to calm her. Finally, Julia stopped playing. Abbie said nothing but moved to the window and glanced downward, lost in thought.

After a long pause, Julia stood up and joined Abbie by the window. Parting the curtains, she could see a long-neglected garden covered in bramble and weeds. Finally, Julia broke the silence. "It must have been so beautiful when you first came here."

"Yes, yes it was." Abbie spoke in a far-away voice.

"Was it a happy time for you?" Abbie did not answer. "I would love to see it as it once was. Would you let me?"

Finally, Julia had spoken words that penetrated through Abbie's gloom. Abbie turned to her with an air of suspicion.

"What do you mean girl? How can you see what is no longer there?"

Julia searched Abbie's eyes as if to unlock her secrets. "I can imagine it. Can't you?" Again, Abbie said nothing, but Julia gently persisted.

"What if I transform the garden for you? Make it just the way it once was or perhaps even better? With your permission. You just tell me what to do, and I'll do it. However you like. Once it's done, we can sit there in the cool afternoon shade. Would that please you?"

Again, there was silence, but Abbie was present again, and that's all that mattered to Julia. Abbie shrugged, as if she had never been disturbed. She softened her tone and turned her gaze back to the garden. "Do as you like. Just tell Howard what you need, and he'll get it for you." Julia smiled to herself. This was progress. To find something that was lost. To restore beauty that has been destroyed. She peered downward and imagined all that it could be. Now, this would be something worth doing, if only she could find the time. She hoped that Abbie would feel the same way once it was done.

Roger McCallum had been true to his promise to visit his grandmother, but so far, he had not run into Julia. Not that he was trying to see her. He had resolved on avoiding her. Whatever strong feelings he had felt on that first day, he pushed them away. Now that he had seen her again, he was restless and unsettled. He tried to resist the thought of her, but the more he tried, the more he was sucked in, like an ebb tide pulling him in deeper.

He made a point of checking her employment records. He wanted to know her name, her age and address. There it was: Julia Estela Eva Mirante. He spoke it softly to himself. He resisted the impulse for several days but gave in and rode by the Mirante farm. It was not so much that he wanted to run into her; he knew he could accomplish that at the cannery. He just wanted to see how and where she lived and estimate her distance from his home. He spotted Marcos, in the distance rounding up cattle, jealous to realize the man's close proximity to Julia. His snooping only left him with feelings of embarrassed self-reproach.

Roger liked to think that he was in full control of his emotions and that he was independent of any outside influence when it came to matters of the heart. Especially his mother's influence. Still, he could not deny that his mother was determined to have her say about any woman he might choose. It was a topic she increasingly raised as he grew older. He even knew that his mother already had her sights on a young woman, because she announced it at dinner one evening.

"I happened to run into Leslie Hampton the other day," Olivia started in. "Do you know her daughter Kathleen just returned from finishing school in San Francisco?"

"And why would we care about Kathleen Hampton?" Celesta suspected a plot.

"Well, because she is well-connected to a prominent San Francisco family and because she's a very accomplished young woman." She turned to Roger. "One you need to get to know." Roger ignored her by plucking up the newspaper and burying his nose in it.

Celesta laughed. "Roger, didn't you hear our mother? She has picked out your future wife. Now, what do you say to that?"

Roger spoke through the newspaper in as indifferent a tone as he could muster. "That would be fine, if I were looking for a wife, which I am not."

"They say she's quite a beauty." Susanna interjected. "And very accomplished! What more could a man want?" The girls giggled. Roger cinched the newspaper closer into himself, as he braced against the bewitching image of Julia galloping on her stallion. He could still see her delicate profile as she slowly read to his grandmother on that first day he saw her, and he heard her laughter ring around the canning shed. There seemed to be no getting away from her.

CHAPTER 28

1878, The Pacific, Welcoming Party

It was now day one hundred fifty-six, and the bark was within twenty-four hours of Honolulu Harbor. The sense of anticipation was so potent that it acted as an elixir to hoist their drooping spirits. Just one day before, they had buried another two-year old at sea, who had been ill almost the entire journey, but the thought of seeing their new islands was enough to pull them out of the gloom and drive them upward to gaze wearily across the horizon, their hearts aching for home.

With little else to do but wait, the passengers lined the galley ways every day, draping themselves over the taffrails, riffling their eyes across the sea over and over. Every face, from the youngest to the eldest, carried the lined forehead and the cocked eyebrows of long-awaited hopes and dreams.

There was one man named Thomas Perreira who was also clutching something, but it was much more palpable than hope. To him, it felt far better, because it was tied to his belt. He never took it off, day or night. Hidden under his shirt was a tightly drawn leather pouch. One evening, as they were smoking out on deck after dinner, he showed it to Miguel. They had been discussing the work they would choose once they arrived on the islands.

"I hear they need workers in the boiler rooms." Miguel commented. "It might be hard work at first. There would be a lot to learn. But it seems to me there is more advancement in it, and it is a good skill to learn. Perhaps a way to supervise the work. That would suit me better than working out in the fields."

"If all goes well, I won't need advancement," Thomas opined. "I won't be on these islands for long. I won't be doing farm work for long. Just long enough to get my passage to the mainland." Thomas patted the bulge under his shirt around his belt on his left side.

Miguel turned towards him with curiosity, "Oh, and just what makes you so sure?"

"Diamonds," Thomas smiled back, as he drew out and untied the leather pouch, which was secured with a draw string. He opened it and shoved it towards Miguel as a signal to inspect its contents. Miguel peered into its depths and was astonished to see what looked to be about a hundred diamonds of all sizes, sparkling in the sunlight. Miguel drew back in surprise.

"Diamonds? From where?" Though he had known Thomas well in São Miguel, they were not close, and he was surprised that the man would confide in him.

"My father gave them to me before we left Funchal."

"But how and where?"

"He and my grandfather worked the diamond fields in Africa."

"But how did he come by them? Did he mine his own claim?"

"No. He was hired help, along with about fifty other laborers. But at that time the diamonds were everywhere. They did not even have to go underground to find them. They were in the river beds. Even on the ground."

"Surely, that was not his pay?"

Thomas laughed. "Of course not."

"Then how?"

"One day at a time and one swallow at a time." Thomas gulped with an intentional look. "Both of them — as long as they worked there. They would each swallow one or two a day."

Miguel raised his eyebrows and let out a low whistle, as he turned his gaze back to the sea. "I bet that was a fun cleanup job."

Thomas laughed. "Oh yes. But well worth the mess."

"Why did he give them all to you?"

"He did not give all of them to me but most of them. You see, once he returned from Africa, he never had the means or the opportunity to sell them in Funchal. He was always afraid he would somehow be exposed. And besides, no one in Funchal knows how to measure or pay for their true value. You have to find the right buyer for them."

"Like in Europe, right?"

"Yes. He thought about peddling them to the German merchant ships that would stop in Funchal harbor, but even then, he was afraid they would take advantage of him or steal them away. The diamonds have never brought him anything but fear at the thought of losing them. So, when I told him I was sailing halfway around the world, he thought it an easy way to unburden himself and to ensure my future. I am, after all, his only son."

"But how can you barter them on the Sandwich Islands any better than he did on Funchal?"

"The Sandwich Islands are only a stepping-stone. Where else do you think I could sell them?"

"America?"

"Exactly. My father never wanted to leave São Miguel. He was too overwhelmed by the language barriers, and he didn't have the right connections. After all, he was just a poor farmer, not a worldly man. So, he simply held onto them until he could see a way to peddle them. Now I will go to the Sandwich Islands, but not for long. As soon as possible, I will head to California. San Francisco is my final destination, where I plan to become a great man."

"You still have to pay for your passage. Will you sell the diamonds to buy passage right away?"

"No. I will be patient and work out my service. I do not want to draw attention to me or to my family. The right time will come soon enough. And then I will not sell them all at once. I must take it one step at a time. No one must know just how many I have, and I will find more than one buyer. I am hoping I will be able to send something back to my father, maybe even send for him and my mother to live with us in California."

Miguel leaned hard against the taffrails, as he considered the possibilities. "Either way, you will be a rich man. You will not have to work by the sweat of your brow like the rest of us. I wish you all the best with your good fortune, but I advise you not to tell anyone else."

"I appreciate that. And I hope I can trust that you will not speak of it either."

Miguel turned to shake Thomas' hand. "You can rely on my word, but how do you plan to get them through inspections?"

Thomas smiled and raised his eyebrows. "My wife is a very good seamstress. She knows how to sew them tightly into many seams. She is especially good at making dresses for the little girls. The entire family will participate in the process without even knowing it."

Miguel shook his head out of appreciation for their cleverness, but he wondered at the man's taking such a chance on telling him. "I guess he is too proud to keep it to himself," he thought. He had not noticed Francisco lurking nearby, listening to every word.

As he left Thomas and circled the deck, it occurred to Miguel that it was time to talk to Francisco. The boy ran away the morning after Paulo died. After over-hearing Maria confront Miguel about Paulo's death, Francisco had followed them up on deck and listened to their conversation. He knew that Maria would never accept him in Paulo's place. He also knew that the girls did not like him. So he disappeared once again.

Miguel tried to find him out in the open. Now he would have to seek out his hiding places. Not long after his conversation with Thomas, Miguel found him playing dice with the off-duty crew up on the forecastle. He came up behind him and tapped him on the shoulder.

"Francisco."

Francisco spun around and shaded his eyes from the setting sun, as he recognized him.

Miguel spoke simply and directly. "We need to talk."

Francisco did not trust him. Why would this man want to help him? Miguel decided to bribe him.

"Come on. I'll get you a grog."

The promise of refreshment was more than Francisco could resist. In spite of himself, he followed Miguel to the larboard side of the vessel, after Miguel grabbed a couple of grogs from the kitchen galley.

Francisco eyed him suspiciously. "Why should I trust you? I can take care of myself."

Miguel backed him into his own corner. "You haven't made arrangements to disembark yet, have you? What are you waiting for? We are just about to land."

Francisco had always planned that Paulo could get him off the ship unseen. He figured that Paulo knew the crew and could talk them into looking the other way. Now that Paulo was gone, Francisco feared he would never make it off and would end up having to stay on ship to work off his fare. He also knew that no one gets on or off the ship without passing through inspections, especially now that they would be quarantined. Like it or not, he needed Miguel's help.

"So, just how am I supposed to become Paulo?" He said with a slight note of sarcasm. "We don't look anything alike."

Miguel gazed down at him, knowing that Francisco had few other options than the one he was proposing. "We've been told we can't leave the ship until my wife delivers. That may not be for three or four weeks. We will still be on the ship long after most of the crew goes on leave, long after anyone who knows Paulo would recognize the difference. You just have to stay out of sight until we depart."

"And then what?"

"If you stay with us, I'll get you work. You may even get to go to school. But that's up to you. It will be easier for you to find work, if you stay with us, at least in the beginning. But I won't keep you. You can go at any time."

"Where can I find you when it's time to get off?"

"Don't worry. I'll let you know. Just keep close to the life boats, where I found you last time."

Francisco nodded, but it was not in his nature to show appreciation. He shoved his hands deep into his pockets and disappeared suddenly. He was practiced at slinking away into dark corners.

The night before reaching Honolulu, the bark sited a smaller ship slowly coming towards them. The ship hovered astride the bark and sent a dinghy of two men with landing instructions for Captain McAllister.

Most of his orders for preparation were a matter of routine. For the crew, there would be two weeks of quarantine, followed by two weeks of leave on shore. Some would stay and some would take the return voyage. For the passengers, it would be the first time they had been on shore in one hundred fifty-five days, and it would be the only home they would know for at least three years.

The last forty-eight hours seemed interminable to those who had nothing to do but wait. They covered only about one hundred thirty-two miles the following day. The breezes were not with them and so they drifted into what seemed like one long slog to the finish line. Some played cards or dice. Some smoked and ranted. Some strummed braguinhas or violas. Some took long naps on deck under the sun while listening to the melancholy tones of the violas.

The Captain spent his time preparing the crew for inspections. He ordered his men to scrub the ship from stem to stern, sending out an order "Forward there! Rig the head-pump!" Three men scrambled to the forward bow of the ship to pump up sea water used to scrub the deck.

The First Mate took an inventory of everything from supplies to food stores to crew members and passengers. All luggage would be ready when they arrived, so that the passengers could disembark onto Quarantine Island. All except those who were too sick to leave the ship. Although they would be confined for fourteen days, the more prepared they were, the more likely it would be that there would be no further delays.

In preparation for quarantine, each passenger underwent a brief doctor's exam that was to be recorded before they landed. Anyone with fever, sore throat, or signs of rash would be separated from the rest of the passengers. Upon arrival, they would undergo yet another exam by the Quarantine inspection doctors and wait fourteen days before they could start work.

Soon, the seabirds came, signaling that land was near. And then it finally appeared, their first land sighting. The girls were all on deck, when the man on the watch gave the cry, "Land ahoy!" Ida glanced to the side of the ship where he was pointing. They could not get to the side of the ship fast enough, everyone running and screaming for position.

The first island they spotted was the largest, the great island of Hawaii. It appeared like a bleep in the distance, but it was enough to excite anticipation. Over a period of one day, they traveled fifty-eight miles and spotted Maui, then Lanai and Molokai.

Next day, they arrived at the Honolulu harbor. The first thing they noticed was Diamond Head, the volcanic ridge that hedges the harbor. "Look *Pai!*" Ida noticed. "It reminds me of the Madeira peaks."

"The natives call it Le'ahi, because it looks like the fin of a tuna fish," remarked one of the crew members standing close by.

Miguel caught his breath. It did remind him somewhat of Madeira and the air felt like the Azore islands, but he could only think about Maria. She was lying below in the heat of the day, sweating profusely, and still, she would not speak to him. One look at the harbor might calm her. It did remind him of the Funchal Harbor with all of its jostling sea vessels.

"If only I could bring her up here," he thought. "She might see that all is not lost. That there is a home for us here. That we are home for each other." But he could not speak his thoughts out loud to the girls, so he responded absent-mindedly to Ida.

"It's not nearly as high as the Madeira peaks. Perhaps it looms larger because it is so near the harbor and seems to protect it."

"Yes, the peaks are more distant from the harbor at Funchal," Estela chimed in. "And much harder to climb, I would imagine. But the weather is so like our island. I think I will learn to like it here very much." She spoke this as she spotted the sandy beaches and felt the breezes that blew through the Acacia Koa trees lining the coast.

Very soon after they entered the harbor, they were greeted by a tugboat Titcomb, which led them through the port. There were several Portuguese representatives on the boat who came onto the ship with gifts of tobacco for the men and baskets for the women.

The baskets were full of mangos, star fruits, lychee, strawberry guava, and papaya, the likes of which they had never seen. The children crowded around and helped themselves to the delectable fruit. They were pleasantly surprised by the welcome.

"We are so glad to see you made it. Your arrival has been very much anticipated by the sugar cane growers who are in sore need of your assistance," one man announced to the listening audience.

The welcoming party of representatives from the Portuguese consul was eager to hear about the journey, knowing that it would be an indicator of whether more of the Portuguese would come. "How was your trip around the Cape?" Everyone shook their heads. It was a memory that had faded but had not been forgotten.

"It's not a trip I ever want to take again," one man groaned.

"We barely survived it. We took in so much water and lost the mast head."

"I've never felt so sick in my life."

There seemed to be a never-ending stream of comments on this topic, but their hosts were eager to give them a reason to forget its horrors. "And hopefully, we will find a way to welcome you, so that you will never need to return again."

Speaking in Portuguese, their hosts turned to a collection of men around them and asked how they were treated by the crew members. Juvenal Terra spoke for the rest of them, "Our meals were paltry at first. We did not eat well, and some of the children got sick. However, when we complained to the Captain, he addressed the problem with the cook. We were also given medical treatment, but sadly, several died from measles, as you know."

"Yes, we are sorry to hear about those who died, but we are glad to hear the crew addressed your problems with their cook. If there is anything else you want to report, then please arrange to meet with us privately on the island." The immigrants were grateful to hear that there was someone who could speak on their behalf.

As they glided through the Honolulu Harbor, they passed a lighthouse and then came in sight of merchant ships and even some whaling ships. There were dozens of floating houses, which gave the appearance of a floating city. People peering out their windows and waving. Sitting on tiny porches and calling out in a language they could not understand. Tossing flower leis into the water at them. Laughing and smiling.

"There is warmth in these people. There is warmth in these islands. I can feel it." Marissa put her arm around Juvenal and gazed up at him. "Now, if only Maria could be well again and find the strength to deliver the baby."

Juvenal signed, "If she could only forgive Miguel. Paulo's death has come hard on her."

"I think she will. She just needs time. Remember when our twins were born?" Juvenal nodded. "She is going to need all of her strength to start a new household. We must stay together so that we can help them."

"Yes. I will ask Miguel if we can arrange to work on the same plantation. If we go ahead of them, then perhaps we can help them get settled in."

"Oh, Juvenal. That would be perfect. That's exactly what she will need. People around her she knows." Just as she finished her sentence, the Captain announced that all of their belongings were ready for landing.

"As soon as we arrive, Mr. Roper and his men will hand you your stowed luggage, and you will be escorted to your quarters on Quarantine Island, where you will remain for two weeks. While you are there, you can speak to your prospective employers and sign up for employment. Those who were not able to pass our medical exam will remain on the ship for now, until further notice."

The Captain turned to Miguel. "Special arrangements have been made to make your wife more comfortable on board. A doctor will assist her, until she can leave the ship."

"Will I be able to come and go, so that I can arrange for our employment?"

"Yes, the rest of your family will remain on the island most of the time, but we can arrange visits for them in between."

"Thank you, Captain."

CHAPTER 29

1909, San Jose, May Day in the Valley

It was an annual affair, a day in spring when time squealed to a stop like a trolley car gear down a San Francisco descent. Families across the Valley briefly put aside their toil to mingle and relax. Even the lazy dogs in the street knew it was time to celebrate, while the egrets, downy woodpeckers, and kestrels made a spectacular showing along the Penetencia Creek slicing through the center of Alum Rock park. The most dauntless hikers scaled up steep cliffs to lay eyes on the best views of the San Francisco Bay from its southern shores.

On this occasion blue-checkered tablecloths lined picnic tables covered with bowls of robust cherries, while Pacific breezes escorted the scent of rosemary-infused barbecue. Farmers and their wives showed off their prize produce alongside their elderberry wine, plum brandy, and freshly-baked cherry-berry pies. No one would go hungry on this day. A steam-powered trolley trundled streams of celebrants back and forth between the town of San Jose and the park.

On the morning of the picnic, both Rose and Julia stood close together frowning in front of the looking glass. Their mother had made them matching gingham-bustled summer dresses trimmed with lace collars and cuffs, Rose in yellow and Julia in blue.

"What sort of man does mother think we'll attract in these getups?" Julia popped out a matching parasol and took a peek of herself in the mirror.

"How can we have fun in these?"

"Well, we certainly won't be riding today, but perhaps we can take a swim in the indoor pool?"

"Oh yes, let's definitely bring our swimwear. If I have to sit around in these get-ups with my pinky over a teacup all day, I'll die of boredom. That's for sure!"

"Let me talk to Mother." Julia offered. "Perhaps she'll let us change back into our dresses later in the day, after we make a polite showing. It will be just too gawd-awful hot to stay in these dresses in any case."

Julia settled plans with their mother. They would pack their dresses and wear casual clothes on the trolley ride so they could swim first and change later for the picnic. After the picnic, there would be a rodeo round-up and a barn dance. "There are changing rooms at the pool, so we'll be able to freshen up before facing the heat again," Julia informed Rose.

It had been a sultry morning; the sky looked as if it was covered with clouds lined in silver. The morning gloom promised to make way for blue skies as the sun rose farther overhead. The cloud-covered mornings provided the Valley with a natural air conditioning system that tiptoed in at morning and often returned after sunset.

The streets were crowded with cars and carriages, horses, and children piled into carts. Anarosa and the girls stood waiting in a long line for a trolley, while the men of the family road in their new Ford truck with all of their picnics supplies. The Mirante women were accompanied by Anarosa's sister Mildred and her sixteen-year-old daughter Maggie from the Central Valley.

When they arrived at the park, Maggie, Rose, and Julia jumped off the trolley and found the natatorium, a large red brick building that enclosed an indoor pool with a two-story ceiling. "We'll be on the west side of the south lawn picnic tables," their mother reminded them, as they parted ways for the afternoon.

The men unloaded the truck and sauntered over to the game area to play baseball and throw horseshoes, while the three young women took in a buzzing scene of mostly young people jumping off platforms, screeching, and splashing. Some were climbing onto a platform so they could fly down a two-story slide. Hot steam lightly sprayed the girls' faces as the front doors closed behind them.

"Let's make our way to the changing rooms. This way back at the left." Rose charged ahead. She could not wait to get into the pool before it was too crowded.

As they were entering the dressing rooms, they almost collided with Susanna and Celesta McCallum. They had not met since the day of the horse show and parade, but the McCallum girls had seen them coming before any of the Mirantes realized who it was. Susanna brushed hard against Julia, as she flew by.

Julia lost her balance, almost fell backward, and dropped her basket. All of Julia's clothes and cosmetics were splayed across the floor. Stunned, both Julia and Rose glanced back to see who it was and if there would be an apology or even a simple "excuse me."

Susanna flung a stabbing glance at Julia, but Rose was not amused. "What was that all about?" Rose's eyes flashed and she called out after the girl. "You could at least apologize."

"Not a chance." The words hung heavily in the steamy chlorinated air, as Susanna disappeared into the pool area. Rose gave Julia an inquiring look. "Do you know her?"

"Don't you remember?" Julia crooked one eyebrow. "The horse show?"

"You've got to be kidding me. That was five years ago!"

Julia shrugged. "Some people just take a long time to get over themselves." Rose smiled back. "I'll say. And some people never get over themselves." As they gathered their things on the floor, their good humor melted away any thoughts of resentment.

Olivia McCallum had lingered behind her daughters and was taking in the entire scene. She had also witnessed her daughter's behavior and was not in the least inclined to correct her. Since Julia had never met the mother, she did not recognize her, but she did glance up in time to lock into her glacial stare. Rose noticed it as well, and the two sisters cast a questioning gaze at one another, as they collected their things off the floor.

Olivia McCallum swept past them, stepping on Julia's hand mirror in the process, and without a word, exited the changing room. Julia and Rose grew even more perplexed. Maggie was also taken aback, "Who is she?" They all yanked their heads in the direction of the retreating woman. It was not until they saw the woman in the bathing area surrounded by her daughters, that they realized it was the mother.

"One thing I'm sure of, Julia. If looks could kill, you'd be dead by now," Rose remarked once they had found a place to park their things. "From what I've heard, she's not a woman to be crossed."

"And just how did you hear anything about her?" Julia was at least curious about the mother of her employer.

"Cathy Jacques knows all about that family. She told me how the mother has mistreated the grandmother and probably wants to see her dead, so she can get all of her money."

"I wouldn't listen to that kind of gossip."

"All I want to know is whether, in all the time you've been visiting the grandmother, have you ever seen her daughter-in-law or her grandchildren? I hear she's always alone. So, there must be some truth in it."

"Now that you mention it, I never do. I think that Abbie McCallum is very much alone." Julia sighed wistfully.

"There you go. I rest my case. Given how that woman just acted towards us, when we did nothing wrong, I think it's all likely true. She cannot be a nice person."

"Let's not worry about it now. Let's just get in the water." Julia took Maggie and Rose by the hand and together they jumped off their first of many platforms. "I'll race you!" Julia cried back at both of them and crawled to the far side of the pool. They spent three hours swimming and diving without another thought about the McCallum girls. But the McCallums never took their eyes off of them. The Mirantes remained the main topic of their conversation all afternoon and into the evening.

When it was time for the picnic, the pool began to thin out. Maggie begged Julia to take her up to the highest platform for one last second-story slide into the pool. "You must have gone down that slide twenty times already. Aren't you hungry yet?" Rose was famished by now and they needed extra time to dress for the picnic. "Please, just one more!" Maggie begged. Julia turned to Rose, "I'll take her up while you start getting ready."

"Just promise me that you'll watch my last slide before you go into the dressing room." Maggie begged.

Rose smiled, "I'll wait until you take your dive."

Julia led Maggie up to the slide platform, while Rose wended her way through the crowd exiting the pool. Just as Rose came to the dressing rooms, she looked up to the platform and waved to show Maggie that she was watching.

Julia and Maggie were nearing the end of the line when an unseen hand reached out and pushed Julia over the side of the platform from the second story. Rose sucked in her breadth, as Julia belly-flopped into the pool. The flop made a slapping sound on the water that left a hiss in the air and drew all eyes onto the welted spot. Maggie thought Julia had jumped on purpose, but Rose saw someone push her. It was clearly one of the McCallum girls. She just wasn't sure which one.

Rose bolted towards the platform, just in time to see one of the girls hurrying away. "Hey! Hey you." Rose ran after her, but whoever she was, she muscled her way into the crowd before Rose could reach her. Then Rose thought of Julia and hurried towards her. By now, Julia was dragging herself out of the pool and Maggie had climbed down from the tower.

"Are you all right?" Rose huffed as she came up to her.

Julia laughed, "I guess I really made a splash. No one will forget that one."

"Yes, and it sounded like it really hurt."

"It stung, but I'm all in one piece."

"Did you see who pushed you?"

"No, not at all. Did not see it coming."

"Well, I'm pretty certain it was one of those McCallums. Did you see any of them in line or on the platform?"

Julia spoke with amusement, "No, I never saw any of them, but I sure hope it wasn't the mother." The girls laughed.

"Given the way she looked at you, I would not be surprised. But seriously, I'm concerned. They really seem to have it in for you, Jules."

"Well, even if they do, it's nothing to me."

"It makes me wonder if the son knows anything about it. He sure doesn't seem to have it in for you. At least not in a bad way."

Julia responded with a shrug and changed the subject. "I'm starving. Let's get out of here." No one disagreed.

After the barbecue, the crowd dispersed to join various games of competition. There were the usual sack races and relays. The men's riding and roping event was eagerly anticipated, especially by the Mirante workers, and the Mirante women gathered on a nearby bleacher to watch.

Julia and Rose were now dressed in their gingham picnic dresses. The McCallums sat not far away. Rose saw Susanna glaring at them. "I swear there is absolutely no getting away from them today."

"Oh, never mind them. Look, Stefan is riding first," Julia remarked enthusiastically, as she pointed towards the corral. Just as she spoke, Stefan broke out and tore after a calf, swirling around it, tossing and roping it, and then jumping off his horse to tie it. A bullhorn sounded. After Stefan came a succession of Mirante ranch hands, Alexio and then Marcos. By the time Marcos was ready to ride, the bar had been set high. It would take some pretty quick and fancy roping to beat Alexio.

As Marcos entered the coral, Maggie let out a sigh, "Who is he?" At sixteen, she was instantly smitten and had not yet learned how to conceal her emotions.

"That's our ranch manager, Marcos D'Angelo."

"You mean he lives at the ranch?" She spoke breathlessly. "For how long?"

"Oh, about eight years. He manages the ranch hands and all the horses and cattle." Rose was a little amused at Maggie; it was clear that she was gushing.

"You mean he lives with you? Is he married?" Maggie's questions came with another sigh.

Rose was hiding a grin. "No. Not married. And he doesn't live at our house. There are separate quarters for all the workers. Why, are you in the market? Don't you think you're a bit young for him?" Rose winked at Julia.

"Never. I'll have him in a heartbeat. Is he taken?"

Julia responded somewhat absent-mindedly. "Yes, taken by himself."

"What do you mean by that?"

"Just what I said: in love with only himself. Save yourself the heartache because he has no heart. Not for a woman anyway." Julia had never quite gotten over the way Marcos had treated her when she was young, although she had learned to tolerate him. They still rode together, but she never considered him as a friend.

Maggie was not the only woman who admired Marcos. As he mounted his horse all dressed in black and bolted out of the gate after a calf, Celesta McCallum had a reaction similar to Maggie's. She remembered him but had not seen him in several years. As she sat on the bench next to her family, she remarked to no one in particular, "Well, look who's here and more handsome than ever."

Susanna turned to Celesta. "And if he shows up at the dance tonight, just what do you plan to do about it?" She spoke just as Marcos's name was announced as the winner. Marcos was collecting his prize, a winner's take of one hundred dollars. Celesta only smiled and said, "In that case, I'll have a little roping of my own to do."

"Well let's just hope he's not too quick for you."

Celesta laughed in response, "Never!" Celesta pressed the issue even further. "I'll bet you I'll have him eating out of my hand by the end of the night. Two dances minimum. Name your wager."

Susanna rose to her challenge. "Your new lace ball gown is mine."

"Agreed."

Later that night, the families assembled into a large red barn which had been prepared for dancing. They took in a scene of plaid-shirted musicians in cowboy hats and lanterns sputtering shadows against the wood-planked walls. People poured in from all sides and coupled up spontaneously as the music started.

Rose and Julia were never without partners, and Maggie enjoyed her first dance. All of the Mirante brothers gave her a twirl, and she could not have been happier, but what she really wanted was for Marcos to ask her. "Don't hold your breath, girl," Rose remarked. "He's not a dancer. As a matter of fact, I've never even seen him dance."

Julia smirked, "I'm sure he wouldn't even know how." They all laughed together, as they spotted Marcos across the room holding court with some of the ranchers in a corner. The men were drumming up a dice game and about to move out the door. "You can see just how interested he is in dancing," Julia remarked dryly.

Just as Julia finished her sentence, she felt a light tap on her elbow and swung around to look up into a pair of searching green eyes. Rose took Maggie by the arm and quickly led her away. Maggie glanced back to see Roger McCallum escorting Julia onto the dance floor.

Maggie shrugged Rose away. "Why did you drag me away just when it was getting interesting? Who is he?"

"Julia's great admirer, although you will never get Julia to admit it. Everyone knows it but Julia."

"Why would she not want to admit it? He's almost as dreamy as Marcos, but not quite."

"The richest landowner for miles around, too. He's our employer. He runs several of the biggest canneries in the Valley."

"Really?" Maggie stared as she watched Roger lead Julia in the dance.

Julia was so caught off guard that she hardly remembered saying yes. Perhaps she never said anything. The next thing she knew Roger McCallum was guiding her into a square dance.

"So, will you be joining us this year again at the Cannery?" Roger smiled down on her. He was determined to engage her in conversation. It had been impossible at the cannery, but this was a unique opportunity.

Julia was again caught off guard. "Why yes, Mr. McCallum. I hope to."

"Whatever you need or want, feel free to come to me."

Julia seemed uncertain, as she tried hard to keep up with him. She was not a practiced dancer and stumbled over her feet. As she started to fall, he caught her and pressed in closer. She experienced an unfamiliar awkwardness and discomposure.

"Well, I appreciate it," she stammered. "But really, it's not necessary, Mr. McCallum."

"It would be my pleasure. But please, call me Roger. I'm not an employer tonight." Julia just stared up at him without a word as the teasing of the other women came back to her, and she realized there was some truth to what they were saying. She blushed again. Before the night was over, he asked her to dance two more times. During their last dance, he brought up the subject of his grandmother.

"I can't tell you how much I appreciate your helping my grandmother. Her life has not been an easy one."

"Well, she is my employer, but I really do enjoy our time together. I would gladly visit her, even if she did not pay me."

He smiled, "Then I won't bother to tell her you said so."

"No, really. I think she is a very special person."

He gave her an affectionate glance, as he realized that she spoke from the heart. "I happen to think so as well. And you are a good influence on her, I think. She told me how you came up with a garden plan, and she seems to have a renewed enthusiasm for things she once enjoyed. I can see an improvement in her garden already. I understand she's going to replant the orchard now."

"Well, I loved doing it, and I enjoy spending time with her there. It has been a pleasure." Just as Julia spoke these words, she noticed Marcos staring in her direction, as if he were searching her every expression. She blushed and again did not know why. As she surveyed the room for the exits, she could not help but notice that all eyes seemed to be turned in her direction. She felt a strange burden of expectation bearing down on her. As soon as the dance was over, she made a beeline for Rose, grabbed her, and dragged her outside. "Let's go now."

Rose turned on her "What's the hurry? The dance isn't over yet. Let's go back inside." Rose stopped when she saw Julia's look of panic; it was so unlike her. "Come on, another half hour won't kill you." Julia was not in a position to explain her mixed emotions, so she shirked them off and followed Rose back inside. She sought refuge with her mother and father, who were sitting at a table on the far side of the room. She slumped down next to them, not wanting to be noticed.

But it was not long before she felt a hand brush her shoulder and a pair of blue eyes peering down at her. It was Marcos asking her to dance. She almost blurted out, "You? You've got to be kidding. You don't even dance." But she remembered her manners in front of her parents and muttered instead, "Oh, but I'm so exhausted. Can I take a rain check?" She smiled weakly. Her mother and father insisted, and she knew it would be impolite to refuse their favorite ranch hand.

As he led her by the hand onto the dance floor, it occurred to her that she had not seen him dance all night. Again, she was taken by surprise, when she realized that he was a graceful dancer and that she had never noticed his dimpled smile. She did not have to think about the next step or stumble over her feet like she had with Roger.

Not far into the dance, she felt Celesta's eyes drill into her and realized that Celesta was probably the one who had pushed her off the platform. Julia could not know that Marcos's only choice of a dancing partner that night was the ultimate revenge on Celesta, nor did she know that there were others who jealously regarded his choice.

CHAPTER 30

1878, Oahu, Landing

For the first time in one hundred fifty-six days, the immigrants were about to touch solid ground. There were no regrets in these initial moments or thoughts of missing the creaking ship they were about to leave behind. Now, there was only the uncertain but hopeful path forward. As they disembarked onto a pontoon, they would not look back, at least for awhile. The pontoon was called a lazaretto, and it sat just opposite the Quarantine Island, where they would remain during the first two weeks of their stay.

Before they disembarked, the passengers gathered around the gangplank with their belongings, while the Portuguese consul and government officials greeted them on board. Once the officials confirmed quarantine procedures with the Captain and his First Mate, Joshua Roper explained the process that would follow, while João Amarel interpreted for him.

"We will call you by family. When we call your name, please step forward with your belongings, and you will be given a number. Once all family members are together, you will be escorted off the boat and onto the lazaretto."

"Where will we eat?" João prompted.

"From there, you will receive food baskets for the day and then the consul members will take you to a waiting room, where you will be examined by quarantine doctors. There is another waiting area beyond the doctor's examination rooms, where you can wait for your family members. Once you are united with all of your family, hold up your numbers and a guide will take you in groups to your sleeping quarters on the island. This will be your home for the next fourteen days."

"What about our work assignments?" João Amarel knew what was uppermost in the minds of the passengers and spoke up for them. They were eager to know where they would work.

The Portuguese consul spoke up. "Starting tomorrow, there will be representatives on the island from many plantations throughout the islands. Each plantation will set up a booth where you can gather information and ask questions. You will be given the opportunity to choose from the available assignments. All transportation arrangements to the various islands will be arranged by the plantations. Don't worry. There is plenty of work."

"What happens if we don't pass the doctor's inspection?"

"That depends upon the diagnosis. We will be looking for any sign of measles, since there has been an outbreak on the journey. You will be separated from other passengers until we are certain you are no longer contagious. Depending upon your health, you can be sent back to the ship."

Since this was one of the first boats to arrive from the islands, there were still a lot of unknowns among the Portuguese about which plantations and locations would be the most desirable. Their contracts were all the same in terms of pay and duration, and they knew they were signing up for three years of service.

As the passengers collected their luggage and descended, they could see a large boat near the lazaretto from which dozens came to greet them with baskets of bread, food, and tobacco. That same boat would be their source of sustenance for the next two weeks of quarantine.

Miguel joined the Terra family, so that he could make arrangements for his wife and family once Maria's baby was born. He and Juvenal planned to choose a plantation together. Before they left the pontoon, there were guards who searched each one of them for contraband. They were looking for liquor, any illegal substances, or stolen goods.

"Place your baggage on the ground. Open your coats and spread out your arms." Miguel quickly complied and waited for the pat down. Another guard rifled through his satchel. Miguel thought about Thomas and his diamonds, looking to see if he was anywhere nearby. What would be his fate if the diamonds were found?

As Miguel let his foot touch solid ground onto Quarantine Island, he was greeted by a blast of tropical breezes. They drifted through the shade trees and gently riffled his hair. He closed his eyes, breathed in the island scents, and tried to identify something familiar. Gardenia and pineapple and salt accompanied by a tickle of liquid wind, he thought to himself. Familiar in some way. He opened his eyes and took in the pellucid skies, thinking to himself. "Just like home." It made his heart smile and hurt all at once. "No looking back," he coached himself.

He turned toward the city of Honolulu. The tall palms dotting the island waved back and forth, as if in welcome. For the first time in many days, he relaxed, even as his drooping shoulders straightened up to take in all the sights and sounds around him. It felt as if a great load had been lifted from him, and he was not sure why.

"How long will you stay on Quarantine Island?" Juvenal broke into his thoughts as they followed their guide to their sleeping quarters.

"Just one night, until I've secured work for me and Paulo. And then I will return to the ship until the baby is born."

"Paulo?" Juvenal snorted. "You mean that little stowaway? Honestly, I just don't understand why you're sticking your neck out for that kid."

"Shhhh," Miguel blenched. He was fatigued at having to defend his actions towards Francisco and deflated at every reminder of Paulo. He would think of the seraphic look on Paulo's face as he wrapped him in his burial shroud. It haunted his waking thoughts and stalked his nighttime dreams. He had told Juvenal about Francisco, because he was hoping that at least one person would take his part in case anyone questioned the boy's identity. He wanted to avoid involving Maria in the subterfuge.

"I already told you why. It was Paulo's dying wish. Don't give me a hard time about it again."

Juvenal could see that Miguel wanted to close the subject, but he shook his head, "I just hope he doesn't bring you trouble or bad luck."

"I'll do what I can for him. The rest is up to him."

Once they were well beyond the guards and settling into their quarters, Juvenal tapped Miguel on the shoulder and thrust a bottle of Madeira wine at him. "Take a look at this."

Miguel started with surprise and cast an ear-to-ear grin at Juvenal. "How'd you manage that?"

Juvenal smiled. "I just wrapped it up in a ball with socks and underwear at the bottom of my baggage. When the guard rummaged around the clump, I held my breath, but he didn't search further. My last bottle." Juvenal sighed. "How long will it be before we get another taste of our heavenly nectar?"

Miguel sighed as well and put his hand on Juvenal's shoulder while he locked eyes with him. "Sip it slowly, my friend. It may be some time before we get another taste of home."

"Perhaps my brother will bring me some when he comes." Juvenal shrugged. "In any case, I will savor every drop."

"When will that be?"

"Soon. On the next ship, I hope. They say there will be one ship a year, so I am hoping to make this bottle last."

Miguel laughed. "Don't waste good wine! Are you sure he's coming?"

"Oh, he'll come. No doubt. As soon as I'm settled, I'll write to him and tell him to hurry."

"You sound optimistic."

"And why not?" Juvenal winked. "We'll just have to start our own plantation."

"Absolutely, my friend. And we'll make our own wine. It may not be Portuguese wine, but it will be very fine."

It turned out that Juvenal was not the only one who had tried to bootleg his wine past the guards. There was more than one creel full of bottles at the inspection station. Some very lucky official would line his cellar with very fine wine. What the guards did not know is that twice as much made it past their inspections.

Their quarters on Quarantine island consisted of rows of cots in a large open-air building under a roof covered in palm fronds. They set their baggage on a cot to claim a spot. Next to the building were rows of picnic tables under palm trees, where they could take their meals and hang their laundry from the conveniently placed wash rooms.

The island was quiet and felt isolated compared to the busy harbor, but it was possible to walk around it. After eating their meal, they walked through the complex and then out to the shoreline. The island was low and swampy, lying on the reef side of the harbor just opposite the city. Quarantine authorities had scraped up a layer of sand from the coral reef to raise the land around the buildings and roads. They were about two feet above water. The rest of the island was submerged, so there were many opportunities to tiptoe into the ocean.

To those who had been languishing on a boat for almost six months, it felt like a luxurious foot bath. They laughed and splashed each other along the shore, their shrieks sailing over the salt-swollen waters. Some were swimming on their backs and spouting water in the air. A sense of relief and relaxation came over them.

Still, no one would be at rest until the matter of employment was settled.

The next morning everyone was up and dressed early, even though there would be several hours before the plantation representatives arrived. After breakfast, they could see people setting up tables. Each table had a sign labeled with the name of the plantation and the island.

Before they left São Miguel, they had all agreed to the same terms of service. In return for their passage and food onboard, the immigrants would be contracted to the sugar plantations for a period of three years. It also included lodging, daily rations of food and garden space, and medical care, as approved by the Portuguese government.

The workers agreed to work a minimum of ten hours per day every day except Sunday. Age, sex, and marital status determined the level of pay. Married men with children were the highest paid. The children would go to school up to eighth grade and could work when they were not in school. From 1878 to 1911, approximately sixteen thousand Portuguese would immigrate to these islands to work in the sugar cane fields. When these islands became a U.S. territory in 1898, the Portuguese were granted citizenship. By that time, many would have already left the islands or started their own businesses.

The lines started forming early in what was known as the "Planter's Shed." Most were interested in the type of work they would be doing, but the island they would inhabit was also of interest.

Miguel turned to Juvenal, "Why don't we divide and conquer? I'll take one side and you take the other. Then we'll compare notes. I'm looking for a position in the sugar mills."

Juvenal was not so certain, "I'm open. I just want to see what's available." Since there was no variation in pay, it was simply a matter of preference. As time went on, they would learn how to earn their way into supervisory jobs with better pay.

Miguel quickly discovered that he could go to the front of any line to read a list of available positions. It was not long before he found what he wanted at a plantation in Kauai. He didn't know much about the island, but he had heard about its beauty. That would certainly please Maria, he thought, and then he waved down Juvenal.

"I think I've found what I want. Why don't you look over the list of jobs to see if there's anything that interests you?"

Juvenal eyeballed the list. "Now this sounds interesting. I like the idea of driving the oxen or plowing and planting the fields. I'd rather do that than cut the cane."

"Let's get in line." Within twenty minutes, Miguel was at the front of the line.

"I'd like to work in the sugar mill." The man taking down the information looked Miguel up and down. He had an eye for quickly gauging the strength and age of a man.

"Have you ever worked in a mill before?" The sugar cane foreman was looking for men who could handle the heat and intensity of working in the mills. He knew that the more experience they had, the more likely they would be able to succeed at mill work.

"No, but I'm familiar with the process, and I've seen a sugar mill."

Miguel's interrogator could not afford to be too picky, but he liked to pretend that he could be. The truth was that he knew it was unusual to find someone outside the islands who already knew how to run a mill. "Well," he muttered. "That is something and you look strong enough. Let's sign you up then." Once Miguel filled out the paperwork and gave him his number, the man asked about his family.

"The rest of the family are back on the ship, waiting for my wife to deliver a baby. Can I sign them up now or can it wait?"

"Well, the boat leaves eight o'clock in the morning the day after quarantine. Everyone needs to be on it."

Miguel heaved a sigh. "We may have to wait up to two weeks beyond quarantine. We can't leave the boat until she has delivered. Is there another way to get to the island?" The man shuffled some papers, as he considered the exception he would have to make.

"I'll tell you what. There's a schooner that comes regularly on Monday mornings from Honolulu Harbor to transport people between the islands. You'll have to make your way over to the Harbor." The man examined his ink-stained finger nails and thought a moment. "Here. I'll write up an I.O.U. from the plantation." He signed it and fixed it with a plantation stamp. "Make sure you send a note ahead to let us know when you are arriving. We'll need to send an ox cart to transport you and your family once you land in Kauai."

"I sure appreciate that." Miguel realized that if they were willing to go out of their way for him, then it must be a good plantation to work for and felt some sense of relief at the thought. And then he remembered Francisco. "I also have a son. He's about fourteen years old. What type of work can he expect?"

"Given his age, we'd probably want to put him in the fields. He can cut cane during harvest and plant and hoe the fields the rest of the time. He might also work in the mill dam certain times of the year, and we always need water carriers. What's his name? I'll put him down for field work."

It did not sound like Miguel had much of a choice, so he nodded and answered. "Paulo. Paulo Mirante."

Miguel walked away and thought about Francisco. He did not know how Francisco would respond to his new work assignments, but he was not going to let it worry him. He knew what they did with stowaways, since another boy had been discovered as a stowaway at the end of the journey. They were not allowing him off the ship. The boy would have to take the return journey and work his way back with the remaining crew. If Francisco gave him any trouble over his work assignment, then Miguel was prepared to make him suffer the consequences.

The next day, Miguel made his way back to the ship with the I.O.U. and work papers. He was hoping this would be good news to Maria. Anything to lift her spirits. Making his way down to the immigrant quarters, he greeted her with a smile and a kiss, and then held up the papers.

"We're all set. I have work, and we'll have a house, a garden, an outdoor oven, and plenty of work for the rest of us, while you take care of the baby. You must come up and see the island as soon as possible. It's so much like São Miguel — with high peaks and tropical winds and sandy beaches. It feels like home." Miguel took her hand and smiled broadly.

He searched her face for some sign of emotion, relief, or gratitude. Any sign of happiness would do. She smiled wanly in return. But she did not let go of his hand. She was tired of the solitude and realized she needed Miguel's optimism more than ever. And a shoulder to lean on. "We will be going to the most beautiful of all the islands. It is called Kauai. It is full of beauty and tropical rain forests and waterfalls." Once again, Maria smiled. This gave Miguel some hope.

"I've brought you a surprise." He took a papaya from his sack and cut a slice or two for her. "This is a fruit from the island that we have not tasted on São Miguel. I also brought you some sliced pineapple."

She gulped it down and smiled at Miguel. "It is wonderful. It's not exactly like our pineapples, is it?"

"No — and the papaya is like nothing I have ever tasted." His expression was filled with concern for her. She had been lying there on her back so still for two full weeks with nothing to do or read and very little company. "Are you getting all you need down here? What can I bring you? Water?"

She shook her head, "I will be fine. Really. Don't worry yourself. They are waiting on me, now that everyone is off the ship. And the girls are trying their best to keep busy and stay occupied." She reached out to touch his hand. "Please don't worry about me. It won't be long now."

"I wanted to tell you, Marissa has offered to come back onboard to help you when your time comes. Even if it's beyond the quarantine period, she has promised to come help."

Maria expressed relief. "It's good to know that I will be in good hands. I was not looking forward to delivering alone with just the ship's doctor."

"And I will be close by," he spoke softly as he kissed her hand. "And now I have a few things to do on deck. You will be alright until I return? Where are the girls?"

"They've been spending a lot of time on deck sunning themselves. They say the weather looks wonderful here."

"Yes. I'll round them up and be back in time for dinner."

Miguel left with the intention of finding Francisco, but he did not want to mention it to Maria and add to her agitation.

CHAPTER 31

1909, Santa Clara, The Grape Tower

Julia turned nineteen at the end of May, just as the canneries were about to reopen. For her, it was a time when life took a deep breath and a long pause, as it twirled her in a state of endless possibility. Filled with uncertainty and yet, full of hope. These were the slowest days in the year, a time when change was almost imperceptible and daydreams floated endlessly across the hearts and minds of Valley people.

The canneries would start up again like a well-worn clock winding everyone into mind-numbing repetition. Julia and Rose were not as opposed to working in the cannery this year. They had made some friends during the prior season and stashed away their money. They liked the idea of stockpiling even more. Rose was particularly interested in buying a new horse, and one more season of cannery work would be enough to get it for her. Julia was still contemplating going in with Luana on her dairy, although she had not yet discussed it with her aunt.

As for Anarosa, she was now determined to see both her daughters married and well-settled as soon as possible. She was currently on a mission to make them all new summer dresses. Any social invitation was snatched up without question, and a new bonnet or ribbon or piece of lace was secured for special occasions.

Frank sat reviewing the bills one evening and protested out loud. "Why so much expense over lace and bonnets all of a sudden?" His reproach surprised Anarosa, since he rarely objected to her household expenses. Anarosa kept her gaze fixed on her knitting. "Well, if you ever want these girls to marry, we're going to have to put out to get back."

"What do you mean, married?"

"Just what I said. It's time." She managed to keep her head down and knit with focused energy as she spoke.

"Time for what?" Frank was genuinely perplexed.

Anarosa kept purling as if life depended upon it but finally eked out a sigh in response to her husband's willful ignorance. "Time that both of them start making a life for themselves. God knows, we can't support them forever."

The thought struck Frank with surprise. It's nothing he ever contemplated. He turned to her with a queer expression. "Who said anything about the rest of their lives? It seems to me that they have plenty of time. They're no trouble. They're good girls and hard-working. What's the rush?"

"What's the rush?" Anarosa stopped her knitting. "Don't you know that women age earlier than men? In just five years, Julia will be an old maid. They are at the peek of their youth right now." Anarosa sometimes found it difficult to imagine that others did not think exactly like she did, even Frank.

"What nonsense. You sound as if they were fruit ready to ripen and not your daughters. Next, you'll be talking about canning and sealing them! Or isn't that the same thing as marriage?" Frank slapped down the pile of bills, apparently unaware that his views on marriage were targeted at the wrong person. "I for one, don't see any reason to rush things, and I'll not have you forcing them to marry anyone they don't care for."

Anarosa softened her tone slightly but remained firm in her convictions. "In any case, this is a time of their lives when new social connections will serve them well. I want to give them every opportunity to marry well, and their husbands do not have to be Portuguese, although I would prefer someone close to the family."

Now that Frank was forced to think about it, he had to admit that he would prefer Portuguese husbands for his daughters. "Perhaps you should invite your family from the Central Valley for a visit. Tell them to bring friends. If the girls are to be married, let's look for a well-established family with a thriving business."

Anarosa felt pleased that he was beginning to see things her way. "I don't want to limit their prospects. And besides, if I wanted my daughters to marry a ranch hand, there are plenty here in the Valley. I don't have to go out looking for them. Although I do like your idea of inviting my cousins. It would be wonderful to see them, even if I will have to put them up for a few days."

Little did Frank and Anarosa realize that Rose and Julia were within ear shot of their conversation sitting on the front porch outside an open window. The girls glanced at each other with concerned looks. They knew their mother wanted them to develop more of a social life, but it had not occurred to them that she was determined that they marry as soon as possible. It was the farthest thing from their minds.

Later that night, Rose climbed into Julia's bed, and they whispered about it from under the bed covers. "I had no idea Mama was so determined to get rid of us. I mean, I knew she wanted you gone, but I didn't think she was ready for me to go with you."

Julia was less surprised than Rose. "I'm the one who's really been feeling it. We were at the market last Saturday, when I realized she was introducing me to every mother who had a son anywhere near my age, even younger! It was positively embarrassing."

Rose smirked, "You must be mistaken. She cannot be that obvious."

"She can and she is. She even made a point of introducing me to each one, even introducing me to much older men. I was waiting for her to find some old man and beg him to take me off her hands."

"She really is trying to push you out the door. What are we going to do?"

"Well, don't worry for yourself. Once I'm gone, she'll back off for awhile. And besides, you heard Papa. He's in no hurry to get rid of us. If she tries to marry me off to someone I don't care for, I feel pretty certain that he'll take my part. For now, that makes me feel safe from her scheming."

Rose thought about it for a moment. "What if you don't meet someone you like well enough to marry? Then what?"

"That is exactly why I'm saving all of my money. If Mama pushes it too far, I'll join Luana at her dairy. I am determined that no one will force me to marry. Not until I am absolutely ready."

"But what about me?" Rose was even more alarmed. "If you escape, then she'll put the pressure on me."

Julia was the sister who would not be intimidated by an over-bearing mother. Since she had proven to Frank that she could ride Coal, she knew she had his ear. Rose, on the other hand, had not learned how to manage her mother. Julia wanted to reassure her. "As I said, I think it'll take some of the pressure off of you for awhile. And if not, we'll all live with Luana and be old maids together, agreed?" That brought a hopeful smile to Rose's face.

"I can just imagine it. Maybe we could even hang out with her at Jake's Place in the Mud Hen slough and find out what all the fuss is about down there." They muffled their laughter by pulling the bedclothes tighter around themselves.

"By the way, do you know why they call it the Mud Hen slough?"

"I'm not exactly sure, but Luana once told me that millions of birds migrate there for the mud."

"Why do they care about mud?"

"Because they eat it. They're a type of water bird, blue-grey water fowl."

"Millions of birds eating mud. No kidding?"

"No kidding."

It was not long after overhearing her parents talk about marriage that Julia decided to approach Luana. She wanted to feel her out about her plans for a dairy. They were putting away pots and pans at the back of the *Serradura* when the day was almost over and in an hour, they would close up shop.

"Luana, there's something I've been meaning to ask you."

Luana stopped her work and turned around to get a full look at Julia's face. She could tell by her tone that what Julia was about to say was important to her.

"Well, fire away, girl. Don't keep me in suspense."

"It's not like that exactly."

"Well, fire away, anyway."

"How would you feel if I told you that I'm saving my money, and I would really like to help you out with your dairy, maybe eventually be a part owner?" Luana could not have been happier. She dropped her drying towel and swung Julia around. "Would I ever?" She took Julia by the shoulders. "But what brought this on?"

Julia's eyes swept away but Luana persisted. "Well?"

"It's my mother. She is determined to marry me off. She must have said something to you about it." Luana could not conceal the truth of it, and she realized that Julia would see right through her in any case. "I do know what you mean. But you have to realize that you'll never be happy if you do this just to get away from your mother."

"No, that's not what this is all about." Julia dropped her gaze to the floor. "Not completely anyway. I just want something of my own. To make my own way and not have her hovering over me to make me into what she thinks I ought to be."

"And how would you feel about getting up before dawn to milk cows? It will tie you down you know."

Julia considered. "It can't be any worse than the cannery. I mean, the cannery is alright, but it's not what I want to be doing for the rest of my life. And, I could be with you. All the time. And save my money. Maybe even go to college."

"Would you like that? What would you do with it?"

"I was thinking of maybe becoming a teacher."

"Just like your *Tia*, Estela!" Luana took her by the shoulders and gazed at her reassuringly. "You can be certain that I will do everything I can to help you make that happen, if that is what you truly want. But what about marriage? Do you ever think about it?"

Julia shrugged away. "I'm in no hurry and there's no one who even remotely interests me. And besides, if I eventually do meet someone I like, why can't I have both?"

"Well then, I see no problem. None at all. I will support you, and I know we can get your father's help, if needed. I know your father. I don't think he'll ever want to hold you back." Luana realized that Julia would always want to consider all of her options.

As they were finishing up their work, Julia glanced over the shop to see if any of the customers needed help before they closed up. There he was again, back in the corner seat; at least once a week, Roger McCallum would come by. He never stayed long and he never spoke to anyone. He would just drink his coffee and go, always looking pre-occupied and in a hurry. Luana followed Julia's glance and wondered if Julia had yet realized his interest in her.

Julia stood cleaning the counter and turned to Luana with a perplexed look. "Luana? Would you mind closing up today on your own?"

"No. There's not much else to do. You go along." Luana could not help noticing that Julia took off her apron immediately, gathered her things, and went out the back door. It seemed to Luana that Julia was aware of the young man's interest and did not want to encourage it. Even if she was not aware, his presence clearly made her uncomfortable.

Luana decided it was time to kick up the dust covers a bit, just to see what might fly out of them. So, she approached the stranger. "Hello, Sir. Is there anything else that I can get you today?"

Roger seemed a bit startled at being noticed and cleared his throat before speaking. "Uh, no. I was just leaving." He remembered his manners and added, "But, thank you."

Luana hovered with a hand on her hip and leaned in just a tiny bit closer. "You don't come from this side of town, do you?"

Roger's posture became slightly defensive. "Well, no, not exactly." He searched for a reason to be there without considering that he owed her no explanations. "I used to be a student at the college, so I am very familiar with this part of town, and my grandmother lives a few blocks away. I come here after my visits to her."

Luana cleared away his plate and softened her tone, "Well, we are always glad to see you, Sir. What may I call you?"

"McCallum." He gulped ever so slightly. "Roger McCallum."

"And I am Luana Mirante, co-owner of this bakery with my brother Domingos," she spoke lightly. "And it is a pleasure to meet you. I just want you to know that you are always welcome."

Luana swung away with a smile at having achieved her purpose. She wanted him to know that he was noticed. She also wanted him to recognize her name, if not the fact that she was a force to be reckoned with. The more he came in, the more she could get to know him.

The day finally came. The cannery doors swung open again. This year, Rose and Julia would not have to fumble around or fear the old crows who hovered above them.

"Where do you want to work this year?" Terry Zuniga was there on their first day to greet them when they arrived. They had since realized that some jobs were more desirable than others. The women were, however, limited in what jobs were available to them. They were well into the cherry season and about to harvest apricots.

"Rather than slice and pit, why can't we label the cans this year?" Rose suggested.

Terry begged to differ, "That group is tight knit and it takes a long time for a spot to open up. Unless someone shows up sick or you know someone from the group, you're not likely to get that job."

"Then what?" Rose whined, and then she glanced over at the soldering shed where the men were soldering cans, and the cappers were getting ready to seal them shut. "Why can't we do what the men do? It doesn't look that hard."

"The can solderers and cappers are the most highly skilled workers and the highest paid," Terry added.

"It doesn't seem fair that women never get those jobs." Rose shook her head and Julia agreed. As they stood grousing about it, Roger McCallum approached them.

"Good morning, ladies."

The three women stared for a moment. Roger smiled and tipped his hat. "I'm Mr. McCallum. Can I help you find your way?" Terry gulped. Rose raised a twitching eyebrow. Julia stood her ground, determined not to be over-awed by his attentions. Then she responded with a pleasant smile.

"Why, Mr. McCallum. It's a pleasure to see you. We were just wondering what positions are available and which ones would provide opportunities to gain the most valuable skills."

"Well, that's certainly something I can help you with." He seemed pleased at the question.

Julia laid dark eyes upon him with an inquisitive look, as she inspected him more closely. "We were just wondering what it would take to become a capper. What would we need to do to get such a position?"

Roger did not miss the gleam in her eye or the challenge in her tone. She waited while he gathered his thoughts and Rose jabbed her from behind. "Well, uh ... miss." He side-stepped her question and turned to Julia in a tone of nonchalance, "Will you introduce me to your friends?"

"This is my sister Rose and our friend Terry." The other two women nodded in his direction and stifled an urge to giggle.

Roger redirected the conversation. "Why don't we go up to the Grape Tower? I think that the women who work there consider it to be one of the most desirable positions."

The grape pickers worked in a special room, known as the Grape Tower, located in a second story loft that was much cooler and quieter than the rest of the cannery. It was generally agreed that it was much easier to sort grapes than it was to work in the apricot and peach pits. The grape sorters did not have to carry baskets of grapes or contend with runners, and the grapes were some of the first fruits to be sorted on conveyor belts. These were the more popular assignments, but neither Julia nor Rose had enough seniority to qualify for them.

Without giving the young women a chance to change the subject or to ask another question, Roger led the way to the Grape Tower and up the stairs to a long, high platform where he turned to a woman who was obviously in charge. "Mrs. Rogers, I believe we have some open positions in the Tower, and I would like to introduce you to three young women who are ready to fill them." He gave her no opportunity to object.

Mrs. Rogers was taken aback. She was not accustomed to receiving orders directly from Roger McCallum. Her supervisor was the Head Floor Lady, Mrs. Clemens, who had told her that she would select her new workers and bring them upstairs mid-morning. Mrs. Clemens was going through the applications and would choose from a select group who had gained priority from the previous year. Mrs. Rogers did not know what to say.

"Ah, certainly Mr. McCallum. But ..."

"Provide them with all the training they need and get them started immediately." Roger knew what she was about to say and that these positions were typically the prerogative of the Head Floor Lady, who wielded a great deal of power. Yet Roger knew that none of the supervisors would dare override his wishes.

Mrs. Rogers started to speak, but he stopped her mid-sentence with a serious "I mean business" look, before she could object. He cocked his head to one side. "Remember, give them all that they need."

He then turned to the three young women. "I hope you will find this assignment a suitable one. Let me know if there is anything I can do for you at any time. Good morning, ladies." Then he walked away, more concerned with the impression he had made on Julia than with the unpredictable outcomes that would result.

The four women stood staring at each other for one long, suspended moment. Julia sensed the truth of the matter, that they now stood in someone's way and that whoever it was would not be happy about it.

After a moment's hesitation, Mrs. Rogers showed them around the tower and pointed to an overhead chute that conveyed the grapes down from above and onto two conveyor belts. Similar to the other sheds, there was a platform above and around them so that they could be observed. Julia did not doubt that they would be closely watched. One step out of line and down into the peach pit they would go.

"The matter of grapes is a delicate one. They turn brown quickly. It is imperative that no brown grapes or stems get by you. Not one." Mrs. Rogers showed them where to stand and explained what to look for and where to discard the excess grapes. She then turned on the conveyor belt and demonstrated the process.

"Now, put on your gloves and let me see you sort this next batch of grapes." A slow trickle of grapes trundled by them. The three young women stood at attention, knowing that their every move was being scrutinized. Mrs. Rogers stood over them while they picked out stems and quickly removed every grape with even a hint of a brown spot. Every few minutes she would correct them. At one point, she noted that they would not last long if there were too many blemishes or stems that made their way to the fillers.

After about an hour, Mrs. Clemens, the Head Floor Lady, approached Mrs. Rogers with obvious surprise. She had three workers in tow, all ready to do the grape picking. It was obvious that they had been promised the positions.

Mrs. Clemens took Mrs. Rogers aside. "What is this all about? I told you I would bring the new workers once they were ready." There was anger in her voice.

"You were overridden."

Mrs. Clemens slanted an eyebrow. "What do you mean overridden? By whom?"

"Roger McCallum."

Mrs. Clemens stood stupefied. "Roger McCallum? Since when does he interfere with our hiring decisions?"

Mrs. Rogers shrugged. "Since today, I suppose."

"Something smells fishy here. Are they related to the family?"

"Not that I can tell. They certainly don't bear his last name."

Mrs. Clemens was getting angrier as she considered how she was going to explain this to her new hires. "You turn that belt on full speed. One false move and these young women are out of here."

"That could work against you if they complain to Mr. McCallum. I overheard him tell them they should come to him if they needed anything."

"Just you let me worry about that. You go on break and turn that conveyor up full speed. You hear?"

Mrs. Rogers sighed. "Whatever you say."

Mrs. Clemens motioned the other women to climb down, and Mrs. Rogers turned to her three workers. "I've got another area I have to oversee. While I'm gone, make sure that no stems or brown fruit get past this conveyor."

The three young women nodded to signal that they understood. Then Mrs. Rogers went to the side panel to turn up the conveyor belt speed and make her escape. It was not long before Julia and her co-workers noticed that the grapes were coming faster and in larger clumps. When they were working under the supervision of Mrs. Rogers, the clusters were no more than three or four grapes a bunch or the grapes would come one-by-one. Now the clusters were filled with stems.

The receiving department was the first to handle the grapes and divided them into smaller bunches. The next group cut the top stems before thrusting them down the chute that brought the grapes down to the conveyor belts. As the belts worked faster, the workers above them kept up the pace.

Rose started to panic. Terry and Julia kept their heads down as the grapes flooded the belts. There was no time to strategize. Rose shouted over the clacking conveyors. "What are we going to do? We can't keep up with this. Shall I make a run for the supervisor?"

Julia kept her head down, "Just keep your eyes on the grapes." Terry was getting jumpy as the belts increased in speed and the stems flew past her in ever-increasing numbers. "We're letting too many stems go by. We can't keep up this pace."

In a single moment, all three of them felt the grapes bearing down hard, and they heard a loud thump and a swoosh as the chute overloaded. They peered up to the wide mouth of the chute, where a mountainous storm of grapes fell down in large clumps onto both conveyor belts. Green grapes were jouncing down in clusters the size of cantaloupes. The young women glanced around at each other, eyes rounding. They had few options, but a single thought came to each of them simultaneously.

Rose shouted "Whatever you do, don't break the line!" and then, in an instant, all three of them dove over the belts using their bodies to dam the tidal wave. They held the line for ten seed-spitting, stem-sticking minutes as the avalanche piled over them.

Finally, someone from above noticed their plight and stopped the belts. Everything went quiet with the exception of their labored breath. Gingerly, they stuck their heads up out of the grapes with searching looks.

Rose was the first to bust up, and then the others joined her. Fear of losing their jobs fell away as tears of laughter streaked their faces. "You look like a grape monster!" Accusations and characterizations came thick and furious, as their laughter swirled around the Grape Tower. They started picking stems out of each others' hair and spitting out the grape seeds.

Their every move was being observed from above. Roger McCallum had come to their rescue and stopped the conveyor belts, amused and impressed by the way they had handled the dilemma. He could easily guess what had happened to the belts, and he realized that Mrs. Rogers was nowhere to be found. Before long, he saw Mrs. Clemens approach the three young women below.

"What do you think you're doing? Do you realize you've stopped production? There are grapes that we can't process. Cans will not be filled until we clean up your mess." She did not stop to ask them what happened, because, of course, she knew. The young workers stood sheepishly silent until they heard a voice from up above.

"Mrs. Clemens, may I have a word with you?"

All four heads ratcheted up and around. There stood Roger McCallum, the unseen hand that had stopped the belts. Mrs. Clemens stuttered a moment, turned around on the young women and muttered a quick "I'll deal with you later."

Mrs. Clemens thought about how to save face as he led her away to his office. Once she was inside his private office, she immediately defended her actions, unwittingly casting herself in an unfavorable light. "These young women had no business being put in these positions."

Roger slowly raised his eyes up at her from his desk and leaned back on his chair. "And just why would they be any less qualified than anyone else?"

She sputtered for a moment, as she groped for justification. "Because they haven't paid their dues yet. These positions are filled only by the best and hardest workers who have proven themselves over time, those who have extensive experience in all areas of the cannery. This is a breech of protocol and morale will suffer because of it."

"And just whose protocols are we talking about?"

Mrs. Clemens blinked. She knew that such favoritism was subjective. It was not morale that she was concerned about but her own prerogatives. She struggled to find words to explain herself.

"Now, Mrs. Clemens, I want you to know that I really do appreciate your hard work and dedication, but in this case, I am asking you to make an exception. As a matter of fact, I am asking you to act as sheepdog over these young women, making sure that they get the best training. I am certain, that if you try, you will find a way to bring them up to your standards." And then he smiled at her sweetly. "Will you do that for me?"

Mrs. Clemens knew she was backed into a corner. "Well, of course, sir. But I don't think your father ever would have thought of doing such a thing." She had to get in her last lick.

He picked at a thread on his jacket as he spoke. "It is true. I am not my father, God rest him. But I will have my way on this, just as he sometimes insisted on his way in other matters. I have the utmost confidence that you will work this out." He looked up and his look was not stern, but she sensed that the conversation was over and that she could not win this battle, so she exited and made her way back to Mrs. Rogers in the Grape Tower.

By this time, the conveyor belts were humming at a normal pace, and the young women were busily hovering over the grapes. Mrs. Rogers gave her manager an inquisitive look but said nothing. Mrs Clemens folded her arms across her chest in disgust and whispered out of the corner of her mouth. "I guess we're going to have to live with this. Mr. McCallum wants me to "ensure that they are successful," as he put it.

Mrs. Rogers turned to observe her closely, and the Head Floor Lady made a final pronouncement on the matter. "I'd just like to know which one of them he's interested in." Mrs. Rogers cocked her eyebrow and took another look at the three young women, thinking that there was no doubt that, whoever it was, it would soon be the talk of the cannery.

CHAPTER 32

1878, Quarantine Island, Twins

The wave-slapped bark sat creaking in the harbor. The crew were on leave, except for a few who manned the ship. To Maria, it felt like she was living in a ghost town. Familiar voices had faded away, along with the drumming of the crew overhead and the notes of the braguinhas strumming across the sea. In spite of Miguel's daily visits, she felt quite alone, as if Miguel were a specter who passed through in grey-lighted dream sequences. Unknown to Maria, there were twins in her belly who also lay still, no longer contending with one other for the last vestiges of space.

Maria had yet to see her new home or to even glance at the island. She listened half-heartedly as Miguel described it all to her with grand gestures. Still, she could not conceive of or grasp her future. Little by little his words gave her strength to move forward, and sometimes she stopped looking back into the depths where her son lay like tentacles sliding across the ocean floor in muffled waters.

For the rest of the family, it had been two long weeks of waiting beyond quarantine. By now, most of the immigrants had left with their employers to start work on the plantations. Boredom stalked the Mirante girls. So they spent their time along the seashore on Quarantine Island, swimming and collecting tiny shells and driftwood, as they skipped stones and played tag.

Wills had searched for Paulo before he left the ship but was disappointed to hear from Miguel that he had already disembarked to Quarantine island and was sorry he had no time to say goodbye. Wills had half-hoped that the boy might join them on the return journey and consider a life at sea. Truth be told, he was going to miss the lad.

The girls and Francisco stayed on the island while Miguel spent part of each day with Maria. There had been some disagreement about what to call Francisco, but Miguel insisted they call him Paulo so that no one would suspect he was a stowaway. Estela approached her father on the matter. "*Pai,* don't you see that just the mention of Paulo's name is hurtful? And now we must speak it out loud all the time to a boy we can hardly trust."

"Hurtful or not, we must do it to protect the boy, and try to remember that we do it for Paulo's sake. In any case, you don't have to be with him all the time."

"I suppose that is so, but he will be living with us."

"Actually, I've arranged for him to stay with the Terra boys in separate quarters. He'll come to our house for his meals, but that's all the interaction you will have with him." Miguel had been thinking about the girls and that it might be awkward for them to share their personal space with a brother they did not know.

Estela squeezed her father's hand in relief. "My sisters will be happy to know that. And can I ask just one more question?"

"What is it?"

"I want to be there when the baby is born." Miguel looked searchingly into Estela's eyes. "Are you certain? It can be very difficult to watch your mother in pain, you know."

"No, I've given it a lot of thought, and I spoke with Marissa about it. She needs someone to help her. I want to help in any way I can."

"You always had a generous heart, and I think you're old enough to handle yourself. I'm sure your mother will feel better with you at her side."

"I have a more practical reason for wanting to be there. I have been thinking that I need to learn a useful skill. And even if there will be some medical care on the island, the women always need good midwives. Marissa promised to teach me. I can attend school, do some plantation work, and earn extra money as a midwife. Perhaps someday I'll have my own business. Either way, I want to learn how to be independent. Marissa and I have agreed to start spending the night with *Mãe*."

"I think that will bring her a great deal of comfort." Miguel squeezed her hand and smiled down at her.

It was not long after this conversation that Maria's birth pangs came on heavily in the night. Marissa woke with a start when she heard Maria cry out in pain. She sensed that Maria was in a panic, so she sat upright in bed and shook Estela. "Wake up! Your mother's time has come. Quick, go up and find Kit. We're going to need his help."

Kit arrived sleepy-eyed and bedraggled. "Kit, we need buckets of hot water and strips of cloth, as much as you can gather. And a ball of twine or string, whatever you can find. Once you round those up, go over to the island and see if you can find a quarantine doctor."

Kit ran as fast as he could and Marissa's face filled with uncertainty at Estela.

"What is it?" Estela felt her sense of foreboding.

"It's not likely we'll find a doctor on the island at this time. We'll probably have to go it alone."

"You've done this before, haven't you?" Estela gulped.

"Yes and without a doctor. The first thing we need to do is ensure the baby is in the right position."

Marissa moved to calm Maria whose face was dripping with perspiration and then she turned to Estela, "Get me a wet cloth." Estela quickly complied.

As Marissa patted Maria's face, she spoke reassuringly. "Maria, I'm going to have to feel around to see that the baby is in a good position. You may feel some discomfort. Don't be alarmed."

Maria rolled her eyes. "So, you really think this is my first time?" Marissa returned a laugh. "No, obviously not. I'm just glad to hear you can find your sense of humor in all of this. Now, just hold on while I try to figure out the baby's position."

Marissa pushed and prodded as Maria moaned. She turned to Estela, "The baby is head down and has dropped low. That's a good sign." Estela smiled with relief and held her mother's hand, "I'm right here *Mãe*. We're going to take good care of you."

After a half hour of listening to Maria's groans, Marissa looked at Estela. "See if you can find out where that boy went to. We're going to need every last strip of cloth on this ship. And help him bring in as many buckets of hot water as you can."

When Estela reached the cook's kitchen where Kit had started a fire, there was no sign of the cabin boy, only a pot over the fire. She scooped up a bucket and started filling, refilling, and delivering buckets down to the hold. It was slow-going, but she managed to bring down three buckets before Kit returned from Quarantine island to find her by the cook's fire boiling more water. Marissa glanced up as Kit entered the room with two more buckets. "Did you find a doctor?"

Kit responded by shaking his head into a no. "There's no one on the island right now, except the rest of your family and the guards. Your father wanted to take off to find a doctor, but they would not let him leave the island. They're sending someone from the guard station to take a message into the city, but they said it could take at least a couple of hours for a doctor to get to the ship."

Estela's brow furrowed. "By that time, it may be too late anyway. Is my father coming back?"

"Yes, as soon as he's dressed and ready."

It took three hours of hard labor before a little boy with a shock of black hair and bright copper eyes made a showing. Marissa inspected and cleaned him before bundling him in cloth and handing him to Miguel. The little boy lay completely still and quiet. "You have a strong little lad." Miguel's eyes glistened as he held him for the first time and then he gave a loving glance at Maria, "We have a boy. Another boy!" He croaked. Maria smiled weakly. She was still in great pain, but she was happy for Miguel. It could never make up for the loss of Paulo, but this little lad would surely bring hope.

Much to everyone's surprise, labor pains did not subside once the boy was born. Marissa was alarmed but tried not to show it. "Let me check inside." Marissa massaged Maria's stomach, but it did not give way; it remained hard, so she reached in to search for the after-birth, but instead, she came across a foot.

She looked at both Estela and Maria. "It seems you're having twins, my dear."

Maria was startled but quickly resigned. "Well, that explains it."

"Explains what?" Estela wondered.

"All the kicking and fighting. And why I'm so big this time."

Marissa was eager to get on with it. "I'm going to have to turn the baby around. It is coming down feet first. I'm going to be pushing on your stomach. Are you ready?" Maria flopped her head up and down. The pain was clawing its way through her, and she felt faint.

"Estela, come here and place your hand upon your mother's stomach. I want you to tell me where the head is." Estela slid her hand across her mother's belly and found a hard spot at the top of her stomach. "I think it's here."

"That's correct. Now, watch me turn this baby down. I will apply pressure along its back and buttocks while you lightly keep your hand on its head."

Marissa gently coaxed the baby downward, but it would not yield or budge. After a quarter of an hour, she declared "This baby definitely has a mind of its own. Even with its brother gone, it does not want to move out of position. We may just have to deliver it this way. Maria, you're going to need to hold on. Estela, take her hand and keep wiping her forehead with cold water."

Within the hour, the baby's bottom began to crown. Marissa gently reached in and maneuvered the baby to its side, so she could slide her hand across a thigh and pull the first leg down and out. She turned the baby to the other side to feel for the other leg when she felt resistance from a tiny but firm foot.

Marissa gave a start and then remarked, "One way or another, you're coming out!" Once the second leg was released, Marissa wrapped the baby's bottom with a cloth and then gently rotated it and applied downward pressure, as she felt for the shoulders and pulled out one arm after another.

"This one's a girl," she pronounced. Maria let out a sigh as she huffed and puffed. "Water, please!" Estela took a clean cloth, soaked it, and then touched it to Maria's lips.

"It won't be long now, Maria. Hold steady." Maria smiled weakly, as Marissa continued to coach her. "Remember, if you can make it around the Devil's Horns, you can make it through this." She turned to Estela with a meaningful glance. "Now, Estela, I'll need your help." Marissa grasped her two fingers around the babies neck over its shoulders with one hand and then placed her other hand on the other side along the baby's cheeks. "As I rotate the head, I want you to apply pressure to the lower stomach with a downward fist. Let me see your fist first." Estela lowered her hand and crimped it into a ball just above the lower abdomen.

"Perfect. Now not too hard. When I count to three, start applying pressure with your hand gently but firmly, just as if you were kneading dough." Estela started massaging her mother's abdomen. "Now, with a little more pressure." After several turns to its side, the baby's head was fully exposed and Marissa turned her over. At first, the little girl was quiet, and Estela caught her breath. "She's not breathing."

"Give me a second while I clear her passageways." Marissa cleaned her, turned her upside down, and gave her a wack. The baby girl let out a yowl so fierce and so vehement, it set her brother to crying. Now, both were crying, but it was music to their ears. The family let out a collective sigh and burst into applause. Marissa turned toward Maria, "You've got a lusty girl. There's nothing dainty about this one."

"Yes, it seems she'll no doubt be a good match for her brother." Maria broke into a grin and there were hugs all around. Maria turned to Estela, "Quickly! Go find your father."

By now, it was six o'clock in the morning. Miguel and Estela climbed up on deck to watch the sun peek out over the Honolulu horizon. As they took in a scene of golden glow with a fresh wind on their faces, Estela murmured half to herself, "Life is wonderful in spite of our sorrows. Don't you think *Pai*?"

Miguel smiled. "Yes, I do. No matter how dark the path we tread, we must always remember that we don't know what is around the next bend or over the next crest of a hill. There are mountains we must climb and rocky paths, but there is the hope of something better that keeps us moving forward. Even a glimpse of something beautiful sustains us on a road that shines ever brighter."

"And what road is that?" Estela examined her father, seeing that he had grown quiet and serious.

Miguel questioned her tenderly. "Why, don't you know?" He gazed back at the beautiful sunrise. "It's the road that leads us back to God."

"But why do we go backwards?"

"Because that is where we started and that is where we must finish."

It took three days before they started to think about naming the babies. Maria did not have the strength to think about it, so the girls sat around trying to agree, while Maria languished in bed as she nursed them. She could not find the strength to care at this point.

"Juvenal is a good solid name for a boy. He is strong; it will suit him well." Ida was insistent.

"But it is too common." Ana disagreed. "I like Carlos; it is a name fit for a king." Back and forth they argued, while Miguel was out making arrangements to transport them to Kauai. Estela spent her time trying to gather what was left of their things while she listened with half an ear. "What do you think Estela?" Ida was looking for an ally.

"I think we should let the day name him."

"And how does that make any sense?"

"Simply this, he was born on the Sabbath, a blessed day. He should be called Domingos. Which means he is a blessed baby."

The three sisters nodded in agreement. "What do you think *Mãe*?" Estela was trying to do everything she could to keep Maria engaged. Her spirits were waning and she was still very weak.

"I like it, but I think your father should make the final decision."

Estela walked over to her mother. "You've been in bed now for weeks. Why don't you let me take you up on deck, so you can get some fresh air? You have yet to see this beautiful paradise we are going to call home."

The other girls coaxed her, and they finally got her to agree to walk upstairs while Ana stayed with the twins. They helped her take a sponge bath, combed her hair, and provided her with a clean dress. Then they wrapped their arms on either side of her to help her upstairs.

The fresh air hit Maria with a blast of ocean spray. She gulped it in like one who has been submerged almost to the point of drowning, yet manages to come up for air just in time. And then she blinked, as her eyes adjusted to the light. The sky was bluer than she had ever seen, and the palms along the shore appeared to be greeting her in soft waves. Estela and Ida held her fast as she slowly surveyed the entire panorama. She spotted Diamond Head and murmured, "Your father was right. It is so like our islands."

"Can you see yourself making this our new home?" Estela encouraged her.

"Yes," she exhaled. "It is lovely." Just as they were taking it in, Miguel bounded up the gangway. Seeing the flush of red in Maria's cheeks, he gave way to a wide grin and enclosed her a big hug, lifting her up and twirling her around.

"So, what do you think, Maria. Is it not beautiful? Can you imagine being happy here?" Maria gave him a tired smile with a slow but steady nod.

"So, when do we make our way to the island where we will live? What is it called again?"

"Kauai — it is called Kauai, which means it is a garden paradise. I chose the garden island just for you. I have received a note from Juvenal Terra. They have secured lodgings right next door to us." Miguel held out one brief paragraph written on a single piece of paper. "He says we have plenty of garden space and our own outdoor brick oven for baking. We can even raise pigs and chickens. What do you think? Shall we have a feast to celebrate together when we get there?"

"Oh *Pai*! That sounds perfect." Ida was cheered by the idea.

The next day they were packed and on their way across the ocean heading to Kauai. Miguel produced the IOU from his new employer. Ida and Ana followed, carrying the twins in baskets. Domingos in one basket and the little baby girl they had yet to name in the other. Domingos lay quiet and content during the entire journey, while the baby girl wailed endlessly.

"It is clear that this one does not like the bumpy ride," observed Ana. Maria shook her head. "She will learn soon enough that life is full of bumps." Maria was not in a mood to tolerate a fussy baby. She was already training Ida and Ana to care for them, but they did not mind. Except for feeding time, they enjoyed doing everything they could for the twins.

It was no easy matter finding their way to the harbor where they would meet the schooner that would transport them to the next island. Kit plied a local farmer who provided an ox cart to take them to their boat. They crowded into the back, covered with hay and straw, and kept company with two very grotesque hogs. It took them all night to reach Hanalei Bay and all the next morning until they were finally settled into their new home.

CHAPTER 33

1909, Santa Clara, Flatfooted Luana

After the Alum Rock picnic and Julia's return to the cannery, Roger's attentions to Julia became a much-discussed topic of conversation within Valley social circles, especially among members of the Mirante and McCallum families. Even Julia could no longer deny Roger's attentions, but she would not speak of it, and no one dared broach the subject with her. Wherever Julia went, Roger seemed to pop up from nowhere. He began to visit his grandmother more often in hopes of seeing her, and he became a regular patron at the *Serradura*. Roger even ingratiated himself with her Uncle Domo by inviting him to weekly card games with his ranch hands.

When Domingos started assuming airs because of his relationship with Roger, it irritated Luana to no end. On one occasion, when she overheard Domingos bragging to some of his friends who were regulars at the *Serradura*, she confronted him. "Honestly, Domo, you've grown such a big head, I can't see anything behind or around you!"

"What do you mean, big head? What are you talking about?"

"You bragging about smoking cigars and drinking brandy with Roger McCallum. I heard you. Don't try to deny it."

Domingos snorted his indignation, "Why can't a man enjoy a good cigar and brandy and even enjoy talking about it, eh little Kokomo?"

Luana stopped her work, flattened her hand on the tip of her broom, and double-slashed him with a stare. "Don't you call me Kokomo! Don't you dare." It was a moniker he had tagged on her back when they lived in Kauai, and he knew better than to press the matter, so he skulked to the other side of the room where he continued to hold court with his friends.

Earlier that day, Roger had been in the *Serradura* sporting with Domingos and his crowd like long lost soldiers regaling each other with stories of their manly endeavors. Roger had dropped his reserve and embraced this lively crowd, even though he did not speak Portuguese; they accommodated him by sticking to English in his presence.

Roger also sensed Luana's proximity to Julia and frequently roped her into conversation by complimenting her business acumen and culinary skills. "Luana, no one can make malasadas like you can. What is your secret?"

Luana glanced up from her work to see Roger seated down at the end of the counter. She was about to make a sarcastic reply, but then she thought the better of it. To Luana, Roger's interest in Julia was his one redeeming quality, even if she did not really trust him. The truth was that when it came to men, she trusted only Miguel and Domingos. At one time, it had been rumored in their little town that Luana was disappointed in love. She had laughed to herself when she first heard it. "No one can stand the thought of a woman who is neither heartbroken over a man or tethered to one. No one can believe that a woman may simply want to be left alone, that she is smart enough to know she is better off on her own."

Her thoughts turned again to Roger. "The secret is in the butter. I make it myself. It has to be fresh."

"Ahh! Fresh-churned butter - nothing like it." He spoke with a twinkle in his eye. "All you need is your own dairy."

Luana wondered how he could have hit on a subject that was so close to her heart, not knowing that Domingos had told Roger all about Luana's hopes of buying a dairy. Roger could be charming, when he wanted to be, but Luana was chary when it came to charming men. She always assumed the worst about the intentions of any man until they proved themselves otherwise. He understood this about her and pressed her further.

"Why don't you wrap me up a dozen of your freshest malasadas pastries to take home with me?" Now she was impressed; with Luana, greenbacks spoke more loudly than flattering words. "You got it! Coming right up."

As she headed towards the back ovens, she thought about her conversation with Gilberto the prior year, when she had promised Rose she would ask him about the relationship between Marcos and Roger. She was hanging out at Jake's Place in the Mud Hen Slough when she spotted Marcos's cousin Gilberto on a stool gazing into a glass of whiskey. He appeared as though he had gulped down a few already, so she figured it was a good time to broach the subject.

Straddling the seat next to him, Luana had picked up on his reflective mood and launched into an inquisition. "So, tell me about Marcos and the McCallums. What's the story?"

"Story? What makes you think there's a story?" He shrugged her off.

"Everyone knows that Marcos did not leave the McCallum ranch on the best of terms."

"That's ancient history. Now, tell me something I don't know."

Luana shifted her approach as she twirled the golden liquid in her glass. "If it was so long ago and it does not matter anymore, then why is there so much animosity between Roger and Marcos, now that the father is no longer around?"

Detecting Luana's eager curiosity, Gilbert locked into her gaze with a sideways glance and a shrug. "Look Luana, Marcos's beef was never with the son. It was the old man who let Marcos go without proof that the accusations against him were true."

"And yet, it's pretty clear that there's no love lost between Roger and Marcos. Rose told me all about it. She saw them glaring at each other when Marcos picked them up from the cannery one day."

Gilberto shook his head. "Luana, for such a shrewd woman, you sure can be blind sometimes."

Luana blenched and swiveled around on him with an intense look. "What are you talking about?"

"I'm talking about Julia."

"What does Julia have to do with any of this?"

Gilberto gulped his last splash of whiskey and set it down as a signal for another pour. "Just about everything." He turned to show her the twinkle in his eye.

Her eyes narrowed at him like a cat ready to pounce. "What are you getting at? Prove it."

"All right, explain to me why Julia was the only one Marcos asked to dance at the Alum Rock picnic. And why Roger glared at them from across the room, or didn't you catch that?"

Now, it was Gilberto's turn to examine Luana closely. He couldn't help but think how adorable she was when she was losing an argument. Luana sat tongue-tied, realizing she was caught flatfooted. Gilberto took advantage of her silence to rub it in.

"And why does Marcos still ride with Julia every chance he gets, even though he doesn't have to anymore? Did you notice the way he practically gave her his prize stallion?"

Luana's eyes dilated, as if she had been staring into the sun for too long. She turned sharply on Gilberto. "And you think Roger McCallum knows this?"

Gilberto toasted her with his next pour, "Bravo!" Luana had never felt so foolish. How was it that she had never seen it? Gilberto could only smile, as he watched the deliciously cute and dumbfounded look that dawned upon Luana's face. When she first came to California, Gilberto had admired Luana, but he had long since realized that falling in love with her was a risky endeavor, something akin to loving a baby cougar. He concluded that it was alright to look but never get too close.

Luana stood pondering this conversation with Gilberto, as she wrapped a fresh batch of malasadas pastries for Roger McCallum. She could not decide which man she would choose for Julia. Both Marcos and Roger were attractive, active men, but Roger was the most successful. Even so, she had to admit Marcos was practically family, and she knew that he had a good heart, but she could not be so sure of Roger's heart. The entire subject left Luana flustered. After Roger left that day, she made up her mind to find the right moment to prod Marcos for his feelings on the subject.

Olivia never forgot the letter she had sent to Abbie by way of Roger, even though it had been several years. When he returned from visiting Abbie on that autumn day when Olivia first gave it to him, Olivia interrogated him. "What did she say when you gave her the letter? How did she look? What was her reaction?"

This only reinforced Roger's first impression that there was something unkind or even sinister in the letter, so he side-stepped her question by simply stating, "I never saw her read it." He then turned his back on her. Roger was relieved when his mother did not ask if he had delivered it into Olivia's hands. He never liked the idea of lying to his mother. From his earliest years, he had developed a healthy fear of her, as he witnessed his father doing end-runs around her.

Olivia was puzzled by Abbie's lack of a response, but when confronted with the possibility that she would have to carry out her threats to expose Abbie, Olivia thought the better of it. For the first time, she considered that it might embarrass her children to spread scandal about her husband's family. She also realized that her son would be the likely beneficiary of any remaining property in Abbie's possession, and as such, she encouraged Roger's visits to her.

Olivia's ambitions had to course into a different direction, so she became singularly focused on Roger's marriage prospects. She was determined that he would marry a young woman of high society and wealth. While Roger was her primary focus, she also invested most of her energies in making advantageous matches for all of her children. The day after the Alum Rock picnic, she gave voice to her feelings at the morning breakfast table regarding Roger's attentions to Julia.

"Honestly, Roger, how could you be so obvious? The whole town is marveling at your choice of a dance partner. Surely you have better taste than that?" Roger remained silent, while his sisters joined their mother in heaping insults upon Julia.

Still smarting from her failure to attract Marcos's attention at the dance, Celesta volleyed the second insult. "Why, she's a common cannery worker in one of our factories and has no real talent for anything. How could you even consider her?"

Susanna added insult to Celesta's injury. "And did you see those dresses she and her sister were wearing? So out of date and obviously homemade!" Both girls tittered while Roger took up a newspaper to cut them off.

The three women glanced at one another when they realized they were not getting through to him. They continued to heap insults on Julia for another quarter of an hour, until Roger had enough. He calmly folded the newspaper and pushed himself away from the table. From a standing position he gave off a triumphant air, as he looked down on them and said what they all suspected and feared.

"You're wrong about Julia. She's intelligent and kind, and she's the most talented horsewoman in the Valley. As strong and beautiful as her black stallion."

He turned and left them incredulous, all knowing that the topic had not been exhausted.

Luana watched from the porch swing as Marcos entered the barn at the end of the day. When she walked in, she found him rubbing down the horses. He glanced up at her but did not speak.

"Marcos. Frank was asking for you. Can you come by for dinner tonight?"

"Of course."

Marcos was surprised to see Luana take up a brush and start grooming the horse next to him, while Luana searched for a way to engage him. She knew that Marcos was a deep well with many secrets and that one must respect that deep well and approach it carefully, if one was to draw water.

Now that she thought about it, she could not think of any woman who had ever interested Marcos, at least not as far as she could tell. Yet, she knew that there were many young women who were interested in him. He sometimes came to Jake's Place, but he was a man's man who always kept his cards close. When young women approached Marcos, he was friendly but kept them at arm's length. If there were any women in his life, he kept it to himself.

Marcos interrupted her thoughts. "Since when did you take an interest in horses?"

"Are you kidding? I used to break horses with the paniolos in Kauai."

"You knew paniolos?" Marcos stopped and studied her for a moment. "But most of them work on the big island. Didn't you come from Kauai?"

"Knew them? I practically was one. And no, they weren't all on the big island. Some came to Kauai."

Marcos shook his head in disbelief. "But that makes no sense. You hardly ever ride anymore, let alone break in horses. Why not?"

Luana was taken aback. She had come in to ferret out his secrets, and now he was putting his finger on one of hers. "Let's just say that by the time I left the islands, I had had my fill of paniolos and their horses."

Marcos hung his arms over a golden palomino with a slightly puckish grin on his face, as he put two and two together. "Why, Luana, I think you were once in love with a paniolo, weren't you?"

This was too much for Luana, who was determined that no man would ever get the best of her, not in verbal combat or in love. She decided to change the subject and take a more direct approach. She popped her head back at him with a challenge. "Not as much as you love Julia."

As soon as her words had landed, she regretted it. Marcos's welkin eyes could freeze boiling water; they were such a deep pool. He quietly finished his work and left her in silence. Luana could see that she had hit his soft spot, but if she wanted to know more, she would now have to approach him through a back door, and that back door would have to be Gilberto.

CHAPTER 34

1878, Kauai, Christmas

Five months passed on their garden island, and the Mirantes were still endeavoring to make it feel like home. They drudged and sighed their days away, sometimes under a downpour of sticky rain and sometimes under a downpour of their own sweat. Their bodies grew sleek and hard and brown as a roasted baru nut. Their only relief from the rays of a merciless sun came when the south-easterly winds would sough through the Kukui trees at night, as the Koloa Maoli ducks nattered from the marshes.

The highlight of their day was when the sun descended upon the horizon, while pasting pink and orange ribbons above the cobalt waters. Everyone collectively stopped and sucked in their breath at the sight of it; in the Azores, none of them had ever beheld such supernal artistry in the skies. They rarely stayed inside for long. Outdoor living so captivated them that they no longer knew how to exist indoors. After long days and nights cramped inside the belly of a bark, they were like butterflies set free from their cocoons.

Coconuts dropped everywhere, and they learned to hack and pop them open, then imbue themselves with their life-giving substances. The children were warned to be careful in case an errant coconut dropped on their heads. They kept one eye upward and one eye across the horizon, as they played feet unshod among the sugar cane fields, forming protective calluses against the cane refuse.

Mangoes and guava were staples at every meal. What the children could not pilfer from the kitchen or garden, they learned to dredge from the rich soil and pluck from the carapace: oysters, macadamia nuts, cashews, berries, Java plums, breadfruit. The men and boys spent their Sundays fishing with the natives, learning to navigate the strong currents, while adopting Polynesian words and new ways to fish and dive for shellfish.

The journey from the ship to their new grass-thatched house had been an arduous one. There had been no place to dock when they landed, so they hauled all of their belongings down a ladder from the schooner to canoes and then to a sandy shore. A wicker bird cage, doves and rabbits, violas, an accordion, and Miguel's braguinha were cluttered among their clothing, bedding, lanterns, pots, and pans.

After climbing and canoeing their way to shore, they waited five hours for an ox cart to carry them and all their worldly goods. The cart accommodated just one person squeezed in with household goods and two hogs. For most of the twenty mile journey through prairies of high grass, Maria and the twins joggled in the back, while baby girl Mirante screamed.

They had yet to name the girl, and when asked by the inspectors to provide a name for her birth certificate, Maria replied, "just write down 'baby girl' Mirante." Maria was so dispirited upon arrival that it took them three days to name the girl. The rest of the family competed to find the perfect name, but Maria took little interest.

"It's clear she has grit," Miguel offered, after they had settled into their four-room thatched roof cottage alongside the Terra family.

"And she's strong as our ox." Estela unwrapped the blankets she had been crocheting for the twins. The first one was green and she gave it to Domingos. She was just getting started on the second, and she had yet to decide on the color. "Well, I have yellow, green, and red. What do you think?" She spoke absent-mindedly for anyone who might be listening.

"Red, definitely red," Ida offered. "That girl is a little fireball."

"But what shall we name her?" Estela was miffed that the baby was three days old and still without a name.

Miguel glanced over at the little ball of fire who was flailing for a twine of yarn like a boatswain after a stubborn mooring line. He gently got up to place it in her hand, but the little one screamed at any attempt to do anything for her.

As Miguel sat back down, he spoke thoughtfully, "I think we should choose a Polynesian name, maybe one that sounds like a Portuguese name we already know."

"I overheard one of our neighbors calling her sister, Luana, and I thought it sounded pretty," Ida chimed in.

"It reminds me of my mother Lorena who passed away; it's musical sounding and my mother loved to sing." Miguel sighed wistfully.

"It's a strong name. I like that about it as well." Maria finally spoke, and her comments gave a sense of finality to the matter.

"That's it then. We'll just have to call her Luana." Miguel confirmed what they were already thinking. "Domingos and Luana."

"Or rather Luana and Domingos, even if Domo was born first," laughed Ida.

By Christmas time, Luana was worming in the dirt outside the chicken pens. As she learned to crawl, she pushed herself off the ground feet first, wiggling after the hens, gasping in delight as she chivvied them, until they squawked and flapped to get away. It was a sound that always produced a spasm of giggles from Luana. Whenever she was not after the hens, Luana would grasp a feather or pull Domingos' hair. She loved to play with his thick dark curls; they were a mirror image of her own. Domingos never retaliated; he was always happy to accommodate his twin.

No one ever thought to cut the twins' hair or anyone's hair. They tried to look like islanders with cocoa brown skin and long glossy dark locks. After awhile, Ana decided it was time to braid and tie back Luana's unruly mane, but every day when the time came, Luana whined and squirmed to free herself from their clutches.

"You hold her, while I tie," suggested Ida the first time. Ana grasped the squirming toddler while Ida quickly and expertly plashed Luana's unyielding locks. When the task was done, the girls signed with relief, as the toddler squirmed her way after more chickens.

The girls had been in school since the end of the harvest season and were learning to read English. Each night they read stories to each other in front of the fire. Estela took on odd jobs after school around the plantation while Ida and Ana spent their time taking care of the twins for Maria, who had not fully recovered from the long journey and the birth of the twins. She was given a pass on plantation work, due to the recent birth of the twins, but at some point, even she would be expected to work on the plantation.

At the end of their workday "pau hana," the women cultivated their gardens with varieties of potatoes, kuala beans, corn, breadfruit, ohia apples, and figs. They also managed to cultivate peppers and garlic for Portuguese sausages and their favorite holiday pork, carne Vinho d'alhos. The Mirantes and Terras also shared milk cows, pigs, and hens.

Unfortunately, the hens did not always cooperate. It was a good day when everyone ate one egg for breakfast instead of mush. The women were in a constant state of anxiety over the number of eggs they would need to bake sweet bread for Christmas, so they began stashing them in pails of cold water. During the final days leading up to Christmas, their families were sustained on mush and poi, a food they had disdained to eat at first. They soon grew accustomed to it, because it filled their stomachs and strengthened them for the long work days.

Maria and Marissa noticed that native women were more successful at egg harvesting and decided to ask for advice. Marissa approached a neighbor by the name of Oliana, who was born on the island. "What is your secret to hen laying? How do you find their nests before the eggs hatch?" With a wink and a smile, Oliana showed her the secret.

The next day, Marissa gathered the Mirante girls together with Sonia and Sophie, and sent them on an egg-hunting mission. She brought them out to the coop where she fed the hens using scraps from the breakfast table. "Now watch this." She cupped her hands around a hen who had just finished eating and held tight, while it flapped. The longer she held it, the more frantic the hen became. "Whatever you do, hold on. Don't let go right away."

The flapping and shrieking escalated while the girls' eyes grew wider. "Get ready to run." As soon as she set the hen on the ground, it took off and Maria motioned them to follow. "You cannot lose a second, or you will never find the hen in the underbrush."

The girls ran after her in rapid succession, leaving a trail of flattened brush in their wake, until Marissa stopped and burrowed her hands down into the brush. They heard the hen clack and scream. Then Marissa bounced up and triumphantly held up two plump eggs, "And that is how it's done!"

"But why did the hen run to her nest?" Ana wanted to know.

"It is the first place they will go when they are frightened or upset. They instinctively look for a way to protect their young when they feel threatened. So, that is how you find their nests," said Marissa.

Within a week, they were well prepared for Christmas baking and eating significantly less poi. They were planning their holiday with a rare degree of enthusiasm. They created new traditions, while infusing old ones with a Polynesian touch. It was important to all the Portuguese that they assimilate without losing their cherished beliefs and culture.

This first Christmas, almost every decoration and costume would have to be created from scratch, using as much ingenuity as their environment could provide. They spent their evenings with the Terra family creating holiday costumes and decorations. They decided they would enjoy their Christmas meals and celebrations together.

"Marissa, how many eggs have you been able to gather for our sweet bread?" Maria inquired.

"Thanks to our secret method, we have more than enough, but I think we could gather even more if we could find a way to keep the dogs away from the underbrush."

"I can build a fence around that area to keep the dogs out," offered Miguel. He turned to Francisco. "Paulo, why don't you help me?" Maria bristled at the sound of Paulo's name.

Francisco was sitting on the floor in a corner, teasing and playing games with Luana. He would take her yarn doll and hide it behind his back and then provoke her to come get it. This was a game she could play for hours. She never minded when she could not find the doll, as long as she could hold his attention.

Francisco, of course, loved to tease her and would move the doll from one hand to the other behind his back. As she crawled around him, gasping and squealing, he would slide it back into his lap. It provided amusement for a short period of time until he announced the end of the game by handing it back to her. She adored him no matter what he did, but she was clearly the only one.

Francisco did not like being called Paulo, and he was never comfortable when he was with the family. The mother would not look at him or speak to him. He knew he was not wanted. The sisters were barely polite and only spoke to him when they had to. He came in for his meals and then left as soon as it was polite to do so. Francisco often slept with the single men in their camp, where the men played dice and cards. At fourteen, he was quickly learning island ways. At other times he slept in the open air. He was used to sleeping under the stars and had come to prefer it.

For his part, Miguel did everything he could to make the boy feel at home, knowing how other family members felt about him. By inviting Francisco to join in, Miguel was hoping that there would be more opportunity for the girls to get to know him. Perhaps they could be friends. His every attempt seemed to fail, as it became clear that neither the boy or his daughters viewed their situation as either desirable or permanent.

Maria sat sewing and never glanced up as she tried to cover over the awkward moment, "How will we create our costumes for this New Year's eve celebration?"

"We've already thought of that, *Mãe*. We were able to save some paper from our school work to make animal heads for our dance," replied Ida.

"And we brought our white robes to wear with them," added Estela. "We could even wear our nightgowns underneath." On New Year's eve, they planned to don their costumes and serenade their neighbors from cottage to cottage.

Ana and the Terra twins sat on the floor making a nativity set out of straw, wood, palm leaves, and rocks. "We will have our *Boas Festas*, even though we are so far from our home, and nothing will cloud our joy," Estela declared as she lifted up a tiny manger.

The girls exhausted their creative energies to create the *lapinha*. They surrounded the nativity scene with tiers of muslin to make an altar, including a grotto made of rocks. Each family member was expected to contribute to the altar. Offerings would include fruits and flowers. Sonia and Sophia added banana leaves to make a tropical backdrop. Once they were finished, they surveyed the scene, which held a prominent position in their somewhat small living area.

Maria clapped her hands together. "We must add some light. A small candle perhaps." Ana rushed to retrieve two small candles to surround the manger, and the scene was complete. As they all sat gazing at the scene in surprised wonder, Miguel lightly strummed his braguinha, and they sang the Christmas songs of The Azores. Even Maria could not help but feel comforted by the familiar scene.

Once Francisco had left the house that evening, Maria whispered her disapproval to Miguel through clenched teeth, "Must you call that boy Paulo? Need I be reminded of my son in such a way?" A bitterness had lodged itself deep in her heart, and it was blocking out the love that had always come so easily in times past.

"I only call him that so that I am in the habit. I don't want to slip up in front of others. It's only to protect the boy."

Maria turned away and muttered, "Just try not to do it in front of me. Call him by his given name in my presence." She could not even manage to say his given name, while Miguel shrugged away from her. He had become too accustomed to her brackishness, and it cast a shadow over their new life.

The next day was Sunday and Miguel listened for the "wagon man," who brought them food and goods from around the island. Miguel had ordered spices to make marinated pork, a dish known as *Vinho d'Alhos*. Maria waited to buy fruit, which she would add to the produce she grew in the garden. By mid-day on Sunday Miguel heard the familiar clang that signaled the arrival of the red wagon. He was not the only one waiting and listening. Others gathered around to gather similar ingredients for their Christmas festas.

After dropping chunks of pork into jars, Miguel added his special marinade: vinegar, peppers, garlic, pearl onions, and salt. The jars sat on the kitchen shelf next to the garlic-spiced linguica sausages hooked and dangling from the ceiling. The sausages had been smoked in the outside brick ovens for hours after being stuffed with garlic and red peppers.

Maria spent her day either in the kitchen or out among the brick ovens baking sweet bread. She and Marissa produced the glossy loaves in a variety of shapes and sizes, some intwined, some rounded and spliced through the center, and some elongated.

All the children gathered around them as she lifted out her prize loaf, shaped like the Christmas angel. It was Maria's proudest Christmas achievement. She intentionally set the loaves down on the highest shelf in the kitchen to cool and then lay down to take a nap while Ida and Ana took care of the twins.

When she awoke, the angel loaf was on the floor with Luana hovering over it: crumbles in her hair, cake-smashed face, gumming her way through it. Ida and Ana were nowhere to be found, but Francisco was in the living area, waiting for his dinner. When Maria spotted him, she immediately assumed the worst and confronted him.

"I suppose you know those loaves were for our holiday celebrations." Hands on hips, she pounced, refusing to give him any opportunity to respond. "Do you know how long it took me to make that angel?" Francisco turned mute. "You're a thief, a plain, ordinary thief. You stole your passageway and you stole my son's place. Now, you steal my food? After all that we've done to save your neck? How dare you, boy. How dare you." Maria flashed at him.

Just as she finished, Miguel came in from outside. "What is going on?" Maria pointed to Francisco. "Go look at what he did to the Christmas angel, and you'll know everything you need to know."

Miguel glanced into the kitchen, startled to see two wide-eyed and innocent eyes surrounded in angel crumbs. By the time Miguel turned back to talk to Francisco, the boy had disappeared. Maria had also disappeared.

Miguel reached for Luana, picked her up, and cleaned her off. When he had finished, Ana and Ida came in from the garden. "Can you girls explain to me how Luana got to the Christmas angel?" By the looks on their faces, he could tell that they were not entirely ignorant. "What happened?"

Ida spoke up first. "Well, we wanted to get a closer look at it, so we took it down from the top shelf and placed it on the stool. At the same time, the pigs got out of the garden, so we ran after them. The rest you could probably guess."

"Was Francisco here when you took it down from the shelf?"

"No. We haven't seen him."

"Where was Luana?" Both girls responded with a shrug. "I need you to keep a closer eye on her. She can be lost in the brush or bit by a rat in the wink of an eye. Is that understood?" Two heads bolted up and down. Miguel mustered up his courage and searched for Maria, who was in the garden gathering vegetables.

Maria shot him a fighting glance, "I warned you about that boy. He's no good."

"You're wrong Maria. He had nothing to do with Luana getting to the Christmas angel. You didn't even bother to ask before you accused him."

"What do you mean? He was the only one around."

"I asked the girls. They took the angel down to look at it. At the same time, the pigs got out of their pen, and the girls ran after them. That's when Luana found the angel. Francisco came in after that. He was never even in the kitchen." Maria moped into a sheepish and resentful manner.

"Now, I'm just asking you, at the very least, you can be fair to the boy. You don't have to treat him like a son. Just be fair to him. Will you promise to at least try?" Maria remained reluctant. As she tried to brush past him, he gently grabbed her arm. "Promise?" She nodded ever so slightly, but he could see the effort it cost her.

CHAPTER 35

1910, Santa Clara, Carnival of Roses

The following spring Abbie's garden came into full bloom. Julia came up with a detailed garden plan, and Abbie spared no expense to carry it out. Abbie's servant, Howard, was in charge of ordering all the supplies, trees, and plants. Work crews cleared the brush and dead trees and overturned the long-neglected soil, while another work crew repaired the fencing. Even Howard joined in the planting and pruning.

Twenty new pear and plum trees encircled the garden and popped open with pink and white blossoms. There were a grand total of fifty new rose trees and bushes that included fifteen different varieties attracting a bevy of hummingbirds and bees. The neighbors noticed the unexpected activity at the old house and peered nosily into the back garden to figure out what could have induced the old woman to rejuvenate the decrepit place.

On a brilliant April day, Abbie lay on a lounge chair overlooking her new garden, while Julia chased a croquet ball through a thread of hoops surrounded by erupting crocuses, hollyhocks, and roses. Julia knocked a croquet ball through a hoop and commented absent-mindedly, "What do you say we enter some of these roses in the Carnival of Roses parade, maybe even decorate a float with them? It would be one way to put it to good use. All we need is a car or a horse-drawn carriage."

Abbie pointed to the old barn at the back of her property. "I'll supply the carriage and driver if you supply the horses."

Julia bounced up with bright eyes. "Are you serious? You have a carriage? Can I see it?" When Julia made the suggestion she was half-joking so she was surprised at Abbie's ready response.

"I'll send for Howard to open the barn." Abbie rang the bell and Howard came out with the tea tray. While Howard went for the key, Julia came up with more ideas. "We'll need help if we're going to decorate in time for the parade. I could ask my sister Rose to help with the cuttings and the decorations. It would give her a great deal of pleasure. Would you mind?"

Abbie lay back to warm her face under the sun, and then she shaded her eyes as she glanced over at Julia and responded languidly. "Of course. Do whatever you like. It'll be your special project."

Julia paused to think about it and then proposed another idea. "And of course, you will ride in your carriage along the parade route." It was not a question. Abbie's face retracted. Julia could see that the thought of appearing in public was a struggle for Abbie; she had been a recluse for so long. Just at that moment, Roger arrived. Having overheard Julia's comment, he sprang into the conversation without fully understanding Julia's proposal.

"And I will ride next to you of course!" Abbie looked up, startled, as Roger gave her his hand and a peck on the cheek. Julia smiled at the thought, knowing that Abbie would be more inclined to ride in the parade if her grandson was at her side. Abbie did not demur in response.

"And Rose and I will escort you on horseback," Julia offered.

"On a black stallion by any chance?" Roger winked at Julia, as if they were involved in a secret conspiracy. It was a wink that Abbie could not help noticing, and for the first time, it occurred to her that Roger had more than one reason for his frequent visits. The thought did not unsettle her; in fact, she admired his taste. She had grown very fond of Julia and enjoyed her as if she was the daughter she had never had. Roger's interest in Julia made her think more highly of him.

As soon as Howard appeared with the keys, Julia hurried off to the barn, excited to see just what kind of carriage they would be decorating. Roger followed. The carriage was tucked in the back corner of the barn and covered with old rugs and sheets. Roger helped Howard pull them away to reveal a nineteenth century white Scottish barouche with a retractable cover. Julia gasped and clapped her hands together; she could not have been more delighted.

"It's perfect. Absolutely perfect. But will it work?"

Roger was pleased that she was pleased and assured her that he would do whatever it took to make it work. "Yes, I vaguely remember playing on this when we were children. It needs a bit of sprucing up, but I think that, with Howard's help, we can have it looking very fine in no time."

Roger inspected the wheels and turned to Howard. "I'll send over my blacksmith. He happens to be very good with carriages and cars. Anything that runs on wheels, in fact."

Howard sported an energetic grin. He couldn't help asking. "And who will drive the carriage in the parade?"

"Well you, of course. If you're up to the task, that is."

Howard's grin grew wider. It was not often that his job involved a bit of fun. Julia, anxious to work out the details with Abbie, left the barn immediately to take tea with her and make plans.

"It's beautiful. Like something out of a fairy tale." Julia spoke brightly as she raised a teacup. "Where did it come from?" Roger could not help but enjoy her childlike wonder and made up his mind to ensure the endeavor was successful.

Abbie began reminiscing. "We sent away for it to Scotland when we first moved into this place. It had belonged to my parents, and they no longer had any use for it. It took awhile to get it here, but it was worth the effort. George put a good deal of money into making it one of the finest carriages in the Valley."

This is the first time Julia had ever heard Abbie mention her husband's name. She wanted to know more but did not press the issue. "Are you sure we're not too late to enter it in the parade?"

"Well, I was a member of the Santa Clara County Rose Society for many years, and I think I may still know a few people there. I don't expect it will be a problem. I'll make the necessary inquiries."

"I hear there will be an aviation show that day in addition to the carnival." Howard interjected as he carried out another pot of tea.

"That ought to make for quite a spectacle." Roger commented.

"Yes, what a day it will be." Abbie spoke airily. Julia had never seen Abbie so enthusiastic about anything and she savored the moment.

"We'll have to plan ahead to keep the roses fresh for the parade." Julia was thinking out loud about everything they would need to make their entry a prize winner. "I wonder when the carriage must be ready? And where will we get the right horses to draw the carriage?"

Roger piped up. "No need to worry. I'll have the carriage and the horses just in time. We'll even take a spin around town ahead of time to ensure that everything works properly."

"Yes, it will be an exciting day, but you're forgetting something. What about the evening?" Abbie interjected with a twinkle in her eyes.

Roger looked quizzically at Abbie, "What about the evening?"

"You're forgetting the Women's Auxiliary ball. People from miles around will go home after the carnival and get dressed up in their finest." Abbie glanced wistfully away, as if she were remembering another time. She turned back to Julia. "Have you ever been, Julia?"

Julia looked up in surprise. "No, never. I have never been in a ballroom for that matter. I wouldn't even know what to wear or how to dance."

"Well then, that settles it. You absolutely must go."

Julia cupped her hand under her chin. "Oh, no. I have nothing to wear that would be suitable."

"Don't you worry about that, young lady. I have plenty of gowns that we can tailor to your taste. For your sister, as well. You must go together. My dear, this is the time of life to enjoy such things. Roger, you will escort them, won't you?"

"It will be my pleasure."

A week before the Carnival of Roses, Julia stood with Rose in Abbie's dressing room as a local seamstress adjusted their ball gowns. Julia's lavender silk taffeta gown was overlaid with three tiers of lace sewn with seeded pearls. The sheer sleeves were gathered slightly off-shoulder around a décolleté neckline. Abbie circled her to inspect the tailoring.

"It fits beautifully, and the color is perfect on you," she pronounced. "All we had to do was remove those exaggerated bustles to give them a more modern look." She turned to her seamstress, "Mary, you did a beautiful job. Thank you so much."

Julia could see that Abbie enjoyed dressing them up. She did not mind being Abbie's project, and it was evident that Abbie had once had quite an eye for fashion. Abbie also had a wardrobe that could fill a museum. When she and Rose were first admitted to her dressing room, they were astounded by the parade of Victorian gowns, some clearly imported from France.

As she peered in the mirror, Julia had to admit that the smoky lavender suited her in a way she had not expected. "They call that shade of lavender "moon dust," Abbie informed her. "It's perfect next to your pale skin and dark eyes." As Julia gazed at herself in the mirror, she was taken aback to realize she was looking at a full grown woman. It was the first time she had ever truly seen herself.

"Our Mama will want to see these," Rose spoke up. "Can we take them home and get ready there?" Abbie had chosen a gold brocade gown over white silk for Rose, which she adored. Rose had not been this excited since her Mama had given her a cocker spaniel puppy on her thirteenth birthday.

"Yes, of course," Abbie smiled. "I'll have Howard pick you up and bring you here. We can toast together and then Roger will escort you to the ball in the carriage."

True to his word, Roger had the carriage ready five days before the carnival. Rose and Julia accompanied Roger, as Howard drove them to Saratoga for lunch. "We certainly don't want this thing to break down in the middle of a parade," Roger chuckled. "It would be a real show-stopper. But I am quite certain that my man will put it in tip top shape. Even gave it a new paint job."

It was a light and breezy day, and the newly restored carriage drew stares from all directions. Roger worked at gaining Rose's good graces by entertaining her with lively stories along the way. On the way back from lunch, he made them both a proposal.

"Rather than riding on horseback, I have an idea that you two should accompany my grandmother and me in the carriage on the parade route. You can sit across from us in the barouche. What do you think?"

Rose and Julia looked at each other and nodded their assent; the idea was appealing to both of them. Later when they returned to his grandmother's house, Roger repeated his proposal and gained immediate approval from Abbie, who could not have been more pleased.

"You know, this is not just a Carnival of Roses," Abbie remarked. "It's a contest."

"Contest? For what?" Rose spoke inquiringly.

"For the most exotic bonnet. The women love to wear their bonnets decorated with ribbons and roses. A competition to see who can come up with the most unique creations.

"Is there a prize for the best bonnet?"

"No, actually. It's what you might call an unspoken contest."

"I don't think we have any bonnets that would do." Rose was disappointed. The idea of bonnet decorating appealed to her.

"Then step up into my attic and let's take a look at my collection." They ascended a third story staircase, and Abbie took out a key to open the attic area located in one of the turrets. True to Abbie's word, she possessed an astonishing array of bonnets from various time periods. "It won't be difficult to find something quite unique in here."

Rose and Julia spent an hour trying on bonnets. With Abbie's help, they also picked out sundresses and parasols that would go well with their selections. "There's just enough time to alter these dresses to fit you," Abbie offered.

For two days they decorated the carriage and their bonnets with pink and white roses in a variety of shades. Every inch of the barouche was covered in roses, down to each spoke of the carriage wheels. On the morning of the parade, the women wore pink, while Howard and Roger wore white with pink roses at their lapels and in the bands of their straw hats. French Lace, Lady of the Dawn, Brigadoon, Moonstone, and Double Delights cascaded from the barouche and from their bonnets.

As Anarosa helped Julia and Rose dress on the morning of the parade, she harried them with instructions on how to behave. It had not escaped her notice that Julia was a favorite of Roger McCallum's and that he was doing her a great honor by escorting her to the parade and the ball. She was already bragging to her friends that her daughter would be the richest woman in the County.

When the subject first came up with Frank, he voiced his concerns. "It does not seem appropriate that my daughters go to a ball with a man we have not met. They must be accompanied by one of their brothers."

Rose and Julia did not object and informed Roger that he would be picking up three Mirantes on the night of the ball, including their brother Alexio. Roger was happy to oblige. Alexio had to buy formal wear for the first time and take dancing lessons, which put him in an ill humor for weeks.

As Anarosa fumbled with twenty five buttons at the back of each parade dress, it gave her time to give the girls a good talking to. "Be sure to sit up straight and don't gobble and slurp your food down or talk with your mouth open."

"Oh Mama. Really? You'd think we were both twelve years old the way you speak to us."

"I'll not be having it said that my girls don't know how to be ladylike. You must try to make a good impression."

"Really, Mama, have you no faith in the way you've raised us so far?"

Anarosa flushed with a perturbed grimace, "Of course. But a few reminders is what you need once in awhile."

The girls had been taking ballroom dancing lessons with Alexio and had been spending their evenings practicing with him in front of the mirror. He closed the drapes so that none of the work hands would see him. "This is as refined as any cowboy has cause to be," Alexio groaned every night, as he twirled both his sisters around the living room in a fox trot or a waltz.

At about mid-morning, Alexio drove the girls over to Abbie's house just before the parade. Their bonnets had been decorated the day before and were waiting for them in the garden next to the carriage. As they arrived and went to the back garden, Howard was giving the roses one last watering so they would last through the parade. The two girls made quite a picture, as they donned their bonnets. Howard laughed as he watched them balance and tilt them precariously upon their heads.

"What we need is a picture," Howard noted. "Wait just one second while I get the tripod and camera." Howard ran back to the house, just as Roger was arriving in his white linen suit and a straw hat. When he saw the girls, he stopped in his tracks and a bemused smile spread across his face. "Careful. You two might very well attract a couple of mourning doves looking for a place to nest."

Rose and Julia laughed. "That's exactly what we need to complete the picture. We would win the 'unspoken contest' hands down in that case." Rose smirked as she put on her lace gloves and opened her parasol. "Does this complete the picture?"

"Beautifully." Roger could not help noticing their bright eyes and soft complexions. They were both beauties, but Julia was all he could see. He had never seen her looking so incandescent. He found himself staring and shook himself to deflect his thoughts. "Uh, have you seen my grandmother yet?" He spoke the words awkwardly, not quite himself.

"Not yet. I'm dying to see what she decided to wear," Rose answered. He made his way upstairs to find her, just as Howard arrived with the camera and tripod.

In a few moments, Roger returned with Abbie, and the girls were amazed at the transformation. Abbie wore an all white summer dress in the latest fashion.

Her hair was shaped into a curled and clustered Gibson knot under an angled wide-brimmed hat topped with white feathers and pink roses. Her green eyes shown brightly, and she looked much younger than they had ever seen her. Julia could not help but think of the young woman in the picture above the mantle. It was plain to see that Abbie had once been a beauty, a woman that many must have envied and admired. No doubt it had brought her fortune, if not happiness.

"You look perfectly wonderful," Julia sighed and gave her a hug. As she released her, she looked into Abbie's eyes and spoke with the deepest sincerity. "I hope this day will be a happy and memorable one for you."

Abbie returned a warm smile and simply said, "Shall we take some photographs before we set off?" Howard obliged her, and they spent a half hour laughing and posing for the camera.

"Now, we'd best make our way to the parade route, shall we?"

Roger helped them each into the carriage and then seated himself next to his grandmother across from Julia and Rose, as the ladies splayed their parasols.

Howard led the carriage down The Alameda into the heart of San Jose. The floats were lined up to the south of Market street, where they found their place in line. The parade route was crowded, and the sounds of the day burst forth like a golden poppy on a Morgan Hill stagecoach trail.

Slowly, the line began to move and Howard lurched the barouche forward. Spectators lined the streets, calling and waving. Roses perfumed the parade route. Women wore picture hats that sprouted flowers, exotic birds, feathers and bows. Delighted spectators gazed in wonder.

As they paused before Obrien's Candies, Roger was just finishing a story that had the three women in stitches. Their laughter filled the air as sunshine splashed around them and drew attention to their convivial party. They were poised to proceed along the parade route, just in time to be observed by Roger's family.

Julia turned slightly to see the stares of frozen astonishment on the faces of Roger's mother and two sisters; she felt as if she were in a slow-motion picture show, the image of their gaping mouths imprinting like a lithograph on her mind. Olivia's eyes shriveled into slashes as she observed the gaiety of her mother-in-law sitting beside her favorite son, while the beautiful Julia returned his warm smile.

Abbie and Roger also caught his mother's withering look seconds later, as the barouche slowly paraded beyond her. Roger felt as if thousands of pin pricks had showered down on him, and he abruptly swiveled away, just in time for Abbie to detect a flicker of sadness in his eyes.

CHAPTER 36

1879, Kauai, The Jackel

After Maria scolded Francisco over the Christmas angel, he started taking his meals in the Japanese camp with the single men and rarely spent time with the Mirantes. Francisco looked down at his bruised and blistered hands, as he sat around the campfire with Jordao, Renato, and other single male workers. The Terra boys and he had been readily transmuted into comrades with the Japanese workers, in spite of the language and cultural barriers.

Their transformation was sparked by the sweat they shared under a relentless sun, but Francisco and his friends also enjoyed the Japanese food and their hot baths. Together, they commiserated with one another after enduring the glower of power-hungry overseers known as "lunas," who only added misery to their long ten-hour workdays. Certain lunas were slave drivers, who felt compelled to torment the workers, fearing that their bosses would peg them as too soft, and they would lose their hard-won position in the plantation pecking order.

Francisco and the Terra boys joined the Japanese in the evenings after dinner with a soak in the Japanese communal hot tubs called "furos." They peeled off their work clothes and donned "yukatas" before slipping into the steaming waters. There was little conversation between the Portuguese and the Japanese, but they learned to speak a form of pidgin English by stringing together short phrases mixed with Polynesian, Japanese, and Portuguese, enough to share food and misery and play cards or toss dice. All it took in the fields was a look to understand and to sympathize with one another, although they had to be quick about it, lest a luna lunge at them or crack a whip close to the ground.

The lunas sometimes rode on horseback and sometimes followed side-by-side with the workers so they could correct them. When the lunas were on horseback, they carried whips as a sign of authority, but they were not allowed to apply it to a man's back. They could crack the whip and would come within an inch of a worker's back. Too close, as far as Francisco was concerned.

That day had been harder than most for Francisco, which is to say, it pushed what little boundary lay between misery and the grim reaper. The next day, Francisco woke to the shrill five o'clock mill whistle, startled out of a bad dream and soaked in sweat. He never remembered his good dreams, if he still had any. He waited to feel the rocking of the ship, even though it had been almost a year since he had left the bark that he now somehow missed. Instead, he listened to the insistent shouting of the lunas, as they crowed "Hana, Hana," and cracked their whips throughout the camp.

Every muscle in his body and every bone cried out to him. "No more!" He heard the moans across the camp and thought to himself. "Were they all thinking the same thing? Now, if I can only get to the wash basin first." To linger was to subject one's face to muddy water. He lugged himself upward, quickly changed his clothes, washed, and relieved himself outside, determined to beat the sunrise.

Colorful Japanese koi kites tied to poles snapped against the wind, as he scudded down the lane to his work field. It was not long before the sun glowed across the horizon. Anticipating its daily torment, he fixed a wide-brimmed straw hat onto his head and tied a bandanna around his neck to filter out red dust from the fields.

Some days Francisco hoed and some days he hacked or stripped the cane; whichever it was, his back arched low to the ground in a rictus for hours at a time and his ankles suffered the jabs of the cut cane. There was no time to stand straight or stretch. Anyone who tried it was quickly singled out and called out as an example to others. He was the best worker on his team, able to sustain his position longer and work faster than any of the others. But with some overseers, his diligence worked against him.

The most hated overseer of all was the one they called the "Jackel." The Jackel was a pestering, weasel-like man, so boney, the sweat would bump, instead of trickle, down his rickety back and leap off of him like tetchy fleas. No one wanted to be near him, as he sniped at them with a hyena's skirl.

For some reason, Jackel had it in for Francisco that day, as if he had lain awake thinking up a plan to get him the night before. Francisco could do nothing right. It did not matter how low he cut the cane; it was never low enough. Jackel jumped beside him all morning, gushing with fetid breath, as he sliced into the boy and shouted his employee number. "Like this, number 1024. Like this!"

Grabbing Francisco's machete, the Jackel attacked the cane, hacking so close that his slices barely missed Francisco's feet. It was never as low as the cuts Francisco had already made, but there was no arguing the matter. When such an incident occurred, which was often on that day, the workers watched with a sideways glance, as they listened to the humiliating snipes of the Jackel.

When the Jackel grabbed Francisco's machete for the fifth time that morning, Francisco's patience waned. The men glanced to the side with curious looks, knowing that number 1024 had become the Jackel's target and realizing that the Jackel's behavior was bordering on the maniacal, even for him. Given that Francisco was the best worker in their gang, they wondered why.

Francisco was tempted to pluck back the machete. In his mind's eye, he imagined himself taking a swipe that, oops, leveled the Jackel to the ground. Knocking him literally off of his feet. "How likely was it that such an accident could take place?" he asked himself. After all, it was not unusual for men to be hacked and then bleed to death among the cane. Francisco knew that no one from his gang would utter a word if there was an accident. He quickly brushed aside these pestering thoughts, along with the sweat off his brow, and retrieved the machete. He furiously hacked away and remained in a state of frenzy until he heard the lunch bell. He stood up and the sweat tumbled off of him like a broken pustule.

All of his comrades stood at attention with sympathetic looks. Words were not necessary, as they motioned him to lunch. One of the Japanese ran for the water boy, dipped into his pail, and ran it over to Francisco to keep him from collapsing in a heap.

Francisco guzzled water from the dipper as if it were with his last breath. Blood trickled from this hands and shins while his blisters oozed. Another sympathetic comrade brought him a water-soaked cloth to wipe his dribbling palms.

The rest of his team led him to a banyan tree where they ate lunch. They quickly opened and laid out their meal tins to share. The Portuguese brought bread, sausages, and fresh fruit, while the Japanese brought smoked fish, rice, and vegetables. They passed their tins to one another quickly because there was barely enough time to eat. One Japanese friend named Kenji signaled to Francisco not to get up. He hurriedly dished up a large plate of food and passed it down to him. No one spoke as they ate, but they kept an eye on Francisco.

After lunch, the afternoon passed as the morning had, with no relief from the Jackel. Francisco endured his taunting, as did the others. When the last whistle finally came, Francisco's entire body caved in, but his pride held him together. He warned the others away from him. He did not want to give the Jackel any satisfaction by showing weakness. By sheer force of will, he straightened his back, shifted his weight from one hip to the other, turned in his machete, and made his way to the Japanese camp. As soon as he was out of the sight of the overseers, his friends gathered around him and led him to the hot steaming bath before they tended his wounds.

After dinner, as they sat around the campfire, they all spit out insults to the Jackel. "Kemono!" "Idiot!" "Monster!" The Portuguese spat out "Fera" and "Monstro." After each new insult, they spat into the fire and watched the flames lick their spittle.

The other workers encouraged Francisco to singe his blisters over the fire. "Watch. It will stop your hands from oozing." Kenji demonstrated by placing his own blistered hand just above the flame. Then he took Francisco's hand, motioning him to do the same. "The fire will stop the pain."

"Hai," Francisco complained. "But bring new pain." The rest of the Portuguese nodded in agreement, but their Japanese comrades insisted that it was their best option to minimize pain. Jordao encouraged him to seek help from Miguel. "Let me run for some medicine. I know Miguel will want to help you." Francisco only nodded. Jordao returned an hour later with Estela who brought witch hazel, coconut oil, and fresh bandages.

"Here. Let me see your hands." She examined his hands. "Keep the bandages on all day tomorrow. Don't work without them." Estela had been learning healing arts from Marissa and from Oliana, who knew how to use native plants and mixed potions to treat workers who could not wait for their weekly doctor visits.

Francisco groaned in pain when Estela first applied the witch hazel, but later he had to admit to feeling better once his hands were wrapped in coconut oil. From that day forward, the entire gang kept strips of cloth and coconut oil to treat their hands.

It was this incident, however, that lodged a deep determination inside of Francisco. He could not wait to complete his contract, as others had determined to do. He would find a way to escape indentured servitude. He would disappear.

Perhaps sell himself out to a merchant ship to gain passage to America. Whatever it took, it was only a matter of time before he found the right opportunity. And if he had to, he would lie, cheat, or steal to make his way.

Once the cane was hacked, gathered, and processed, the soil was tilled, and the cycle of cane growing began afresh. It could take up to two years to prepare a field for planting again. Juvenal Terra had signed up to till the land, but he had no real idea what he had signed up for.

There was nothing more resistant than land that had to be reconditioned after caning. The bits and pieces of cane that lodged themselves deeply into the earth were pulverized and eliminated before a new crop could be planted. The soil required two feet of digging before planting, so it had to be worked over numerous times. The furrows must be straight and deep and then fertilized with ground pineapple skins and cane tops, weeded, and then watered.

The luna looked Juvenal up and down on his first day, assessing his size and strength. Since Juvenal was not a big or brawny man, the luna looked doubtful, but he shrugged his shoulders, figuring that the bosses had recruited him with good reason. "First, I'll show you how to tie and tether the oxen. At the end of the day, I'll show you how to remove their yokes safely and where to take them for water and food. Tomorrow you will do it all yourself. Understood?" Thanks to João's nightly lessons on the bark, Juvenal knew enough English by this time to nod affirmatively.

The luna removed three team of oxen from their stalls pulling them by their leaders. Using a stick, he guided them to the front of the wagon and tied them, starting with the team closest to the driver. Then he placed a single beam upon their shoulders and above the neck of each team. He then tied rope through the ox bows that would tether all six together. Juvenal watched, as the luna jumped on the wagon and ground the first row of cane refuse. A group of young boys followed to club rats or other pests who infiltrated the aftermath in the wake of the cut cane. Another group of boys hoed the weeds after them.

"Climb up and let's see you do the next row, while I sit beside you." Juvenal took the reins and using a stick, he started the train down the row. Try as he might, he could not get the oxen to furrow a straight row. Over and over, the patient overseer showed him what he was doing wrong. It took about an hour before Juvenal had successfully tilled one row.

The overseer jumped down, looked up at Juvenal and said, "The furrows must be two feet deep before we can plant more cane. Every row has to be straight or you must do it all over again. It may take twenty times before the refuse is broken enough."

Juvenal did not realize that this was something he could not do in one day. Every time he managed to furrow one row straight, he looked back at the next one only to find he had run over the previous rows. To pass the time, he named the oxen and called out to them. Cain and Abel were the closest to him. Sophie and Sonia were in the middle. Preto and Branco were in the lead.

"Come on my Sophie and Sonia, stay together. Do not stray." He whispered over the ox bows. He spoke to them with cajoling words, as sweat poured over his brow. Occasionally, he would curse them. The strain on his arms, shoulders, and back was more than he could bear. By lunch time, he had covered only one acre. Lunch finally came, and he motioned to the water carrier who ran over to him. He slid down the wagon and fell on the water bucket, gulping water and washing his seared palms repeatedly.

Five hours later, he brought in the oxen. As he slid down from the wagon, he tried to walk, but his legs felt as if his feet were ensconced into concrete pilings. He tried to put one foot in front of the other, but just dragged his feet on the ground. Sweat, red silt, and sunburn radiated from his entire body. The luna looked at him askance, thinking, "this guy is never going to make it."

Without a word, the luna took the leaders tied to the oxen and showed Juvenal how to coax them out of their yokes to food and water. He could see that Juvenal could barely walk, so he left him sitting on the ground while he led the oxen back to their stalls. When he was done he came back to where Juvenal sat in the dirt with his hands on his head. Juvenal saw him coming and stood up with great effort.

The luna looked Juvenal in the eye and placed his hand on his shoulder. "Don't give up. It will get better. The first day is always the hardest." Juvenal bobbed his head up and down as best he could and shuffled his way to camp, gathering some sense of relief from the wind that whistled, as it blew through the Kukui trees lining his path.

Marissa was sweeping the porch, when she spotted him in the distance. She shaded her eyes, took one look at him, and sensed that something was terribly wrong. She ran to him, noting his blisters and the arch of his shoulders.

"Juvenal, what is it? You look as if you were beat up by the lunas!" Juvenal smiled weakly, "In a way, you could say that I was beat up. But not by the lunas. I've never worked so hard in my life. I just don't know if I'm made for this kind of work." Juvenal said no more and Marissa took him inside to nurse his wounds.

CHAPTER 37

1910, Santa Clara, Auxiliary Ball

It was fortunate for Roger that he had brought his formal attire to his grandmother's house, where he was planning to prepare for the ball after a light supper. He was relieved that he did not have to return home and face his mother. Abbie had observed him closely after the encounter with Olivia on the parade route and noticed the change in his demeanor. His gaiety and natural good nature diminished in the light of his mother's displeasure.

Abbie had long known that she herself was an object of Olivia's disdain, but she now wondered if Julia was also a target of Olivia's ire. How much Olivia knew about Roger's feelings for Julia was something Abbie could only guess. What Abbie now realized was that her grandson was a man deeply in love and that Julia was unlikely to meet her daughter-in-law's expectations for an advantageous match.

Abbie sat in the parlor overlooking the garden and pondered why Olivia was so driven, even to the point of denying happiness to others. How could it make sense when she already possessed so much? With regard to herself, Abbie realized long ago that any filial devotion she received from her son and grandchildren was an object of Olivia's jealousy; it was the reason Olivia kept them away from her. Abbie concluded that while Olivia no doubt coveted wealth and prestige, what she really coveted was absolute control. Abbie was sad to realize that Olivia's ambitions threatened her grandson's happiness.

Abbie sat sipping a glass of anise, when Roger came in from the dressing room and interrupted her thoughts. "How do I look?"

Abbie turned a glowing smile on her handsome grandson, as he straightened his tie in a mirror and searched for a glimpse of her approval. "Wonderful. You look absolutely charming. If you don't dance every dance, you will leave a flood of disappointed hearts in your wake." She winked.

"Ah hah, I see you are a flatterer."

"No, not at all. I take pride in the fact that I am circumspect in my compliments."

"I suspected that about you," Roger replied warmly, as he bent down to give her a peck on the cheek. Abbie saw that his spirits had improved and was glad of it. She was determined to draw him out while she had him to herself.

"Has Howard left yet to pick up Rose and Julia?" Roger inquired.

"Yes, yes. He just left," Abbie replied. "He should be back shortly. Now, why don't you come sit beside me, so we can have a chat." She patted the seat next to her on the divan. Roger poured himself a drink and joined her.

"Here's to today in all its glory," he toasted her. "Now, what shall we talk about?"

"About you, of course. About your future and your heart."

"My heart?" Roger smiled weakly and thumbed his pocket watch. "Such a serious subject."

"It is a serious subject. I am eager for your happiness, and hearts have everything to do with happiness, you know. I want you to know that I think your heart has chosen well. The only question is whether you have the courage and the wisdom to follow it."

He gave a start, suddenly realizing that she read him perfectly and that there was no use in denying it. "Now, that is a serious subject, grandmother. I see you examine me closely."

"She is lovely, you know. To my mind, she possesses all the qualities that would make any man happy. She is not only beautiful; she is strong and good and kind."

"I could not agree with you more and I am glad of your approval, but I am not ready to make any long-term commitments to anyone."

"Then it would be unwise and unkind to lead her and her family to think otherwise," Abbie cautioned.

Roger took out his gold watch and peered into it, as if the time had suddenly become a matter of urgency. His grandmother prompted him again for a response until he finally gave her one. "I don't believe that is the case, actually." Roger had never really thought about the perceptions of others in the matter, because he did not see himself as an open book.

"If I can see it, do you really think others cannot?" While Abbie felt certain of Roger's feelings, there was nothing in Julia's demeanor that suggested that Julia returned his feelings. Nevertheless, understanding the constraints on Roger made Abbie want to protect the girl.

He shrugged, "I don't imagine they can. After all, you have superior knowledge of me. And, I suspect, keener insight than most into matters of the heart, as you put it."

"You flatter me, but either way, take my advice and err on the side of caution. Unless, of course, there is some other reason that you hesitate." Abbie looked inquiringly into his eyes. "A man your age, who is established in the world, cannot make a commitment where he truly loves? Do you honestly believe that?"

Roger had no response. As he groped for words, Howard arrived with Rose and Julia. They could hear the young women chattering downstairs as Howard took their wraps, and they ascended the staircase to the upstairs parlor. Abbie and Roger looked meaningfully at each other and then Roger stood to greet the newcomers.

Julia appeared on the landing wrapped in "moon dust" lavender, her curls falling in soft waves down her back. Roger flushed, feeling his grandmother's eyes upon him. At a loss for words, he was grateful when Julia spoke first.

Julia smiled and motioned Alexio towards them. "I'm so pleased to introduce you to my eldest brother Alexio. I think you two will have a great deal to talk about."

As the two young men shook hands, Roger said, "So glad you can join us this evening. This is my grandmother, Abbie McCallum."

Abbie raised her hand to Alexio, and Julia was pleased to see him take and kiss it. Rose could not help but say, "Alexio, if you're not careful, you'll be transformed into a true gentleman by the end of the night." Alexio smiled and turned to Abbie unpretentiously.

"But this smart lady won't be fooled. I hope you don't mind my rough hands and my rough ways. I work with cattle all day."

"On the contrary young man. I admire the rugged outdoor type. No soft hands in this drawing room will do. And are your cattleman's feet prepared for a waltz or two tonight?"

Alexio made a short bow, "You can be sure I will do my best. My sisters have put me to the test all week long."

"Well, I am certain you will make them proud. And be sure to keep them dancing all night." She winked. "Forgive me for not standing. The day has been a bit taxing for me, and I will be retiring early. I wish you all a splendid evening."

Abbie turned to Howard, "Howard, are you ready to lead the way?"

"Yes, quite, Madam."

"Another ride in the barouche. Shall we?" Roger followed them all downstairs.

The ball was well underway when they arrived at the Vendome Hotel in downtown San Jose. The room was brimming with the scents of a thousand roses and the soft lights of candelabras against a backdrop of violins and the hum of low-toned voices. Rose sucked in her breath and cinched her gloves as she took in the elegant scene.

"Rose, this is clearly your night," Alexio turned to her and offered his arm. "It's all for your namesake. And guess who gets the first dance?"

"You honor me, brother."

"Who else can I torment with my toe-stepping?" He spoke with an amused air and led her to the dance floor before she could protest.

That left Roger to offer Julia the first dance. "Shall we?"

It took Roger a few moments to collect his thoughts as they glided around the ballroom. He was still thinking about his grandmother's cautions and had determined not to dance with Julia a second time, when he spotted his mother and sisters staring in his direction. The effect of their stares brought home to Roger his grandmother's references to the expectations of others. He said nothing until Julia spoke first. "I see your family is here tonight. Will you introduce me?"

Julia had also seen their stares. She knew that it was Roger's prerogative to introduce her to his family, but she intentionally pressed the matter. She even smiled as she considered what a conversation would be like with her former rival. Nothing about it intimidated her.

"Why, of course," he replied with a catch in his throat. Julia noticed that he had no encouraging responses.

When the dance was over, Alexio and Rose immediately joined them. "Shall we find the refreshments?" Alexio was already looking for a break from the dancing, his new shoes being a bit too tight.

"Absolutely," Roger's response was eager, as he sought to put off the unavoidable introductions. No sooner had they rounded up the champagne than Roger's mother advanced upon him with a heavy step and a determined gaze.

"Well, Roger. I see you made it to the dance after all. We were beginning to wonder if you would be here when you did not come home." There was a touch of reproach in his mother's tone that no one present was likely to miss.

"I believe that I did mention I would be leaving from grandmother's house." Roger replied evenly.

"Perhaps," Olivia touched her fan to her chin, her back slightly turned away from Julia. Standing beside her were Roger's sisters with Leslie Hampton and her daughter Kathleen.

Before Roger could make his own introductions, his mother made hers. "Roger, you've met Mrs. Hampton and her daughter, Kathleen, haven't you?" Olivia shifted her stance as she spoke, her back now turned fully away from Julia and her companions. Neither Rose nor Alexio could see beyond her.

Roger hesitated and Olivia spoke and acted quickly. "Why don't you dance with Kathleen Roger? She has just arrived and has yet to dance." Olivia's hand was on Roger's elbow, and he was in no position to protest; in no time, he was on the dance floor with Kathleen. Olivia immediately turned to the rest of her party and hustled them to the other side of the ballroom without a backward glance at Julia or her party. Julia and Rose looked at each other, both aware but also amused by the obvious snub from Roger's mother. As soon as they could get away, Rose turned to Julia.

"The nerve of that woman. How does she live with herself?"

Julia shook her head with an incredulous smile. Before she could respond to Rose, there was a tap on her shoulder and a pair of eager eyes waiting behind her. A new suitor had come to ask Julia to dance.

"But of course," she replied to the young man. "As a matter of fact, I think I could dance all night." He smiled an enthusiastic smile at her. She winked behind his back at Rose and spoke as she was being led away, "And you too, Rose!"

As the night trailed on, Rose and Julia were never without partners, while Roger was monopolized by his mother and the Hamptons. But Roger kept his eye out for Julia. He watched her dance with every other man in the room and envied each one. If she danced with one partner more than once, he winced. He listened for her laughter and her voice. It was as if all other gaiety except hers receded into the background whenever she was near. He could still smell the scent of her after their first dance and all he could offer the Hampton girl was disjointed, empty remarks. His mind played tricks on him. By way of consolation, he thought to himself that if "Julia dances with me again, she will surely be my wife."

Roger was not the only one in the room who was lost in thought. At one point, Rose passed Alexio dancing with Susanna McCallum and clearly absorbed in conversation. Rose watched as the dance ended and he led Susanna back onto the dance floor. Not once, but twice more. As soon as Rose could find Julia, she took her aside. "Julia, did you see who Alexio is dancing with?"

"No, I haven't seen him all night, now that you mention it. I hope he's having a good time."

"I'll say! He's been dancing almost every dance with Susanna McCallum."

Julia and Rose put their hand to their lips, suppressing laughter. When Rose finally composed herself, she spoke with an amused tone, "And to think, all this time the mother was guarding the son from the lowly Mirantes, when she should have been guarding the daughter." They looked up to see Roger coming towards them with a strained and serious brow.

"Look who's coming. The guarded son," Rose whispered behind her fan.

Roger apologized. "I hope you haven't been feeling neglected. Family duty called me away."

"Not at all," Rose was eager in her reply. "We've been having a wonderful time, actually. Dancing the night away, in fact."

Roger wondered if there was a bit of sarcasm in the remark but deflected it and turned to Julia. "I hope you saved the last dance for me," he spoke graciously. The two seconds it took her to respond felt like an agony to Roger, until she smiled and obliged him. He was happy again.

Rose watched them as they danced. She could not help thinking that they made an especially handsome couple. Yet, she understood her sister well enough to know that Julia was holding back something from Roger and that Julia would not be easily tempted, even to a man as rich and handsome as Roger McCallum. As she watched Roger lead Julia away, she noticed another couple: their conversation was intense and earnest and their eyes were bright; it was Alexio and Susanna. Across the ballroom, she looked up and saw Olivia examining the two couples as well. Her eyes were not so bright.

The ride back to Abbie's house was a quiet one with everyone lost in thought, as the sound of clip-clopping and Howard's soft whistle accompanied the quiet mood. Some in the carriage were clearly more satisfied by the events of the evening than others. Alexio seemed pensive and hopeful. Roger was conflicted and cautiously optimistic. Julia was serene. Rose was smiling because she had danced every dance except the last; there had been so much to see in that last dance.

CHAPTER 38

1880, Kauai, The Evil Eye

It was not long before Maria discovered a close friend in her neighbor Oliana, who had lived on the island all of her life and was known to be a *curandeira* medicine woman. Some of Maria's friends said that Oliana used witchcraft magic, but Maria believed that she was a healer. All she knew was that Oliana seemed to know things that others could not know or did not want to know. She had an aura about her, always confident, never worried about her life or what the future might hold. This was something Maria did not understand, but it was a quality she desperately wanted to possess.

Oliana saw the world in two dimensions, one physical and one spiritual. She insisted that the physical world was the one we would die to, but the spiritual world would last beyond death. She therefore considered the spiritual to be more important than the physical. Maria hung on Oliana's every word. Oliana told Maria that, with these powers, Maria could protect her family, ward off evil, and even defeat death and illness or even speak to Paulo through conjuring. Maria became obsessed by these possibilities.

Every Monday, Maria prepared a basket of her choicest fruits, vegetables, and baked breads, as an offering to Oliana. It was an exchange for power. She was seeking the good of Paulo's departed soul and learning wisdom from the one she called the wise woman, "Mulher Sabia." In return for her offering, Maria gathered "pearls of wisdom" from Oliana for one hour each week.

One evening Miguel saw Maria exit the front door with a bag of sea salt. He followed her out the door after dark under a full moon, and he watched from a safe distance, as she slowly walked in a counter-clockwise circle and sprinkled salt on the ground. He spoke abruptly out of the darkness, "Why are you wasting the salt?"

Maria jumped when she heard his voice and pierced him with a look of accusation and annoyance. "Shhhhh, evil spirits will hear your unbelief and remain in our house. The salt will keep them at bay. We must remove all negativity. Who knows who lived in this house before us?"

"Why would you think there are evil spirits? There are no evil spirits here, Maria." With a toss of her head and a dismissive glance, Maria unfurled the remaining salt when she reached the front door and then spoke derisively under her breath.

"What do you know?"

Her words jabbed at Miguel. "I am your husband. That makes me your protector."

"Like you protected me when you brought me here and threw away our son?" Miguel stared helplessly in the face of her accusation, realizing that the trust between them had melted away. He had hoped he could win her back, but it was more apparent than ever that it would be a long fight. "Perhaps she is lost to me forever?" he thought sadly, as he turned from the darkness and went back into the house.

Once inside, he was overcome by a powerful scent that infiltrated their four-room cottage. Something was burning in the oven. Maria had placed garlic in the cast iron stove and left the door open. "What is this smell?"

"Never mind, it will chase away the evil spirits. It will release us from illness."

"But no one is ill. Why do we need to be released?"

"It is to ward off future illness, then."

"The children are all happy and healthy. What is this nonsense?" Maria looked disgusted at Miguel and turned her back on him. She ordered him with more derisive words, "Never call it nonsense again."

Not knowing what to expect next, Miguel watched her closely from that moment forward. One night he caught her licking the twins' foreheads, while reciting a kind of chant. She licked their foreheads exactly three times. After reciting the chant, she spat in the dirt.

Alarmed, Miguel could not help but ask. "Why do you lick our children? Why do you spit in the dirt? You act like a crazy woman!"

"Don't you know that children are vulnerable to the evil eye? We must protect them." Maria patted their little round heads. He could see that there was no arguing with her. Any denial of these strange beliefs would only be met with further disdain, so he walked away.

One day Estela walked into the kitchen and found her mother cutting up dough for sweet bread. She was shaping them to look like crows.

"*Mãe*, these are very strange. What are they for?"

"You and your sisters will use them to find the men of your dreams."

Estela threw back her head and laughed aloud.

"And just how can a piece of bread help me find the man of my dreams?"

Maria took one piece of toast and wrapped it in cloth. There was no mistaking her excitement, as she shoved the toast at her daughter with determination.

"Just take this over to Jordao at breakfast time tomorrow. When he's not looking, place it in his coffee."

Estela wanted to bubble into laughter again, but she held herself in check, seeing that her mother was deeply serious. She gently pushed the toast back to her mother and said, "*Mãe*, how many times do I have to tell you? I do not wish to marry Jordao."

"But we all expect it and now you are at the right age. Why won't you accept this honorable, and I might add, handsome young man? Here then, if you won't take him the toast, then let me cut a lock of your hair and give it to Marissa. She will sew it into the seams of his trousers."

Estela backed away. "*Mãe*! You are not going to cut my hair. How can I convince you? Marriage is simply not what I want. At least not now."

"And what else is there for you?"

Estela turned to her mother. "I happen to think there is a lot more to life. I love going to school and I love to read. If my English is good enough, I may be able to work in Honolulu. And I am enjoying my work as a midwife and learning about healing. Oliana has taught me how to use sea water, seaweed, and kelp for their healing properties. I can mix herbs into medicines. I've seen how much they help with the burns and injuries from the sugar cane fields. Helping people gives me joy and satisfaction."

Maria examined her closely for that look of pain she had seen in her eyes many times before. "Are you sure it's not because of what happened to you on the ship? Be honest now."

"No, *Mãe*. I am certain it is not about that. I'm to the point now where I rarely think about it anymore, and if I do think about it, I have learned that, with God's strength, I can overcome it. The memory of it no longer has power over me."

"You know, Estela, not all men are like that. The marriage relationship is not like that. At least, not with the right man." Maria stopped herself. It made her realize that Miguel had always been the right man for her, and in that moment, she felt some regret for the way she had been treating him.

"Please don't worry about me on that account, *Mãe*. I am beginning to enjoy life again. I love the people that I help, and it fills me up to see their babies born and to become part of our lives. Maybe someday I will marry, but it just isn't now, and it isn't Jordao. I know that will disappoint you and the Terras, but I cannot help the way I feel. He is a wonderful young man, but he is not the one for me."

It was not long after this conversation that Maria approached Oliana with a grave petition. She prepared a special basket that day. She took a chain that Paulo had worn as a baby, one of her favorite momentos of him, and she tied it around a bouquet of rainbow plumeria. As she lay the basket before Oliana, she looked up with tears trickling down her cheeks.

"My goodness, Maria, what is it that you desire today?"

Maria trembled as she spoke, "Please Mulher Sabia, I beg you. I must speak to my son. I am in torment day and night, thinking that my son's spirit lies at the bottom of the sea and is unable to leave his body or the deep, cold ocean waters. I must know that he is not trapped. That he is not crying out to be released from he bottom of the sea."

"Have you called his name out loud in the past year since he left you?"

"I do not think so." Maria thought for a moment and then spoke with hesitation. "I, I cannot remember," she stuttered. "I know that my heart has been crying out for him. Why do you ask?"

Oliana placed her hand on Maria's hand, "If you cry out for your loved one too soon, they may not want to leave the earth. They may cling to their bodies. If you wait at least a year, then you can ensure they are safely on their journey to another life."

"But he was at the bottom of the ocean. How could he possibly hear me and how can I know for certain if he remains?" Maria felt over-whelmed by what she was hearing. She considered all of the possibilities and could find no comfort in them.

Oliana gave her explicit instructions. "There is a way you can speak to him. Now that it has been over a year, build a small altar in your home. Cover it with white cloth and any pictures you may have of him. Set a white candle beside it and a glass bowl of water. The water is what the spirits use to carry our messages to the departed. Make the altar a beautiful place, where you can meet with him. Keep fresh flowers beside it. Whatever gives you joy or reminds you of him. Even his favorite food. Whenever you are missing him, go there. Tell him about your hopes, your dreams. Share your heart with him. Share your family life with him. This will give you much joy and benefit both you and your family."

Maria smiled thankfully. "Then there is hope?"

"There is more than hope. There is everything to hope for."

Maria thanked her profusely and hurried home to build the altar. When the family asked her what she was doing, she simply said, "I am building a memorial to Paulo. This is where we can meet with him and he can hear our prayers. Even if he is still at the bottom of the sea, we will comfort him there."

Estela reached out and placed her hand on her mother's shoulder, "But *Mãe*. I am certain he is not at the bottom of the sea."

"Even so, wherever he is, he will hear us. Bring him gifts from the island, so that he knows we live in a paradise. It will comfort him." The rest of the family looked at one another and knew that the matter was settled. After that day, Maria no longer reproached Miguel for dropping Paulo's body into the sea.

Miguel operated under an assumption that life could and would get better, no matter how high the mountains before him. The will to live fully and to improve life for his family was strong within him, but the desire to make peace with those around him was an equally powerful force. These two opposing forces sometimes worked at odds with one another, creating a tension that gave birth to frustration, but he kept his eyes forward.

Things were not what they seemed when he was on Quarantine Island. When he arrived, he was denied the position he requested to work in the boiler room. He cheerfully took up whatever work was available to him, under the assumption that he could somehow cut out his own path with hard work and endurance.

He was not entirely wrong. For a time, he cut cane in the fields and performed strip work, cutting away the leaves from their stalks. There was no job too lowly for him. He even worked with the women to stack the cane into the ox carts. Before long, he was working in the mill. Either way, he knew that he was close to meeting the obligations of his contract, and if things did not work out well, he would seek other options on the islands when he was released.

Francisco's perspective was more myopic; he never saw beyond his current situation. This was true even while he was stowing away on the ship. He very quickly grasped that there was no future he wanted on these small islands. He envisioned something far more expansive and enterprising.

Francisco had watched Miguel closely, unconsciously wondering if this was a man he could respect or grow into. He was curious to know what drove Miguel and could hardly believe that his relentless cheerfulness could be genuine. One day, after watching Miguel take a tongue-lashing from the "Jackel," he could not help himself. "Why do you put up with that man? Knock him off his feet!"

Miguel addressed him composedly, "And just what would that accomplish? To make him more of an enemy than ever? To lose my job for insubordination? That would only leave my family without food and shelter."

"Do whatever you have to, but at least tell the managers what he's doing. Gather a group of men who will report their grievances against him. Anything but sitting back and taking it!"

"Paulo, my boy, you must learn to pick your battles. Timing is everything, and everything passes away, even this evil man. He is a small man. I would have to become small myself to fight against him. I would never want to be like this man."

Francisco's blood ran hot. "I am NOT Paulo! I am not your boy! I will NEVER be Paulo. Stop calling me that."

Miguel was startled and shaken. "And why would it be such a bad thing to be Paulo?"

Francisco said nothing. Miguel thought for a moment and then spoke very quietly, as he turned away from Francisco, "Yes. Of course, you are right. You could never be Paulo."

Francisco looked away as well but could not help but call after him. "It is not who I am. I am not your son and I never could be."

Francisco knew that he owed this man a debt of gratitude, but he was somehow unable to repay it. There was a gnawing sense of dissatisfaction that came from being cruel. He knew Miguel did not deserve it, but he could not help himself. Still, another part of him very much wanted to impress Miguel, though he did not understand why.

CHAPTER 39

1910, Drawbridge

Luana awoke with a grunt and a thud as she rolled to the floor. She wondered why she was on the living room floor and not in her bed and then rubbed her disjointed neck. She pulled herself back up onto the settee and then flung herself back down on it with another groan. Why did I end up here? And then she remembered: she had stayed up late last night hoping to catch Rose and Julia when they returned from the ball. They must have passed her without a word.

Anarosa loomed over Luana, as she lay prostrate. "Never made it to the bed, I see. I knew you must've come in late. Another night at Jake's Place?" Anarosa shook her head in response, served up her most indignant look, and then cranked her head back and forth to straighten her neck. "No. I was not at Jake's." She quickly rousted her brain for an excuse. "I was up late reading." She yawned largely.

"Reading what?" Anarosa looked around for reading materials and saw none, while Luana pretended it did not matter. "Oh, I must have left it in the outhouse." Luana spoke innocently. "And now that I think of it, I need to go there right now." She jumped up and bolted out to the back porch, where she found a book, and then ran to the outhouse to plant her reading material. As she was leaving, Rose was coming towards her.

"Just the person I want to see," said Luana.

"And why would that be?" Rose spoke coyly.

Luana leaned into Rose and jackknifed a finger at her. "Details. I want to hear every detail about last night."

"Well, you're just going to have to wait until I've had some breakfast." Rose sang out in a teasing tone, as she twirled past her.

Luana called after her, "I'll tell you what. Get dressed and I'll take you into town for breakfast. On me." Luana was thinking she would get more information if no one else was around.

"On you?" Rose snickered at the idea of Luana paying for anything. "Is that a bribe?"

"Not unless you intend to withhold information."

Rose smiled a mischievous smile, "Not likely."

"Then meet me on the front porch in fifteen minutes."

At breakfast, Luana prodded Rose for the details. The most interesting bit of news was about Alexio and Susanna. Luana wanted to know exactly how many times they had danced.

"At least four times the entire night, as far as I could tell."

"You don't say," Luana placed her elbows on the table with her cheeks ballooning into her knuckles, as she thought about it. "And you say that Susanna's mother did not look happy about it?"

"And I'll say it again. If looks could freeze hell over, then hers would have done the job."

"And what about Roger McCallum and your sister?" Luana got directly to her point. "Do you think Julia is in love with him?"

Rose sputtered into her coffee. "I have no idea; she's a complete mystery to me. But one thing's for sure," she paused.

Luana waited with wide-cocked eyes. "And, what's that?"

"He sure is in love with her."

"And what makes you so sure?" Luana did not doubt it, but she wanted to hear why Rose thought so.

"Well, let's just say that, he looks at her in such a way that most women can only envy. And not just every once in awhile but almost every time he lays eyes on her." Rose let out a sigh.

"And do you think he's a good match for your sister?"

Rose put her coffee cup down thoughtfully and settled into her seat. "Well, she could sure do a whole lot worse. And would my mother be happy about it!"

"Forget your mother. What do you think is right for Julia?"

"Well, you know her as well as I do. What do you think?"

Luana was not expecting the tables to be turned on her, but now that they were, she trusted Rose enough to confide in her.

"Because I have reason to believe there's another man who's just as much in love with her, and if it was up to me, Roger would not be my first choice for Julia."

Rose leaned in with an arched brow. "And who might that be?"

"You really have no idea?" Luana could not really be surprised that Rose did not know; after all, she had not guessed it herself.

Rose shook her head slowly, searching her mental index for candidates. "It could be any number of men. I've no doubt that Julia has many secret admirers." Rose shrugged.

"Someone very close to this family. Someone who is also a bit of a riddle."

"I give up. Who?"

"Marcos."

"Marcos?" Rose tossed an incredulous look. "But Julia has always hated him."

"When she was younger, of course. But things are different now. They're older. He's nearly twenty-seven and she's twenty."

"Maybe different for Marcos. I'm not so sure about Julia." Rose wrinkled up her nose. "Are you sure about this?"

"Trust me. I have it on good authority. From someone who knows Marcos very well or as well as anyone could."

"Then why doesn't he stand up for Julia?"

"Because of Roger. Don't you see? He sees a man he dislikes courting Julia, and he does not want to get in the way."

"I don't get that at all. If he loves her that much, then he would fight for her."

"Actually, I've given it a lot of thought, and I think he's testing her. They are such very different kind of men. He needs to know that Julia would choose him."

Rose spat her disgust, "Men! Why can't they just declare their feelings?" She crossed her arms as she contemplated the idea. "I mean, if that's what he's doing, then it's just not going to work. And if he believes he's the right man for her, then he's doing her a disservice. Why, she could marry the wrong man!"

"Agreed. And that's exactly why we've got to help him along."

"So, what did you have in mind?"

"Well, for one thing, they need to spend more time with each other. Give Julia a chance to see he's not the teenager she once knew."

"And just how are you going to help that along?"

"A date. I've spoken to Gilberto, and it's all arranged. Gilberto suggested we all take a day and go to Drawbridge together. We'll fish and dig clams and hang out with the locals."

"You mean a double-date? Really? You and Gilberto?" Rose leaned in with a teasing smile.

"Now, don't get the wrong idea. It's only to get Julia and Marcos together. I can assure you that Gilberto and I are nothing but good friends."

"Sure you are." Rose winked and Luana rolled her eyes.

It was a brilliant summer day at the tip of the San Francisco Bay near the Coyote slough. A northern harrier swooped down onto the marshy waters, scooped up its prey, and then flapped up to the skies like the slap of a whale's tail. Marcos steered their scull boat through the salt ponds towards the north end of Drawbridge. Julia sat back and periodically sliced the water with one hand, while Luana and Gilberto searched for the right spot to dig up mud clams.

"Over there. Let's head for the shallow end." Marcos guided the scull, while Gilberto shaded his eyes and pointed to a dense area of grasses where the tide was low. Just before the scull was about to run aground, Gilberto slipped into the waters, dressed in hipsters and rubber boots, and then pressed his feet along the bottom.

"This is it. I can feel it. The bottom is loaded with them." He reached down and scooped up two or three clams from the mud with his rubber gloves. "And a good size." He held one up to the sun. "Let's rake them in."

Never one to be left behind, Luana reached for a pail and a clam rake and slipped into the water. Julia sat in the scull shading her eyes, as she watched them. Luana was breathless in her efforts; within no time, she had filled one pail and glanced over at Julia, "Come join us."

"No, it's so much more fun watching you drabble around in the mud. And besides, just how many buckets of clams can we lug back?" Just as Julia finished her sentence, Luana lurched, wobbled, and fell over with a splash. Gilberto lunged down, offered a strong arm, which was accepted, and hoisted her up, dripping mud. Luana laughed it off.

"Oh, great. I'll be in good shape for dinner in Drawbridge."

"Do you really think anyone in Drawbridge cares?" Gilberto smirked. "They're like crawdads here; they live in mud!"

"It looks like you two will be awhile." Marcos uttered. "I'll take Julia out to where the waters are deep enough for fishing. We'll come back for you in about an hour or two."

Gilberto waved them on, and Marcos steered the scull northward, as they slid through the marshes. A great egret arrowed itself across the grasses, while a black-neck stilt ushered its young along the shore.

"It's so peaceful here," Julia sighed. "It's as if it were a land beyond time, another world. I can see why people love to come here, but I can't understand making a life here."

"The northern part of the island is filled with cabins, mostly duck hunters, who come in the winter or on the weekends. Most of the permanent residents live to the south."

"But what do they do with themselves and how do they survive here? There are no grocery stores, schools, or even churches."

"They follow the train tracks using their own push carts. They call them skateboards."

"But to where?"

"All the way to Alviso. That's where they go for groceries and school and whatever else they need. And remember, there is an abundant supply of oysters, clams, fish, and duck. Even shrimp."

Marcos slowed the scull as they approached deeper waters and tossed an anchor. He grabbed a couple of fishing poles. "Have you ever fished?"

Julia wrinkled her nose and shaded her face with her hand. "Not hardly."

He sat down opposite her and laid out his equipment. "Are you willing to try?" She agreed.

"Here, let me show you how to bait your hook." Marcos demonstrated and then cast a line for Julia. He sat next to her and handed her the pole.

"Now what?"

He looked back at her. "You wait."

"For what?"

He raised an eyebrow with an amused grin. "A tug. Don't you know anything about fishing?"

"About everything I ever needed to know up until now."

"Here, let me show you what to do when you feel that first tug." He sat beside her, wrapped his hands over hers, and helped her ease the line into her body and manage the reel. "Like this," he shot her a crosswise glance to see if she was getting the feel of it. She had never been so close to him, and their eyes locked momentarily. She felt herself flush as he released her hands and moved to sit opposite her. He cast his line in the opposite direction.

He shrugged, "You need to get out more. Try things, you know?"

"I do get out. Just not to the salt marshes."

"And where do you 'get out'?" He spoke teasingly.

"I was in the Carnival of Roses parade."

"I know. I saw you," he said flatly. Julia sensed something like disapproval in his tone.

"I even went to the Auxiliary ball," she bragged. Marcos knew about the ball, and he knew about her date. He clammed up with a brooding stare into the deep waters. They sat in silence for a full ten minutes with nothing but a light breeze between them and sunshine splashing around them. The water lapped rhythmically against the sides of the scull.

Marcos broke the silence, "The people here, well, they really know how to live."

Julia looked doubtful, "In mud?"

"People see what they want to see. It's not about the mud. It's about a way of life. It's about a way of thinking and living. Not bound by rules that other people make up for you or based on someone else's expectations. Refusing to base your life on what you can accumulate just to impress others. Living life on your own terms. Yes, that's the beauty of this place," he spoke decidedly. "It actually takes a special kind of person to see beyond the mud."

"Then, why don't you live here? Are you that kind of special person?" Julia spoke with light sarcasm.

Marcos paused and tossed Julia a serious look. "I could live here. But my first love is the land, the Valley." He gazed outward, towards the Valley. "The scents of high mustard grasses in the winter and the cherry blossoms in the spring. The sticky hot fruit in the summer. The feel of the dew just before dawn. The twilight rides up the mountains. Horses." He turned and looked at her. "Our rides." He searched her eyes to see if what he said had resonated with her.

She glanced away, but she couldn't help being curious about him and his plans. He was such a mystery, she thought. "I wonder why you don't have your own ranch, if you love it so well."

He shrugged, "I do."

Her eyes searched him skeptically. "What do you mean, you do?"

"I've already bought twenty acres, but I'm not ready to farm it, so I've leased it out. When I can buy the equipment I need and a few more acres, I'll start my own ranch."

"So, you will leave us?" She did not mean to sound accusatory, but there was slight disappointment in her tone.

"I'll continue to help your father, as long as he needs me. After all, a man can do more than one thing at a time, can't he? And besides, your brothers are getting old enough to manage the ranch themselves. Your father won't be needing me forever."

"I suppose," she shrugged and then leaned back. They sat for a half an hour in contemplative silence. During that time, Marcos reeled in two fish. It occurred to Julia as they sat there that Marcos had never been a man of many words, yet the silence between them was not an awkward one. Finally, Julia felt a tug on her line and a jolt of excitement. "I think I've got one! What do I do now?"

"You're doing just fine. Reel it in a bit." She struggled.

"Keep reeling. Just let me know if you need help." Marcos knew Julia well enough to realize that she could never be satisfied with anything she had failed to accomplish on her own. In no time, there was a hefty fish flapping in her face. "Now what?"

Marcos took over and smacked down the fish.

"We're not having this for dinner, I hope?" Julia looked a bit horrified, as the fish ceased struggling.

"No, I'm taking you out for an early dinner, remember? To a wonderful place, where you will meet some very special people."

"More special people. I confess you've made me curious. I'm starting to think they walk on air around here."

"Not hardly. As a matter of fact, they have their feet planted firmly on the ground or the mud, if you prefer." He laughed and she realized how it softened him. "Come on! Let's go get Luana and Gilberto. Do you think they're done mucking around in the mud?"

The only way into Drawbridge was along the railroad tracks. There were no roads or sidewalks into or around the town. The town's various buildings were conjoined by boardwalks. As they walked along the tracks, Luana looked around at the houses and buildings and remarked. "It looks like a shanty town. Maybe even a ghost town."

"Not at all. There's a whole lot of life here. You just need to know where to look and how to look." Marcos was quick to defend the place. For him, it had been an oasis, a quick getaway that cured many ills, a place of refuge where one could find true camaraderie.

"And when to look," Gilberto chimed in. "During duck hunting season, the entire place erupts. People bunk by the side of the tracks. Wherever they can find a place to lay their heads. And when the sun goes down, they really know how to have a good time."

Marcos stopped in front of a towering water tank. "Well, here it is, the town's water supply." Their heads craned up to the tank raised high up onto a wooden platform. They heard a sputter, then a motor churning.

A sturdy-looking German woman came out from the side of the tank brushing her hands, looking downward at the pipes that carried water to the townspeople. She was anxious to ensure there was no leakage. Her shoulders were broad, her hands worn from hard work, her apron a permanent fixture atop a white cotton dress. A top-knot twisted tightly at the top of her square head, as if it were bolted in place.

"Marcos, my friend. We've been expecting you."

"Good to see you Mrs. Sprung. I see you keep that water pump going. I've been hankering for some homemade German sausages. I hope we're not too early."

"Too early? When I heard you were coming, I made sure I had a fresh batch. Just let me know and you can eat any time you're ready. You been out digging today?"

Marcos patted his stomach, "Clam digging and fishing work up a hearty appetite. I've been dreaming of potato latkes to go with those sausages, washed down with your home brew. Tell me you're not out."

Mrs. Sprung smiled with a twinkle in her eye. "Anything for you."

"No one can whip up a meal like you can." He gave her an appreciative smile.

Mrs. Sprung turned towards Gilberto. She made it her business to remember everyone who had ever come to Drawbridge. "Welcome back Gilberto. Who do we have here with you?"

Gilberto introduced the two young women, and then they made their way to the Sprung Hotel just beyond the water tower. It was one of two hotels in Drawbridge, servicing vacationers, duck hunters, and fishermen from all over the Bay Area and beyond. The wooden barn-like hotel was encircled by a wraparound covered deck with a screened-in porch that kept the bugs from the salt ponds at bay.

Mrs. Sprung showed them to a dining hall just inside the front porch across from a well-equipped kitchen leading them to a large table covered with a white table cloth. Everything was clean and comfortable in the well-lighted room. From the window beside their table, they could see the seagulls swarming in the western skies, as the sun was completing its daily rendezvous with the horizon.

The table was soon filled with large bowls of hot German dishes ladled with steaming vegetables, sausages, and potato latkes. Mrs. Sprung brought out a pitcher of her best home-brewed beer.

"Now this is just what we need after mucking in the mud all day," Gilberto poured one for Luana who slurped it down.

"You should have brought some of those clams with you," Mrs. Sprung remarked. "I would have been glad to shuck some for you. They go best with German food, you know."

Gilberto laughed, "We would have, but we weren't inclined to haul them in over the tracks without a skateboard."

At that moment, Mrs. Sprung's husband Joe came out to greet them. "Marcos, my man, you fixing to play tonight?" Joe clapped him on the back. Beyond the hotel bedrooms was a well-occupied card room, where the men of the town gathered regularly, and Marcos was known to be one of the best players in town.

When Joe saw Luana and Julia, his eyebrows shot up. This was the first time he had ever seen Marcos in the company of beautiful women. "Oh, I see that you have other things to do, tonight, perhaps?" He spoke with a wink. "Who are your friends?" Marcos introduced Luana and Julia.

"Oh yes, I know your father well," Joe commented to Julia. "He is a fine duck hunter. And you are his sister?" Joe turned to Luana with a doubtful look.

"His baby sister," she was quick to reply.

"Yes, I was going to say. You don't look old enough to be his sister." Joe stood conversing with the group for several minutes more and then made the rounds as other dinner guests arrived. The German dinners at the hotel were a favorite among locals, and like his wife, Joe made a point of getting to know everyone who passed through.

Just as the group was finishing their meal, the front door opened to four men looking for a card game. Luana looked up to see Domingos and his friends, followed by Roger McCallum.

"Hey, little sister, what do we have here?" Domingos had clearly been drinking and was in a particularly friendly mood. Roger stood staring over his head. Marcos stiffened. Luana froze. Julia was made uncomfortable by the flush that came over her face. She did not appreciate Roger's vaguely accusing looks.

Domingos did not pick up on the awkward moment. He just continued babbling. When he did not get much of a reaction from anyone, he began moving to the back of the hotel, but he shot back at Marcos, "Marcos, join us for cards later?" Domingos's question was met with silence, so he shrugged.

Sensing an opportune moment, Gilberto turned to Luana and Julia. "Shall we leave this joint and go to Jake's place?"

Shaking off her discomfort, Julia spoke up, "You would take me to Jake's Place?"

Luana smiled a conniving smile, "As long as you don't tell your mother."

"She'll never hear it from me." Julia laughed and for her, it was as if the awkward moment had never happened.

CHAPTER 40

1881, Kauai, The Sugar Mill

As time passed, more ships arrived, and the Portuguese blossomed across the islands as they were reunited with their loved ones. More ships also meant more Madeira wine, malasadas, violas, braguinhas, and rajaos. The rajao was called the taro patch fiddle, because it was not uncommon to hear them thrumming from the taro fields during break time. Portuguese music was a life-giving force, tumbling down from volcanic peaks to serenade the native dancers, as they swayed to the hula.

Some of the newcomers were practiced in the art of crafting their unique instruments by sawing thin strips of koa wood, wrapping them around a mold, and gluing them together. These craftsmen set up businesses on the side for profit, while they fed the island's natural love of music. The natives were hungry to acquire them, and the Portuguese were even hungrier to earn the means to escape the drudgeries of plantation life. It was not long before the braguinha was played before the court of King Kalakaua and dubbed the "ukulele," meaning "jumping flea."

Miguel and his family were just a few months away from the end of their contracts. Those first plantation workers were now faced with decisions regarding their future. They had learned English well to advance in the trades. While some became lunas and stayed on the plantations, others started their own businesses or saved their money for passage to the mainland. A steady stream of the Portuguese earned their way to California, where most of them took up farming or set up tanneries and dairies. They learned very quickly that plantation work was not a path to riches or even independence, and independence was what they craved.

Holding high hopes for their future, Miguel approached Juvenal Terra with an idea of going into business together, a business to support new immigrants to the island. "We were the first ship from the Portuguese islands, and it has been two years since we came here. We can help our people adjust to life here and ensure their success. And not just our own people."

"And just how do you propose we do that?"

"We start with a grocery business and then we branch out."

"Branch out, how?"

Miguel spoke with confidence born from what he considered to be a well-laid plan, "It will be a grocery business like no other, not like the plantation stores, where wages are attached at the end of every week and prices are so high that the worker loses all his wages to the stores and the plantation owners."

Juvenal thought about if for a moment. "I like that idea. We'll need to make it easy to get to, not too far from the plantations. But how do we make money if we charge less than the plantation stores?"

"We offer more than groceries. We offer goods and services."

"Services? What kind of services?" Juvenal looked doubtful.

"How to negotiate wages, what plantation jobs to choose, how to become a luna, how to manage money or learn English. Think of all the things we had to learn when we arrived, and there's no end to what we can offer."

"But how can they pay for these things?"

"We won't charge for the services, at least not at first. We will operate on a small profit for awhile but with enough to earn our living. Eventually we'll buy land to grow crops to sell, but in the meantime, we'll rent the land. We're looking for high volume to get started, the more people the better. Word will get around that we can help them adapt to island life. As the immigrants become more established and save their own money, we will have gained their trust. Eventually, we can charge for more. The girls are keen to teach. Over time, we can expand our offerings. Our store will be the gathering point for new arrivals, a familial place, with the advantage of gradually undercutting the plantation stores."

"Hey, I have another idea. We can write home and ask our friends and relatives to bring some of the goods we will need. Things that are unique to our homeland. They can be the means of providing a variety of goods. Things we can't get here. We pay them upon arrival and then make a profit."

"More Madeira wine?"

Juvenal's eyes twinkled, "Yes lots more wine. And seeds, herbs, and cuttings for our gardens. Ones that can make the crossing."

"And home-brewed beer bottled in soy sauce jars. I'm sure the Japanese will help us out with that." Miguel winked.

"Perhaps we can recruit others to sell their homemade wares in the store. Whale oil lamps, mosquito netting, hala seed pods for fueling their fires. We'll offer something for everyone." Miguel clapped Juvenal on the back, as they began their work day with high hopes.

On this particular day, Miguel made his way to the mill, near the boiler rooms, where he spent most of his time. Past a string of bamboo huts; through a kukui grove; listening to the trills of the rose-ringed parakeets as they preened in bright green and splayed their long tails. He was beginning to feel at home on this garden island, and his heart beat faster as he dreamed of a prosperous future for his family.

Maria seemed softer and more forgiving. She stopped throwing salt around their home. She was less afraid. He was proud of his girls who had learned to read and write in English. Ana was about to marry one of the Terra boys, and they were planning a wedding for the first time. He smiled as he imagined that day, when the taro patch fiddles and the ukuleles would fill the camps and the dancing would last through the night, just like the old days. Everyone would be invited.

He passed an ox cart, weighted down with wet cane stalks bound for the mill, where it would be dried and crushed. He whiffed a scent of syrupy cane juice as the warm Pacific breezes riffled his hair. Flowing waters called to him from the mill dam along with the plashing and grinding of the mill wheels. Before entering the mill, he watched as a group of women turned over piles of wet cane for the drying shed, where the juices were squeezed before using the cane to stoke the never-ending mill fires.

Miguel never knew what tasks he would be completing on any given day; it all depended upon the workload and the available workers. He had become so versatile in his work that he could do just about any mill or boiler room job. At the mill, the cane was ground and its juices extracted and clarified before flowing to the boiler room. He watched as the mill workers mixed powder and water into a large iron pot to coagulate impurities from dirty cane juices, gently stirring in a little at a time.

Each worker was caked with sweat, soil, and powder from the hot, steamy room, where there was no respite from the heat, a heat which came at them from the inside as well as the outside. They longed to open the windows and the doors but they did not dare, as the insects and dust could easily invade the cane syrup, especially when there were strong winds.

Miguel tapped a man on the shoulder. The man was clarifying the newly squeezed cane juice. He nodded and handed Miguel the large paddle used for stirring and skimming. Miguel explained how much powdered lime to add to the pot. "Be careful. If you use too much milk of lime, the sugar grains will grow dark, which does not bring a very high price at market. We want to keep the grains as light as possible."

The man nodded in understanding. "And you cannot use the same amount with every batch, because the sugar content can vary between batches. The trick is to add a little at a time and watch for discoloration as you stir. Wait for the juices until they are just under a boil and then collect the scum. Once you've scraped it off, then let it boil another ten minutes before letting it settle again. After that, it takes about thirty to forty minutes before you can draw clear juice off the top to be sent to the boiler room."

Miguel stayed with the worker for an hour to show him the entire process. After inspecting the mill workers and finding everything in working order, he went to the boiler room, which was located in a large barn-like structure. The boiling room was where juice was transformed into crystals, the more crystals per batch the better. Miguel surveyed the boilers where there were three rows of long brick ovens lined with pots of varying sizes and one tester to oversee the process.

Beneath the pots, there was a steady stream of native island workers in loin cloths slick with sweat and constantly stoking the fires with wood and cane stalks from the drying sheds. The flames cast the workers in large shadows against the walls of the boiler room, as if ballooning phantoms were writhing against them.

The only job Miguel did not do was that of boiler room tester, a very fine art. The skill of a tester was critical. The success of the sugar cane process came at the very end, where the judgment of the tester could make or break an entire batch of sugar. If the tester misjudged the texture or temperature of the final vat, large quantities of cane juice would have to be thrown out.

Miguel was so close to leaving plantation work that he no longer cared about becoming a tester, but he worked closely with the testers to strike the right temperature before cooling the cane juices. He took up a wooden ladle and listened closely for the tester. His first task was to fill the first pot with fresh cane juice and then move the juices from pot to pot just at the right time, while skimming off the scum.

Throughout the room, voices resounded with instructions, "More wood, stoaker! We need to raise this heat now." Miguel ran to ladle juices from pot to pot. The tester poked a long pole into the last pot, lifting it while dripping juices into the water and then testing it for the right consistency. "Strike it now! Not a minute to lose!"

Miguel jumped forward, ladled the last pot into a spout which transported it to the cooling vats in the next room. He emptied the entire pot and then worked backwards to move the fluids from pot to pot, finally refilling the first pot with fresh cane juice from the mill. He then repeated the process over and over for four sweat-drenching hours. After one break, he helped pack sugar cane into barrels for another two hours. The work was exhausting, but Miguel was accustomed to it.

Just when he thought he was done for the day, the mill manager approached him. "The mill workers all went home with a sweating sickness. We have to keep the grinder going for at least another hour. Can you fill in?" Miguel was never one to say no, but he had not finished packing all of the barrels. The mill manager went to find another worker to relieve him and came back to find Miguel.

"You'll need to supervise the mill on your own for awhile, since we have no one for backup. Do you think you can manage it?" Miguel nodded in the affirmative, and the manager, having the greatest confidence in Miguel, left him on his own.

Working the mill grinder was a monotonous process. Cane stalks were fed into three heavy cement rollers powered by steam and water. Being a mind-numbing job at the end of a long day, Miguel soon found it difficult to keep his mind on the work. Daydreams of what he would be doing in six months, when his contract ended, relieved the monotony.

Unlike many of his peers, he had saved a somewhat substantial sum of money by taking on odd jobs and encouraging family members to do the same. At the end of each work day, he gathered wood and dry dung and sold it to his neighbors and friends to keep their outdoor ovens burning. Maria and the girls baked extra bread and sold it to the red wagon. Ida and Ana took on babysitting and provided laundry services for the single men's quarters. Estela contributed some of the money she earned as a midwife. Economizing had become their way of life for three years and it had paid off.

Miguel now had enough money to rent his own place. He was thinking about renting a storeroom in a nearby village; it had two stories with three rooms above the store, where the family could live while they were getting started. Ana would be married soon, and Estela had already planned to rent a room, now that she was able to pay her own rent.

Miguel's head bobbed up and down, as sweat trickled down his back. The warm day made him groggy, creating a swimming sensation in his head, floating dreams of times gone by across his mind. Nodding, starting up, nodding again, drifting. Eyes blurring, feet stumbling, as he fell over the grinders. First his hand and then his arm were sucked in, crushing him between the cement rollers. Water continued flowing, while half of him jammed up the rollers and the other half was mortified with spasms of searing pain. There was no one around.

He tried to yell, as the air came sucking out of him. He did not know how long he lay across the cement cylinders. Passing in and out. Blinking and tearing up. Blood-letting. The boiler room manager finally noticed that the cane juice coming in from the mill was not just dirty; it was running red.

As in a dream, Miguel heard pounding feet, frantic voices calling to one another, close by and then fading away. Waters coagulated. Wheels groaned. Cranking, carts rolling, screaming. Were they his screams or someone else's? A hatchet, more blood-curdling screams and blinding pain. He could no longer feel his arm, and the rest of him went numb. He fell and then floated. He looked down at the bloody scene and then his spirit slowly slipped away.

Francisco finished his work day and stopped by the Mirante cottage. Maria was out at the ovens, and Ida was in the garden watching the twins. Luana sat in the dirt gnawing on a rag doll, spotted Francisco, and threw it to the ground. It had been at least a week since she had last seen him. She dropped everything and squealed with delight, raising up her arms for his embrace.

Luana was the only one who ever seemed happy to see him; it's what kept him coming back. Waving pudgy, dimpled arms at him, she anticipated his usual greeting, his arms sweeping down, lifting her high above his head, eyes locking into hers and waiting for her gasp, as he swung her back down and up again. Luana erupted into squeals of delight.

Ida let Domingos slide from her hip to the ground and smiled as she surveyed the scene. "She just can't seem to get enough of you, Paulo." Francisco gave a start. Neither of them could be more surprised to hear her speak Paulo's name. Miguel was the only one who had ever called him that, and since their latest encounter, even Miguel had stopped using the name. Ida started as well, as if she had just picked up a hot iron.

"I'm sorry. I guess I just don't know what else to call you. Does it bother you?"

Francisco turned away and paused. "If people outside the family are around, I suppose that's what you should call me, but otherwise, I would prefer that you use my real name."

Ida recognized the pain it caused him just to mention the matter. "I'm sorry. I know the family have not been kind to you. It's not your fault. It's just difficult to be reminded of Paulo. I hope you understand." He nodded back but remained silent.

At that moment, the plantation bells and bull horns began to sound an alarm. At first, it did not concern them, but when they continued with increasing urgency, the two stood at attention. Prolonged alarms meant there was a fire or something worse.

Francisco shaded his face with his left hand, his eyes riffling across the horizon. "There's no sign of smoke. I wonder what it could be?" By this time, Maria had returned from the ovens with a basket of bread and opened the gate to the path back to the kitchen. They all remained silently watchful.

Something that tasted like bile was rising up in Francisco and caught in his throat. He let Luana slip slowly to the ground, and she began to wail relentlessly. Her cries added a chilling accompaniment to the sirens.

Francisco turned to Ida with a frozen stare, "I have to go see if they need me." Ida felt the rising sense of fear, like a dog who has picked up the scent of a wounded animal. She grabbed Francisco's arm, "Please come back here right away and tell us what is the matter." She did not know why she clung to him. He murmured his assent, shrugged her off, and then sprinted towards the mill.

Francisco was not the only one running in the direction of the mill. Dozens of people converged on the spot where Miguel lay near a darkening pool of blood. Francisco watched, as the doctor hovered over Miguel. It was too late to save him. Before long, the doctor pronounced him dead.

The mill manager, who had left him alone and then chopped off his arm, was overcome with guilt and grief. With the help of the doctor, the workers tied off what was left of his arm and cleaned up the body. They wrapped him for burial, so that his family would not have to see the horrific state in which they had found him. The severed arm had been removed from sight. They closed his eyes, his expression a blank gray.

CHAPTER 41

1910, Santa Clara, Escape

Marcos had failed to tell Julia the whole story regarding his land and why he was not farming it. He stayed at the Mirante farm for her only, and he had bought the land in hopes of her. All of these hopes lay so fallow in his mind that it was something he had not admitted, even to himself.

Soon after seeing Roger at the Sprung hotel, it now occurred to Marcos that he had been waiting for Julia to get over Roger, or perhaps, to grow up and somehow see that Roger was not the one for her. Now he was not so sure that would ever happen, as he detected persistence in the eyes of the man who stood over Domingos at the Sprung Hotel. That look had rendered Marcos helpless with uncertainty.

Sensing this, Gilberto finally addressed what had been an unspoken topic between them one night at Jake's Place. "I was surprised to see Roger McCallum the other afternoon at the Sprung."

Marcos shrugged, "Yes, he's been hanging out with Domingos."

Gilberto tested the waters, "Can you guess why? I mean, they don't exactly run in the same circles, if you know what I mean."

Marcos looked up and Gilberto volleyed an inquiring look, wondering if he could ever get Marcos to talk about it, yet sensing that now might be the right time. Marcos looked deep into his glass and remained silent.

Gilberto pressed further. "You know he hangs out a lot at the *Serradura*, don't you? Some people say he's there for Julia." Given the pained expression that clouded Marcos's face, Gilberto knew he was pushing it, but he ventured a question, "You know her as well as anyone. Do you think she'll have him?"

Marcos shook his head slowly from side-to-side. "She's a hard one to read. On the one hand, I know that if she were dead set against him, then it would never have gone this far."

"And on the other hand?"

"What can I say? He's rich. He's influential and well-connected. He could have any woman in the Valley."

Gilberto's tone went low. "You know. If you love her, you're going to have to do something about it." Marcos gave a start and slanted Gilberto a look of self-preservation, "Am I really that obvious?"

Gilberto shook Marcos on the shoulder, "You forget, my little cousin, that I know you better than anyone. If you're wondering if she knows, then I would have to say 'no,' based on what I saw in Drawbridge. That's because you're like an iceberg; no one knows what's below the service. And she...." Gilberto grappled for the right description. "She's clearly a woman whose heart is not easily touched."

"You don't understand." Marcos took a hard slug of his drink and shook his head. "It's absolutely hopeless. I made life a misery for her when she was young, and I don't think she could ever see past that now."

"Well, I'm certainly no expert on women, but one thing I do know is, if a woman does not show her feelings," he paused with a meaningful look, "then she just may need to know how you feel first. After all, knowledge of attraction is a powerful invitation. Or do you just want to sit back, do nothing, and watch her marry someone else?"

Agitation set in as Marcos pondered this possibility. "I've never looked at it that way. You're close to Luana. What does she say? And don't try to tell me you haven't talked about it."

Gilberto grinned. "Luana is the right one to talk to; that's for certain. She's the one who told me that Roger hangs out at the *Serradura*, and she keeps a pretty close eye on how he treats Julia. She would definitely know."

"And, what does she say?"

"Oh, she's pretty certain of how Roger feels. She just wonders if Roger will do the right thing by Julia. After all, he has more at stake than most men when it comes to marriage."

"But what does she think Julia will do about it?"

Gilberto tipped his glass. "Now that my friend, is something even Luana cannot say. It's a mystery to her, as well. Right now, she's careful not to push Julia, but I think if she believed the stakes were high enough, she might intervene."

"That leaves me with nothing," Marcos spoke fatalistically.

Gilberto gave Marcos a meaningful look along with a firm shake of his shoulder. "So, now you know what you must do."

Olivia lost no time letting her son know what she thought about his attentions towards Julia. The day after the Auxiliary ball, she laid her cards on the table and held nothing back.

"Don't think I don't know that your grandmother is behind this."

Roger grew dumbfounded. "She has absolutely nothing to do with this. And you will not tell me how I should feel about anyone."

"She would do anything to defy me." Olivia fixated on Abbie.

"On the contrary, I think you're the one who would do anything to defy her," Roger challenged. He was beginning to see how things were, that his mother was the reason they never saw his grandmother. Since Abbie never spoke of his mother, it was obvious that she was neither resentful nor divisive.

"I better never see you with that woman again, or..." Olivia spluttered.

"Or what, mother? Just what are you going to do about it?"

Olivia said nothing, but Roger gathered that his life would be a misery if he continued to pursue Julia. It would certainly test his love for her.

"I think it's best if I move out. It's time," he spoke quietly. He started up the stairs, but she called after him.

"And just where do you think you're going?"

"That's not difficult. We have any number of properties. There's the old McKinley farmhouse. It's been vacant for awhile. I could fix it up or build a new place. Either way, it's time I struck out on my own."

"If you do, you will never get a penny from me." Olivia stood with eyes blazing. She had now been reduced to her ultimate threat.

Roger knew that, while his mother owned their homestead, Abbie's land was held in a trust for him and his three siblings. They would divide it among themselves when Abbie passed away, but they had full access to it in the meantime. Abbie had asked her solicitor to ensure that her land would not pass into Olivia's hands. When Olivia discovered this after Jack died, she was furious. Jack had withheld this very important detail from her on the day he returned after Abbie's illness, and Olivia could not forgive either of them for it. Roger now suspected that this was, in large part, the reason his mother held such a malevolent grudge against his grandmother.

The canneries were a more complex matter. Jack retained complete control of the canneries in his lifetime, but Roger and his brother Samuel shared ownership with their mother after his death. Olivia's shares would fall to them equally upon her death, as stipulated in Jack's will. If she could persuade his brother, they could vote Roger out of management until her passing. The only problem was that Roger's brother Samuel loved ranching and managing the canneries had never interested him.

As Roger packed his things, he thought it through. Just what more could his mother do to him? She might persuade Samuel that they could hire managers to replace him. He was thinking he would just have to take that chance or pre-empt his mother by having a serious talk with his brother. Either way, he would not be persuaded to give up Julia or pursue another, just for financial advantage. He packed his bags and left.

Marcos traced a path adjacent to Coyote Creek along the Mount Diablo range, as Julia followed closely behind on a horse they had borrowed from the landowner's stables. After ten miles of riding, Marcos led them away from the creek through the chaparral and Valley oaks under a low-swinging sun. The chittering of western bluebirds and vireos accompanied them, as they made their way up to the eastern slopes overlooking the southern tip of the Valley. They had been riding for several hours in silence, until he stopped at their first lookout.

"Now this is worth the journey," Julia pronounced. "Can we stop here?" She was surprised when he dismounted and helped her down; it was not his habit to stop or to help her down. She ran to the top of the lookout and he followed.

"Now, that's a sight for the angels," Julia spoke with awe as she shaded her eyes to take in the scene. The sun was beginning to set on a late May Day over the narrowest tip of the Valley. Across from them, the Western range sat parallel to the Pacific coast and ran north to south inland.

They sat upon the rocks overlooking the Valley in front of a field of fiddlenecks, sun cups, and lupine, a vast sea of yellow, orange, and purple. The sun was quickly melting into a puddle of orange and pink, as Marcos grabbled for the right words. After a long silence, he finally spoke.

"If you could live anywhere, where would it be?"

His question surprised her. It never occurred to her that she would live anywhere else. She had thought of visiting Hawaii to see her relatives, but this would always be her home. "I would very much like to visit my aunts and uncles and grandmother in Kauai, but honestly, I can't see myself anywhere but here. It is home to me."

He paused before asking her another question. "Where do you see yourself in ten years?" She wanted to laugh out loud, but she sensed his seriousness.

"Definitely ranching or teaching — here, in the Valley, of course. Why, where do you see yourself?"

"On my ranch. Maybe dairy farming. But definitely here." After a few moments, he got up and bounded over to another high rock and stood still, as he watched the sun go down. After another five minutes, he jumped down and started pacing. He came towards her with an anguished expression.

"Julia, you just can't."

The sun had set and his silhouette stood against the orange marbled skies. She shaded her eyes up at him to see him more clearly. "Can't what, Marcos? Ranch or teach?"

He came closer, struggling for words. "You just can't — marry him. Of all people, not him." His words struck her like an ocean wave slapping her back upon the sea shore. A vague realization came upon her, as she put the pieces together. She knew who he meant, but she wanted to hear it from him.

"And just who is it you think I can't marry?"

"You know who. McCallum."

"And just how is that your business, I'd like to know?" A kind of fever seized her, as she tried to control the anger rising up in her throat, catching her on her last word.

"Because I know him. Because I know what he's made of and what he's not made of."

Julia sprang up to face him, arms entwined tightly together. "And you don't trust my judgment in the matter?" Her response caught him off guard. It made him think she was determined to have the man. Dread came over him and he stepped back.

"That's not what I meant. You know that's not it."

"Then just what is it?"

"I know him better than you do, because I worked with him. I lived on his father's ranch. I'm also older than you are. That gives me a superior knowledge of him."

"Superior?" That's the only word Julia could hear. "Of course, you always considered yourself superior. Especially compared to me. Well, I won't have it. I won't have you, or any other man, telling me what I can or cannot do or how I should feel about anyone." She flounced away.

Marcos saw that he had lost the argument. It would do no good at this point to declare his feelings. He watched as she untethered and mounted her horse and started down the grade. He mounted his horse and followed her back through the brush at full speed, until they reached the ranch and returned the horses to the stable manager. Marcos drove Julia home through twilight without a word spoken between them.

Two weeks later, Marcos packed his things and left the ranch, after a heartfelt discussion with Julia's father. "I just need to get away. See some of the world before I settle down," were his words to Frank. He was determined to get as far away as possible, whatever it would take to forget her. He could not watch her marry Roger McCallum.

For the first time, he even considered selling his land. Gilberto had been looking for property and might want to buy it, but Marcos thought the better of it. He was constrained by his dual loves, for the Valley and for her. "Well, you are welcome back at any time, and you will be missed," Frank told him. "I don't think I'll ever find anyone who could replace you."

It was not until after Marcos had left, at dinner that night, that the rest of the family heard about it. Rose was startled and projected a meaningful glance at Luana, who was just as surprised as anyone. Julia stared into her plate and said nothing, but Luana intuited that Julia knew something that no one else knew.

The next day, Luana found Julia gazing into space, dangling on a makeshift swing that had been roped years ago to an old Valley oak. Luana asked her what she knew. Julia could not hide from Luana; she admitted that she may have had something to do with Marcos's departure and described their interaction.

Luana had the same reaction as Marcos, somewhat alarmed that Julia seemed determined to marry Roger. Luana decided it was time to have a serious talk with Julia. Kneeling down in the grass, she placed her hand on Julia's knee and searched her eyes like she used to do when Julia was a child. "Don't you see, Julia?"

Realizing that her *Madrinha* was being quite serious, Julia squinted at her, "See what?"

"He's in love with you."

"Roger?"

"No, that's not who I meant. I'm talking about Marcos."

Julia looked away and scanned the horizon. Shaking her head, she spoke softly, "That can't be."

"Why can't that be?" Luana challenged her.

"Because he knows I've always hated him."

"Hate is a powerful word, *Afilhada*. Is that what it really is?"

Julia looked down at her feet. "Well, maybe not hate. More like resentment, I guess. And he well knows it, but that's never stopped him from tormenting me."

Luana looked lovingly at Julia, "Don't you remember how he helped you when you were determined to ride Coal?" Julia shook her head. "Yes, but very reluctantly, and only after my father insisted." Julia crossed her arms tightly and grew pensive, "And only after he made my life a complete misery."

Luana forced Julia to look straight into her eyes and spoke insistently, "No, Julia. You're not seeing clearly at all. He made you work hard, because he knew you were capable of great things. He believed in you. Don't you see that now?" Julia glanced away, not ready to see the truth of the matter.

Luana pressed her further, "What about when you were strangled with grief over Therese? How he took you out riding? And how he came to our rescue through the great quake and many times more in countless ways? He may be quiet in his love, but he does love well. Perhaps it's time you grow up, little *Afilhada*. Grow up and open your eyes."

Julia stared ahead and Luana said no more; she simply returned to the house. Luana's purposes were now set in motion. Her instincts told her that now was the time to exert her influence as Julia's *Madrinha*, and the duty of every *Madrinha* is to guide her charge onto a life-giving path.

CHAPTER 42

1882, Kauai, Diamonds

It had been a year since Miguel's death and there were many changes. Maria, Estela, and Ida followed Miguel's dream and started a grocery business in the village with the money they had saved. They lived above the store, just as Miguel had planned, and established strong ties with the other shopkeepers and local community.

The Terras rented land to supply the store with produce and dairy products. Estela rented a back room from them and traded with Ida to care for Luana and Domingos in the daytime. Marissa and Estela continued working as midwives, and Estela taught English lessons in the evenings and on weekends. Estela wanted to be a teacher and was saving her money to attend a teaching college in Honolulu.

Ana married Renato Terra when she was sixteen. Renato worked multiple jobs so they could eventually buy their own farm, and Ana worked as a laundress for the men's camp, while babysitting and helping out at the store. Renato farmed with his father and brothers, but also took up Miguel's old job of collecting firewood to sell at the camps. He traveled monthly to Honolulu to buy supplies for the store and farm.

When she was not at the store, Ida helped Ana with her laundry business. Using large paddles, they were dropping laundry into large oil drums over open fires one day, when they spotted Francisco heading over to the men's camp. They had not spoken to him or seen him since the funeral, and he had grown leaner and much taller since then. He was now eighteen and looked like a grown man with a full beard. It took a moment for Ida to recognize him, but once she did, she burst out loud. "Paulo! Over here." He launched a withering look at her and kept going. She ran to catch up with him. "Will you at least wait a minute? I only want to see how you are."

"I'm no longer bound by contract, so you don't have to call me Paulo. That's all you need to know." He was in no humor to be friendly, and he had decided some time ago to avoid the Mirante family. He had no stomach for any of them, although he sometimes missed little Luana.

"I apologize. Just wait a minute, won't you?" She reached for his shoulder and he turned to face her. Breathlessly, she implored him, "Luana misses you. She cries for Pabo."

"Then you should tell her it's not Paulo. It's Frisco." Ida stifled a giggle. "As in San Francisco?" Francisco's shoulders relaxed and he managed to look straight down at her. "Well, that is where I'm headed."

Ida was curious. "When and how?"

"I'm leaving as soon as I can make my passage to the mainland."

"What will you do there?" Ida longed to know.

"Whatever I can and however I can. This island is not for me. I've slaved enough. I'm going to make my own way now. Be my own boss." He started to leave.

She put her hand on his arm and searched for his eyes, "Before you go, I want to thank you for being there at that awful time. For being with us in our grief. You could have disappeared then. You certainly did not owe us anything. It seems you did care for my father, at least a little." It was true. Francisco grieved with them. What little sense of family he possessed had kept him with the Mirantes the entire week of the funeral.

Francisco would never forget the sight of Miguel stretched out on a long table in their front room, his right arm carefully hidden from sight. His left hand was placed over his breast and wrapped with rosary beads. The rest of him was shrouded. The table had been specially made by a local Portuguese craftsman for Miguel's funeral. It was brought into the Mirante home just for the viewing and would thereafter be used hundreds of times more for funerals throughout the Portuguese community.

At the wake, the scent of island flowers permeated the overly capacitated room, accompanied by the keening of dozens of mourners. Francisco could no longer stomach the heavy perfume of tropical flowers, so much so that just a whiff would now churn his stomach. He could not walk by the mill or hear its grinding without clenching every inch of his body, from his teeth to his hands and feet. He knew he had to escape the sugar cane.

At the funeral, Maria sat in a chair at Miguel's side swaddled from head to toe in black. She did not move from the chair throughout the vigil. Her daughters implored her to come away to rest, but she refused. Every time a newcomer entered the room, outbursts of wailing would begin afresh, as each one tried to comfort the inconsolable widow. It was their custom to speak of the dead in a wailing tone, as if in a dirge.

Juvenal Terra knelt down and belted out a long sing-song tribute to Miguel in a high-pitched lament. "Never has a man had so close a friend. Like a brother. He would do anything for anyone, even without asking. And so wise! He was so wise." The entire room crying, weeping, moaning, swaying back and forth.

Juvenal continued, "When I could not find the strength to take this journey, he helped me find it. Without him, I would not be here. We would have starved in the Azores." Juvenal swung his arms upward. "My family would have starved!" As he said this, he looked up and peered intently, as if searching for Miguel.

Maria clenching her fists, tears streaming down her cheeks, writhed up from her chair in torment. "But my husband and my son would have lived had we not come here!"

Estela was at her side to quiet her, "But *Mãe*, you know *Pai* did what he thought best for us. He only wanted to give us a new life with hope for a good future. Please, please do not cast blame."

When all was quiet, Juvenal went on gulpingly, "Whenever I needed help with my farm back in São Miguel, he was the one I turned to. He always knew the right thing to do. And when I could not endure the ox carts here on the sugar plantations, he found a way to get me another job, even at the risk of losing the good graces of the lunas. He always sacrificed for others, not thinking of himself. He even loved my children, as if they were his own. He lived well and he loved well."

"*Sim, Sim!*" The whole room cried out in agreement.

Francisco stepped forward, knelt down before Miguel, and cleared his throat, speaking in very low tones. Ida had to strain her ears to catch what he was saying. "He was like a father to me. In fact, he was the only father I ever had. He kept me on a straight path. I would have been gone by now. Maybe even in jail, had it not been for him. He showed me how to work hard and how to be patient. Many times I did not listen, but now I realize that I learned from him most, not by what he said, but by how he lived."

The girls teared up when they heard these words. They too realized that they had been the beneficiaries of a loving father who spoke louder by actions than by words.

Jordao Terra stepped up and knelt before Miguel's body. In the voice of a siren, he made this pronouncement. "When we all thought we could not survive the Devil's horns, and darkness overcame us in the hold, he was a light showing us the way. He held fast. He held fast to life and to his family and to his God. Truly, he was a wise and holy man." Jordao choked up, "Oh God, words cannot express how much this man will be missed. We rejoice only that he is now in your care."

Weeping, more wailing and moaning. Hundreds of people streaming in and out of the room all day and all through the night, spilling outside to the porch and the garden. People bringing chairs with them. Passing coffee around to stay awake all night long. Telling stories of their homeland. Wondering what Miguel was thinking and doing now that he was gone. Thinking out loud, where has he gone? Wailing profusely.

One man spoke for so many others, quietly putting words to their emotions, "He cannot come back to us, but some day, we will go to him and see him again."

It was customary to describe the illness and death of the departed, but no one could talk about it, and no one was up to the task. Finally, Juvenal asked the local priest to say the final words. When he told the priest how Miguel had died, the priest raised an eyebrow. "The family may not want to hear these things. It is a very sensitive matter."

Juvenal nodded. "Yes, I could not agree with you more and that is why only you can speak of it. I know you will find the right words. I cannot." The priest nodded. Such is the role of a priest, to find the right words in the right moment. He arrived the next morning, as soon as the coffin was built and the burial ground secured. He cleared his throat and with rosary and missal in hand, he groped for and found his elegiac voice.

"He died faithfully, as he lived faithfully. Always willing to do the hard work that others would not do. After a long day of work, he took on one more task, because in his mind, all must be done well. He did not question it, because he would never refuse to help when needed. He died feeding the cane, so that it might feed others. He died nobly. His work was a blessed work. He did all that he did, because he loved his family and his community. May he forever live in peace and rest."

The sign of the cross was made and a line formed. At least two hundred people waited to kiss the corpse over a period of two hours. After each kiss, the sign of the cross was repeated. Maria wept softly. She was the last one to kiss the corpse. But when it came time to leave, she could not do it. She clung to him and cried out, "Miguel, my Miguel. If you only knew. If you only knew how much I loved you. Now it is too late, too late."

Her daughters helped her away and the wailing intensified. Everyone gathered around to make the trip to the burial site, groaning like a great whale who realizes its life is ebbing away from one thrust of a harpoon. After the casket was lowered and the priest pronounced a final blessing, each mourner filed by the casket with a handful of dirt, and one-by-one, they tossed it over the casket, as the fragrance of flowers pulsed into the air.

When all was quiet and the drumming and wailing had ceased, and the people had retired to their cottages, and night fell over that burial sight, there remained one solitary figure. Francisco would not be moved deep into the night. As he kept his lonely vigil, a strong urge to get as far away as possible lodged itself deeply within him. And so, he plotted his escape before morning dawned on him again.

After the funeral, Francisco soon realized that it would take far more time than he wanted to earn the money for his passage to the mainland. He tried working multiple jobs, but he could not earn the money fast enough or get away soon enough. He also tried gambling, but it only set him back.

Seeing Ida again, a year later, stoked his sense of urgency to depart as quickly as possible. Francisco decided it was time to carry out another plan, one more daring but potentially more rewarding, than his original plan. He knew that Thomas Perreira and his family lived on the very edge of the plantation and that Thomas was about to move his family to the mainland, so Francisco did not have a moment to lose.

On Sunday, when everyone was in church and no one was around, Francisco skulked around the Perreira cottage, checking for ways to access the back bedroom where Thomas and his wife slept. All of the children were in one back room and Thomas and his wife in the other. He discovered that he could easily get in from the front window. All he had to do was figure out where the diamonds were kept while Thomas slept.

He watched and waited outside the dimly lit room for several nights by hiding in a kukui tree that hung over the cottage. From his perch, he observed

Thomas and his wife's nightly routine and the time they normally went to bed. It was not until the third night that he noticed Thomas remove his belt and then slip something under the mat just beside him.

Francisco now realized that he could not waste any more time, but he noted that the house was very dark under the kukui trees. He would need to wait for a full moon to light his way. He waited two full weeks for a full moon, climbed the tree, watched until the family were all asleep, slid down the tree, and burgled into the house.

Slowly, Francisco made his way to Thomas's bedroom, crouched down, and listened for rhythmic breathing and snoring. Luckily, he heard snores loud enough to muffle his tread. He crawled his way to the left side of the bed and found Thomas facing the opposite direction. He used one hand and then two hands to creep under the mat, reaching and groping quietly. It was not difficult to retrieve the pouch. The difficulty would be in replacing it once he was done. He needed more light.

Francisco made his way to the window in the front of the house where there was a full moon. How many was too many? How often did Thomas count his diamonds? One diamond would make his passage. Francisco knew that was all he needed, but greed took over. If he could just pilfer a couple more, it would get him off to a good start in the new land. After all, if Thomas discovered the missing diamonds, who could he complain to? If Thomas spoke up too loudly, someone might question him about where he got the diamonds. Someone else might want to steal more from him. All of these thoughts were swimming around Francisco's mind on the night of his vigil over Miguel's grave.

Francisco weighed all of the risks and decided that out of four or five hundred diamonds, Thomas could spare six. Surely Thomas would not notice six missing, at least not for awhile. Francisco did not know what he would do with them, but it did not matter. He only knew that once he made it to California, it would help him start a new life, a life that was not dependent upon working for someone else.

He counted them out, making sure that he took sizable diamonds but not the biggest diamonds. It might be some time before Thomas counted them, but he was sure to figure it out sooner if the largest diamonds were missing. Better that Thomas was far away in San Francisco, when Thomas finally figured out that he had been robbed. He picked out the diamonds and placed them in his pocket. Then he pulled tightly on the pouch, so that no others could escape, and skulked back to the bedroom.

Thomas had turned over and was on his back, his snores vibrating the ceiling. Francisco would have to place the pouch closer to the edge of the bed. He inched his way closer and then he slid the pouch slowly, until he heard a grunt and a sputter, and the snoring stopped abruptly.

Francisco flattened himself low to the ground. The pouch was secured but not far enough under the mat. Francisco slid his hand and pushed the pouch into position just in time to back away. Thomas jumped up, seized the bed pan, and spouted a steady stream. Grunting, shifting, sliding, pulling up his pajamas. Falling back into bed.

Francisco remained at the foot of the bed and sighed and waited for the rhythmic breathing to return. Twenty minutes later, the light breathing resumed. Francisco raised his head slowly and crawled to the door. He turned and saw Thomas' wife sit up. He bolted and then he heard a scream. By the time the entire household was awake, Francisco was almost back to his camp. There was not a sound as he slipped into his bunk.

CHAPTER 43

1910, Santa Clara, Crossroads

It was time again for the canneries to open, and Julia was eager to return, not that she was especially fond of cannery work. She was longing for pre-occupation and camaraderie. Something to keep her wheels turning and anything to fill her thoughts. The days felt to her as if they were endless roads of nagging restlessness. She spent more time with Abbie and offered to work for Luana and Domingos at the *Serradura*. She even helped her mother with the first wave of canning that year.

Her work at the *Serradura* brought Julia in continual contact with Roger who continued to pursue her. Julia never seemed particularly eager in response, but she did not avoid him either. Her phlegmatic manner made her a puzzle to both Roger and to those who knew her best. Luana and Abbie were growing uncomfortable over Roger's persistence but for slightly different reasons. Neither woman could put her finger on exactly why, but both resisted the temptation to interfere.

From Abbie's perspective, there was reasonable concern that Roger's intentions could not possibly lead to marriage because of Olivia. She did not doubt his sincerity, but she calculated that Olivia's disapproval could only end in heartache for both Julia and Roger. Abbie had not spoken to Roger about Julia since the ball, and he had apparently failed to take her words of caution to heart on that occasion. From what she could tell, his behavior indicated that he was more determined than ever to continue pursuing her. Abbie searched for ways to warn Julia, but it was a delicate matter.

On one particular occasion, Julia was helping her rearrange her downstairs parlor and organize a scrapbook. "I love these paintings of Stirling, Scotland," Julia remarked. "What was it like growing up there?"

Abbie gazed into space, "The most beautiful land at the heart of Scotland. A paradise in its own way but like a rose with a thorn, dark and treacherous in winter but wondrously beautiful in spring and summer. Filled with fields of heather flashing across miles of rolling hills. Rivers and brooks splashing through the spring."

"And there's a castle, isn't there?"

"Yes, indeed. Right next to the Church of the Holy Rood. Set high on a hill. A place where there were very great power struggles. A place that protected the Queen of Scots for quite some time; it's where she was crowned."

"Were you born there?"

Abbie smiled at the question, "No, actually. I was born not too far from there in a village called Linlithgow. I share a birthplace with the Queen of Scots."

"And is that where you met your husband, George?"

Abbie considered for a moment. "No, actually. I met him in the capitol city of Edinburgh. My parents sent me to live with an aunt, so I could attend school there. That's where we met."

Abbie thought about it for a moment and then taking Julia's hand, she led her over to a floor-to-ceiling mirror positioned in a corner of the great room. They stood side by side, Julia looked curiously at Abbie who paused to consider how she might impart some essential truth.

"Look, Julia. Look ahead. Try to imagine yourself at my age. I was once beautiful, just like you are now. I had nothing but high hopes. I loved a man who could give me everything I could want in life, except his heart."

Julia looked back at Abbie through the mirror. "But he must have loved you?"

"Yes, of course. He spoke of love at that time, so he could win me. But for a man like him, winning was everything. Unfortunately for me, once something was won, it lost its allure. At some point, he lost both the will to love and the language to love. In the end, he brought me disillusionment and heartache."

"But why? How can that be?"

Abbie returned a tender look. "I now believe he just never had a heart for love, and it was something I did not want to see in the beginning. We all make the mistake of seeing only what we want to see. Now I see. I see that those who marry for love often find love illusive in the long run. Those who marry for other reasons often find marriage tedious, but at least they come into marriage with low expectations."

"But still, isn't it better to marry for love? You still believe that, don't you?"

"Yes, absolutely. But it's not everything."

"What then?"

Abbie paused to choose her words carefully. "Compatibility and financial security are important, but I think respect is even more important. And more than that, it's all a heart matter. If you want to choose wisely, then you must learn to read hearts. It's a highly under-rated skill but one very much worth having."

Abbie mentally groped for something more concrete. "You know, my grandson is a good man. I don't doubt it. But he is very much like his grandfather. He thinks himself independent, but in his heart, he is driven by the ambition that his mother bred in him, much more than even he realizes."

Julia did not return Abbie's searching gaze as she took in her meaning. There was no mistaking that Abbie wished to warn her away from him. She hardly understood her own feelings in the matter, and for the first time in her life, a wave of uncertainty came over her, an emotion more enigmatic to her than a starlit sky.

Julia and Terry took the stairs to the grape tower two at a time. They arrived early on their first day, so they would have time to catch up. "I heard you are getting married soon," Julia said to Terry. "Will I be invited?" Julia grabbed an apron and then tied her hair back. No one had arrived and they took a seat at a nearby workbench while they waited for everyone.

"Of course you'll be invited. As a matter of fact, I'd be honored if you'd be my bridesmaid."

Julia smiled. "Well, I've never been a bridesmaid before. I think I would be the one being honored."

"Then, that settles it," Terry responded. "I just hope you don't mind wearing pink." Julia laughed, "Pink, really?"

"No, purple actually. Just as dreadful."

"So, where will it be?"

"At the Mission church with a reception afterwards in the hall."

"I'm so happy for you. How long have you known your fiancé?"

"Oh, we grew up together. Our families have known one another since before coming to California." Just as Terry finished her sentence, they heard a commotion down below.

"You promised you'd have five hundred cans soldered for me by the start of the season and look where we are. Not even a hundred. Production starts in an hour. That won't even get us through the first week!"

"That's not what I said." The angry retort spun into the air.

"That damn well is what you said. I'm tired of your excuses."

Julia and Terry looked at each other. Julia immediately recognized Roger's voice tinged with an anger she had never heard from him. Terry took her hand and they peeked out from the catwalk in time to see Roger reach out and shove the man. The man lunged back at him.

"Get out! Get out now!"

The man sneered, "And just who do you think will do your soldering now?"

"That's no longer your concern. Just go and never set foot in here again!" When the man hesitated, Roger struck him in the face. The man wiped his cheek with a disdainful stare and then spat on the floor and left.

Terry receded into the shadows, but Julia remained fixed to her spot. She could not move. She had never heard or seen anything so violent. Feeling her gaze, Roger glanced up and could not miss the disappointed look in her eyes. She shrank back and ran down the back staircase of the tower out of the cannery, where people were beginning to mill around waiting for their work assignments. She kept running and then realized that someone was running after her. His steps grew closer and closer.

"Julia, wait! Stop!"

She turned to face him with an accusing stare. He reached for her and she shrugged him off. "Don't touch me!"

"Julia, it's not what you think."

"How would you know what I think?"

"Because I can see it in your eyes. It's not who I am."

"Or is it just not who you want me to think you are? I saw you strike a man, Roger. There's no excuse."

"Julia, you don't know all of the circumstances. All the things this man has done," he heaved.

She turned and started to walk away from him. "I know all I want to know." He reached for her arm and again she pulled away but stood still. They stood facing each other.

"Just hear me out. Julia, don't you know? Don't you know how much I love you? That I want nothing more than to marry you? I've thought of no one but you. I've planned for no one but you. I've left my mother's house for you."

"So, you think that changes things?"

"Yes. Yes, I do. As a matter of fact, I think it changes everything."

"Well not for me it doesn't." Julia paused, "And probably not for your mother."

"You don't know me."

"And now you've made sure that I don't want to know you."

His eyes grew pleading, "Marry me. Marry me and I promise I'll make it up to you. I'll never do that again."

Roger searched her eyes and she searched his in return. "Tell me you'll be mine. Soon," he pleaded again, as he moved closer and cupped his hands softly around her shoulders.

She looked off in the distance, sighed, and then looked back at him squarely. Her next words rushed out, almost involuntarily. "I can't."

"You can't what?" She stood silent, looking down and away. "There has to be something more." He paused to consider the possibilities. "Is there someone else then?"

Her eyes suspended distantly. "No," she shook her head. "That's not it." Even as the words slipped out of her mouth, she began to doubt them.

"I can't believe that," he whispered.

"Even if it were so, I know you are not for me and that I cannot give you what you want." Tearfully, she turned away. Julia felt a sense of certainty lodge its way into her heart. He reached for her hand and she stepped back and looked down.

"I'm sorry. You must let me go now." She spoke so softly that there was no mistaking the finality in her words. His face grew pale with unfulfilled longing. He released her and watched her walk away for what seemed like an eternity. She faded slowly into the distance like a kite that slips out of the hand of a disappointed child, followed by the shocked realization that it will never return. Dread swarmed his heart like a sandstorm.

It took Julia almost two hours to walk the six miles home. When she arrived, Anarosa spotted her coming down the road and ran outside to meet her. "What happened? Are you sick?"

"No. Not sick. Just sick and tired. I'm not going back to cannery work, Mama. Don't ever ask me to go back again. I'll find some other work."

Anarosa started to protest, but sensed there was no use in arguing the issue further and went inside. Julia parked herself on the porch swing and gazed into the Western skies, while Pretty Boy chittered happily over her presence.

As Luana was coming home from the *Serradura*, she spotted Julia from a distance and called out to her. Julia did not look up, and Luana knew instinctively that something was terribly wrong. She mounted the steps to the porch swing one by one, while Pretty Boy's trills provided a peculiar backdrop to Julia's sad mood. "What is it, *Afilhada*? Why are you not at the cannery?"

Julia did not look at Luana. "I'm not going back there. Will you take me on full-time at the *Serradura*?"

"But of course. It will give me more time to investigate my prospects for a dairy. But there is something more behind this, isn't there?"

And then there was a long silence until Julia stated flatly, "I want you to know that I am not going to marry Roger McCallum."

Luana straightened up and then sat down abruptly to face Julia. "Well, this is a revelation. What happened?"

"It doesn't really matter what happened; what matters is that I now know that we will never marry. Please do not mention this to anyone."

Luana looked at her tenderly. "But of course. I always knew you would find your way, even in the dark." Julia looked up and laughed painfully at her *Madrinha*, "And I suppose that you will always claim that it was with no help from you?"

"Well, you know it is my job to give you a little push when needed." Julia put her head on her *Madrinha's* shoulder with a sigh, "There's just one thing I'd like to know." Luana glanced down at her, "And what is that?"

Julia stared at the distant mountains. "Do you think he will ever come back?"

Luana shook her head up and down slowly and thoughtfully. "If he knows what is good for him, he will come back." She turned to Julia with a meaningful look, as she gently lifted Julia's chin. "And I think he is a man with enough good sense to know what is good for him."

CHAPTER 44

1882, The Pacific, California Bound

While Francisco did not really know the value of the diamonds in his possession, he was certain that at least one of them would pay for his passage to the San Francisco Bay with enough to spare. He thought about bartering with others to purchase a passage on his behalf, but he worried that word would get back to Thomas Perreira. Francisco just needed to find a way to sell it for a reasonable sum. As for the other diamonds, he would figure out how much he could get for them when he arrived in California.

He was right in assuming that Thomas Perreira was not likely to sound an alarm about the theft. After all, the man had close to four hundred diamonds. What harm could there be in a few stolen? Why would he dare draw attention to himself? Francisco presumed that Thomas might now wonder whether Miguel had told others, not knowing that his words had been overheard by the stowaway. Now that Miguel was gone, that could never be known. After waiting a week, during which there was no indication that the theft had been made public, Francisco decided it was time to plan his escape.

There were many Asian and Portuguese workers interested in travel to the mainland, and there was a constant buzz of conversation around the campfires about the easiest and cheapest ways to make the journey. Francisco kept his head down and his ears open until he felt certain he could move forward without arousing suspicions about how he had earned his fare.

He planned his first step: he would journey first to Honolulu, so he could sell one diamond and then purchase his passage on a steamer. He went in private to his Japanese friend, Kenji, whose uncle in Honolulu traded precious gems imported from the Orient. One day, at the end of their work day, Francisco took Kenji aside and showed him one of the diamonds.

"I need to talk with you. See this?" Kenji's eyes popped open. He looked up at Francisco. "Where'd you get it?"

Francisco put a finger to his lips to quiet him. "I need your help and your confidence. Your uncle, will he pay?" Kenji looked back down at the stone and then up again at Francisco with a quizzical expression.

Francisco elaborated, "Will it cover the fare for a ship to California?" Kenji crackled with a somewhat toothless smile, "And more. You will also need money for lodging and food." Kenji jogged his head up and down before speaking. "This should get you there with plenty to spare. More than plenty."

Francisco's excitement grew. This was exactly what he wanted to hear. "Can you write a note for me so I can get me a fair price?" Kenji agreed once more, excited for Francisco, knowing how much he wanted to get to California. Francisco pressed him, "How much should I ask for?"

"My uncle will tell you."

"But what do you think?"

"I would say two hundred dollars is a good price, maybe three hundred."

"Can you ask him in the note?"

"Yes, I will, and I will miss you, my friend."

Francisco thrust an arm around Kenji's shoulders and shook him heartily. "And I you. But let's keep this a secret, just between friends. Agreed?" Kenji smiled up at him. "Yes, and I will join you someday, soon."

"Yes, soon."

The next morning Kenji brought Francisco a letter, written in Japanese and labeled with his uncle's name and address.

There was just one thing Francisco had to do before catching the schooner to Honolulu. He had to find a way to say goodbye without letting anyone know that he was saying goodbye, especially the Mirantes. He did not want his Portuguese community to know that he had left until well after his departure. There were a few gambling debts he was leaving behind, and he wanted to avoid confrontations.

Early on a Friday, when he knew Ida would be taking care of the twins, he borrowed a horse and rode to the Terra farm. The Terras were away working at the store. Ida was in the garden with the twins, who were now almost five years old.

Luana was making mud cakes and slapping them into Domingos's lap, while Ida was tending the garden. Once Ida was out of sight, Luana slapped one cake onto Domo's head. Each time she'd slap another one on him, both of them would erupt into laughter, causing such a ruckus that Ida came running. "Luana, stop putting mud cakes on your brother's head." This process repeated itself three times before Domo was caked from head to toe.

"Now look what you've done, Luana. Your brother will need a bath before noon!" Ida should have known by now that Luana never followed her instructions. Just as Ida was pulling Domo out of his mud bath, she noticed Francisco coming towards them.

Luana followed her Tia's gaze and ran to Francisco with arms outstretched. "Cisco, Cisco!" She had learned his new name and loved to hear it spoken. Francisco could not help but smile and raised her up to the skies with a swooping hug. They looked into each other's eyes. No one had ever touched Francisco's heart like Luana, except perhaps Miguel. Francisco loved this little daughter of Miguel's more than he could say.

Ida crossed her arms and watched them closely. She could see the special bond between them. Perhaps Luana was just like Francisco, she thought, or perhaps she was something of a combination of Miguel and Francisco, the best of both of them. Whatever it was, she had to admit that it was something special. Ida sensed the uniqueness of that moment, and before she knew what she was saying, she turned to Francisco. "It's time, isn't it?"

Surprised by the direct confrontation, he nodded back at her. She turned away, suddenly feeling sorry that he would actually go. She walked a few steps away from him and then turned back around to face him. "You know she'll miss you. She still asks about you all the time." Luana picked up on their mood and her brow knit into a frown.

Francisco set her down and looked into her big grey-slate eyes puddling with tears, "Luana, I am going away for a time."

"No Frisco, don't leave." The child wrapped her arms around his legs and he squatted down to her eye level.

"Sweet one, I know how hard it is to say goodbye. When you get older, you will understand. People come and go, but that does not mean we will not see each other again or that I don't love you."

"Are you going to be with *Pai*? Did you get hurt like *Pai* did?"

"No, Luana, not like *Pai*. Not like that." Ida had to turn her back when she heard this.

"I promise that you will see me again, and that no matter what, you can write me anytime, and I will answer."

"But I don't write."

"Maybe not yet, but in the meantime, your Tia can write for you. You tell her what to say and she'll write it down for you." Luana considered all of this and began to cry. "No. No. You can't go. You can't leave me too."

"I must go. Just for a little while. Trust me, I will find a way for us to be together again." Luana whimpered and Francisco slumped. Then he released Luana's arms as gently as possible. He remembered being abandoned by his mother, and his heartache weighed on him. He wanted to run. Instead, he turned to Ida. "Take care of the girl. I will write you and send my address as soon as I am settled. Promise me you will find ways to keep me in her heart." Ida nodded.

"And please, do not tell the family until I am well on my way. Promise me," he insisted.

"I promise. But before you go, there's something I would like to do for you. My mother's extended family live in California. My grandmother's maiden name is Fernandes, and her father João and his family live there and run a dairy farm. They could help you get started. Let me give you their address. They are in the Santa Clara Valley, just south of San Francisco. I will write to them and tell them who you are and that you are on your way."

Ida ran inside and came back with a piece of paper with their name and address and handed it to him. "Be sure to tell them I sent you." Francisco nodded in appreciation and turned to go.

Ida understood that he must get away immediately. As he crossed over the garden to the gate, Luana spouted a wail, and Ida took hold of Luana and held her tight. "Come back. Cisco, come back!" It reminded Francisco of Miguel's vigil, when Luana lamented relentlessly, so much so that it still haunted his dreams.

Francisco understood that Luana's loves would always be as strong as her hates, and she would never let go of anyone she might choose to love or hate. Francisco loved her all the more for it. As soon as he was out of her sight, he jumped on the horse and surged forward until the horse broke into a sweat.

The next afternoon, Francisco packed his few belongings into a duffle bag while most of the camp was still at work and shambled softly out of the camp in the wake of the afternoon. He waited an hour for the last schooner to Honolulu, hiding in shadows and peering around to ensure that he remained unnoticed. At five-thirty in the evening, he boarded the schooner.

It was early the next morning, when he reached the busy Honolulu port. He made inquiries of a crewman on how to find his way to Kenji's uncle. Kenji's uncle's shop was close to Chinatown, and Francisco immediately took off to find it.

Once in Honolulu, locating the shop was no easy matter. In Chinatown, the streets were filled with people shuddered around outdoor market stalls. Patrons jammed him up and blocked his every step. Francisco had never been in such a densely-occupied place. He soon discovered that one false step took him off in a wrong direction. He tried thrusting a piece of paper in front of market vendors, who would shake their heads angrily and shrug their shoulders at him. It took several attempts before someone finally stopped, looked at the paper, and pointed him in the right direction.

The shop was tucked into a morass of causeways surrounded by, what seemed to be, a never-ending sea of dead ends. Francisco spotted it at the end of an alleyway, a frowsy lean-to. The look of it did not inspire confidence. Francisco entered a room overstuffed from top to bottom redolent with stale incense. There were cases of gems on tables, a ceiling filled with hanging lamps, lanterns, and kaleidoscopic kites. Fusty, incense-filled air.

An old man with a gray beard resembling a streak of smoke, snored in a corner. "Ahem, sir?" The old man looked up, eyes blurry.

"Mr. Watanabe?" He nodded and shined a tobacco grin.

"My name is Francisco. I bring a message from Kenji." Francisco presented the letter, and the old man unfolded and looked it over somewhat suspiciously. He jolted his head upward, and with his eyes narrowed, he sliced them up and down Francisco.

After a pause, the old man spoke, "You are Kenji's friend?" Francisco nodded. "You have the gem? Let me look." Francisco removed the second largest diamond from a small pouch tied to his duffle bag. "Here."

The old man clawed the gem out of Francisco's hand and quickly fastened an ocular to his eye to examine it closely, as Francisco waited impatiently.

"Yes, I will pay. It's very fine. I've not seen anything like it. Where did you get it?"

"The gem comes from Africa. I brought it all the way from Madeira island." Francisco did not want to appear too reticent, so as to arouse suspicion of ill-gotten gains. He thought he would give the old man just enough information to keep him curious but quiet. "How much?"

"You are a friend, so I will give you two hundred and fifty dollars."

Francisco instinctively countered. "I need three hundred fifty." The old man resisted slightly and after a pause, said, "I'll give you three hundred."

"No, I need three fifty."

"You are going to America? For how many days? You will need food and a place to stay while you wait for the ship. I will put you up at my house. Will you take three hundred ten?"

"Yes, with food and a place to stay for a few days. I will take three hundred and ten." Francisco grinned widely and reached out his hand to cinch the deal. Mr. Watanabe smiled faintly, knowing that his was the much better end of the bargain.

Three days later, a full-pocketed and dressed-out Francisco boarded a steamer bound for the San Francisco Bay. He had enough fare to pay for his own room with enough money left over for room and board to last at least several months once he arrived in California. In seven days, he would be on the mainland.

He bounded up the gangway in his new traveling clothes and proudly presented his boarding pass. He would no longer be stowing away, hiding in shadows, playing dice in corners, and pilfering food. He was clean-shaven, a man with a purpose and a man with means. He felt brand new, all grown up.

It occurred to him that if Miguel could see him now, he would be proud of him. On second thought, Francisco realized that Miguel would never approve of the way he had purchased his fare and how he used Miguel to do it. He quickly brushed such thoughts aside, as he searched for his room.

Francisco would not be traveling in steerage with dozens of laborers. He was astonished when he finally found his stateroom. It was a palace compared to the places he had lived for the past eighteen years of his life. He knew it was an extravagance and that he should be saving his money, but it was too much of a temptation to resist. With five more diamonds sewn into the lining of his new traveling clothes, he could afford a little luxury. And at least this way, no one was likely to recognize him.

Once he was in his room, a porter arrived with his trunk of new clothes. The trunk was a gift from Mr. Watanabe. The old man could afford to be generous, knowing he would sell the diamond for double what he had paid for it. Francisco suspected as much, but he did not care. All he wanted was to get on the ship and get on with his new life.

Francisco unpacked for the seven-day journey, freshened up, and went out on deck for a stroll. He wanted to watch the ship disembark and view the islands as he sailed away. On the promenade, he bought a lemonade and took in Honolulu harbor one last time. The sun was bright, and the beaches were dotted with multi-colored umbrellas and bathers. Francisco reclined in a deck chair and raised his face to the sun. For the first time in his life, he could relax and toss away every care. He basked in the glow of that first-time moment of security and optimism. Just as he was dozing off, he heard a sound, "Hey mister! Pssst!"

Francisco thought he was dreaming and willed himself back into a doze. But the sound pestered him awake. "Hey mister! Pssst!" He could not will it away. Finally, he opened his eyes and stared into the eyes of a poor urchin peering down at him. He started up out of a fuzzy day dream. "Who are you and what do you want?"

"Please sir, do you have any food?" The boy was tattered, skeletal, about thirteen or fourteen years old, anxiety-ridden, and he smelled like the bottom of a fish barrel. Francisco saw himself in the boy's muddy face, as if he were looking at a reflection in a clear crystal pond. Francisco wanted to turn away, but he hesitated, somehow knowing that his own little boy would always be lodged deep inside. Those eyes, those lost and lonely eyes. "Where do you come from, boy, and what is your name?"

"My name is Gilberto. Gilberto D'Angelo. I came from the camps, but I had to escape. They beat me regularly." Knowing the camps and what they were like, Francisco suspected the child was telling half-truths. Still, there was just enough credibility in what he described to be believable. "Where are your father and mother?"

"They are far away. When they could no longer take care of me back in Sicily, I hired myself out on a ship to come to these islands. But the work has been too hard with so little pay. I can hardly survive. Please sir, won't you help me?"

"How old are you? Tell me the truth now."

"I am thirteen." Five years younger than Francisco.

Francisco heaved a sigh of resignation. It only took him a moment to say, "Yes. I will help you. You can sleep on the floor of my cabin, and I will give you some new clothes. But first, let's watch the sunset and the ship depart. After we get you outfitted with new clothes, we'll eat our first night in the dining room. Would you like that?"

Gilberto was dumbfounded. Why would this man want to help him? "Of... of course, sir."

Francisco stood up and put his arm around Gilberto and smiled down at him like one who has been given a new lease on life. "Call me Frank."

"But I heard the porter call you Francisco. Isn't that your name?"

"So, I see you have been spying on me. And just what was it that made you single me out?"

"Uh, nothing. Nothing sir. Perhaps you had a kind face?" Francisco looked doubtful.

"Or perhaps the face of a sucker?" The boy shriveled back, but Francisco only laughed and put his arm around the boy. "Well, if we're going to be friends, you must first stop calling me Sir."

Francisco then steered Gilberto away from the deck. "And second, you must never tell anyone that I was once called Francisco. From now on, you must always call me Frank. Agreed?"

"Yes, of course, Frank. Is that your new name?"

"Yes, my new American name." Frank's face colored with pride.

CHAPTER 45

1911, Santa Clara, Luana's Dairy

After Marcos left, life took a sudden turn for the Mirante family. Their lives shifted one by one, like chess pieces moving around a playing board. Julia's brothers took on more responsibility for the ranch. In their free time, Frank helped Alexio build a house on a property he had bought adjacent to the Mirante ranch. Julia started learning how to manage the *Serradura's* counter service with Uncle Domos's help, while Rose took over the baking in the back of the store. People came from miles around to taste her specialties, fruit pies and blackberry brandy. Rose also learned to play the ukulele, and when she wasn't working at the dairy, she gave lessons to children at the elementary school.

Like most grand schemes in Luana's life, her best laid plans were hatched over a bar stool at Jake's Place. "So, have you heard from Marcos?" It was not the first time Luana nudged Gilberto on the subject, and it would not be the last.

Gilberto shook his head slowly from side to side and put down his shot glass. "Not a word."

"Do you remember what he said to you before he left? Did he mention Julia?"

Gilberto shook his head decisively. "Not a word about her. Just that he wanted to travel, see the world. Why? Do you think he left because of her?"

"Yes, I do. I think he thought she'd marry Roger McCallum, and he didn't want to stick around to see it happen."

"Well, the marriage hasn't happened. Do you still think it will?"

Luana stopped to consider whether she could trust Gilberto. On second thought, she realized that Gilberto just might be the one to get word to Marcos at some point. "I have good reason to believe that it will never happen."

Gilberto glanced down at her with a surprised expression. "We all thought it was just a matter of time."

"I know. But we didn't know our Julia very well."

"So, you think it was her doing?"

"I don't know, but I don't think it really matters. I mean, you must have noticed that he never comes to the *Serradura* anymore, and he used to come almost every day."

"Yes, Domingos mentioned it to me. They were good friends for awhile there. We never see him playing cards in Drawbridge like he used to either."

After thinking about it for a moment, he turned the subject back to Marcos. "You know, Marcos owns land here, so he's bound to return at some point."

It was now Luana's turn to be surprised. "You don't say? I never knew that. He sure keeps his cards close, that one."

"Yep, right next to my land."

Luana almost dropped her teeth and turned roundly on him. "You own land too?"

Gilberto grinned down at her, "Why? Are you jealous?"

Luana sighed and turned back on her stool. "I've been looking for just the right place myself. The problem is, I can't afford to build a dairy from the ground up. I need a farm that already has a dairy barn and the herd to go with it. And one that I can buy for the right price. I just haven't been able to find it, and I don't want to leave the Valley." She sighed, "So, you see, I feel stuck."

"Well then, why don't you use my dairy barn? I don't plan to use it; I was going to tear it down. And there's land adjacent to mine you might consider buying, where you can grow alfalfa and wheat for grazing."

Luana's eyes brightened like a glacier reflecting the summer sun. "You would do that for me?"

Gilberto faced Luana with a smirk, "Yes, Kokomo. I would do that for you."

Luana creased her brow at him, realizing that her twin had told Gilberto a story that he was supposed to have kept to himself. Something about Luana at her sister Ida's wedding when she was sixteen.

"That would make us partners then, wouldn't it?"

Gilberto cocked his head with a sly look. "If you want to look at it that way."

Luana harpooned Gilberto with an icy stare. "Well then, partner. Just don't ever tell anyone about Ida's wedding."

Gilberto grinned widely. "Only on one condition."

"What's that?"

Gilberto stood up, leaned down towards her, and whispered in her ear, "That you marry me." Before she could object, he cupped his hands around her face and gazed deeply into her astonished eyes. Then he kissed her soundly, taking her breath away and lifting her off of her stool. Like she had never been kissed before.

He was gone before she could stop her pounding heart. Vaguely aware that all eyes were on her and that she couldn't care less, she shook her head from side-to-side, slapped her thighs, and laughed out loud. The convivial crowd obliged her by applauding.

The next day, Luana waited at the bakery, wondering if Gilberto would come by and seal the deal, but there was no sight of him. A week went by, and she still did not hear from him. She grew mad and then anxious. She wondered if Gilberto had been making sport of her. Then she would remember his kiss and smile to herself. She kept it close to her heart like a little boy with a toad in his pocket. Frequently throughout the day, she would take it out and giggle out loud at the thought of it. Julia started watching her closely, noticing that something was very different about her *Madrinha*. Back near the ovens, Rose mentioned it.

"What is up with *Tia*?"

Julia shook her head. "I've never seen her like this."

"Yeah, I know. Except for maybe that one time she got drunk on watermelon brandy. She was glassy-eyed for two days after that."

"Yep. That about describes it. Giddy almost. It's kind of scary." Julia wiped down the butcher block and then wiped the steam on her forehead with the back of her shirt sleeve. She was not accustomed to an uncertain Luana, one who is anything but a source of strength. Her *Madrinha* was always the most indomitable presence in any room. Goofy was definitely not a typical demeanor for Luana.

"Well, do you want to ask her what's going on or shall I?" Rose prompted.

Julia tossed down her rag. "Go ahead and finish up. I'll see what I can get out of her." After Rose locked the front door and left, Julia came out to the front of the bakery and found Luana staring out the window.

"Penny for your thoughts?" Luana was startled and tried to laugh it off. Julia made eye contact with Luana and raised her eyebrows, "*Madrinha*, just what is going on with you?"

Luana ran her hand through her hair and let out a sigh. "Oh, Julia. I can't hide anything from you, anymore than you can hide anything from me." She groped for the right words. "Remember the day I found you out on the front porch gazing into the horizon? Wondering if Marcos would ever return?"

"Don't remind me."

"Exactly."

"What do you mean, 'exactly'?"

I mean it's a pretty miserable state to be in, right? You try not to think about it, but you can't help but think about it, because it's driving you crazy. Right? Isn't that what it's like?"

"Definitely a miserable way to be."

"Well, you and your *Madrinha* share the same boat now. That's what it's all about, I'm afraid."

Julia couldn't be more surprised. She leaned back, elbow to hand, fingers on her cheek, with an astonished look. "You don't mean....?"

"Yes, just say it. Say it. Come on, spit it out."

"You're in love?"

Luana flashed Julia a look that was both apologetic and deeply embarrassed, as if she were letting Julia down in some way. "Yep, that pretty much says it without me having to say it, thank God."

Julia clapped her hands together. "Why *Madrinha*. That's amazing. And wonderful. Rose and I always wondered if you and Gilberto would get around to it."

"Yeah, well. He got around to it over a week ago at Jake's. And then he left and I haven't seen him since." She shrugged. "And now I'm miserable."

Julia put her arm around Luana, "Now, finally. I get to comfort you. You know, as you grow older, I'm the one who'll be looking out for you and not always the other way around?" Luana smiled and gave her hand a firm squeeze.

Gilberto was not trying to keep Luana in suspense. He had laid his cards on the table, but now he was experiencing a combination of relief and dread. Relief that he had finally done what his heart told him to do but dread that she might not be able to reciprocate. He had not planned it; he had just seized the moment. He also knew Luana well enough to realize that she would need a few days to let it sink in. He decided to pay Frank a visit, but not before he asked Domingos about Luana's schedule to be sure she would not be around.

He arrived at the ranch on a beautiful May afternoon and found Frank outside, supervising the spraying of the prune orchards. Spotting Gilberto from a distance, Frank jumped down from a ladder and waved him on. "Gilberto, so good to see you, my friend." He slapped Gilberto on the back. "To what do I owe this unexpected visit?" Before Gilberto could respond, Frank guided him to the farmhouse kitchen. "Let's go inside and get something cool to drink."

Once they were settled on the back porch, Frank berated his friend for not coming around. "I suppose you are busy getting your crops ready for planting? If you need my help, let me know. My sons have pretty much taken over the ranch, and I find myself at leisure more often than I care to admit."

"I just may take you up on that," Gilberto tipped his glass at Frank.

"Do you need help taking down that dairy barn?"

"Actually, I may need help repairing it."

"You're not going to tell me that you'll take up dairy farming now, are you?"

"Not me. Your baby sister. I've offered my barn for her use. But I'm sure she'll want to tell you herself."

Frank slapped him on the back. "No kidding. What a perfect idea. She's been hankering for a dairy for some time now. Just looking for the right opportunity. I'm surprised I didn't think of it myself. It's perfect."

"Frank, there's more. That's what I came to talk to you about. I've made her an offer, you see. But it's more than a business deal. I've asked her to marry me." Gilberto searched Frank's face for approval, knowing his affection for his baby sister.

Frank looked up, happily startled. "Why, you are one cagey fellow. How is it I never knew? You know I would like nothing better than to have you in the family." Frank's face moistened with delight.

"Yeah, well. There's just one problem. It's been a long time coming. I mean, Luana never struck me as the marrying kind. That's just it. I asked her, but I didn't stick around for an answer, and now I'm not sure if I can convince her."

Frank rubbed his chin and considered for a moment. "Well, I can't disagree with you there. Luana has always been allergic to the idea of marriage. That's for certain."

Gilberto gazed at Frank hopefully. "Do you think she'll have me?"

Frank grabbed Gilberto's knee and gave it a shake. With a straight face, he said, "If she won't have you, then I'll make her have you."

Gilberto laughed out loud. "Frank, you can't do that. You can't force someone like Luana to marry, if she doesn't want to. We'd make each other miserable under those circumstances."

"Either way, you have my blessing. You know, I have a great deal of influence with my baby sister. I could put in a good word."

"I appreciate that more than I can say. But it's not necessary, really. I just wanted to know if you had any insight into her that I can't see. Any encouragement you can give me."

"Don't hesitate. Go to her as soon as possible and reassure her of your intentions."

"That's it?"

"No, actually. There's something you should give her. Wait right here." Frank went into the house and was gone for a good ten minutes. When he came back out, he was holding a tiny silk pouch in his hand. Frank took Gilberto's hand and placed the pouch in his palm. "Give her this and she'll love you forever." He winked.

Gilberto examined it quizzically, opened it, and turned it upside down. A sparkling one carat diamond fell out. A look of utter surprise spread over his face and he spoke with disbelief. "Frank, I can't take this."

"It's not for you, my friend. It's for my baby sister. Any man who could deserve her deserves to give it to her. Of course, you will have to go to a jeweler to have it cut."

"But, where? How?"

"Don't you remember when we were working on the docks in Oakland? I told you when we'd had enough and that we didn't need to work anymore?"

"Yes, but ...."

"Well, this is how."

"I don't know what to say." He choked up. "You are more than a friend. You are more than a brother."

Frank squeezed his arm and leaned over. "And now we will make it official, eh my brother? I have a good feeling about this. If Luana is to marry anyone, then it has to be you."

Later that week, Gilberto showed up at the bakery and asked Luana if she would walk with him to the college. He led her to a bench in the rose garden by the Mission church and on one knee, he let her know that he had loved her for as long as he had known her. When she looked skeptical, he handed her a black velvet box and searched her expression desperately like a dog biting for fleas.

Never failing to appreciate the value of the dollar, Luana's eyes grew moon-sized, as she was blinded by the sparkling light. Gilberto smiled a most endearing smile. "So, is it a yes? Please say yes."

"Oh yes." Luana was never one to gush but she became a virtual geyser in that moment.

"Now, be honest. You're not just saying yes because of that sparkler and my land, are you?"

She replied mischievously, "Well, let's just say that I like the WHOLE package, but even that's not the best part of the package."

"And just what is?"

"Your kiss," she said softly.

"Well then, I'll just have to give you lots of them."

"Oh yes." And so he did.

Frank shaded his eyes as he surveyed the finishing touches on Alexio's new two-story red farmhouse. It contained five bedrooms and a large kitchen with an icebox and a cast iron stove. It even had an indoor commode. The two brothers had been building it in their spare time during the past year, after Alexio purchased five acres of land adjacent to his father's orchards. The farmhouse was bigger than Frank's house, two stories with a well-laid-out back garden surrounded by a row of weeping willows and pasture land for grazing.

Anarosa joined Frank followed by a cart full of household supplies, including rugs, kerosene lamps, food for a well-stocked pantry, and furniture.

"Now we just have to build the tank house and we'll be done," Alexio wiped his hands on his dungarees with a look of satisfaction.

"I don't think you can find a better-looking farmhouse in the entire Valley," Frank spoke admiringly.

"You better be careful. We might all move in with you," Anarosa laughed. "I'll get this food in the kitchen."

Three months later, they gathered at the Mission church for a small celebration of marriage uniting Luana and Gilberto. Rose and Julia attended the bride in their gingham May Day dresses, while the bride wore a dress of silky white with pearls. Frank walked his baby sister down the aisle, his eyes filling with tears, as he gave her away to his best friend.

They celebrated late into the night around a candlelit dinner at Alexio's new house. Gilberto spared no expense on the food and wine. Rose and Luana had baked for three days at the *Serradura*. There were two tables filled with Azorean dishes including Cozido das Furnas, a spicy meat stew with linguica sausages and plenty of Madeira wine to wash it down. Three large bowls of fresh fruit spilled over and around the cakes and pies.

Rose turned to Alexio as they were finishing their meal, "Now, big brother. Just how do you plan to fill this great big house? You surely don't expect to live here with a bunch of farmhands, do you?"

Alexio winked. "Don't you worry baby sister. I will make good use of this establishment and with no help from you."

"*Sim, sim*," everyone cried.

There were many toasts at the candlelit table that night. Once they had depleted the wine, they switched to cachaca, a fine rum. But there was one toast that Julia would never forget. Her father had rarely ever spoken of her grandfather, whom she never knew.

When Frank had consumed his fair share of wine, his eyes glistened and took on a far away look. He raised his glass of cachaca and his voice turned solemn like a prayer, "To the man who showed me the way. A great man. Your grandfather, Miguel Mirante."

"*Saude*," everyone responded as they raised their sparkling glasses.

Rose touched her father's sleeve, "Tell us Papa, what was he like?"

His children had never heard Frank speak of him before.

"Endlessly selfless. Endlessly optimistic. A humble but great man. He took me on when my life was worthless and I was lost. I would not be here today were it not for him."

"*Sim, sim*."

Frank raised his glass again, "And to Paulo, the son I could never be. The one who gave me his place with his last dying breath." Frank was overcome, as candle lights cast shadows around the walls of the large dining parlor. "Miguel so wanted me to be him, but I couldn't. I just couldn't. I'll never understand. Why him and not me? I deserved to die. He never did." Frank broke down.

Anarosa was taken aback. She had never seen Frank cry before. He had always been her rock. The room grew silent, as he wiped his tears. Rose wrapped her arms around her father's neck and pressed her cheek to his. "Oh, Papa. Please don't cry.... We have so much to be grateful for tonight."

"*Sim. Sim.*" Everyone joined in.

Frank wiped his cheek with a handkerchief. "Yes, of course. I have all of you. But I can't help thinking that I would not be here were it not for Paulo."

CHAPTER 46

1882, The San Francisco Bay

For seven breathtaking days across the Pacific, Frank and Gilberto traveled in style. They danced and sang; they played at cards with the first class passengers and afterwards threw dice in steerage. They drank and ate well, dressed and groomed well, laid out in the sun and breathed in the salty air. They hung over the sides of the ship smoking and laughing as dolphins bounced aside them. Even had their shoes shined.

Frank could not help comparing this trip to his last. There were no storms, no billowing sails, no slop buckets, or hard tack. Every meal was a feast to those who had been pilfering and starving. Frank took to drinking whiskey, smoking cigars, and eating sardines.

The night before their approach to the San Francisco Bay, Gilberto and Frank shared one last meal in the dining room with two businessmen. Frank's English had greatly improved, and he could talk his way into or out of almost any situation. He was a conniver and a charmer, but he was no bounder.

"So, where are you boys headed?" The question came from a Mr. John Carver. The man was the owner of a lumber and imported furniture business. Gilberto glanced up at Frank, never quite knowing what he might say.

"Wherever the road takes us," Frank spoke with a certain air of confidence. Mr. Carver was carrying furniture from the Orient, dressed up for the San Francisco market. He assumed that Frank might be green and malleable, which to a certain extent, he was.

"Will you be looking for work right away?"

"Yes. We're open to all possibilities."

"Anything in particular that you have in mind?"

Frank sucked on a cheroot, spewed smoke in the air, and watched as the smoke curled into slow-motion tendrils, "Like I said, wherever the road takes us."

"Then maybe you might consider coming to work for me. I need good strong men like you on the dock in Oakland. It's an easy, quick way to earn the cash you'll need to see you on your way."

"Well, I do appreciate that offer. Perhaps we will take you up on it." He considered that it had not been his immediate plan, but it may just give him more traveling cash.

The man took out a pencil and paper and scribbled a note. "Here, take this to dock number seven and ask for a man by the name of Carlos, Carlos Becerra. Tell him I sent you, and he'll take care of you."

"Again, I sure do appreciate that, uh, Mister?"

"Carver, John Carver."

Francisco took the piece of paper and folded it into his pocket. He and Gilberto spent the rest of the night playing dice. "We may as well have fun while we can. From here on, it will be nothing but hard work."

The opening to the San Francisco Bay was like the maw of a yawning whale. The gateway looked deceptively easy to navigate, but overconfidence upon approach was ill-advised. Ships were known to tumble up against boulders mistaken for benign aquatic landscapes. And yet, whatever the ride, the bay always dazzled its first-time onlookers like an initial gaze at the Crown Jewels; until it is experienced, its glories cannot be fully appreciated.

Francisco and Gilberto hung over the ship's railing soaking up the sights, and they did not move until they disembarked. Neither of them had ever seen anything like it, not even the busy port city of Valparaiso. Rolling hills lined the bay to the west, dotted with tents and campfires and ships docked in the foreground. Abandoned ships and boats of every kind were anchored everywhere. Buildings lined the wharves stuffed with cargo, and workers conveyed goods from ship to wharf and back again.

The sight was one of endless hustle, people moving back and forth. The sounds of growth were buzzing everywhere, and the churning of industry was endlessly chawing and spitting out its refuse. The city bore all the signs of human appetite for accumulated wealth, and it easily captured Frank's imagination.

Their steamer crawled its way to the Oakland docks, dodging the multitude of anchored boats along the way. Upon arrival, they went through a brief immigration process and were granted naturalization papers. Immigration officials at the dock asked them a few questions.

"Where are you from and where are you headed?" Francisco answered first, so Gilberto would know what to say. He had been schooled by those back on the islands who were privy to the process.

"I've come from Kauai where I worked on a sugar plantation. I have already found work in the San Francisco bay."

"Have you ever been in prison or resided in a lunatic asylum?"

"No never." Frank was quick to reply.

"That'll be fifty cents tax." Frank handed him the money, and the official gave Frank his naturalization papers, which he would later use to apply for citizenship. Next, Gilberto repeated the same answers, paid the immigration tax, and received his papers. As soon as they were out of range, they celebrated.

Frank shook Gilberto's shoulder. "Let's have lunch and then find this man Carlos Becerra, what do you say?" They discovered a vendor near the dock who served up clam chowder, fish stew, fried mussels and shellfish. They gorged themselves and washed it down with cold lager ale, changed into their work clothes, and returned to the dock to find Carlos Becerra. Frank handed him the note from Mr. Carver. Carlos looked them up and down and then sent them over to a supervisor who put them to work immediately.

After a long day of hauling cargo, Frank asked the supervisor where they could find a place to stay. The man pointed to a long row of shack-like buildings across from the harbor. After surveying each one, they knocked tentatively on the door of what seemed to be the largest establishment. An Asian woman peaked around the corner of the door.

"Hello, Ma'm. We're looking for a place to stay while we work on the docks." Her eyes contracted. "How long will you stay?"

"Uh, we're not certain but at least one week."

"The longer you stay, the less you will pay."

"Let's say one week." The woman nodded and opened the door. Truthfully, Frank did not know how long they would last on the docks. He was now at the point where he wanted to preserve his remaining funds and get the lay of the land before moving on. He considered traveling around the state before settling.

For six days they hauled cargo off ships and into waiting carts. The work was difficult but not nearly as back-breaking as cutting cane or driving oxen in sweltering heat. They soon discovered that the weather around the Bay was tepid and mild. Cool breezes acted as a natural air filter, flowing through the docks, no matter the temperature.

At nighttime, they gathered around local watering holes, meeting people from many different lands speaking a multitude of languages. Frank was a good listener, eager to discover where he could find the best opportunities. What was the best way to make money quickly here? What industry would be most suitable for him? It was not long before they ran into other Portuguese, who could speak their language and show them the ropes of living in America. Some were very friendly; some were distant and resentful.

As they left one canteen to find another, Frank felt footsteps behind them. The footsteps were soft but steady and increasingly persistent. Frank placed his hand on Gilberto's shoulder. "I think someone is following us. Don't look back." They dipped into the next tavern and shimmied up to the bar. Frank waited one moment and then glanced behind but did not see anyone entering after them.

After they left the establishment, he heard footsteps again. Surely they were being followed, but why? Before they reached their lodge, four men grabbed them from behind, fired gut punches into them, taking the wind out of them and knocking them off their feet. Once they were down, their antagonists bombarded them with a flurry of stabbing swipes. Frank tried to get a good look at them, but he could not see them in the dark. He did recognize their Portuguese accents. "This will teach you little "kanaka-portagees" to come around here taking our work."

After pummeling them into a stupor, the four men spat upon them and rifled through their pockets, taking all of the wages they had earned that day, but failing to find the diamonds sewn into Frank's trouser seams. As they fled, Frank groaned, rolled over, and passed out.

Frank woke to the shrill cries of seagulls circling overhead in the early morning hours, just before dawn. His head throbbed like a mambo drum beat, blood encrusted into the seams of his neck. He turned to look for Gilberto. The boy's face had been beaten purple and his eyes were swollen shut. It scared Frank and he shook Gilberto. No response. Frank managed to get on all fours. "Gilberto. Wake up!" Gilberto groaned and he sighed.

Frank looked around and spotted a water pump, dragged himself over to it and put his head under it, gulping in water and air. He felt slightly better. He looked around again and found his hat, collected more water, and brought it to Gilberto.

"Here, gulp some of this. It will help." After two trips to the pump, he took a handkerchief and wiped his own face and then handed it to Gilberto. "Here, wipe yourself up. You'll frighten the landlady."Gilberto's lips were distended and his eyes black and blue. He managed to croak, "How will we go to work today?"

"That's easy. We won't."

Gilberto opened one black eye, "What do you mean we won't? We have to work."

"No, we don't have to." It had been almost a week. Frank had thought they could spend a month on the docks, but he no longer had an appetite for it.

"I don't need this job. We've made enough money to travel."

"Travel to where?"

"I've been talking to some of our people. They say there is a Valley just south of here. Some have described it as an enchanted Valley. A Valley like no other, where many of our people have started their own farms, dairies, and businesses. We will go there and make a new life, a life where we answer to none other than ourselves and no one can tell us what to do or beat us up."

"But how do we get there?"

"As for how we get there, I will inquire. Our landlady may be able to help us. But we won't go back to the docks. And as for how we get started, I have a connection." Frank took out the piece of paper from Ida. There is a family there, the Fernandes family. They may already know I'm coming."

Two days later, they traveled by stage coach to the little town of Santa Clara about fifty miles south of San Francisco, arriving just before dusk. From there, they could see the westerly high peaks which mirrored the easterly peaks on the opposite side of the Valley. The peaks resembled two giant hands cupping a bouquet of grasses and flowers pouring ribbons of flowing waters into the bay at its southern shore.

Frank and Gilberto left their luggage with an attendant at the station and strolled through the little town around Mission Santa Clara, the college, and its nearby environs. The town was surrounded by a patchwork of orchards, trees, flowers, and farms. Frank stopped to breathe in the earthy scents of mustard flowers, pollinated grasses, and ocean air.

It was getting late, and they wanted to find the farm before it grew too dark to see.They stopped a stranger to inquire where they could find the Fernandes farm. "It's about five miles east of here. Go down The Alameda, where you can catch a trolley. Just before you reach the town of San Jose, take a left onto Santa Clara street into the town. From there you can take another trolley or hire a cart down the road just about two miles to the farm."

"How will we recognize it?"

"You can't miss it. It's the first farm on the left beyond the town. Look for a light blue farmhouse with white trim. There's a sign inscribed with the family name at the end of the lane." Frank thanked him, and the two young men went back to the station and asked if they could hire someone to drive them. For two bits, they skipped the trolley lines and hoisted Frank's trunk and a duffle bag of extra clothes onto a horse-driven wagon.

As they passed through the center of San Jose, just beyond the Farmer's Market, both of them craned their necks upward to examine the San Jose electric light tower. Frank inquired of their driver, "Do you mind if we stop for just a few minutes?"

The man grunted but pulled over. Frank and Gilberto jumped down and circled the base of the structure, feeling the frenetic heat of energy in the night air. Frank and Gilberto had little experience with electricity, except briefly in Honolulu; for almost their entire lives, they had spent their nights covered in a blanket of darkness. From its base, the tower appeared to them like a canopy of twinkling stars, perhaps like Jacob's Ladder, thought Frank, lifting angels to heaven.

The tower was close to two hundred fifty feet, illuminating the entire town. Six concentric arc lamps of varying sizes were set within the tower framework, providing as much light as a full moon. "Have you ever seen anything like it?" Gilberto was transfixed. Their driver grunted again, and Frank turned to Gilberto, "We'd better be on our way, before we lose our ride and our luggage. Reluctantly, they jumped back on the wagon and gawked back at it, until they reached their destination.

Their driver came to an abrupt halt in front of a large park dotted with poplar trees. "Whoa boy. Here you go. You fellas can manage your own luggage, I take it?" It was Frank's turn to grunt. They hoisted Frank's large trunk and carried it down the lane in the dark with Gilberto's duffle bag in his left hand and one side of Frank's trunk in his other.

"I sure hope they're not too surprised to see us. Ida said she'd write them ahead of our arrival. I just hope her letter beat us to it." Frank knocked on the front door of the Victorian, which was situated in front of a large white barn.

"Looks like a pretty big dairy," Gilbert commented. "All I want right now is some hay to sleep in."

They knocked at the door and waited, until the front door cracked wide open. Under a lantern, they could see the shadow of a dark and ruddy face sporting a bushy black mustache. The man was stocky and muscular, maybe five feet eight inches tall. In his eyes, they saw a hint of curiosity and just a gleam of merriment. They smelled the remnants of smoking tobacco. The man's eyes were friendly, and he spoke with an engaging voice, like someone who is accustomed to welcoming strangers. "Uh, who goes there, fellas?"

"The name is Francisco. Francisco Mirante, the son of Miguel and Maria Mirante. But, please, call me Frank. And this is my traveling companion, Gilberto D'Angelo." It occurred to Frank that Ida would use the name Francisco and that he should identify himself that way.

The man raised the lantern upon the faces of the two young men, his face displaying astonishment. "You are the son of Miguel and my sister Maria? But I don't remember them having a son named Francisco."

"Please, call me Frank. Yes, my father was Miguel, Miguel Mirante of São Miguel."

"What do you mean "was" Miguel?"

"You don't know? I am so sorry to tell you that he passed away over a year ago."

"What?! Miguel Mirante is no more?" A woman came up behind the man. "João, you forget your manners. Invite the young men inside to warm themselves by the fire."

"Yes, yes, of course. It was just such a shock to hear about Miguel. Please come in and set your things down on the front porch."

"This is my wife Colleen." The woman was tall and slender, fair with ginger hair, intelligent-looking aquatic eyes, and a mouth like a plump tangerine. She smelled of violets and smiled with good cheer. She had an elegance that her husband utterly lacked, but Frank would soon learn that they were ecstatically happy with one another.

The woman was the one to offer hospitality. "Please sit yourselves down in front of the fire and tell us everything. Let me take your coats. Would you like something to drink?"

Once they had settled in with two cups of coffee, Frank made further inquiries. "Do you mean to say that neither Ida nor Maria ever wrote to you about what happened to Miguel?"

"No. But my sister Maria was never one to write." João shook his head. "Now that I think of it, I am not certain that she ever learned to write, especially not in English." João chuckled, as if he was remembering a long-forgotten joke.

"You see, we knew the Mirantes back in São Miguel, but Maria married Miguel after I had already left the island and joined the Portuguese army. Still, it must have slipped Maria's mind. In her grief, she must have forgotten. Are they well enough now?"

"She did indeed grieve terribly, but the family is doing well. They have some farmland and a grocery business in Kauai."

Colleen spoke up, "Tell us, how did Miguel die?"

"It is difficult to talk about actually." Frank gazed down at his feet, not wanting to remember. He spoke with a far away look on his face. "It was a horrible accident at the mill. He bled to death after falling on the grinders."

"*Meu Deus!*" João crossed himself. "I am so sorry to hear. He was such a good man."

"Indeed, he was." Wanting to change the subject, Frank quickly thought of something else he should mention. "Did you know they had twins who are five years old now?"

Again, the couple looked surprised. "Thank you so much for bringing us news. You can see that we have lost touch. Any family of my sisters is certainly welcome here, but I still don't know why we didn't know about his son, Francisco."

"Truthfully, I am not Miguel and Maria's natural son. They adopted me, after they lost their son Paulo to measles on the boat journey to the islands."

João and Colleen drew in a breath and looked at each other again. "Paulo is gone too?"

"Yes, I'm so sorry to have to tell you all this bad news. I should have mentioned it sooner. It's just difficult to know what you may or may not have already heard. Paulo died on the journey during an outbreak of measles."

João choked up suddenly, and a tear pooled in one eye, as he sucked on his pipe and gazed into the fire. His mind grew deep and serious and his voice went low. "To think, when we left São Miguel, we never thought we'd see our family again." He shook his head in wonder. "Yet, here we are in the midst of loss and yet, uniting with new family members. Life comes full circle and renews itself, does it not?"

There was a long silence as each one in the room was lost in thought, and the crackling blaze lit up their faces with an ocherous light.

After a few moments Frank broke the silence and softly tossed grateful eyes at João. "Yes, it is wonderful. Our parents never could have imagined it. Your welcome means everything," he gulped.

Frank then shifted the mood by asking a question that was firmly on his mind. "Your niece Ida promised to write you about me, but it's possible you have not yet received her letter."

João looked up suddenly, lost in thought. "No. I have not received a letter from Ida, but you know, the mail can be slow from the islands."

"Of course. After all, it has only been a few weeks since I left her. Perhaps her letter will come soon. She told me she would write to tell you we were coming and to ask you to help us find a place to live and work. I'm guessing that when the letter arrives, she will have sent news of the rest of her family and how they are doing."

João agreed and looked relieved. He got up and paced the room excitedly. "Your timing is perfect, my friend! I just lost two good farmhands. We do not have a big house, but there are plenty of bunks in the barns. If you are interested, you can both start tomorrow!"

Frank was looking for something a bit more specific. "You see, sir, I want my own farm. I will definitely work for you, but what is the quickest way to earn the money to buy a farm here and how much money do you think I will need?"

João slapped him on the back. "Ahh! I see you are a man with ambitions. I like that! It will take you some time to save enough, but you can take on extra jobs. I could also use a man to haul hay. That is another side business you might consider. "

Frank was delighted. "I see I have many options, and you can be sure, I will take advantage of every one." Frank was thinking that he would hold on to his diamonds, work for a year or two and then buy five acres to start. Gilberto could help him. Just as these thoughts were running through his mind, he heard laughter and singing from the kitchen. He stopped to listen. Someone was playing the viola and someone else was singing in a clear soprano voice. "I see that your family is musical, sir. Do you play?"

João shook his head, "No, no. But all my children do."

Frank turned to Colleen, "And just how many children do you have?"

"Two girls here, still at home, and three boys who are old enough to be on their own. The older ones are João, Jr., who farms in Fresno with his brothers Jorge and Tomás. Jorge and Tomás sometimes work at the canneries here in the summer. Would you like to meet my daughters?" Frank and Gilberto bobbed their heads up and down.

Colleen went to the back kitchen, and after speaking in a soft voice, she returned with two young women. The eldest was Mildred, petite with amber eyes deeply set into a pale complexion, like brown topaz in a white satin-lined jewelry box. Her black hair curled voluminously around squared shoulders, and she crooked a viola in her left arm, as if she had been born with it.

The younger daughter, Anarosa, was the singer and a redhead like her mother. Her voice carried the lilt of a lark. She was slightly taller than Mildred with the same petite stature. She smirked at Frank from behind cat-like green eyes framed in red freckles, as if to say, "I dare you."

Frank was instantly bewitched, and he knew in that moment that he had finally come home.

Two days later Ida's letter arrived. Two years after that, Frank and Anarosa were married in a grand celebration held on their new farm, which was bought, in part, from the sale of one sizable diamond. When Frank kissed Anarosa at the altar, she tasted like spearmint and anise. The whole town of Santa Clara celebrated with a plentiful supply of Madeira wine, and Anarosa sported a diamond that was the envy of every woman in the local parish.

CHAPTER 47

1913, Santa Clara, Gloaming in the Valley

Julia never stopped seeing Abbie. After she started managing the *Serradura*, she could only come on weekends. When she heard from Howard that Roger never came on Sundays, she came regularly after church to visit Abbie at lunch time.

Abbie was quick to notice the change and not just because Julia had taken on a full-time job. Roger came less often now and never lingered. He used to ask Abbie about her visits with Julia; there was a time when he wanted to know all of the details. Now he remained silent on the subject. Two years passed and neither of them spoke of the other to her. Abbie was curious but decided it was best to respect their privacy.

One day, in the middle of winter, Julia came at her usual time, but the house was strangely shuttered. The rain pelted her as she mounted the steps to the front porch. She knocked several times while shaking out her umbrella, but Howard did not answer the door. Since Abbie was always at home, Julia grew alarmed. She left a note inquiring after Abbie, but a week passed and she received no response. The following Sunday, she tried again without success, so she left another note. She decided to take time off from work to visit during the week, and Howard finally answered the door.

"Howard, I've been so worried. Why has no one answered my notes? Where is Abbie?"

"She passed, Miss." Howard gave off an apologetic look.

"Passed?" She looked him up and down. "I don't understand."

"She passed away after a brief and sudden illness. She was in the hospital for a week before she died. The house has been closed. I've been instructed by her attorney to act as caretaker, until it's decided what will become of her estate."

Julia stepped back, suddenly aware of a misty dew in the air that sent a chill through her. "But, but... what about a funeral? Will there be a wake?"

"Only for the closest family members, Miss. It will not be open to the public."

Julia stared at Howard, as she tried to take in his meaning. Her stomach churned and she tasted bile rising in her throat. She shivered and glanced down and around. Finally, she looked up at him and spoke shakily, "But I haven't had time to say goodbye. It's very important, you see, that I … say goodbye." She faltered, as she remembered the time she had spoken those words once before.

Howard looked at her sadly and said nothing.

Julia gathered her thoughts. "Can you at least tell me when it will be, so I can visit the gravesite after the service?"

"Next Saturday morning miss, ten o'clock. There will be a service at the Episcopal Church and then a brief graveside service in the Santa Clara cemetery. At the family plot."

The following Saturday, Julia dressed warmly and made her way to the old Victorian at about nine-thirty. She waited by the tank house. And then it began to pour like a baptism. She tucked in her coat and huddled close to the frame. Rain fell off of her in sheets and disguised her tears. She thought about the time when she and Therese had spied on the old house from the platform, and she pondered her first encounter with Abbie. She watched as Roger arrived with his two sisters and his brother. They did not spend a long time in the house before Howard followed them to Roger's car. There was no sign of Olivia.

Julia made her way to a back door, where she knew she could enter the house. She climbed the stairs to Abbie's bedroom and ran her hands across the soft bristles of Abbie's hairbrush and the thinly carved lines of her porcelain jewelry box. She picked up a bottle of rose oil and dabbed it on, as if she could somehow capture the essence of her friend. She closed her eyes and breathed deeply, as she remembered Abbie wearing the familiar scent. She returned to the front parlor. The emptiness and silence of the room weighed on her like a bill that could not be paid when it came due.

It seemed to Julia that every knick knack and every painting had a story to tell about Abbie's life. She gathered up her memories in her mind and tucked them away carefully. And then she paused before the portrait of Abbie and gazed at it for a very long time. Finally, she heard herself say, "I had to say goodbye, you see. I had to find some way." As tears misted her eyelashes, she remembered Abbie's words about Therese the first time they met.

"You must have faith. You must believe that you will see her again. That you will join her when the time is right, even though she will not come back to you here. Can you do that girl?"

"Yes, yes. I will try hard." Julia now gulped the words softly to herself.

When she looked up, her eyes ran down to the small painting that had once reminded her of Therese. She remembered the sun on her face and the glow in her eyes. An inner voice spoke to her, "Take it. It's yours. No one will miss it." She longed to take it, but resisted the temptation, left the house, and slowly walked away. She made her way through the familiar purlieus of the old cemetery and then positioned herself near the family plot where she could remain unseen as she listened to the service. The funeral was brief, a few prayers, the lowering of the casket, and the tossing of roses. Julia closed her eyes. Long after the family had left, she remained and tossed her own roses.

Every Sunday after that, she brought flowers to Abbie's grave. She bought two porcelain vases and refilled them every week, a practice that had become her custom since the day Therese had left her. Now, she had two graves to visit. When winter turned to spring again, she brought a bouquet of white roses. As she was placing them in a vase, a voice overhead gave her pause.

"You loved her. I know."

She looked up to see Roger standing over her. It had been almost three years since their last encounter. Julia occasionally heard of him from her cannery friends, and sometimes her mother reminded her that she needed to try harder to make him marry her.

Roger, on the other hand, avoided any possible mention of Julia, but he kept his ears open enough to know that she had not married. He wondered why. He had felt so certain that there was someone else. As the months passed, he noticed the flowers at his grandmother's grave and deduced that it must be Julia who brought them. He had come to try one more time.

"Yes. She was a dear and special person." Julia stood up to face him. "How are you and all of your family?"

Roger took one step towards her. "We are well. Thank you for asking." There was an awkward pause. "Julia, I have to ask you. Have you missed me at all?" He glanced at her hopefully.

Julia was not without feelings for Roger. At one time, she thought that she was in love with him. She had even seriously contemplated marrying him. Now that she was unsure that Marcos would ever return, it put her in an awkward position, but she could not turn back.

She shook her head up and down slowly. "Yes, I would be lying if I said that I did not miss you."

"Then you do care for me still? You do think of me?"

She nodded again.

"Then won't you give me a chance to prove we belong together?"

"That's just it. I care for you. I respect and admire you. Perhaps I even love you. But ..."

"But what?"

She clinched her hand and looked at him tenderly, "I can't say why, but it's not enough. It's just not enough."

"But why is it not enough?" he gently prodded.

"It's something your grandmother said to me once. About how she loved your grandfather but love was not enough. There had to be something more that binds two people in a way that makes for a happy life. I just can't get over this feeling that something is missing between us. Right now, it feels like a small crack, but as time goes on, I somehow know it would become a breech as deep and wide as a canyon that would come between us." She looked at him with eyes pleading for understanding.

He shook his head and backed away in denial, like one who has lived a painful moment over and over again and cannot accept having to live it again. "No, Julia. I don't believe that. We can have a good life together. I can make you happy. I believe that with all my heart."

"And I too must trust my heart. I tell you quite honestly that it has not been easy. I am gratified by your love, but I am not captivated by it. Nothing has changed since I last saw you. Even if I wanted to, I cannot make my doubts go away." She backed away and spoke sadly, shaking her head from side to side. "It pains me to know that I have caused you pain. I am so sorry for it, and I wish it did not have to be."

She turned and walked away. This time, Roger did not wait to lose sight of her.

A month later, Gilberto was painting the dairy barn for Luana with Alexio's help when he spotted a figure coming from a long way off. Every few minutes, he shaded his eyes to see who it might be. As the stranger came closer, Gilberto detected a familiar stride. He slid down the ladder and ran towards him.

"Marcos, my man!" He gave his cousin a bear hug. "Where have you been? We've been worried about you. Not a note. Not a word."

Gilberto stepped back and surveyed his cousin who had grown tanner and leaner over the past three years. "You didn't think I'd leave all my land to you, did you? I had to come back to see that it was being properly cared for."

Gilberto grinned. "I figured you'd be wondering about your property some day." Gilberto wrapped an arm around his shoulder, "Come let's go inside for a drink. I have some news to share with you."

As they settled in with two cold beers on the front porch, Marcos toasted Gilberto and said, "Now then, out with your news!"

"Would you believe it if I told you that I am happily married?"

Marcos's eyebrows shot upward, "You, married? I thought you were a confirmed bachelor! Who's the not-so-lucky gal?"

"Guess."

Marcos ranged his mind over Gilberto's history with women. "How could I possibly guess? You never showed a serious interest in any particular woman in your life."

"Luana."

"You don't say? That little jalapeño pepper?" Marcos slapped his thigh in surprised wonder.

Gilberto jogged his head up and down with a wide grin. "Yep. I find I have an unquenchable taste these days for jalapeños!" Laughter spilled between them, just in time for Luana to come home. Hearing the commotion, she approached the porch slowly and rounded the corner to see Marcos laughing uproariously.

She dropped her things and spread her arms out wide. "Well, there he is. Finally! Where on earth have you been, stranger?"

Marcos got up and smothered her in a bear hug. "Now we are related. So, what do you think of that? You can't get rid of me."

"I don't intend to get rid of you." She looked him up and down. "As a matter of fact, I'm needing a good dairy and ranch manager about now. What'd ya say partner?" Luana was always quick to seize her opportunities.

"I say it's good to be home."

Later that night, as they were getting ready for bed, Luana pelted Gilberto with questions. "So, did he ask about Julia?"

"Not a word."

"Did you tell him she did not marry Roger?"

"Everything in its own good time. He'll find out soon enough."

"Well, not soon enough for me. I've got a pretty good feeling about those two. That it's about time they get together. And it can't happen too quickly."

Gilberto rolled his eyes, "Well, we sure took our time. A lot of wasted years, I'd say. It didn't seem to bother you none."

Luana threw his dirty socks at him and a clothing fight ensued, ending in a heavy-breathing wrestling match.

The next day, Alexio and Gilberto stopped at the *Serradura* for coffee after a hard day working on the barn. They arrived at the end of the day, after the girls had left and Domingos was closing up. "Domo, my brother. How about two malasadas and a dozen to take away? And why don't you join us before you end your day?"

Domingos came back with three cups of coffee and the pastries, then sat down with them. "So, how is the painting going?"

"Almost finished. In the meantime, we're milking five times a day and buying more cows every month. Luana can't get enough hands to help her. We're so busy."

Domingos considered, "She'll be back here before you know it."

"I hate to contradict you my brother, but I really don't think so. She loves working outdoors."

"Well, Julia and Rose are doing a good job. I can't regret taking my little nieces under my wing."

"They're not so little anymore."

"That's for sure."

"So what's the gossip at the *Serradura* today?" It was well known that anything you wanted to know about the Portuguese community could be heard at the *Serradura*. Gilberto did not stop in often, but when he did, he made sure he caught up on the latest.

Domingos looked around to be sure that Rose and Julia were no longer around and then he leaned in, "Well, here's a piece of news. I heard today that Roger McCallum is getting married."

Alexio looked perplexed. "You mean he proposed to Julia?"

Domingos shook his head, "No. He's marrying that Hamilton girl. No one can figure it out. We all thought he was completely stuck on Julia. I made sure she didn't hear about it, so don't say anything to her."

Alexio was concerned. "But someone has got to tell her."

"All I know is I couldn't say a word when I first heard it. But it's the talk of the town, so she's bound to hear soon." Domingos spoke through a mouth full of custard.

Alexio started up, "Well, I'm not going to let her hear it from anyone else but me. That's for sure." Without further explanation, he shot out the door and then popped his head back in. "Gilberto, I'm going to need to borrow your truck."

"And just how am I supposed to get home?"

"I'll be back as soon as I can." Gilberto held out his keys with a shrug.

Alexio jumped in the truck and flew home, considering how he might protect his sister before others could tell her. He wanted to act as a buffer that would save her from the truth or at least catch her when she fell. He bounded up the porch, taking two steps at a time, and cracked open the front door. Finding that no one one else was home, he called for her, anxious to hear her voice. There was no answer, but his instincts told him to search the house anyway.

He found her, calmly reading on the back porch as the sun was setting. He looked at her intently, and after a moment, she returned his gaze. The serenity of her face spoke all that he needed to know.

"So you know?" He asked breathlessly. "Who told you?"

She turned away and smiled a faraway and mysterious smile.

"You knew before we did." Prompted by her silence, he stated it again more insistently. And then sat down across from her and tried to meet her gaze. He shook his head side-to-side in a sudden awareness. "You always knew."

She continued to look off into the distance, but he felt no resistance, so he probed further. "How? When? When did you first know?"

She finally looked at him. "That he would never marry me?" It was not Julia's intention to tell anyone that she had refused him. It was better that way. The secret would always remain locked away in her heart.

Alexio persisted. "How could you not know what everyone believed for so long? Even his own family believed it to be inevitable. Are you saying he never proposed?" The questions came thick and furious.

Julia ignored the latter question but freely answered the former. "From the moment he first set eyes on me. Well, maybe not that early," she dissembled, "But it's been a while now."

It came back to her in a flash, that first day at the *Serradura*. It startled her to now realize what his intentions had been on that day and how fully unaware she had been. She had not thought of that day until now. Anyone who had observed them together since might think that she had never really returned his feelings, but her brother was not one to be put off so easily.

"But based on what? There must have been something more."

"It was his grandmother. She did love him, but she also warned me in her own way. It's not what she said, but more what she did not say. She knew him well, better than he knew himself, and she knew what he was made of. That he was more like his mother than he wanted to be and would never resist her influence in the end. Never really knowing himself. Unable to choose the best."

Alexio now felt some sympathy towards the man. He glanced up at Julia with a deeply-determined gaze. "He will regret you. If not now, then in the long run. You know that, don't you?"

She smiled back at him, with a slow smile. "I am not looking for consolation."

"No, I cannot imagine that you would."

Alexio looked at her tenderly now, steadied by the love and respect that he had always felt for her. He wrestled with his own thoughts awhile longer, but he did not speak them out loud. Whatever the reasons and whatever had passed between them, he understood that it was her heart, and not Roger's, that had brought them to this end. And that with all of Roger's wealth and influence, she had resisted him, even though it had been a struggle for her and that she did not care whether anyone else realized it or not. And most importantly, he saw that she was not crushed, and he was greatly relieved.

Julia turned sharply away from the penetrating gaze of one who knew her too well. Even to a beloved brother, she would not describe how she had struggled to protect her heart. Her eyes darted away. Away from his gaze, like a magician practiced at sleight of hand.

Alexio left her lost in thought.

She stood and turned towards the sun that nightly strokes the skies above the Santa Cruz mountains, mottling them with shades of a orange and pink. Plunging down and away, the sun incarnadined the sky, as it melted into crimson and submerged the last gap of powdery blue daylight.

Then came the steely fog, seeping over the mountains, ushering in a cool stillness that nightly transfixes the Valley in its gloaming. Just like lights in the distance so clear to the heart of a little boy who would never make it across the sea to an island filled with pineapples and sugar cane. Or the beautiful Estela who struggled and triumphed over her shroud of darkness, one that she had never asked for but fought and overcame. Julia held her light for them and the strength inside of her that came from the father who struggled and survived, took her uncle's place, and gave her life.

She also knew that beyond the gate and blossoms of the fruit trees, there was a dairy, full of promise, and it was this promise that sustained her and enabled her to move forward, even after the loss of her childhood friend and a love she was now afraid was gone forever. She held onto her visions of a time and place where she would forge her own gold. And like those with the courage to risk everything to give her life, with face like flint, her mind turned ahead without counting the cost or looking back at what was lost, never to return. She simply was not capable of stumbling backward.

Julia walked to the front porch facing east toward Mount Hamilton, and the gibbous moon unveiled itself by swinging low, as a backdrop to an unexpected and unforeseen shadow. Julia watched as it slipped slowly away from the cypress trees, until she could make out a dark but vaguely familiar outline.

Marcos stepped out into her lamplight. Though it had been three years, it felt much longer than that to Julia. Had he overheard her conversation with Alexio? She wondered, but it did not trouble her.

His smile released her from any awkward feelings that remained after their last encounter. He relaxed as she returned it. He hardly knew what to say to her, even after practicing from every city and port he could find to get away from her. "Did you think I would never return?" He spoke softly. Luana had told him in the morning that Julia and Roger were not married and that she doubted they ever would be. It gave Marcos hope that he could find a way back to Julia and that her heart was still free. A hope that had drawn him out of the shadows.

She moved towards him and her eyes searched for and met his in the gray light. "I was such a little girl when I last saw you. So lost in confusion. Such a little fool. Can we forget the past now?"

Marcos smiled at her borrowed use of the sobriquet he had once pinned on her. That she remembered and could speak of it meant a great deal to him now; he could see that she had grown up. In that moment, he dared to hope. "Will you walk with me into the gloaming?" He held out his hand and she accepted it.

They circled the orchards, talking about his travels and what she had been doing since he left. He longed to know her heart and knew that she was not one to reveal it easily. He recalled the child who would not cry out in the face of his demands. He had assumed, like everyone else, that she would jump at the chance to marry Roger McCallum. He determined that he would never give her another opportunity to get away, if it was now in his power to do so.

After some silence, he spoke first. "So, Luana wants me to be her business partner."

Julia smiled slowly, "Do you know she made me the same offer?"

He laughed lightly as he looked down and traced their footsteps together in the gray stillness. "It seems our Luana has been two-timing us." His eyes sought hers. They were now standing on the front porch under the pepper tree.

"Yes," she smiled in return. "Perhaps she calculated it that way, that we would all be partners."

In response, Marcos reached for her hand and his eyes searched hers again. He stopped her in her tracks and pressed her hand softly. "Dear Julia, I have waited so long for you. Being away changed nothing. Now, the only partnership I want is not a business partnership but one that binds you to me forever." He searched her face for some sign that she could possibly return his feelings. "Tell me now that your heart has changed towards me or release me, and I will never mention it again."

The clenched fists of the little girl inside of Julia fell away. That girl was dismissed and gone forever. She looked at Marcos clearly, as if she was seeing him for the first time. Remembering their long rides into dusty sunsets. Recognizing his care and concern for her and everyone around him. His strength in the face of tragedy and loss. She let herself free-fall into his sapphire eyes. Her smile and her touch was all he needed, along with one very long moon-laced kiss.

From behind them came a flurry and a chirp, a hop, and a twitter. "You're in trouble now, boy!" You're in trouble now, boy!"

Followed by teary-eyed, gulping laughter.

CHAPTER 48

1894, Kauai, Paniolos

It had been twelve years since Francisco left his baby sister on the island of Kauai, and now the sixteen year-old Luana pranced barefoot down the road from Poipu beach to Koloa. A copper pony tail brushed across bronze shoulders and refracted brightly off the relentless sun. She carried a basket of fresh fish in her right hand and a fishing pole over her left shoulder and sucked in a taste of salty breezes, as she made her way home.

Luana stood five feet four inches tall with round muscular thighs and calves that gave off a feminine athleticism wrapped in a short holoku strapless dress. Since she had learned to walk, there was no physical feat that was beyond her, whether it was body surfing, horse breaking, cliff diving, or vaulting up the highest peaks of her Kauai home. The island was her playground from the day she was born. Her favorite trek was the Makawehi Lithified Cliffs, where she and Domo would hunt for fossils and explore ancient burial grounds. The views from the cliffs made her feel like she lived on top of the world, which perfectly suited her personality.

Luana began every day by swimming and fishing, and then made her way from the market to the beach and back again, where she delivered fresh fish to the family store. She ended every day surfing or riding horses along that same shore.

Domingos watched as she jogged down the road with her fresh catch. "What's on special today, Kokomo?" He loved to call his twin Kokomo, ever since Ida's lavish wedding in Kokomo on the island of Maui. Luana almost stole the show from Ida that night; you might say she was the talk of the wedding. She over-imbibed on Madeira wine and ended up singing a song on a table top to the entire wedding crowd.

It was the first time Domingos had ever seen his sixteen year old sister drink too much, and he would never let her forget it. For a time, she was the talk of the family, as she was always pushing social boundaries to her mother's dismay. Maria was grateful that the incident had taken place far from home.

Luana cared very little about her reputation, but with Domingos' greeting, she remembered her mother's stern warnings the day after the wedding and her response to them.

"For goodness sakes, *Mãe*! It wasn't as if I was dancing naked on that table."

"You are no longer a child. The worst thing you could do is get inebriated, especially in front of strangers. Men will take you for a loose woman and take advantage of you in such a state!"

"Oh, *Mãe*. We were with family, and you know that Domingos is always with me. And besides, I can take care of myself." Luana raised an expressive eyebrow at Domingos so he would support her, but he rolled his eyes to let her know he would not get involved.

She now called out to Domo lightly as she swung the basket open for his inspection. "A good day for Ahi and Mahi Mahi. I even caught some Ono." After Domingos nodded his head with approval, she took the basket of fish around to the back room where she washed and prepared her catch for sale.

Luana possessed an energy that could light up a midnight sky with fireworks. She never sat still and was as industrious as a badger, constantly on the lookout for new ways to earn and save money. Her dream was to visit Frank in California and start her own business. Every day she reminded Domingos of that dream because she was not willing to leave without him. She knew she would have to pound the idea into his head a million times before it took shape in his mind.

As she wedged the fish into packed ice, she chirped, "You know, if we're going to make it to California some day, we're both going to have to find extra jobs outside the store."

"And just when am I supposed to find time for that?"

Luana ignored her twin's pessimism, a common response whenever he was resistant to her will. "Well, Renato told me I could earn as much as ten dollars just to break in one horse. You know I'm good at it." Renato and Ana had expanded their farm and were now raising and selling horses. They hired paniolos to help them work the ranch.

"And how is *Mãe* supposed to take care of the store all day long?"

"We can trade off with each other or get Ana to help out. You know she and Renato are always looking for extra spending money. You can break horses as well as I can. Between the two of us, we'll make enough money to get us there before we're seventeen."

"What makes you think that life in California is so much better than here?" Domingos always considered Luana's dreams of California as a figment of her grand imagination, but he was beginning to see that she was dead serious about it. He knew his twin well enough to realize that when she really wanted something, she would not be kept from it.

"It's bigger. And bigger means more opportunities. Look how well Francisco has done. He already has twenty-five acres of his own. And I've never even met his wife and kids. They just had their second baby girl. I'm dying to meet them all. Ida told me that his wife has red hair. Red hair! Can you imagine?"

"You forget; he calls himself Frank now, and you think too much of him. You know it's been twelve years since he left. Of course, he's done well by now."

"Either way, he has connections, and he can help us get started with our own business." Luana had been writing Frank from the day he left. At first, Ida would write the letters for her, but as soon as she was old enough to write, she would send him a letter every month. Frank was the best of penpals; even when he was working twelve hour days and could barely stay awake at night, he would write as soon as he received her letter.

That night Luana sat down to write Frank:

Aloha Frank,

Thank you for your last letter. Your new baby girl Rose sounds wonderful, and I am so happy you named her after our grandmother who passed away recently in São Miguel. I wish I could have known her. Mãe grieves deeply, because she promised her mother she would come back for her but never did. She says that had she known the journey would be so difficult, she would never have come here. That is hard to believe, but she believes it so completely that I do not dare contradict her.

I must tell you that, while life on the islands is beautiful in so many ways, I am restless to join you. Everyone else has made a life for themselves here, but I don't see a future for me or Domingos. Estela is now teaching and loving life in Oahu. Ana and her husband will soon be doing most of the work at the store and will be supporting Mãe who can no longer do as much. Ida says she and her husband love Maui and will not be leaving now that they are established. So, I ask, where does that leave us?

The only question that remains in my mind is how we can earn the passage to California. Recently, I came up with an idea that may help us get there. Renato owns a ranch now, and he pays as much as ten dollars to break in one horse. I was thinking of breaking horses to earn our passage to California. If I wait to save enough money by working at the store, it may take me as long as five years, and I don't want to wait that long. If you can find a way to help me, I will work for you on the ranch or help Anarosa with the housekeeping, until I can start my own business. You know I would love nothing better. I am longing to meet Julia, little Rose, and Anarosa. And the boys, of course! Please write soon and tell me what you think of my plan.

Your loving sister,
Luana

Luana and Domingos were relieving one another at the store, so they could spend more time at the ranch. Horse breaking opportunities were sporadic and based on seniority. Most of the time, they were cleaning stalls and baling hay and sometimes training horses, but at least once or twice a week, they were able to break a horse.

"If we each make twenty dollars per week, we should be able to save enough for our passage by the end of the year."

"But we'll need some spending money for the journey and for traveling expenses once we get there." Domingos responded. "And you have not yet told *Mãe* about your plans. You know she won't take it well."

Luana looked away. "I don't like the idea of disappointing her, but we must make our own way and live our own lives. I don't see the point of telling her until we've actually made enough money to go. You know she'll try to talk us out of it."

"It will come hard on her. First, she loses Father and Paulo and now her mother. How can we leave now?" Domingos shook his head. "I don't want to be there when you tell her."

"Nor I," sputtered Luana. "But someone will have to do it."

As they were speaking, a couple of the ranch hands were watching them from across the paddock. Eduardo was tall, sinewy, dark, and lean and had a way with women. Fernando was the younger and the sweeter brother but just as accomplished a horseman. The pair were experienced paniolos, born and raised on the island of Hawaii, and they had come to Kauai to start their own ranch and horse breeding business, but first they had to save some money to do it. They had never seen a woman ride and break horses like Luana, and she had attracted their interest.

"She's a fine philly, isn't she?"

Fernando followed his brother's gaze and was disappointed to see that the girl had caught Eduardo's eye. "She's an excellent rider and she has an unusual talent when it comes to winning over the horses." Fernando admired Luana just as much as Eduardo, but when it came to women, he always took a backseat to his brother. It was not like him to interfere with Eduardo's romantic conquests, but this girl was different; Fernando was truly smitten.

"Perhaps the girl could use a little breaking in herself. I just wonder who the boy is. She's always with him."

"No, Eduardo. Leave her be. She is related to the ranch manager, and this is her community."

"Oh, I can be very gentle when I try." Eduardo laughed to see Fernando's concern for the girl. "You needn't worry anyway; when I'm done, you can have her."

Fernando deflected his brother's crude remarks and bit down hard on a piece of straw, as he groped for an incentive that might keep him away from the girl. "Anyway, she seems to be taken. As you say, she's always with the Mirante boy."

"Not for long, she won't be. I'm going to find out where she lives and then never let her forget me." Fernando flattened a lopsided wide-brimmed hat onto his head and loped away with hands thrust tightly into his pockets.

A few days later Luana was on the road to Poipu coming back from fishing, when she spotted Eduardo standing by the side of the road with two other paniolos. Luana recognized them but did not look at them. With her gaze straight ahead, she walked right by them.

Just as she passed them, Eduardo called out, "What's your name, cowgirl?" Luana kept walking and fixed her eyes on the road.

He shouted louder, "Little cowgirl, I think I love you." This was the kind of approach Eduardo often used and for the most part, it worked well for him, but Luana was not so easily taken in. His appeals persisted, and the boys started following her down the path as Eduardo continued to whistle and call out to her.

She turned back hard on them with a stomp and spewed a blistering response, "I recognize you. I've seen you at the ranch. But I don't know you and I don't want to know you." She turned her back abruptly away.

"But you will want to know me," he smiled confidently. She flushed hotter. "What's your name?"

"Whatever it is, I don't give it out to strangers and especially not to the likes of you stinking paniolo." With that, she reached into her basket, pulled out a greasy squid, and threw it at his feet.

Eduardo was caught by surprise, while the other paniolos erupted into laughter. No woman ever got the best of Eduardo, and he hardened his gaze with determination as he shouted after her. "Oh, but you will know me very soon. You will see me at the ranch again, and I will find out your name."

She kept marching up the dunes but not before she caught his parting words, "You'll find I'm not so easy to get rid of little cowgirl." By the time she reached Poipu, Luana was fuming.

CHAPTER 49

1914, Santa Clara, Julia's Gold

Nothing could stem the tide of Anarosa's excitement over the wedding plans of her eldest daughter. Her other children had disappointed her when it came to marriage, so it was no surprise to anyone when Julia suddenly became her favored child, at least until the next wedding. It only took Anarosa a day to adjust to the idea that Julia was not going to marry Roger McCallum, something she had practically announced to her friends and family. It did, however, give her pause to hear that Roger McCallum was about to marry someone else. She spent about a day mulling it over with anyone who would listen.

Julia refused to say a word about it; she simply shrugged her shoulders and said, "Whatever gave you that idea?" when her mother asked why he had not proposed to Julia. Luana was slightly more obliging when Anarosa cornered her one evening, after she and Gilberto arrived with Marcos for dinner and they were alone in the garden.

"So, what do you make of this business with Roger McCallum?"

Luana decided to take on the burden of explaining things to Anarosa without actually explaining them. "I for one never thought it would happen."

Anarosa looked Luana over suspiciously, "What do you mean? You know very well that the whole town was talking about it. And that he clearly favored her."

Luana shrugged, "Well, I just never thought it would come to be."

"And why not?"

"Too many obstacles. I suspect that the mother had something to do with it. She's a very grasping sort of woman, you know. In the end, the son married a socialite."

Anarosa grew silent when she heard this. The idea that her daughter was not good enough for that woman's son inflamed her. Luana smiled to herself, grateful that her words had mollified Anarosa to the point that no further explanations seemed necessary.

Luana retreated to the front porch, where Rose and Julia were sewing lace and burlap tablecloths for the wedding, while the men were outside inspecting Alexio's new tank house. Alexio was away on business in San Francisco and had asked them to ensure that everything was in good working order before he returned.

Luana sat down next to Julia and whispered, "So, I think I have finally provided your mother with an explanation that has satisfied her curiosity, even if it arouse her indignation."

Julia smiled a crooked smile, "Do tell." Rose perked her ears.

"I tried to imply that Roger's mother did not think you were good enough for him."

Rose rolled her eyes, "Well, from what I could tell at the Auxiliary ball, you can't be too far from the truth. The woman was so rude to us. Practically turned her back on Julia, as if she did not exist."

"In any case, it silenced your mother. I don't think I've ever seen her so speechless. And she's no doubt stewing about it now."

Julia sighed, "Well, I hope it puts an end to her gossiping about it. I'm concerned that she'll go on about it in front of Marcos. Honestly, if I never hear the name McCallum again, it can't be too soon."

At dinner that night, Anarosa remained unusually quiet while the men talked on about Alexio's new tank house and property. As they were finishing supper, a messenger arrived with a telegram for Frank. Since it was not often that telegrams were delivered to their door, Frank gave out an inquiring look and the table went silent, while he examined its contents. The look on his face was enough to keep everyone on the edge of their seats. Frank was so thunderstruck that Anarosa snatched the telegram out of his hands and ran her eyes over it.

"I don't believe it," she cried. The two looked at each other.

"Frank, don't keep us in suspense. Did someone die?" Luana's comments brought them to attention.

Frank muttered, "No. No one is dead, thank God. It's Alexio. It seems he did not go to San Francisco on business after all."

Anarosa took over. "He did go there, just not on business. Alexio eloped." As soon as the words were out of Anarosa's mouth, the rest of the table erupted with questions. Frank raised his hands to silence them.

"He has eloped with Susanna McCallum."

The light dawned in Rose's eyes, as she remembered Susanna dancing with Alexio at the Auxiliary ball, and Frank could not help noticing the change in Rose's expression.

"What do you know Rose?" Frank looked at her inquisitively and everyone listened, as she explained what she had seen at the ball.

"Of course, Julia was there as well. But honestly, I don't think we've seen the two of them together since that evening. And it's been over three years! They sure have kept it a secret."

"No doubt they had to elope because of the mother," Luana chimed in. "She never would have approved."

This raised Anarosa's hackles. "To think, now we have to be associated with that family!"

"I don't know, Anarosa. My guess is that the mother will disown her." Luana was shaking her head, somewhat sorry that she had turned Anarosa against the mother.

"And now we know why Alexio was so keen to build on his property. He needed to have a place for her to live before they could marry," Frank surmised. "That cagey son of mine."

Julia finally spoke out. "Whatever the circumstances, she is family now, and we must find a way to make her feel welcomed. Especially if her own family disowns her." She shot a meaningful look at Marcos to let him know that she was looking for his support. She knew that Marcos would not harbor any resentments against the McCallums, but she wanted him to know that she felt strongly about it. Before Marcos could respond, Stefan piped up.

"That's right. She's the one you beat in the county horse show. That's awfully big of you, little sister."

"Well, that was a long time ago now and best forgotten." Julia hastily replied. "Papa, does that note say anything about when they will return?"

"Not for another week. I suppose we can all adjust to the idea by then and welcome our new daughter-in-law with open arms. Wouldn't you all say?" No one could disagree.

Later that night, Rose crawled into Julia's bed and whispered about it under the covers. "How could we have been so blind all of this time? I mean, the way they looked at each other that first night. We should have known."

Julia smiled, "No. I don't think we could have known. After all, at that time, everyone thought I might have married Roger."

"Tell me the truth. When did you really know?"

"About Roger or about Marcos?"

"Whichever came first."

"It was Marcos. Not long after he left. When he was gone, there was this hole in my heart. I tried to fill it up by keeping busy, but it never worked. And then I knew. The hard part was, I didn't know if he'd ever come back."

"Did you tell Roger that?"

"No, I never spoke of it to anyone. Except Luana just seemed to know."

Rose sighed. "Love sure is a strange endeavor. It'll take you by surprise. I mean, look at Luana. She's still as giddy as a schoolgirl and at her age! Who would have thought?" They broke into laughter.

A week later, the Mirante family was prepared to welcome Susanna McCallum. All of the women stumbled over themselves to greet her and to help her with her new household. They arrived on the first day with baskets of baked goods, fruits and vegetables, linens, and smiles on their faces. Julia made a point of taking Susanna aside, when the time seemed right. "Now that we are sisters, I want you to know that I would be honored if you'd be a bridesmaid at my wedding."

Susanna was genuinely pleased and embraced Julia, "I do hope we can forget the past and become good friends." She seemed to have grown up quite a bit since their last encounter.

Julia also broached the subject of Susanna's family as gently as possible. "I assume that your family knows about your elopement."

Susanna seemed relieved that Julia was the one to bring it up. "Yes. Of course. But I don't expect that I will be seeing much of them. I'm sure it won't surprise you to know that's why we had to elope. My mother would never have agreed to the marriage. She made her feelings known the night I met Alexio. I'm sure this does not surprise you, since no doubt you know that she also did everything she could to keep Roger from marrying you. I just want to say how very sorry I am for it."

"Please. Don't be. Things ended up just as they were meant to be. I have no hard feelings about the matter." Julia was quick to reassure her and was glad that Susanna was taking a practical approach when it came to her family. "Do you think your mother will come around eventually?"

"Yes. Actually, I think she will. Maybe when there's grandchildren." Susanna shrugged. "Even if she won't, I know that it will be her loss. You see, I know you knew my grandmother. And now I realize that it was my loss that I never took the time to know her. I'm quite envious of you for that. My mother was always so against the idea. I still don't really understand why."

"Your grandmother was a very special lady, and I will always treasure the memory of her." Julia was relieved to see that she and Susanna were destined to be good friends.

It was a sparkling April day when they all gathered at the new Five Wounds church in San Jose to celebrate the marriage of Marcos and Julia. Anarosa was in her glory. Frank never looked finer in his striped tux and tails. Luana was six months pregnant and radiating like a glowworm. Rose and Susanna wore lavender instead of the old gingham May Day dresses.

When Marcos slipped a stunning diamond on Julia's finger at the ceremony, everyone assumed he had bought it on his travels; probably somewhere in Africa, it was whispered.

The champagne never stopped flowing as they gathered at the new home of Marcos and Julia not far from Luana's dairy. As usual, there was a bevy of toasting. All of the men were quick to out-do one another in their pronunciations. As the father of the bride, Frank was the first to toast.

"To my new son-in-law. It's so good to know that you will not be leaving us again, even if you will be a ways down the road." Everyone laughed. "But seriously, I could not have imagined a better husband for my daughter. May God keep you always."

Much later, Frank turned a misty-eyed gaze at Anarosa. "Can you believe it? Two of our children married. Wasn't it only yesterday that you and I were celebrating our wedding?" Anarosa raised her glass to him. "Frank, you can be hard as nails, but with a little Madeira wine, you turn into a sentimental old fool."

"*Saude*," he laughed.

Once the celebrations were over, the couple left on a honeymoon trip to Kauai, where Julia met her grandmother and all of her aunts and uncles. They even stopped in Maui to visit with Ida and her family and made a trip to Oahu where Estela taught school and lived with her husband and three children.

When Marcos and Julia returned to their ranch house, there was a certified letter waiting for Julia. It had been sent to Frank and Anarosa's house, but Alexio took the trouble of bringing it over to the newlyweds' house, since it looked important and had come by special courier.

"Who is it from?" Marcos asked.

Julia opened and read the letter, "Some attorney in San Jose. He says he wants to discuss a legal matter and would I stop by his office next week?" Julia raised a questioning glance at Marcos.

"Any idea what it's all about?"

Julia shrugged. "We'll just have to see, I guess."

The following Tuesday, Julia put on a dress and a hat and took a trolley downtown to the legal offices of a Mr. James McMahon, Esquire. After a brief wait, a serious-looking secretary in horn-rimmed glasses ushered her into the leathered law office of Mr. McMahon. He sat at his desk chewing on a cigar thoughtfully, and when she came in, he stopped himself abruptly and eyed her with a curious up and down glance. After a moment, he remembered his manners and shot up to greet her and shake hands.

"It's a pleasure to meet you, ah, Mrs. D'Angelo?"

Julia had to think about it for a moment. "Why, so it is. I was married just recently and it's only been a few weeks, you see."

"Please, have a seat," he motioned to a chair opposite him.

Julia made herself comfortable, while Mr. McMahon gathered up some papers. "Now let's see. I just have a few questions before I show these papers to you. How is it that you became acquainted with Abigail McCallum, Mrs. D'Angelo?"

"Well, it's been a few years. I was retained as a companion through a friend of hers by the name of Gertie Cantell."

"And what year would that have been?"

"Well, I can't remember exactly. But I think it was about seven years ago."

"So, she employed you?"

"Yes. She paid me."

"And just what kinds of things did you do for her?"

"Well, I was mostly a companion to her. I would read to her. Play music. Actually, we did a lot of things like gardening and dressmaking. I would occasionally shop and do errands for her. I'm curious to know why you are asking?"

"I ask because a few years before she died, she came to me to make a change to her will. And she included you in the will upon the event of your marriage. Now that you are married, I can tell you the terms upon which she left you a great deal of money."

"Terms? What kind of terms?"

"In accordance with her wishes, her estate was not to be liquidated until you married. Now that you have married, I can execute those terms."

"What if I had never married?"

"The will states that if you have not married within ten years after her death, you would still inherit from her."

"That is a very curious set of conditions."

"And there's more that's curious. As a matter of fact, I've never written a will quite like this in all my years of practice. You would inherit nothing at all if you had married her grandson, Roger McCallum. Now that you have married elsewhere, everything belongs to you, including her house and grounds and about five hundred thousand dollars in gold deposited and waiting for you in a San Francisco bank."

"That's an amazing amount of money."

"It would make you one of the richest women in the county, no doubt." Mr. McMahon looked up to study her reaction.

"I don't know what to say." Julia fidgeted and paused, studying her nails. "And if I refuse this money, what happens to it?"

"It all goes to charity and the family is notified."

"Family? What family?"

"Why, the McCallum family, of course." The attorney looked down at his papers. "I am to notify Olivia and Roger McCallum upon receiving your acceptance of this inheritance. As a matter of fact, I am to notify them of any decision you make."

"Is that absolutely necessary?"

"It is my duty to execute the terms and conditions of this will, and I will carry out my duty."

Julia paused to consider why Abbie would make such a will. "Would it be possible to accept the house but not the gold?"

"That's entirely up to you. Either way, I must notify the family of your decision."

"Then I accept the house but not the gold."

"Are you absolutely certain, Mrs. D'Angelo?"

Julia gazed down and nodded her head up and down slowly. "I am certain."

"Do you mind if I ask why?"

"Because I have everything I could ever want or need. And because this kind of money changes people."

"You could use it for good."

"And it will be used for good. But besides that, there's nothing about my life I want to change with one exception. I did love Abbie McCallum and her house would mean a great deal to me."

"Well, it's not my job to talk you out of it. Only to execute on the wishes of the deceased. I will draw up the papers to sign over the gold to the charities listed on the will and change the title on the deed of the property. Can you return next week?"

"Yes, of course."

"You're absolutely certain?"

Julia stood up and looked him in the eye. She extended her hand with a winsome smile, "Thank you, Mr. McMahon. I am certain."

He ushered her out the door and watched from his office window as she walked down the street. Then he sat quietly puzzling for some time, flounced across the backdrop of his mind, stood up, and looked out his window overlooking the Valley. Brown bovine blotches dotted the green foothills, as a light spring rain stretched itself over them; it was accompanied by a rainbow that shone over the mountainsides.

He stood thoughtfully, sucked on a cigar, and scratched the back of his neck. He knew he had seen her before, and while he could not fix the time or place, he felt certain that his faint memory of her was a pleasant one and that it was somehow associated with excitement and wonder. He just had to place her. Where was it? It took him a quarter of an hour and one long smoke before he made the connection. A broad grin arced across his face. "But, of course," he puffed, "the girl on the stallion." He admired her then; he admired her even more now.

CHAPTER 50

1894, Kauai Girl

The next day, and every day for an entire week, Eduardo followed Luana from Poipu beach to the village. He went to great lengths to find out everything about her. He now knew who she was and where she lived. He also knew that Domingos was her twin. Luana looked away every time he came near and refused to speak to him, but when Eduardo followed her all the way to the village, they attracted the attention of the townspeople.

One day, just as she was entering the village, he approached her and put his arm around her shoulders. Infuriated, she brushed him away as if he were a gnat on her shoulder. He laughed, catching the attention of nearby onlookers. It did not matter that she resisted him; the gossips of the town found reason to blame her for his attentions.

She found Ana pounding out dough one morning at the back of the store and asked for her advice. "This man will not stop pestering me. Now it's the talk of the village, and they say it is all my fault. If *Mãe* hears of this, she will also assume it is my fault."

Ana punched down hard on the dough and spoke with ironic resentment, "Life is not always fair to us women. I do not think you should walk the road to Poipu anymore by yourself. At least not for awhile."

"But that's not right. Why shouldn't I do what I want and go where I want?"

"When you were just a girl, that was possible. Life was free and easy for you, and you could run all over the island. But when a girl becomes a woman, she can become a target, whether she wants to be or not. Don't get me wrong. Not all men are on the hunt, but you seem to have caught a real predator."

Luana protested. "But it was not that way for you."

"That's because I worked at home and I married early to a close family friend. This is the way of our people. Women must be protected."

"But I don't see why women must marry and why the men cannot leave us alone when we make it clear we are not interested."

"It would go better for you if you simply accept the way things are. You may not like it, but you must act wisely. Once a woman gains a reputation, it's all over for her. You must avoid it at all costs."

"Why must it be all over for her? Why?" Luana was incensed at the idea that her life hung in the balance between her freedom and everyone else's opinions. Especially since men did not suffer the same consequences. Luana valued her independence over everything else in life.

Ana used her thumb and forefinger to pluck at the dough as she considered the possible consequences for Luana. "Please, Luana. Change your routine for awhile, just so he does not catch you on the road or in the village. Take Domo with you as much as possible. That may be enough to discourage him. Perhaps you should also explain the situation to Domo. You know he will look out for you."

"I can't be with Domo all the time. We work different shifts at the ranch."

Ana threw down the dough and massaged her hands with a towel tied to her waist. "Then let me talk to Renato. He can also look out for you, and if needed, he may need to talk to the man."

Luana did not like the idea of needing a chaperone, but she had to admit, it was a plan that might persuade Eduardo to take her seriously.

The following Sunday, Luana, Domingos, and Maria attended mass at St. Raphael's Church in Koloa. As they entered the church, heads swiveled left and right in their direction. Luana felt all eyes on her and heard hushed whispers as she walked down the aisle. Maria felt it as well and wondered at the darting glances.

After Mass, Maria approached Marissa Terra. "Marissa, why are the people staring and whispering at us?" Maria sensed that Marissa knew something she had not yet told her. "Tell me everything." Marissa took her apart from the crowd.

"It's Luana. She's been seen with a man alone on the path from Poipu beach, not once but several times. And the other day, Mary Freitas saw him put his arm around her." Maria's brow darkened over, and she bristled. She assumed that all the rumors were true and that it was probably Luana's fault.

Marissa tried to calm her. "Don't berate the girl. She may not realize how it looks to others."

"She has always been so reckless. I knew she'd live to give me nothing but grief." Maria's tone spilled out of a bitter heart. It was something Marissa had witnessed many times before. She was forever encouraging Maria to look for the silver lining out of her many misfortunes, but her efforts came to nothing.

"Try to consider just what life would be without Luana and Domingos. With all you've lost, you still have family all around you." Such admonitions could not lessen Maria's resentment.

On the walk home, Maria made her feelings clear to Luana. "You have brought shame upon your family."

Luana tried to be gentle with her mother, but her own sense of indignation was too great. "*Mãe*, I have done nothing I am ashamed of. He is not my boyfriend. He's just a man from the ranch who will not stop pestering me."

Luana had not yet had an opportunity to explain her problem to Domingos; pride had held her back. Concerned, Domingos offered advice. "Just tell Renato to have a talk with him. Or I'll have a talk with him."

"No, don't threaten the man," Luana did not like the idea of Domingos getting into an altercation with Eduardo over her. Eduardo was bigger than Domingos. Besides, Domingos was not a fighter; he was a lover, and Eduardo was just the sort of man who would welcome a fight with a boy like Domingos.

All Maria could think of was the damage done to the family's reputation. "I never thought to see the day when one of my daughter would be ruined."

Luana turned on Maria with a stomp. "Ruined? Ruined? My whole life must be ruined over one incident that meant absolutely nothing and was not even my fault? I will never accept that. If that is true, then I must find some other place to live, where such notions are unacceptable."

Luana hurried away to the ranch before she said more to Maria than she was ready to say. She was almost on the brink of telling her mother about their plans to leave for California, but she and Domingos had not yet saved enough money. A few more months and then they would be able to tell her. There was no sense in telling her now; Maria would only make life a misery for her in the meantime.

Domingos ran after Luana, "Luana, wait for me." He caught up with her breathlessly. "You mustn't tell *Mãe* just yet. It will come hard on her."

"No, Domo. Don't you see? This was actually a good thing. It will now be a relief for her to be rid of me; she won't have to hang her head in shame at the village or in church. She may miss you, but I am convinced she will not be sorry to see me go."

"You can't believe that."

"Yes, I can. And besides, I know I will never be the good Portuguese girl that she wants me to be. I don't intend to bring her shame, but I don't want the life she wants for me. I am like Estela who would not marry the Portuguese boy next door, just to please her. Now I know how a woman can so easily lose her children by imposing her wants and expectations upon them. If I ever have children, I will not make that mistake."

That night, Luana sat down to write another letter to Frank:

Aloha Frank,

Things have come to a head for me on the island. Mãe says my reputation is ruined, because a paniolo who works at Renato's ranch has been giving me a hard time. I tried to tell him to leave me alone, but he followed me everyday, and now the whole town is talking. I hope you will agree that this is the perfect time to get away, as Mãe will not regret my absence and is unlikely to forbid it.

The only problem is that we still do not have the money for our passage. We will need another hundred dollars to make our way. Would you consider advancing me that sum? I cannot stand to stay around these gossips another moment. Please write and tell me if you can help us.

Your loving sister,

Luana

Luana waited for Frank's response for two unbearable weeks. He did not disappoint her. In exchange for work on the farm, he agreed to advance the money that would convey the twins to California as soon as possible. He also gave her instructions on where to go in Honolulu to retrieve the wired money and book their passages. Luana was ecstatic and relieved. She ran to tell Domingos.

"We can start packing our things. Frank is going to advance the money. It will be waiting for us in Honolulu." Domingos was astonished. "Like, right now?"

Luana waved her arms up and down with urgency. "Yes, immediately."

"Who will tell *Mãe*?"

Luana hardened into a stony stare, "It must be you Domo. You know it must be you." His face grew downcast, but he agreed.

Their departure date came at last. The skies were achingly blue, but Luana's heart beat furiously, determined to push away any thoughts of nostalgia or regret. She had not weathered so many storms to turn back now.

She and Domingos went shopping for traveling clothes, which turned out to be a trying experience. She wondered how she would ever grow accustomed to wearing shoes. They packed their new clothes and dressed casually for the journey to Honolulu. Ana and Renato and their two children were taking them to the dock where a schooner was waiting to transport them to Oahu.

Maria refused to come with them. Luana was not sure if her mother resented her more for her public humiliation or for her going away. It seemed that both reasons gave her enough grief to last a lifetime. "I hope, *Mãe*, that in time, you will forgive me, and you will consider coming to California."

Maria was silently resolved. Luana knelt down and placed her hand on Maria's arm and spoke in low tones, "Surely you can see that it's better I go away now and make a new start in a place where no one knows me."

Maria sniffed and Luana detected a tear pooling in one eye. Luana searched her expression to find some indication of her true feelings. And then Luana did something that neither of them expected; she put her arms around her mother and hugged her with all her might, "I see that you do love me after all." Maria did not deny her or resist.

Luana released her and looked at her searchingly. "Ana and Renato will take good care of you. And if you ever want to join us in California, you know you are welcome anytime."

Maria shrugged, "It's not likely I would ever want to take a journey across the Pacific again. No, my life is here, and it always will be. I will be buried by your father's side."

Luana pondered her tenderly, "You love him so very much, don't you?" Maria nodded. That would be Luana's final image of her mother, and the last time she would hear her mother's voice, even though she did not want to believe it in that moment. Much later she would remember Maria's final words, "I will be buried by your father's side," words that would echo in Luana's heart to the end of her days.

As Luana and Domingos waved goodbye to her sister's family, Luana caught a glimpse of another face. One that she barely recognized. She turned away, but then she heard a voice calling out. "Come back Kauai girl. Please come back." She could not resist the urge to see who it was, mortified that it could be Eduardo, but it was not Eduardo; it was Fernando sadly waving as the schooner slipped away. And then she heard his last words, "I love you Kauai girl."

Luana sighed, "At least he was the nice one." She waved back.

Domingos heard it as well. "Well, I'll be. Strike me with a stone," he murmured. "It seems you had more than one admirer little sister."

Luana stared at her brother, "I am NOT your little sister."

"Oh yeah! Who was born first? Tell me that?"

"That doesn't count. We're twins."

"But I came first." They simultaneously cracked a smile at each other and then erupted into a cachinnation that floated across the plashing seas.

That night, Maria dreamed again that she was back in São Miguel. She was walking just before dawn towards the neighborhood where she and Miguel had lived when they were first married. Their house sat in a jumble of cottages at the end of a country road just outside the village. She remembered the open gardens behind the cottages and the dooryards filled with children and critters. It was once a place with an abundance of bougainvillea and the sounds of children's play tumbling over porches and verandas. Nature was creeping across stone walls, archways and gardens filled with the scents of sweet peas and honey bees. She remembered that Paulo once played for hours on a rocking horse near the front door.

In Maria's dream, she approached the cottages and felt nothing but dread. As she drew closer, she saw that the cottages were shuttered, as if encamped against her; she was shut out. Her mother's home was boarded up. She looked for her cottage across the lane, where a lone mouse frittered on the doorstep, and the air smelled of over-stewed plums. She heard the creak of the abandoned rocking chair, as the wind whistled through the dooryard. Maria shivered and jiggled the door knob; it was locked, and her heart caved into itself. She struggled against the thought that this was no longer home, and it startled her awake.

Maria turned in her bed with a groan. For a moment, she could not remember where she was. She felt the distant pounding waves and smelled the salty air. She waited for the ship to rock. Just then, she heard Ana and her children downstairs, preparing for the day's work. She smelled herbs from the garden breezing through the curtains from the opposite window and closing her eyes, she lifted her face to take in its warmth. She heard the pother of grandchildren, as they scudded up the stairwell towards her. Her life came into focus. She turned and smiled and then got up, got dressed, and left her dream behind.

HISTORICAL NOTES

There were approximately 29 ships that brought the Portuguese from the Azores and Madeira islands between 1878—1913 to the Sandwich islands, now the Hawaiian islands. Most of these ships were steam ships, but a few were barks. Based on the Harbor Master's Records from the Hawaiian archives, the first ship to leave Funchal in 1878 was a German bark named Priscilla. It transported 80 men, 40 women, and 60 children. I took the liberty of making this ship a British bark with a British crew, and I based some of the stories of the journey on the Journal of the Thomas Bell, another bark which arrived in the Sandwich islands in April of 1888. I could not pinpoint whether Quarantine Island existed at the time of the first landing, but I included it, because it was a significant part of the Portuguese immigrant experience when they reached the islands.

Some of the stories related here were based on true stories from family members and some were adapted from journals about this time period. While there are a few names in the story which are family names, they are commemorative only and do not describe actual events related to these named persons.

Dr. William Hillebrand and Jacinto Pereira are non-fictional characters who were principally responsible for sponsoring the Portuguese to travel to Hawaii, believing that the people from the Azores were uniquely suited to the islands' climate and way-of-life. Additionally, Joe and Hedwig Sprung were the actual owners of the Sprung Hotel in Drawbridge at the time of the story.

The folk story of "Little Bean" told to the children on the ship is adapted from a series of Portuguese folk tales. Stories of Portuguese folk magic were adapted from *The Souls of the Departed: A Brief History and Sampling of Portuguese Folk Magic* by Darlene A. Sousa, Ph.D.

While much of plantation life described was based on the Grove Plantation in Kauai, the story in Kauai takes place in a slightly different location and is adapted for story-telling purposes. The stories herein do not represent any actual events associated with the Grove or Koloa Plantations or any specific plantation of its time.

BIBLIOGRAPHY

The Portuguese in Hawaii by John Henry Felix, Ph.D and Peter Senecal, Ph.D

Portuguese Hawaiian Memories by J.F. Freitas

The Diary of Anna Maud Gould's Trip Aboard the Ship Berlin, edited by Laura Penny

Historical Footnotes of Santa Clara Valley by Jack Douglas and the San Jose Historical Museum Association

The Journal of the Thomas Bell by João Baptista d'Oliveira

The History of the de Harne Family in Hawaii by Mary de Harne and Josephine de Harne Jones

Almost Forgotten: Pen and Inklings of the Old Santa Clara Valley by F. Ralph Rambo

Grove Farm Plantation by Bob Krause with W.P. Alexander

Pau Hana: Plantation Life and Labor in Hawaii by Ronald Takaki

Sugar Islands: the 165-year story of Sugar in Hawaii by William H. Dorrance and Francis S. Morgan

For the Souls of the Departed: A brief history and sampling of Portuguese folk magic by Darlene A. Sousa, Ph.D

The Story of Koloa: A Kauai Plantation Town by Donal Donohugh

In Pursuit of their Dreams: A history of Azorean Immigration to the United States by Jerry R. Williams

The Last of the Prune Pickers: A Pre-Silicon Valley Story by Tim Stanley

San Jose's Historic Downtown by Lauren Miranda Gilbert and Bob Johnson

The Portuguese Californians by Alvin Ray Graves

Maui Remembers: A Local History by Gail Bartholomew

Two Years Before the Mast by Richard Henry Dana